THE
DEACON'S TALE

A *Sword of the Stars* novel

ARINN DEMBO

Kthonia Press
www.kthonia.com

Portions of this book were first published in 2008 by Lighthouse Interactive.

Sword of the Stars™ is a trademark of Kerberos Productions, Inc.

DEDICATION

Dedicated with loving respect to Martin Cirulis, a.k.a. "The Director".
You are magnificent, *Var Kona*. We are invincible under your command.

ACKNOWLEDGMENTS

The author would first like to thank Albert Koenig, whose careful eye as editor has improved the text of this novel greatly. Thanks are also due to the seasoned professionals at Electric Story and the Innsmouth Free Press, who helped prepare this text for publication in electronic and print formats respectively; their support and mentorship has been extremely helpful. Artist and graphic designer Ken Lee also deserves a word of thanks for the help and support he has always provided in bringing *The Deacon's Tale* to press; he has contributed to both this edition and the first printing.

Above all, this book owes its existence to the many fans who demanded it. They beat their shields and raised their voices to have the full text written in 2007, unsatisfied with the few fictional "teasers" the author had originally intended. They have kept up a steady drumbeat for the novel's re-publication since its first printing sold out in 2008. Without the steady stream of questions about the fate of the novel on the Kerberos company forums, it is very likely that this edition of the book would not have existed. I would like to take this opportunity to thank them for their enthusiasm and support over the last few years.

Like its protagonist, this book has had to overcome many obstacles to return to print. I apologize for the long wait, and welcome you back to the *SotS* universe. The Man in Black awaits. This is his first story.

1 | THE SHRINE OF THE PHYSICIST

Cai Rui sat in a curving pew at the back of the dimly lit cenotaph, his black hair and uniform blending into the shadows. As always, he felt vaguely guilty to sit in a house of worship built by another faith. A tour of school children had come to visit the cathedral on this occasion; he could hear them for several minutes before they came into view. The light patter of footsteps echoed throughout the halls above his head, and the rare acoustics of the building brought the voice of the tour guide down into the vault and directly to his pew. For several minutes Cai Rui listened to the familiar lecture, given now in English, broken by the loud whispers and occasional bursts of chatter from the children.

"All right, my dears. Please gather here along the wall?" The sister's voice was warm, encouraging. The male teacher cut in more sharply, demanding obedience. The group fell silent, as well as they were able. There were still the busy, furtive moments that youth could not restrain.

"We've come now to a very special place. This is the Shrine of Jupiter, the tomb of the famous physicist Blasky Yao Hsiang! Do all of you know the story of Blasky Yao Hsiang?"

A firm young voice rang out, with an accent from the Australarctic Consortium. "Yes, *sorora*. He created the Node Drive and discovered Node Space."

The pleasure in the woman's voice was unfeigned. "Very good!"

"But he can't really be buried here, can he? Not really." The child hesitated, uncertain about challenging adult authority. "Didn't he die on Jupiter?"

There was a brief pause. "Very good, young man. You are quite right. Blasky's tomb is meant to be symbolic. His mortal remains could not be recovered."

"Is that why they call it the Shrine of Jupiter?"

He heard rather than saw the woman's smile. "Let's go see for ourselves, shall we?" There was a rustle of anxious young bodies moving forward. The nun descended the spiral stairs into the cylindrical tomb. The Shrine was a tube of cool marble and glass, sunk into the bedrock and soaring to a tall peak in the mountain sun above; the resemblance to a missile silo was doubtless unintended by the builders, given that they were a pacifist sect.

He looked up to see the hem of an unbleached cotton robe, swinging just a few inches above the tops of a woman's poor sandals. The grown man wore a black teacher's gown, his shoes just as worn. Many of the children who came after wore trousers which had once been black also, but were now softened to gray by repeated washings. Their ragged cuffs often hung too long or too short, exposing knobby bare ankles.

Orphans, he thought. A pang of mingled emotion twisted in his chest. He remembered the ragged clothes, his feet wrapped in rags when the winters were cold.

The woman turned as she reached the bottom and let the children file past her into the cool gloom, forming a loose milling knot on the glossy black marble floor. Already there was a hush of awe as they craned their heads and turned, trying to take in everything at once. Smiling slightly, Cai Rui sat back in the dark and looked up with them. The ceiling and walls above ground level were made of blue acidglass, divided into panes with delicate whorls and spirals of black lead. The dome was built on one of the highest points in the city, and at this time of day the glass was soaking up so much radiation that the colors were at their darkest, deep violet-indigo mottled with slowly moving veins of smoky lilac. It was the color of Node Space itself, a cool shifting sea of sinuous light and matter.

By force of habit he found himself looking away from it quickly. No one but a raw recruit would spend more than a few seconds staring out the portals at the real thing, and the simulation here was a little too good for comfort. The hologram of Jupiter, by contrast, was reassuringly solid and mundane; in the center of the mausoleum it was generated at full power, almost luridly bright, the turbulence of the great gas giant crawling in real time against the active background of Node Space blue.

He looked back down at the tour group, smiling at the upturned faces and the open mouths. All of the children were contemplating the Jupiter Shrine, except for one; she had stepped away from the others and was quietly drifting through the shadows toward him, her eyes fixed with glassy, hypnotic intensity on the white marble sarcophagus of the physicist.

Her face was pale and flat and round, her black hair shorn to a nearly invisible dusting of fuzz on her vulnerable scalp: it was common for rearing institutes to shave the children thoroughly, as a precaution against lice. Someone had given her a pair of hand-me-down spectacles to wear, badly oversized for her face. The frames were made from heavy plastic, lenses square and thick. Behind the watery glass her almond eyes were magnified, a heavy epicanthic fold giving her the expression of a sleepy owl. As she crept forward she bit her lower lip. Her front teeth were large, rabbit-like, parted by a wide crooked gap that no one would likely pay to correct.

She cast one last furtive look over her shoulder and then reached out with a small hand to caress the marble face of Blasky. Cai Rui surged to his feet just a split second before her fingers touched the surface, already wincing with sympathetic embarrassment. As a child himself, many years ago, he had made the same mistake. Now, wakened by her touch, the old recording activated. A second hologram appeared, hovering several inches over her face—at eye level, to the average adult—and the dead began to speak.

"Hailing all frequencies. My name is Blasky Yao Hsiang, Chief Scientist of the Sol Primus solar research project. I have survived an extraordinary accident during the testing of my new solar scanning array. At present my craft is trapped in a decaying orbit around the planet Jupiter. By my best guess, I will enter the upper atmosphere in approximately six hours…"

The whole tour group jumped, not least the girl herself. She stumbled backward and fell, gaping up at her hero's disembodied head and shoulders, which hung, like the planet Jupiter, in mid-air. Cai Rui looked into the serene black eyes of that golden face with a sense of vertigo. This recording was not the authentic footage from Sol Primus, but an idealized artist's rendering created for the benefit of tourists. It was a composite drawn from earlier holos and vids. During his cadet years at the Academy, Cai Rui had watched the real footage several times, and he remembered a very different face, pale and haggard behind the speckled glass of a fouled helmet, eyes crimson with burst blood vessels and haunted by the certainty of impending death. It was from that mask of anguish and fear that this voice of reason, gentle and calm, had come, quietly passing on the details of the most important failed experiment in human history.

It still gave him a shiver to hear it, and for a moment he almost mouthed the words along with Blasky: "…but I intend to spend the time remaining to transmit the data I have collected to posterity, in the hope that it may be of some use to the people of Earth."

The nun turned to see what had happened and found the child on the floor, her threadbare crèche uniform gray and shabby against the polished surface of midnight black and twinkling stars. Standing beside the tomb itself was Cai Rui. Casually he reached out and flicked the concealed switch on his side of the sarcophagus, cutting off the old flight recording in mid-sentence.

"My apologies." He spoke in English, and added a curt military nod to the crowd; they had all turned to gape at him. "I was hoping to slip out quietly, so as not to disturb others. Very clumsy of me."

"*Lux!*"

Keyed to the sound and volume of her voice, the sconces all around the room blazed into life. Every corner of the shrine was abruptly lit, and the holograms faded to near-invisibility. Cai Rui tried not to squint in the sudden glare. After over an hour in the darkness, it was blinding.

The nun's hand had automatically gone to the Tertium hanging outside her habit, reaching for the comfort of the Three Arrows when startled. She was quite young, he saw, a fragile European face made even more vulnerable by the shorn scalp of her sect. Now her hand dropped from the golden pendant and she stepped forward, reassuring her tour group with a stiff smile. "Not at all ... sir. We didn't see you."

Cai Rui stepped forward, hands folded behind him. Some of the children took an involuntary step back, cringing away. For a moment, he saw himself reflected in their eyes: a dark stranger, his black dress uniform emerging from the blue depths, his brow split by a pale scar, a ceremonial steel boarding blade hanging low at his hip. To all eyes present he must seem the very embodiment of violent authority, just as the Consortium soldiers and police had been when he was a child.

The nun and the teacher moved as one, and instinctively put themselves between Cai Rui and the children. He felt a moment of pain as he looked at them, instantly mistrustful, expecting the worst. Then he turned away and bent to offer his hand to the little girl on the floor. She stared at his open palm dully for a moment, as if unable to understand the gesture. When she looked up at him, she searched his face deeply, her eyes hooded and suspicious.

No, he thought sadly. *No trick, little one. None of the world's cruelty is here.*

As if she heard his thought, she suddenly smiled—a bright beam of joy that split her face into beauty. She took his hand, and he raised her to her feet.

He bowed and spoke softly in Han, muttering so that only she could hear. "Are you all right?"

"Yes sir," she breathed, bowing back—in a voice so tiny even he could barely make it out.

The nun hurried forward; she put her hand on the child's shoulder and drew the girl back so quickly that she stumbled and nearly fell again. "I'm sorry…" The woman hesitated, glancing at the golden tabs fixed at his collar. "Captain?"

"Commander," he corrected.

"I had no idea there was anyone in the shrine. Generally we allow visitors—"

"—by appointment only," he said mildly. "I am aware of the policy. I always make an appointment to visit your Temple when I am in Davos."

"I see." She hesitated, and she searched his face more thoroughly, as if looking for some hidden redeeming quality. "Were you once a member of the Utilitarian faith, Commander?"

He shook his head. "No, Ma'am. I was adopted by a different Church, when I was a boy."

"I see." The tiny glimmer of hopeful light in her eyes died, and the grey pools crystallized once again into ice. She drew the little girl away from him firmly, retreating toward the rest of her tour group. When he did not turn immediately to leave, she spoke again with forced joviality. "Out of curiosity, may we ask what draws you to our Jupiter Shrine?"

He raised an eyebrow. "The man you honor here was a member of Sol Force. A personal hero of mine. It seems only right to pay my respects to a fellow serviceman. He did give his life in the line of duty."

A ripple of anger twisted her features. "Blasky Yao Hsiang died in service to humankind, Commander. Not in war."

He acknowledged her statement with a small nod. "And according to the teachings of your faith, the two are mutually exclusive."

She drew herself up tall. "Yes. War is the antithesis of every Utilitarian ideal."

Despite his best intentions, he could not suppress a snort. "Including survival, I gather?"

The teacher cut in smoothly. "Yes, of course. Sol Force never fails to remind us how necessary they are to our…'survival.'" His nasal Australarctic voice dripped contempt. "It amazes me that the human race ever managed to exist, before you lot came along."

Cai Rui smiled thinly. "What amazes me is how quickly the human race could cease to exist, if we were gone." He paused, and looked down into the faces of the children. Many eyes already reflected the same zealous hostility that radiated so ardently from their wardens, but here and there he saw a flicker of doubt. From the one girl whose hand he had touched, there was a beaming ray of such humbling hero-worship that it made him both sad and strong.

When he spoke again, he looked into her eyes. "There are many ways to serve humankind." Just for her, he smiled.

"I'm afraid I will have to ask you to leave, *Commander*." The nun's voice had risen an octave; her hand gripped her Tertium tightly. "We do not allow Sol Force to recruit on the premises."

"And yet Sol Force allows your faith to recruit new members anywhere and everywhere, sister." He cocked his head with a wry smirk. "Under the circumstances, which of the two institutions would you say was more...enlightened?"

Before she could respond, Cai Rui turned on his heel and marched up the staircase. He took the first few steps at a mundane clip, but as he rounded the first spiral turn he lengthened his stride, bounding up the remaining stairs in three long, heroic leaps. From below he heard the children gasp, and a quickly stifled babble of response. He suppressed an impish grin as he walked away, still holding his chin high with unabashed military correctness.

Nothing like a little high-g training, he thought. *Always a big hit with the kids.*

2 | A COMMENCEMENT ADDRESS

He stepped up to the podium and turned to face the crowd, looking down into the darkened auditorium. Each seat below had been embedded in the center of its own miniature communications terminal, ringed by a bank of screens like a coral atoll. The trainees had risen from their places when he took the stage, and now gave him a wave of polite applause as ordered. The noise died immediately and the group sat back down when they saw him touch his throat, activating the transmitter of his data shunt.

"Ladies and gentlemen. Congratulations are in order." His normally quiet voice rang through the hall, amplified through the podium, and he suppressed a wince at the unaccustomed volume. He swept a glance over the class. They were a good bunch, well-disciplined and wary. He noted with approval that they had spaced themselves well, each man or woman keeping a comfortable margin of distance to the nearest neighbor.

"As of today, you have all completed a difficult course of training. Everyone in this room will graduate into service with the Sol Force Intelligence Corps." A gentle wave of sound rippled through the room, a whisper of indrawn breath. "As a ranking officer and Section Leader, I am here to welcome you all."

He paused a moment to let the announcement sink in. "As you know, the end of the training course for SIC is randomized; there is no pre-set expiration date for the Games. This is part of the ordeal: a trainee does not know in advance when it will end. Even now, some of you may be wondering whether this is only the beginning of another test."

There was a murmur of nervous laughter, and a few guilty glances were exchanged. Cai Rui nodded encouragingly. "After some of the things you've been through, that is to be expected. I assure you, this is not an exciting new psy-op. In fact, this particular training period has run longer than average. You have survived three weeks more testing than students from the previous year. Even by SIC standards…you are very hard apes. The Director is impressed, and he looks forward to seeing what you can do in the field."

He watched them for a moment, as the reality sank in. Victory. They had all worked hard to get here, and worked harder still to remain. The SIC program accepted only those with special commendations on record, and seven out of ten candidates from every branch of service still washed out before the end. It was a long, hard road. He remembered it well.

For many, he could see, this was an occasion for grim satisfaction. Some faces remained impassive, carefully schooled masks. For others, there was a dawning light of incredulous joy spreading, and he saw several grins of wolfish delight. All of these emotive tendencies had been logged over the course of the training period, and in many cases would be used to determine placement of a successful trainee. "Giving good face" was a key skill for domestic and diplomatic operatives, but a combat officer wouldn't need a ready smile. In some xeno-operations, a tendency to emote could even be fatal.

"Everyone in this room has passed through the most rigorous training course Sol Force could devise. We've done our worst; you've done your best. From this day forward, you will all be members of SIC. I am here to tell you what that means."

He let the last few words echo in the acoustics of the large auditorium. The room represented an ostentatious use of space and resources, even by planetary standards. This stadium-raked, climate-controlled, lushly appointed theater in Davos was designed to hold the maximum number of applicants that could ever begin SIC training on a given year. In the first hour of Day One, 500 men and women from every corner of the empire had been sitting in this room, eager to begin the course and join the Force's most elite branch of service.

Over the course of the training program, however, this large echoing room taught its occupants a valuable lesson. Every seven days the trainees were brought here for a briefing, and saw first-hand how many of their fellow applicants had disappeared. The end of the first week might sometimes lull them into a false sense of security; ninety percent of the applicants could make it through the first seven days. By the end of week two, this hall was always half-empty. By that time, those remaining had begun to realize that they were not ordinary soldiers, and would never be again.

He touched his throat and murmured a subvocal command to his PDA, activating the cybernetic adjutant he had added to his wetware. "Cicero. *Praebe gladium Damoclitis.*"

An oversized hologram appeared in the empty presentation space above the podium, a slowly spinning reproduction of the Intelligence Corps logo. The massive blade hung over his head, golden and twice the height of a man, suspended as if by an invisible thread.

He reactivated the speakers, letting his voice ring through the hall. "The Sol Force Intelligence Corps is the point of humanity's sword. Our purpose is to gather the information that our Director, our Legators, and our scientists need to effectively promote the interests of the human race." He paused. "Regardless of where we are assigned, all Intelligence operatives have a single mission: to reveal, investigate and neutralize any and all threats to the well-being of our species. But we live in a complex universe, ladies and gentlemen. Today's enemy can be tomorrow's ally."

The giant sword disintegrated into a shower of golden particles and reformed as a holographic map, a three-dimensional representation of 250 nearby solar systems in the sector. The cloud of systems shone in the darkness like a net of burning jewels.

"At this moment, we have achieved an uneasy peace with all three of the starfaring empires that we have encountered." The political boundaries appeared on the map, four amorphous, semi-transparent shapes representing zones of control. It was not a cleanly divided sphere; all four empires were misshapen, extending pseudopods of expansion and intrusion into other zones. He set the image to rotate slowly. "Sol Force possessions are represented here in green. The Tarkasian Empire is marked in red. All systems claimed by the Hiver Imperium are yellow, and what we know about the Liir presence is represented in light blue."

He turned away from them, keying his microphone to sub-vocalize the command to his PDA. "Cicero. *Procede per tempora.*" Reactivating his microphone, he spoke to the crowd. "Watch this sequence carefully. I think you will find it instructive."

The map began to move, an animation slowly peeling back the years of history. The red core of Tarka space held strong, stabbing out an arm occasionally to pluck a lightly-defended prize from Liir blue and human green; its spinward border with Hiver space seethed, war sweeping back and forth over a chain of contested worlds on the front. The Liir demesne separated into a series of smaller blue bubbles; past cartographers had noted the location of their fleets in deep space or mapped their hidden worlds as they were discovered, without any true understanding of the territory they held or the nature of their intelligence. The Hiver Imperium shattered into multiple shades of rust, orange and yellow, as various factions battled savagely from star to star during the Interregnum.

Regardless of the behavior of other colors, however, the most obvious pattern on the stellar map for the past thirty years was the relentless expansion of green. In just three decades, the human race had gone from one badly battered planet and a lightly developed solar system to forge an empire of thirteen charter worlds, including three fully terraformed jewels that could cradle their species for millennia to come... provided that *Homo sapiens* had the strength to hold onto them. In this expansion they had shouldered aside the red presence of Tarka settlement on two border worlds and taken up a good deal of territory lost by Hiver yellow during their civil war. Only the Liir had not lost a world as yet... but no fewer than three of their colonies were within a single Node jump of the human border.

He turned back to the audience, letting the animation repeat itself as he spoke. "Rest assured, we apes are not the only species that can read a map. You and I can see this pattern; so can a Hiver, a Tarka or a Liir. Ask yourself now, if you were a loyal son of Radiant Frost—how would you advise your Mother to deal with these rapacious mammals?"

A few of the trainees shifted uncomfortably in their chairs at the mention of the Queen, as if the mere thought of being Hiver made them want to climb out of their skins. "If you were a Tarkasian Lac-Tar, what would you suggest the Supreme Commander do about the upstarts on his flank?" His black eyes bored into them, relentless and calm. "Would this map make you feel safe, if you were Liir?"

He stood for a full three seconds in silence, giving every member of the audience a chance to reflect in private. "Questions like these have not been part of your training, thus far. You've dissected the Other, put their tissues under the microscope, and learned a few words of their language. We've taught you every way we know of killing, incapacitating, torturing or bribing them. But the fact remains: we can kill a thousand Hivers and still be no closer to understanding the thousand-and-first."

The star map disintegrated and coalesced into a new image. He had sampled the most infamous piece of combat footage in history, broadcast from the documentary cameras set to record the launch of the Nova Maria. From the famous two-dimensional images, he had extrapolated his own hologram. Now he looked out into the crowd, a sea of faces lit by the pulsing glow of burning wreckage. Their eyes reflected an old horror as the infamous Hiver dreadnaught turned its ugly insectile prow planet-ward, to begin the bombardment of Earth.

A familiar sight: all of them had grown up on this event, the scene branded into them afresh on every Remembrance Day. Three generations of Sol Force recruits were battened on the hatred this attack had invoked, drinking the mother's milk of war. Now the massive ship turned again with ponderous grace, slow and majestic, moving in for the kill.

"When we began our war with the Hiver thirty years ago, we thought we knew everything we needed to know. We had been attacked. We had been attacked by Hivers. All Hivers looked the same to us. All Hiver ships looked the same to us." The forward batteries of the dreadnaught opened, raining death on the Asian continent below.

"Cicero. *Insignum maximum.*" The great ship froze, and suddenly the camera view swooped toward its hull. The symbol on its nose was magnified, marked in black and silvery steel: a dark circle, ringed by the bright corona of a white star in eclipse—the clan symbol of a Hiver princess called Obsidian Crown.

"For the first ten years of the Hiver War, universal orders were to fire on sight when any Hiver vessel or colony was encountered. Very few resources were devoted to decoding their transmissions. The stated goal of Sol Force Command was to wipe their species from the galaxy with all possible speed. It was absolute war, genocidal and pure."

A series of different Hiver clan symbols began to flow across the display, one steadily shifting to the next. Strange abstracted beasts, black against a variety of brilliantly colored fields. Flowers and trees, geometric patterns, musical instruments: there were hundreds of symbols. "We had no grasp of Hiver language or culture, at the time. We knew just enough about their technology to find their home systems. Where we found them, we waded in with weapons blazing."

The final symbol shattered and re-formed into a new scene, a Sol Force battlegroup poised in orbit around the planet Rhychopre. The broken remains of the colony's defense fleet drifted behind them, tumbling debris. As the image solidified, the forward cruiser opened fire, beams raking through the thin clouds over the southern continent.

"*Insignum Hiveris maximum.*" The camera once again plunged toward the hull of a Hiver ship to reveal the insignia—a branch blazing with blue flames. "We had assumed that the Hiver, like us, were a unified species. By the time we realized our mistake, we had launched first strike attacks on over a dozen different Hiver clans, which had previously been at war with each other. Not one of them had ever seen

17

or heard of a human before. The fleets and colonies we encountered had no alliance with the clan that first attacked us. The great victories we won at Rychopre, Tisketis, Rizdet...were in many respects, a slaughter of innocents."

He could feel the wave of outrage from the crowd; he met it with a cold smile, teeth clenched tight. "Some of you may doubt me. There is no reason to take my word for it, ladies and gentlemen. Those Hiver transmissions are still on file today; you'll have access to them from the moment you leave this room. Educate yourself. If you passed the Hiver language exam, please feel free to download and translate the recordings at your leisure. You have earned the security clearance it takes to hear to a desperate mother beg for mercy...or plead in vain for her children's lives."

He paused, as if to invite challenge. The crowd was silent, and he continued. "The high command, as you know, has not released this information to the general public. It should be very obvious why they do not. Even decorated veterans of the Hiver War often do not realize that the enemy they fought was not a united species. Too many on both sides have suffered, sacrificed and died. We cannot tell families still grieving today that their loved ones were martyrs to our stupidity."

The rumble of protest was audible this time; he slashed through it without raising his voice. "Yes, my fellow apes: stupidity. We lashed out blindly, without understanding. In the process, we became the very enemy we hoped to defeat. Attacking at first contact, without warning or provocation. Raining fire on civilians. Killing strangers who could not understand what we wanted, or know what cause we had to hate them. Making dangerous enemies, in places where we might have had allies and even friends." His eyes narrowed. "What is stupidity, ladies and gentlemen, if not the lack of Intelligence?"

He let the words sink in, and then continued. "There may still be a price to pay for these errors." In the air above him, the blazing branch gave way slowly to four other clan symbols. Three red blades, arranged in a circle. A cluster of green fruit. A honeycomb of delicate yellow lines. A flaming sun. "Although the Queen has made peace on behalf of Her people, five Hiver clans have taken a vow known as 'metz'ekqua' against our species—the nearest translation would be 'infinite vengeance', although I've been told that 'endless hate' also works well." The camera suddenly drew back from the flaming sun, and the audience could see the ships upon which the symbol was painted—the first wave of attackers at Algol, one of the most brutal battles of attrition ever recorded.

"This custom goes beyond the usual human understanding of war and vengeance. According to our Hiver sources, metz'ekqua requires every member of a clan to bend each waking day toward the destruction of the chosen enemy." The first wave of destroyers at Algol detonated into a wall of fire. Through the burning wreckage the second wave came on, pouring ballistics into the lead cruiser of the defenders. Hivers had died by the thousand in this battle, to smash one of the largest picket fleets Sol Force had ever assembled, and annihilate a budding colony. The smoldering ruins on that once-green world would remain lethally radioactive for another two million years.

"There are stories of clans who have spent decades, or even centuries gathering the necessary resources and laying plans for a decisive strike. This is a sacred vow... and it cannot end unless formally rescinded by the princess of the offended clan. What a mother does not forgive, her sons cannot forget."

The Hiver sequence ended at last with another symbol, a delicate white filigree snowflake, each of its points tipped with crimson: the sigil of Radiant Frost. "Not even the Queen can command forgiveness. These errors of the past may yet have unforeseen consequences in the future. So I urge you, as Intelligence operatives, to take your duties very seriously. The lives of billions may depend upon the work you do."

The last Hiver symbol slowly faded, replaced by a new scene. A Tarkasian freighter was coming about for a landing at the starfield on Mars, its hull shimmering with promise. "As Intelligence operatives, we cannot afford to ignore the errors of the past—but we also cannot wallow in them. Our duty now is to find hope for the future. And you could not have graduated at a better time, to assist in this process."

The scene at the loading docks gave way to a second view, a seemingly endless line of small cargo ships from every race lined up for inspection by the customs fleet at Junction. "The Corps is presently divided into six operational Sections; within a few weeks, there will be a seventh. Since the peace treaties were signed, Sol Force Command has received over 5,000 applications from civilian transport owners, requesting clearance to carry cargo to and from the border worlds of Biima, Ko'Seth, and Rozokor. There's money to be made, and our people want a taste of it."

The scene gave way to an image of civilian freighters loading up at a dock on Ko'Seth. Sweating humans in coveralls worked side by side with half-nude Tarka in the blinding heat of a tropical sun. "We couldn't stop this process if we wanted to—and we don't. Our orders are to infiltrate the new trade relations on a massive scale, and place operatives on every possible route."

The scene shifted to Earth orbit, a Han Consortium low-orbit vessel docking with a massive Hiver transport for inspection of its cargo. "There is a long list of prohibited goods, of course, and the Consortia have imposed a list of tariffs the length of your arm. But our job is not to collect taxes, nor to enforce the law. Where there is a flow of goods, there will be a flow of information—and we need to be there to collect it. Once these pipelines open, even war will never shut them down completely. Radiant Frost may lose her taste for this alliance, but her Children won't lose their taste for cheese."

A soft, almost inaudible chuckle followed. The dark mood he had invoked was lifting, as intended. The projection sphere dissolved all images into rolling mist, a holding pattern of light. "All of you have been placed into the general staff for the moment, but we will expect you to review your options within the next fourteen days. By then you will have filed a transfer request to three possible Sections, in order of preference. Take your skills and assets into account. The duties you request should reflect a genuine ability to perform them. Trade section will be looking for people with past experience as pilots, gunners, and mechanics. People with a background in the outer colonies or in civilian transport roles will blend in more easily, on the frontier." A few people stirred in their chairs. "I think some of you know who you are."

Six hanging swords emerged from the primal mist, each blade shining with a different metallic color. "There are other options, of course. Some of you may have served in the past with operatives from Red, Yellow or Blue Sections. At least one Intelligence liaison is commonly attached to any vessel larger than a destroyer. These operatives are specialists in the language and culture of Tarka, Hiver and Liir military fleets. They serve as consultants during Contact situations, and there are never enough of them to go around."

The six swords joined their points together and spun to dissolution, transforming into a Sol Force cruiser under steam toward the Nodepoint off Midway. "If you are exceptionally gifted in languages, this is a good way to find yourself on the bridge of a major ship of the line. Operatives who take this route can re-enter the chain of the command after a period of training and be eligible for promotion like any other bridge officer. With hard work and meritorious service, you could easily achieve a command of your own. At present, there are four cruisers commanded by Intelligence TFC's."

The cruiser warped and shifted into a deep scan vessel, slowly turning against a blazing blue star on the border of Liir space. "If you have served aboard a scanning vessel, your commanding officer was a member of Green Section. All Signals officers above the rank of ensign are trained and certified through SIC. Those of you looking to join an exploratory task force might consider this option."

The scan ship gave way to a heavy-bellied colonial transport, its mission section re-painted with the warning symbols of biohazardous cargo. "If you have ever been involved in the transport, incarceration or disposal of non-human sentients, then you've already met the members of White Section. White has a strong relationship with the Research and Development Corps, and they are always looking for people with the right kind of education and experience. It is definitely a path to consider, if you have an interest in xenobiology."

The cargo ship disappeared, fading into darkness. "And then, of course, there is Black Section."

The darkness deepened, and a pale rim of white appeared. It was the horizon line of a distant world, as seen from the shadow of its night side. Something moved toward the camera, emerging from the massive shadow of the planet: a huge octahedron of armored black, two pyramids joined at their bases into a single ship. The sides of the vessel were covered with strange hieroglyphs of silvery steel.

"There are things in the universe, ladies and gentlemen, which we cannot presently explain. While exploring the systems within a fifty light-year radius of our solar system, we have encountered a number of ships of unknown configuration. At present, we know very little about most of them. In many cases, the only thing we can say for certain is that the technology they represent is not familiar."

An emerald beam speared forth from the tip of the top pyramid, sweeping toward the camera. The image of the mysterious ship suddenly vaporized into green fog. "Any encounter that cannot be easily and immediately classified is placed under the jurisdiction of SIC's Black Section. It is our duty to investigate all ships and phenomena on the famous 'Black List' maintained by Sol Force Command. At this sitting there are a number of threats under investigation. We call this one the 'Von Neumann' vessel. It's named for the historical physicist who first suggested the idea of an infinitely self-replicating machine."

Already several of the trainees were sitting up straighter in their chairs. Now they watched in fascination as the fog slowly resolved into a second scene: a dense asteroid belt in a system on the frontier. A rolling mile of raw nickel-iron obscured the camera view for a moment. As it passed, a Tarkasian destroyer was revealed, drifting helpless in space. The ship was gutted by combat, its engine section black and cold. Several smaller craft surrounded it, flitting to and fro like flies on a corpse.

"Like the Von Neumann vessels, many items on the Black List are independent mechanisms. These Swarm ships, for example, are pilotless drones. We have yet to find any sign of biological life aboard these craft, although we've studied them extensively. Sol Force has encountered them three times in resource-rich areas; they appear to have been designed as some sort of automated mining system."

The camera view moved closer, approaching one of the wasp-like drones as it settled on the destroyer's mission section. Several members of the audience winced as it began to gnaw and cut away a panel of the hull, its segmented forelegs feeding broken fragments of armor plating into a gnashing mechanical maw.

"These small autonomous units are programmed to collect metallic ores and heavy elements. They carry their cargo back to a central collection point. The 'nest' of the Swarm is a hollow asteroid which serves as a base. Inside the hollow rock is a mother ship, a highly advanced ore processor and refinery: it converts the raw materials delivered by its drones into parts and energy, which it uses to refuel and repair the gathering units."

The small craft, its belly full of Tarkasian armor, rose from its perch and flew away, leaving just in time for another to land. The camera followed the Swarmling's drunkenly weaving flight through the tumbling mountains of stone, but paused safely out of range as it landed on a non-descript asteroid. The alien ore-carrier crawled into one of several dark caves dotting the surface and disappeared.

"Recent evidence suggests that the 'Swarm Queen' processors are able to manufacture new drones. They may even be able to reproduce themselves and make new central processing units, given the time and resources. Both Hiver and Tarkasian informants have reported finding Swarm infestations in more than one adjacent system. Mechanical or not, these Swarms, like the Von Neumann vessels, may be multiplying."

The projector shifted to a new scene, the voluptuous clouds of a shimmering nebula serving as backdrop to a strange firefight. A trio of agile Liirian destroyers circled an enemy craft, their forward lasers stabbing repeatedly at the one turret bolted to its hull. As they slid warily around behind it, the enemy vessel lurched clumsily, as if trying to track their movement. The port side was revealed: there was a gaping hole in the side, as if a large part of the ship had been torn away. This was a derelict fragment of a greater whole, its automatic defenses still blindly firing at any nearby threat—the turret set like a watchdog to defend a master long dead and dust.

"Many Black List entities appear to be the lost or abandoned technology of a highly advanced culture. Apparently there were technological giants once, in this neck of the galaxy... and they left our sector littered with some highly dangerous toys." The sleek destroyers continued their attack, burning the alien turret to a glowing, helpless lump.

"This being said, not every unknown menace is purely mechanical, or passively waiting to be found. Some Black List targets appear to be very much alive. We see them only when they choose to be seen."

The scene shifted again. The resolution was poor, the image washed by rhythmic waves of pixellating static, but this was clearly a camera view in orbit above a frozen world. Pristine glaciers sparkled with prismatic albedo on the planet's surface below. The unmistakable time stamp of a Sol Force defense platform rolled in the bottom right corner: the date was over twenty years in the past.

An ugly jumble of metal appeared against the snow white field, sliding into view like a roach on a white linen tablecloth. The indistinct angles were obscured by the red glow of a hot fission engine, washing across the camera's light receptors in a wave of shimmering heat distortion. For a split second, it was possible to see the ship separating into two distinct parts, as a circular disk broke free from the rest of the craft. Then guns flashed and the camera view exploded into sparkling dust.

"The official designation of this target is Black List Thirteen—also known as 'the Rippers'. This footage was recovered from an attack on the Spica colony, in the year 2413."

Someone in the audience stirred, and a young female voice rang out with military precision, delivering information in a burst between two sharply barked honorifics. "Sir! Spica-wasn't-founded-until-'15-Commander sir!"

He looked down into the pit, seeing her black silhouette standing at attention. The corners of his eyes tilted with a repressed smile. "At ease, ensign. Spica was re-founded in 2415. The first human inhabitants of that world landed in 2411. To this day, those early colonists remain... unaccounted for."

A dark mutter went through the audience and a crisp new image formed above the podium. Again, it was obviously a platform camera, this time above a desert world. The information stamp was written in *Ri'kap-ken*, but for those who could read and translate its date, the scene was over eighty years in the past.

"Since the peace treaties were signed, new channels of information have been opened between SIC and our Hiver and Tarkasian allies. These empires are both much older than ours. They have their own records of Black List entities. Some of the things they've run into are completely outside of our experience—but we also had footage of a few things that they'd never seen before. The one thing that all three empires had in common...was Black Thirteen."

Against a mosaic of velvety golden sand and the shining green water of irrigated fields, the ship was a stark, brutal mass, a black shadow bristling with sharp angles and ugly intent. Again, the saucer-like section broke away from the main hull. This time the camera continued to roll as it descended through the thin atmosphere, dropping with ominous speed toward the Hiver city below.

"They hit the Hivers at Chis'ka-tet in 2362. There was another strike at Etos'che in 2390. Xheketch'is was a small outpost, lost in 2417; they blamed us for the loss of the colony for nearly a decade, before they had time to investigate the scene fully. Once there were trained Intelligence officers onsite, the Hiver recognized the signs of Black Thirteen."

A series of still pictures passed, images recorded by brothers who had come too late to help. The pictures flowed from the abandoned ruins of one colony to the next, from small outposts to whole towns and even cities standing empty: doors and windows hanging ajar, tools and trash strewn through the streets, vehicles smashed or seemingly torn apart, hatches ripped from the hinges as if to yank the occupants from the interior.

The images continued to flow, but the shift between the distinctive hexagonal lines of Hiver architecture and the flowing lines of Tarka dwellings could not be mistaken. Despite the belling curves, brilliant colors and ornate panels of enamel, glass and steel, the scenes were chillingly similar: the aftermath of sudden, wrenching violence, leaving behind an empty world.

"They hit the Tarka at Ka'Saak, in 2350. So far as we know, Ka'Saak remains the earliest attack on record. Apparently the system's defense platforms did some damage to the attacking ship before they were destroyed. It must have set the Rippers back on their haunches. Black Thirteen didn't return to Tarka space until 2415, when they struck at Ku'Van. The system was poorly defended at the time, and apparently our friends found that...encouraging. They attacked again almost immediately in 2416, and wiped out the Tarkasian outpost on Ko'Rorkor. Those two strikes were too close together for the public taste. They sparked a rebellion that eventually cost the Supreme Commander his head."

The images came more slowly now, focusing on specific details. Shattered glass, still stained with dark fluid. Wood splintered under the blows of something like a pick axe, and torn asunder. "Given the ability to compare notes with our near neighbors, it has become clear to SIC and the High Command that Black Thirteen is a more serious problem than we had first supposed. This enemy seems to arrive in small numbers, but their attacks result in mass disappearances: once a system's defenses are overwhelmed or circumvented, the Rippers are able to kidnap thousands at a time. And regardless of the defenses available on the ground, they seem to meet with little resistance, once they land. An entire division of Tarkasian armor was lost at Ko'Rorkor, a home defense force that should have been easily able to cope with a few raiders."

The cycle had come around at last to the photos of the long lost colony at Spica. Scattered signs of human life made the desolation even more poignant. A table in an abandoned dome, plates and cups still set out for a meal half eaten—the room now bound with successive layers of ice. A book lying in the mud, pages soaked into a sodden clump beneath a ruined spine.

"They take our people," he said quietly. "They snatch up their victims whenever and wherever our backs are turned, anywhere that they find our defenses weak. By the time we can react, they've vanished without a trace. The ones we lose are never seen again."

He let the last image linger. It was a churned expanse of muddy ground, the surface trampled by hundreds walking through an open field. A series of stills moved closer and closer to the footprints, the tracks of heavy-treaded boots and atmospheric work units mingled with thermal shoes and household slippers. In the final close-up, a single track had been captured, driven into the near-freezing mud of a summer thaw and then fossilized by the returning ice. It was the slim silhouette of a child's foot, toes splayed and bare in the punishing cold.

"Wherever you go, and whatever Section you choose—keep your eyes open, apes. There are regular dispatches to all SIC members on the Black List entities. Read them. Memorize them. And if you see anything out there, something that doesn't belong? Report it. Don't be afraid of repeating what we already know, or telling us what we don't want to hear. We need whatever help you can give us."

The final image faded and once again the golden sword hung in space, point-down above the podium. "That's all I have to say. Congratulations to you all—and God speed."

He gave them a quick martial salute and turned to step down from the podium. An uncertain smattering of applause followed him as he moved toward the side exit.

"Sir Commander sir!"

It was the same high feminine voice, the same staccato Ground Force delivery. He turned sharply toward the woman standing in the audience. "Ensign?"

"Black-Thirteen-the-Rippers-sir! What-do-the-Tarka-people call-them-sir!"

25

He raised an eyebrow. "Why do you ask?"

She hesitated. When she spoke again it was four words in flawlessly idiomatic *Urdu Kai*, delivered with the same abrupt Ground Forces rhythm. *"Daiko! Yan'-sara, dai!"*

Sir, I want to be sharp, sir.

Despite himself, he smiled. *"Kala du'kai,* ensign. And your accent is good. For the record, the Tarka name for Black Thirteen is very informal. They call them by a general term, *'massaaku.'"* He shrugged. "'Slavers.'"

3 | AN OFFICER AND A GENTLEMAN

Thatcher was waiting for him in the hall, leaning with one shoulder against the opposite wall. She held her data pad in one hand, playing a puzzle game with her stylus to pass the time; she glanced up at him briefly as he slipped out the side door of the auditorium, and then looked back down at the pad. "Wonderful speech, boss. Very inspiring."

"Thank you," he said cautiously. He gave the words the upward lilt of a question: after four years, he knew that too-casual tone too well. "One of my better efforts at public speaking."

"Oh, definitely! Great message for new recruits. Welcome to Sol Force Intelligence: learn to think like an alien, the Hiver War was 'stupid', and no matter what section you're assigned to—you'll be working for me."

He smiled. "Very succinct. I should have had you write it for me. I wouldn't have missed lunch."

She snorted irritably. "The Director is going to love that transcript." Scribbling another few letters with the stylus, she added sarcastically, "Four-letter word, English. 'Stultus, stulti'?"

"'Fool.'" He refused to rise to the bait; arguing with Thatcher only sharpened the pain of desire. He turned toward the end of the halls and the elevators. "The Director won't need to read the transcript; he was listening. He has a feed on Mars."

Thatcher winced. "Note to self: find myself a nice safe landing place for the day they take you down." The tip of her stylus tapped on her data pad, cycling rapidly through security and password screens as she entered their codes.

The elevator doors slid open smoothly and he stepped inside, reserving comment until both of them had entered their thumbprints into the security reader. The doors shut silently and the car began to descend.

"Cicero," he murmured. "*Congelat'elevator. Caecus surdusque.*"

The elevator stopped abruptly, and the indicator lights of its security camera began to flash a steady pulse of red. Thatcher looked up at him sharply. "Have I mentioned that it's extremely creepy when you do that?"

He regarded her gravely. "Margaret. We need to talk."

Her eyes dropped, and the side of her mouth quirked into a bitter smile. "Funny. When I say that, it never works."

He took a deep breath and released it slowly. "I was promoted." He had repeated the words so often that the excuse now sounded threadbare, even to him. "And that is not what we need to talk about."

She lifted her stubborn chin, her blue eyes focused stonily at the panel over his right shoulder. "I see. What did you want to discuss, *Commander*?"

He cocked his head as he looked her over. Standing in this small elevator, alone as only Cicero could make them, made him realize how long it had been since he had really studied her closely. She was nearing thirty now—when was her birthday?—and her thick mop of ginger hair had taken on a few threads of paler gold. She had lost weight, likely dropped under fifty kilograms: the unrelieved black of her uniform hid the loss, but it pained him to think how far the ribs must be jutting beneath it. Above her collar, the proud high bones of her face had risen higher, pointed chin and razor jaw honed to an even sharper edge. The laughing lines around the eyes and mouth, the frown lines of concentration between her brows were more deeply etched into her tanned skin.

Her eyes turned to confront his directly. "Well?" she demanded.

"Do you believe that I care for you, Margaret?"

Her jaw clenched and she looked away, eyes shining with angry tears. "I really don't know what to believe, sir." She hesitated, and spoke again more softly. "If you do, you've got a funny way of showing it."

"There's nothing funny about it, Lieutenant. Do you really believe that I would let you suffer for my politics?"

She frowned. "What are we talking about?"

"The topic of conversation was 'safe places to land.'" He took a step closer, to the outside limit of an arm's length, trying to engage her eyes. "Do you honestly believe that I have made no provision for you, if something should happen to me? After all we've been through...do you really know me so little?"

Her mouth trembled, vulnerable as a wound, and still she would not look at him. "If what should happen to you?" she said unsteadily.

He held her locked with his unbending black gaze. "If I should die," he said. "Where would you like to be assigned?"

Her breath caught in her chest and she looked up at the ceiling, as if for a way out. "Feeling a mite peaked, are we?"

He closed the distance between them, took her shoulders in his hands and squeezed gently. "Back to White Section? Dr. Kliggerman would be happy to have you back, any time. He says as much every time I see him."

She twisted free and angrily dashed a sparkling tear from the corner of her eye. "And go back to scooping Hiver-dung into his petrie dishes? Hell no. I'd rather take the dirt nap my own self." The colonial dialect had broken through her usual flattened speech—a sure sign that she was upset. She gave him an accusing look. "What's all this mortuary talk for, anyway? It was only a joke, Cai. I wasn't serious."

"Yes, but I am." He backed away again. "These are dangerous times, Margaret. I am a Task Force Commander. The moment I accepted these, I became a target." He touched the gold circles at his collar with his fingertips, a gesture curiously similar to checking the knot of a noose. "The same was true of anyone close to me."

Her eyes widened suddenly. "Is that why you—?"

"I was promoted," he said firmly. "Over a corpse. I had no time to maneuver when Commander Otomi died. I was understandably worried. I am still worried. Her shuttle crash was written off as an accident, but she was an expert pilot. And she wasn't the only high-ranking officer to depart the ranks feet-first, when the Hiver Armistice was signed."

Thatcher's eyes flashed anger. "I heard things," she admitted. "I thought it was just talk. You're saying that there really were murders in the ranks? Over that?"

He nodded silently.

She shook her head in disbelief. "That's insane. What's not to like about peace? Call me a simple country girl, but fewer planets burned to bedrock sounds pretty good to me."

"All right. You're a 'simple country girl,'" he said, obliging her with a smile. "And not a Legator who rose through the ranks by glassing Hiver nestworlds. Or a colonel who lost half her crew during a boarding action with the Tarkasian fleet." He spread his hands. "Not everyone is ready to stand down."

She frowned. "No. Guess not. Plenty of civilians grumbling about the wars we didn't 'finish', much less vac officers. My brother wouldn't shut up about the damn Hivers, last time I was home." She shrugged. "I just don't see what any of that has to do with us. Why would anyone kill Otomi? Or you, for that matter? Black Section is nothing in the scheme of things. We have to fight for our share of the paperclips, for God's sake. Even Kliggerman gets more funding than we do."

A rueful shake of his head. "Every Section is part of the whole. You cannot control the Force without Intelligence—the fist is no use without a head." He ran a palm over the crown of his bristling black hair, sighing. "As for Otomi…. Not everyone was fooled by her smiling old Mama-san façade. She built most of the security systems in the empire and designed half the cybernetic wetware in the Force—my own included. She was a dangerous woman. Her Section will always be dangerous, however small."

She raised a dubious brow. "Yes. They are wise to fear us," she intoned sagely. "We pour new water over spent coffee grounds, and it has made us strong…"

He shrugged. "A low profile has its advantages. Otomi ran a lean operation for good reason; she didn't want anyone looking too closely at what she was doing. If anyone had realized how much power she had at her disposal, they would have moved against her sooner."

Thatcher shook her head. "I honestly can't see it. Sorry."

"No need for apologies. I didn't see what she had either—until I had to wield it." He held up his hand, ticking off the competition on his fingers. "Red, Yellow and Blue are all much bigger Sections than we are, heavily staffed and funded. On paper, they seem much more dangerous. Red alone has four times the roster that Black does, and ten times the budget. But privilege has its price." He quirked the corner of his mouth into a smile, inviting her to share the joke. "Carroll, Nguy Sen and Maldonado are all slaves to the Finance Legate. They're chained to their desks; it's been years since any of them did any field work. And while they account for every ape and dime, in triplicate, every one of them is still bound to a limited jurisdiction. They each have a strong power base, but they rarely coordinate with each other unless our enemies do, and even then it's reluctant. They compete directly for resources. They never miss the chance to stick a knife in one another—there will never be any love lost there."

She nodded slowly. "Sure. I follow you that far."

"Meanwhile, when their poor relations in Black Section show up unannounced to rifle through their databases, interview their sources, or commandeer a team of specialists…?" He let the words trail off suggestively.

She grinned. "…they have to cooperate," she finished.

He nodded. "Or go on record as having refused, yes. And in twenty-eight years, they never said no to Otomi."

"Or to you," she pointed out.

"Or to me," he agreed mildly. "No one wants that kind of responsibility."

She frowned. "What about Kliggerman, or Vance? You'd think if it was just a matter of broad jurisdictions—or even seniority!—they would be the first to go. Those old spiders have been here forever. I think that Vance and that chair of his are fused into some kind of cybernetic centaur."

He winced. "Hardly charitable, Margaret."

"I'm not in a charitable mood." She folded her arms stubbornly. "And I don't want to go back to White Section."

He smiled. "All right. How do you feel about Trade?"

She gave him a skeptical squint. "Everyone wants to get into Trade. If you happen to know who the new TFC is going to be—by all means let me know. That job is supposed to be the fast track to Legator. Maybe he'll need someone to polish his brass."

He raised an eyebrow. "What if it was a woman?"

She smiled thinly. "I'm an equal opportunity brass polisher."

He rolled his eyes heavenward, pleading for patience. "Margaret, what if that woman were you?"

She stopped dead, thunderstruck. "Me?"

He nodded, smiling. "I think you have a good chance. I've broached the matter with the other Section heads—delicately, of course. Kliggerman didn't have a serious candidate of his own, and he still has a soft spot for you. Obviously he'd like to see one of his trainees make Commander. Both of us have already put your name forward as our first choice. He's also nominated one of his own people, as a cover—I believe you know him, a man named Cusick. We've both taken him as our second choice. Carroll, Nguy Sen and Maldonado also have their pet candidates, of course—but all three of them would gladly eat broken glass before they'd let one of the others take this plum. They won't risk voting for each other, even as a second or third selection, unless they see absolutely no alternative. I suspect they'll pick the Black and White Section candidates rather than risk doubling the power of their rivals."

Her arms were wrapped tightly around her narrow chest. "You...and Dr. Kliggerman...put my name forward?" Thatcher's voice was small.

"Well...yes." He hesitated. "I thought you would be pleased."

"As...your first choice?"

She looked up at him, her eyes strangely luminous, and suddenly Cai Rui felt the heat rising into his cheeks. "Well…yes," he stammered. "That is…your record is exemplary… and you have the right background for the job…"

And suddenly she was on him, in a breathless rush, arms flung tight around his body and her soft mouth on his. For a split second his body roared in response, a sudden consuming surge of flame that brought his hands up to her thick, fragrant mane and the silken heat of her cheek. In that moment he closed his eyes and let himself feel every inch of her wiry warmth pressed against him, every petal-soft millimeter of her lips on his, reliving every carnal sin they had committed—

—and then he stepped back, gently taking her wrists to disentangle her arms from his neck. Blood thundering in his ears, heart pounding, cheeks burning, nonetheless…he was once again Cai Rui, a man who belonged to himself… and to God.

"Thank you," she gasped. The ring of gratitude was unmistakable, and so was the light of joy in her eyes. "Thank you so much."

He nodded wordlessly, swallowing the lump in his throat.

"What about Vance?" she asked. "What did he say?"

"He was Vance," he croaked, and paused to clear his throat. "He said he would consider it, but the man has always been a little hard to read."

"I can't believe it." Her face was flushed with girlish excitement; at that moment she looked at least a decade younger, if not more. "I can't believe you nominated me."

He smiled reassuringly. "You can do it, Margaret. You were born for the job. You have all the right experience. And let's face it—polishing someone else's brass really isn't your strong suit, is it?" He winked.

She laughed out loud. "I'm sorry, I'm just…" She spun in place like a child, data pad pressed to her chest.

"It isn't a sure thing," he warned. "There's no way to predict it a hundred per cent—the final decision is with the Legate and the Director, and they sometimes have ideas of their own." He raised his hands, helplessly indicating himself. "And it's a big jump in rank. They could always balk at boot-strapping a Lieutenant so high all at once…"

"I know." She spoke gently. Her head was tilted, regarding him with eyes brimming with such radiant affection that he felt the blood suffusing his cheeks again. "I know, Cai. But that doesn't matter. What matters is that you had enough faith in me to try."

He folded his hands behind his back and nodded, a slight formal bow of acknowledgment.

She took a deep breath and let it out with a whoosh. "Wow. What a day. When will they announce it, do you think?"

"I believe there will be some sort of formal ceremony on Remembrance Day. The candidate will know earlier, of course. Two months at the most."

She bit her lip. "Long time to wait."

He shook his head. "Not long at all. If you do get the job, you'll have to be ready to step into your new office. I would suggest you do what all the other candidates are doing—start going through personnel files and briefings in your off hours. See who you want on your staff, set your mission parameters... and write your acceptance speech, of course." He grinned. "It isn't as easy as it looks, I assure you."

Thatcher hesitated. "Cai... what are you going to do if I—?"

He raised a hand to forestall her. "Please. Your old Section Leader will simply have to soldier on without you."

She shook her head, giving him a pitying look. "That's not going to be pretty."

"Oh ye of little faith! Who can resist an exciting career in Black Section? Why, I'm sure that my thrilling speech today has already netted me a few fish."

"Sure it did—for Trade section," she said acidly. Her fingertips suddenly flew to her mouth. "You didn't."

He shrugged it off with one negligent shoulder. "I thought it would be easier to build a new section out of new recruits. You don't want other Section heads planting too many of their own people too close to you—it takes a while to learn who you can trust."

Her eyes were shining brightly again; Cai Rui held up his hands defensively. "Please. No more thank-you's! I've been warned about my blood pressure."

Thatcher turned up her nose and showed him the impudent pink tip of her tongue. "Chicken."

His hand moved toward his chin to reactivate the data shunt, but Thatcher reached out, catching his wrist.

"Wait." Her eyes were grave. "I wanted to tell you, while no one can listen— you got another flower, Cai. One of those Tarka things."

He nodded, trying not to let the reaction reach his eyes. "Ah. Another piece for my collection. What color is this one?"

She looked him straight in the eye. "It's the color of Rome." Her grip on his wrist tightened, briefly—an affectionate warning squeeze. "Be careful, Commander. She isn't as subtle as she thinks."

He nodded, moved by another momentary pang of tenderness: how like her it was, to have known and said nothing. He raised her tiny rough hand and placed a light, chaste kiss above the knuckles. "As always, I heed your advice." He stepped back, returning to his formal posture. "Cicero, *restit'elevator.*"

The elevator resumed its swift descent, the onboard camera's indicator light green. "I told you it was nothing to worry about," he said, picking up the tag end of an imaginary conversation. "Check the net; I want to see if I've caught anything."

Thatcher rolled her eyes. "With that speech? Please."

"Ah, there was at least one who couldn't resist the siren call of cosmic mystery! What about that little ground pounder—hasn't she already applied?"

She cycled through screens quickly, and finally shook her head her head in seeming disappointment. "Yes she has. Poor thing! I'll have to schedule her for a medical exam." Thatcher entered in the codes. "She may have taken a recent blow to the head."

4 | CORRIGENDA

The box rested on top of a vertical stack of paper in his hotel suite, the collected debris of even a brief stay away from his home office on Mars. It was finely carved, a fragile shell of perfumed wood in the shape of a stylized insect. He sat down at the desk, turning the object in his hands to admire the gold leaf and the brilliant shades of lacquer. At last he found the hidden catch that opened the wing-cases to reveal the inner chamber.

Inside the prize rested in a nest of folded paper, artfully creased in a spiral pattern to suggest a pearlescent whirlpool of green water and foam. Even at first glance it was an extraordinary piece, a perfect reproduction of the Tarkasian lotus. Only the sheen of protective oil betrayed the fact that the blossom was made of sintered steel. Every exquisite petal was sharp as a razor, ruby red and enameled with golden veins. It was beautiful and dangerous, like its creator—the product of an ancient empire and a people with centuries of decadence behind them.

The calling card of the Iron Lotus.

He reached into his breast pocket and took out one of his thin cotton dress gloves, put it on, and carefully plucked the blossom out of the box. He took the base between a gloved thumb and forefinger to avoid leaving fingerprints, and held the flower up to the light before his eye. In closer detail the golden tracery of veins was incredibly fine, so natural that one would swear that the ponds of Kao'Kona were littered with steel lilies like this one.

Deliberately he took the forefinger of his free hand and touched the tip of a single petal. The point penetrated skin effortlessly, without resistance, bringing up a perfectly round bead of blood. With the cotton-gloved hand he dabbed away the potential rust spot and put the red flower back into its delicate box.

Another thirteen such flowers already rested on their lacquered boxes on a small shelf in his private quarters on Mars. He had given a drop of his blood to each one; the one time he had forgotten the blossom had self-destructed within a day, and taken a significant portion of his file cabinet with it.

The boxes alone would bring over a thousand credits each—the little lacquered carvings were popular collector's items. The flowers, ranging in color from canary yellow to a shade of velvety purple so deep it was nearly black, were considerably more rare. Tarkasian knick-knacks of sintered gold and other soft metals were often offered for sale as luxury trade—but these were the only frivolous objects of sintered steel that he had seen.

He sat and performed a breathing exercise, contemplating the shining box as his heart rate slowed. One part of him had the impulse, as always, to go home, gather up every single one of these flowers and ship them off to Sol Force RDC at once. There must be a reason that the Supreme did not want any sintered Tarkasian steel leaving the borders of his empire. These tiny blossoms might hold the key to everything from the armored plating of his warships to the simple, deadly resilience of the shatterproof Tarkasian vac-hammer, which had brought more than one human boarding action to an ugly end.

But there would be questions, he thought. *They would want to know where the flowers come from. And if a single lie were to unravel… they might unweave the whole carpet.*

He smiled. It was a thin excuse to possess things of such beauty. In the end, he had no legitimate reason to keep them—if he was not going to do his duty and give them to the Research and Development Corps, then he should toss them into the nearest fusion torch. It was only common sense. It was madness to put a traceable artifact from a high-ranking Tarkasian contact on a shelf in plain sight, even in his private home. If he were ever exposed, this collection would be seen for what it was—a brazenly displayed symbol of divided loyalty and broken protocol.

No. In the end, the truth was that he kept them because she had made them with her own hands. Like her trust, he treasured them. Her art was no less deadly and subtle than the creature herself. With each message she intentionally placed herself in his hands, knowing full well that she might be betrayed—and she reminded him that trust, however precious, could cut as deep as any blade.

He rose from his seat and headed for the lobby. It was not too late to catch the last afternoon shuttle to Rome. A red blossom meant that she had sent an emissary to meet him in the holy city, just as the yellow meant that her agent would be haunting the starport on Arcadia, and the pale blue pointed to an obscure dive on Junction. The Iron Lotus had news for him—news that must be delivered in person by someone she trusted.

Before the southbound train had traveled more than a few minutes, his PDA notified him of an incoming message. Cai Rui pulled a data pad out of his satchel and opened his communications suite, curious. There were only three possible channels for a message that the PDA would not re-route immediately to his office. He had spoken directly to Thatcher less than an hour before; it was unlikely to be his second in command.

The letter was encrypted with the cruciform key of the Holy See. Cicero opened it effortlessly, but it might have taken a hostile specialist hours to break the treacherous protective code, and without care the embedded executable buried in its defensive sheathe could destroy an enemy system. The document, once opened, was titled simply *"Vos Summonemini"*. There was nothing further in the body of the message.

You are summoned. He closed his eyes briefly and erased the message with a flick of his stylus. There were few coincidences in his profession. A Tarkasian agent awaited him in Rome with urgent news; if the Vatican had sent a summons on the same day, the two were likely related.

Doesn't have to be bad news, he tried to tell himself. The pit of his stomach disagreed, and remained stubbornly queasy all the way to Rome.

✳ ✳ ✳

He put on his orarion as he passed through the second gate, slinging the embroidered sash with its seven crosses over the breast of his uniform jacket and snugging the fit under his left arm. As he buttoned it at the shoulder, he moved into the first of several enclosed courtyards. Every flagstone thronged with people, all clumped into loose knots—some jabbered excitedly, some huddled together to speak in low worried tones. Looking more closely, he could see that these were crowds of deacons and lay parishioners, each group in the company of a bishop in full liturgical dress. A score of ethnic groups and hundreds of parishes were represented, including a few recognizably belonging to the outer colonies.

As he approached the security station, a pair of men armed with long black halberds stepped forward. They wore the colors of the Swiss guard. *"Praebete crucem, si placuit,"* one of them said—in the bored tone of routine. *"Arma reliquenda sunt."*

He reached under the standing lip of his collar and found the steel chain of his dog tags. The golden weight of his pectoral cross hung alongside them, and he presented it to the notary, who ran it over the scanner. The man looked up, checking the face before him against the identification image on his screen.

"*Nomen?*" he asked.

"Rui Cai." He unbuckled his sword and placed it on the security counter, tapping it meaningfully with his fingertip. "*Do't detes, non?*"

The notary smiled humorlessly and switched to English. "Of course, Archdeacon. I will see to it personally." The man took the blade in its scabbard and placed it into a claim box, setting the code with Cai Rui's crucifix. He handed the steel chain back across the table. "Cardinal Amato has requested your presence. We will escort you now."

Cai Rui nodded coldly, hiding his surprise behind an expressionless mask. He put the chain back over his head and waited as the men behind the counter exchanged a few quiet words. Curious, he tried to quell his anxiety by reading their lips—until he realized abruptly that they were speaking Romansch. In the meantime, he tried to check his racing pulse. He had come to the Vatican City hoping to meet his Tarkasian contact and receive a communiqué; now suddenly he was "escorted" to the Prefect of the *Congregatio pro Doctrina Fidei*—the oldest of the nine congregations of the Curia and still by far the most dangerous.

One of the two guards apparently lost the argument and gave Cai Rui an impatient wave to come along. Shouldering his black halberd, he double-marched swiftly through the city, leading his charge down an echoing colonnade toward the Palazzo del Astra. As they marched swiftly along the wall, they passed another dozen anxious delegations, each led by a long-suffering black-robed notary toward the Curia.

He quickened his pace, drawing up within a half-pace of the pikeman's right elbow. "What is happening? I have never seen the city so crowded."

The man glanced back irritably. "*Corrigenda.*" His eyes snapped forward and he quickened his pace, stepping ahead to keep his place in the lead.

Cai Rui fell back, frowning. *Corrigenda*—a list of items to be corrected. He had heard of such meetings, when the bishops and archbishops of past times were summoned to Rome to receive corrections of doctrine. In the century preceding the formation of the Consortia, the *corrigenda* had been nearly constant, with the Holy Father summoning His bishops once a decade, sometimes more, to cement the True Faith against the onslaught of countless heresies. But such a meeting had not been held in over two hundred years. Why now?

There could be only one answer: Amato. The Prefect had held his post for just over three years, and already the bishops of several worlds had learned to dread his Doctrinal Notes. These reprimands would swoop down out of vacuum, announcing "dangerous errors" in everything from the Easter mass to the catechism; if the error was not explained or recanted immediately, the man would wield the Papal ban like a sledgehammer. Countless parishes and sects had already faced interdiction and excommunication—some after having held their doctrines for over two hundred years.

The Cardinal's firestorm crusade against heresy had inspired a number of unkind political cartoons, now taped to refrigeration units throughout the thirteen worlds... cartoons pointing out that the "Congregation for the Doctrines of the Faith" had once had a much simpler name: the Office of the Holy Inquisition.

The guard turned at the end of the quarter-mile walk and led him through a second security checkpoint. After a few words in Romansch, the second set of guards scanned Cai Rui's cross and waved him through. The two of them passed beneath a shadowy arch and emerged into the open air of a secluded garden, its gracious paths lined with crushed stone. The grass and trees were subdued and gray, still not wakened from their winter sleep, and the ancient marble fountains were bone dry: the water rationing within the city had not allowed them to be filled within living memory.

Still, the silence of the place alone was a luxury, especially in contrast to the panicked mobs of St. Peter's square and the Curia. Upon the bare branches a few dried berries remained, and the tiny flitting sparrows of Rome had gathered around a scattering of seed that some kindly hand had strewn. Cai Rui drank in the peace of the place as they walked, and silently he smiled. *Dei semper gratia.*

At last they came to the double doors of the Palazzo, and the guard hastily left him in the hands of a red-faced secretary in a fluttering gown. Cai Rui glanced over his shoulder, watching as the man with his halberd practically ran back the way they had come, and a cold weight settled in his chest.

"*Gratia, gratia,*" the man muttered, looking back repeatedly to be sure that he was followed closely as they ascended the winding stairs. Cai Rui, tempted to stop occasionally to examine the paintings and sculptures more closely, nonetheless took pity on the balding little cleric and stayed at his heel, keeping his eyes fixed politely on the stairs beneath his feet.

At last he was led into an empty parlor. "*Cupietis aut biber'aut cenare? Num carebitis quoquam?*"

Cai Rui looked around the room, distracted, and answered in English. "No. Nothing, thank you. Will His Eminence be long?"

"*Ut Deus vult.*" The priest indicated a chair. "Sit, please."

Cai Rui took the seat reluctantly, perching himself as lightly as he could on the silk brocade. The secretary pulled the door closed behind him with a quiet click, locking his guest into a gilded prison.

He looked around uneasily. Rooms like this one never failed to make him uncomfortable. The décor and furnishings were ancient and opulent, relics of centuries past. The chairs and tables stood on delicately curving legs of painted wood like white gazelles, and looked as if they would snap under the unseemly weight of a grown man; everywhere there was gold, glass, porcelain and alabaster, a veritable army of winged cherubim and stern seraphim standing guard over mirrors, decanters, and archival cases filled with paper-and-leather books. Wherever there was an empty space against the burned velvet wall-paper, someone had hung an oil painting or a cross: at least three of the latter he recognized immediately as survivors of the Conflagration.

The carpets under his feet were woven silk. Looking down at them, he couldn't help but lift his boot to check the sole. Perhaps he had tracked some unseemly filth onto the cerulean field with its entwined white lilies and yellow *fleur-de-lis*...

The door handle gave him only a split-second of warning; he was on his feet instantly, turning to face the Cardinal as he entered.

"Eminence." He stepped forward and dropped to one knee, offering the crown of his head in a bow.

Amato hesitated, as if debating, and finally placed his palm on Cai Rui's shoulder. "Archdeacon. Welcome. We do not have much time to spare."

"Yes, Eminence." Cai Rui stood and folded his hands behind his back as the Cardinal went to his desk and settled himself into its wing-backed chair.

Amato unbuttoned his stole and let it slip to the back of his seat. Looking up again, he sighed somewhat irritably and shook his head. "No, no. Please do sit, Rui Cai. This is my hour to dine. A soldier standing at attention will do nothing for this old man's digestion."

"Forgive me, Eminence." Cai Rui resumed his uncomfortable perch. "I am sorry to intrude."

The old man pursed his lips and waved this away with his ring hand. "Not at all, my son. I did not expect you so soon. My summons was sent to Mars only this morning."

The ice in his veins seemed to thaw a half-degree, but still he did not dare to lie. "I had other business on Earth, Eminence."

"*Bene, bene.* Simple good fortune. Some news is not improved by delay." Amato reached beneath the desk and pressed a hidden button.

The secretary's voice came quietly from a speaker beside the door. "*Si, Cardinale?*"

"*Ferte cenam ad studium, Johanne. Amabo te.*"

"*Cardinale.*"

Amato rested his elbows upon the shining desktop, his fingertips steepled prayerfully before his face, and closed his eyes. Cai Rui studied the man, watching as he took a single cleansing breath.

Like many clergymen, the Cardinal did not indulge in modern vanities. For practical reasons, he had maintained the vigorous body of a man in his mid- to late forties, but his face showed every year of ninety. The flesh had fallen into a thousand seams over the iron mask of his aquiline nose, prominent brow and slanting cheek. What little hair remained on his pate was snow white, shaven in a traditional Dominican tonsure about his ears; his Cardinal's cap did not quite cover the bare skin.

"Forgive me," he said at last. The black eyes opened, sharp and shining like jet. "If there is a better way to say these things, I cannot find it presently. Perhaps I am just too tired. I must tell you this: we have word of your mentor, Archdeacon. Bishop Tourneau has gone to God."

Cai Rui froze. His mouth opened; after several seconds he realized that no words would be forthcoming, and he closed it again.

"Apparently his mission has been destroyed. The word of it has been late in coming, to you and to others; I must accept the blame entirely. My fellow Curate, Cardinal Turion, has been ill this winter. I had agreed to assume some of his duties temporarily, in the hopes that he would soon recover. Instead, his condition has worsened, and I have been simply overwhelmed." He spread his hands. "I had thought, given the *Pax Tarkana*, that our people in these outlying missions would be safe. Clearly I was mistaken." His eyes narrowed and the lines of his face deepened with suppressed rage. "These pagan reptiles will answer for the crime, be assured of that."

Cai Rui was on his feet. "The Tarka did this?" The words tumbled out without thought. "Is that... is that possible?"

The Cardinal shrugged. "They are a savage race, my son. They bow before idols and worship a thousand devils, from what I hear. Only a man as brave as Tourneau would even *try* to bring such heathens to God."

Cai Rui staggered a step to the side, knees weak, and abruptly sat again. "F-forgive me, Eminence," he stammered. "I am…"

"Please. Do not apologize. He raised you, did he not? And he was your pastor, of course."

Cai Rui nodded. The tears sprang up in his eyes, and he swallowed painfully. *Not now.* "How did this happen? Is there… any further information?"

The Cardinal's lip curled with distaste. "The report we have received is very vague. They say our mission is lost, that the parish has been attacked by some sort of raiders—"

"Raiders?" The blood had risen in his cheeks. "Was that the exact word they used?"

Amato raised an eyebrow. "You doubt our veracity, Archdeacon?"

Cai Rui stiffened. "Not at all, Eminence. I have learned some of the Tarka language in my work. There are many words to describe different sorts of attack. I had hoped there might be some clue…"

"Ah." The Cardinal shook his head. "Such subtleties may be lost in translation. Our notaries are perhaps not so attuned to matters military."

Disappointed, he lowered his eyes. "I see."

"We have reason to believe that they lie, of course. But we do not expect them to admit openly to their persecutions—nor to their preparations for war against humanity."

"Preparations for war?" Despite his best intentions, Cai Rui could not keep the note of incredulity from his voice.

The corner of the Cardinal's mouth quirked wryly. "Indeed. You are not our only friend in MarsDome, Archdeacon. What you do not choose to tell us-others pass along."

A chill went through him; he gathered the shreds of his tattered composure and measured his words carefully. "Eminence, forgive me. I mean no disrespect. I had heard nothing of this, and I have been…very diligent in cultivating my contacts within Tarka space."

The old man raised an eyebrow, steepling his fingers before his foxy old face. "So we have heard."

He felt the flush rising to his cheeks and nearly spoke again. Just then, a light knock came at the door, and the Secretary appeared, carrying a silver tray. Cai

Rui looked up and rose clumsily to his feet. "Eminence, I...I am interrupting your meal. I should leave you in peace."

The Cardinal dismissed this graciously with a wave of his hand.

"Before I go, may I beg your leave to investigate this matter personally?"

Amato hesitated, eyes narrowed in brief calculation. As he sat in thought, his Secretary hurried to lay out the contents of the tray, leaving a single glass of wine, a Spartan serving of antipasto and a half-loaf of bread on the desktop. "Perhaps you have a good thought there, Archdeacon," the old man mused. He rapped the desktop decisively. "Yes. You will do this thing."

Cai Rui lowered his eyes. "Thank you, Eminence."

Amato rose. "Truly, I am sorry to have so little time. Father Tourneau was a fine man, Commander. He will be missed."

Cai Rui lowered himself once again to his knee, shaking. "Yes, Eminence."

The Cardinal offered his ring. "May God bless you, Archdeacon. I will look forward to your report."

He choked out the words again, his throat constricted. "Thank you, Eminence." Unable to say more, he pressed his lips briefly to the chilly platinum band. As he turned to follow the Secretary to the door, he had no trouble ignoring the fine paintings. It seemed that the light had gone out of the world.

The sound of the double doors closing behind him seemed to echo in the darkness. Somehow he stumbled down the steps and into the gardens alone, until he passed into the shadow of a stone fountain and fell to his hands and knees on the crushed marble path.

His whole body seized, a wrenching spasm that crushed his belly and lungs like a giant fist. Around him, the abandoned seeds were still strewn over the walkway; the sparrows had gone with the light. He sobbed in a breath and forced himself back to his feet, making his way blindly along the white path and out along the shadowy colonnade until he reached the second gate.

"*Signore!*" the notary called as he staggered past. "Your sword—!"

He turned to see the man rising from his seat and numbly went back to the desk. Like an automaton he buckled the blade around his hip, and without a word reached up to yank the orarion from his shoulder. He turned on his heel, leaving the torn fabric to lie in the cobblestone street.

5 | A BROTHER IN THE FAITH

Many hours later, the crowds of the city finally thinning after midnight, he came to the scorched façade of an ancient church on the Capitoline mountain. The growth of the new city had pressed in tight around it, but the solar sconces outside the three doors still glowed softly in the darkness, welcoming seekers as they had for over a thousand years.

Cai Rui hesitated on the step and then went inside, moving down the center aisle through the pews toward the high altar. The Lady of Consolation gazed down on him with gentle eyes from above, the child in Her arms raising two fingers in benediction.

He let himself fall to his knees before Her. As he looked up, a shadow moved over the ceiling, a robed and hooded figure caught by the floor lamps below. He turned his head. A stoop-shouldered cleric in brown homespun stood behind him in the nave, half-hidden in flickering light of a hundred tiny candles.

Cai Rui turned away, closing his eyes. Silently, urgently, he waited for the words of a prayer to form in his mind, but try as he might, nothing came to him. It was as if his soul had been smothered inside him, with an empty void where the love of God should be.

The voice from behind him came softly at first, a rich low sound delivering the Latin of the archaic hymn with paternal authority:

"Deliver me, Lord, from death eternal
on that day when we must tremble
when the heavens will be shaken, and the earth
until You come to judge the universe through flame."

45

As he listened, the stone within his chest seemed to crumble. Cai Rui lowered his face into his hands, and the terribly beautiful, alien voice lifted itself to the next register, filling the church with a clear ringing tenor of lyrical pain:

"I am set a-tremble, I am afraid
while surrender comes, and the approaching wrath..."

The figure moved closer, the voice rising still higher, soaring toward heaven as no adult human throat could ever lift it:

"That day, the day of wrath!
Disaster and suffering!
The great and intensely bitter day.
Eternal rest grant to them, Lord,
And let never-ending light shine upon them..."

Cai Rui's chest hitched with a silent sob. A gentle hand descended to rest upon his shoulder, offering a moment's comfort; he reached up to cover the rough fingers with his own as the tears flowed freely. The voice lowered and sweetened, ringing with love.

"Into paradise may the angels lead you,
May the martyrs receive you upon your arrival,
And may they guide you into the sacred city, Jerusalem.
May the chorus of angels receive you,
And along with Lazarus, once poor
May you have eternal rest..."

The voice dropped once more to the deepest timbre to complete the song:

"Deliver me, Lord, from death eternal...
On that day when we must tremble...
On that day when we must tremble."

The silence lasted for several seconds when the last note faded. When at last he trusted himself to speak, Cai Rui's throat was thick with emotion. "Thank you," he said simply.

"*Habas yan*," the Tarka answered. "I share your grief." He threw back his hood, and with a pale golden hand he offered a torn band of fabric—the orarion Cai Rui had left at the Vatican gate. "But we have much to talk about, Brother Cai."

* * *

The stairs were black, claustrophobically narrow and reeking of boiled cabbage and paraffin. The power had been cycled away from the residential areas of the city hours ago. Only a few of the rooms in the building still stirred with any signs of battery-powered life—music softly murmuring in the dark, or a crack of light as someone sat awake until dawn.

Cai Rui passed the beam of his pocket lamp over the heaps of trash at the landing, startling a trio of fat, red-eyed Roman rats from their foraging. They slunk away reluctantly, one of them still carrying a scrap of garbage in its mouth. He grimaced, and took the remaining steps with a few graceful bounds.

The room was on the third floor, the final door to the left. He let himself in with a pair of old-fashioned keys, stepping in quickly and locking the bolts behind him; the sound of his footsteps in the hall had roused someone from sleep, and he had no desire to be seen or confronted in this part of town. A slanting ray of moonlight filtered through the window and fell across a table just opposite the door. As he watched, a slim figure dropped from the rooftop above, catching itself gracefully with one hand and foot on the windowsill. The Tarka lifted the sash and let himself into the room, his bundled robe under his arm. Once inside, he turned away and modestly dropped the rough homespun gown back over his head, concealing his nearly-nude body and lithe tail.

"My host does not wish me to be seen," he explained, speaking softly. "He does not want it known that he rents rooms to 'my kind'—Catholic or not. The arrangement suits me; I find it more comfortable to climb the building than the stairs."

Cai Rui nodded wordlessly.

"A moment, please."

Mateo bent to the tabletop, lifted a darkened sphere and rubbed it rapidly, rolling the ball back and forth between his palms. Within the depths of the glass globe a flickering red light appeared, rapidly increasing with the friction to a cheerful yellow glow. He set the ball back in its cradle and made a welcoming gesture, inviting his guest to sit within the circle of light.

Cai Rui pulled out one of the rough wooden stools. "Tell me if you can what is happening, Mateo. I don't understand the things I'm hearing. They say that your people are preparing for a new war with our empire, that my Bishop was martyred by Tarka persecution—where do these rumors come from?"

The Tarka gave a practiced human shrug as he set down his samovar and a pair of chipped china cups on the table. "I cannot tell you, Caido, but believe me—we would dearly like to know who is spreading this dangerous nonsense."

"Is it nonsense?" He stated the question flatly.

Mateo's eyes flashed red with annoyance. "Of course. If the military caste were planning a war with *Humaanu*, rest assured that my Aunt would know it."

Yes. But would she pass on that information to me? He left the words unspoken.

"Communications with your people have become increasingly difficult of late. We suspect that there are forces within MarsDome moving against us...but their means are subtle. More and more often, we find that messages have been garbled, lost—perhaps even revised, at times. We seldom receive the response we hoped."

Cai Rui nodded silently.

"As to Ko'Grappa...that is a complicated matter. But not a subtle one. The thing was not done by Tarka hands—on this I would wager my soul." Mateo's eyes were clear and pale as ice. "But a persecution? Yes. Perhaps."

Cai Rui took a deep breath and released it. "I was told that the Tarka called the attacking force 'raiders.'" He used the English term, as Amato had, but he moved his hand in the classic Tarka interrogative. "Does that mean what I think it does?"

Mateo blinked assent. "Yes. *Massaaku.*"

"I see." The weight beneath his breastbone seemed to double, and once again it became difficult to speak. Mateo's eyes were pale violet with sympathy. "Well. Best...to start from the beginning, then."

"As you wish." The Tarka rose. "From the beginning and until recently, all seemed to be well." He went to the counter and opened a black enamel strongbox, chill vapor rising as he exposed its interior to the air. "Our bishop sent regular missives to Rome, and received news as usual. Our work among the people of Soth'ram seemed to be progressing. Several of the leading clans have attended masses in the vulgate, and many of the younger brothers have been baptized. The will to believe is there. We have only to show them the way."

He removed a glass bottle full of white liquid from the case and a tin of chocolate powder. The Tarka poured milk into the brass belly of the samovar, eyes twinkling green with visible delight. "Forgive me. Perhaps it is un-Christian, but I have a weakness for this drink. And I cannot bring myself to share my rations with your 'rats.'"

Cai Rui made a face. "Even St. Francis was not so generous. But please—continue. You've said communications are difficult. This began when, exactly?"

"Seven, perhaps eight cycles ago." The Tarka clapped his hands beneath the samovar, igniting its tiny flame. As the milk warmed, he spooned chocolate powder generously into the two cups. "Difficult to say. The progression was slow. First, there was a delay in the feedback signal from our Node array—as if it were taking longer for a message to reach its intended target. We thought our equipment unreliable, or perhaps our signal met some sort of interference. But we could not find the problem."

Cai Rui sat back, nonplussed. "Nearly a year, then."

Brother Matthew shrugged again, and the ill-fitting robe slipped down over his slim shoulder. "From the eyes in one's tail, yes. But at the time, it seemed nothing. We had other worries." He lifted the lid of the tall brass kettle and stirred the scalding milk with his battered spoon, and then decanted some of the steaming liquid into a cup, using the same spoon to blend the chocolate. "Only in the past four cycles has the problem become serious. Now it seems that many messages never reach Rome at all—or are deliberately ignored. When I brought news of Ko'Grappa, they told me that our Prefect, Cardinal Turion, was indisposed. This other Cardinal—Amat'o?—gave me a very cold reception. When I told him what had happened, he behaved as if I had done the thing myself. And there are rumors that our mission is to be closed—all our people excommunicated."

Brother Matthew handed him the freshly mixed cup. As he accepted it, Cai Rui looked the Tarka in the eye, studying the shape of his pupils with care in the golden lamplight. "Are you certain about Ko'Grappa, Mateo?"

"*Yan. Massaaku.*" Even as he poured hot milk into a second cup, the Tarkas's leaf-green eyes flushed brilliant red, pupils narrowing to icy slits of hatred. "Very certain. I have not seen it with my own eyes, but I have heard that all the signs are there. It was a powerful strike. The destruction is…complete."

Cai Rui closed his eyes wearily. "So the mission is destroyed. The cathedral, the town…gone?"

Brother Matthew froze, his pupils widening with surprise. "No. I do not think you understand, Caido. This attack was not upon a single *ko'di*, mission or no mission. *All of Grappa is gone.* Over a million souls—the slavers have taken them all. The planet has been stripped bare."

He felt the blood drain from his face. "Impossible."

"My aunt said the same. But her soldiers have made their survey on the southern continent. The report has left the matter in no doubt. *Massaaku.*"

He clenched his fist. "I must have that report."

The Tarka nodded. "Yes. She thought so. She said I was to give this to no one else."

He pulled a gold chain from beneath his robe and removed a crystal pendant. "She has done what she can. Her fleet confirms only that the mission has not been spared—she gave them strict orders to leave the ruins undisturbed."

"That is appreciated."

"She gives you and your folk until the end of the cycle to do what is necessary for your dead, and to investigate on behalf of your empire. Then the loss must be announced and an official reason given for the planet's fall. The Nine have debated the available lies to cover such a catastrophe. The Supreme presently favors 'an outbreak of plague'—he will burn the ruins to glass from orbit, claiming contagion, and re-settle over the ashes in the coming year."

Cai Rui took the crystal in his hand, still warm from the Tarka's body, and nodded.

"She says...that you should use this time wisely." Brother Matthew sipped his chocolate, and his eyes shifted back to a leaf-green shade of pleasure. "But you will not have long, *Caido.* I am sorry."

Cai Rui rose to his feet. "Give her my thanks." He held up the crystal in his fist. "This cannot wait. I must be going."

The Tarka tilted his head graciously. "You will not stay to drink your *kok'latl?*"

"Forgive my rudeness. Next time."

"Ah well." The Tarka deacon's green eyes sparkled mischief. "I suppose we must not let it go to waste!"

6 | THE INCIDENT AT KO'GRAPPA

"Thatcher, wake up."

There was a long delay before she answered; in his mind's eye he could see her rolling over to look at the clock. When at last she punched the comm, her first words were grim. "Six a.m., Commander."

"I know. I've been waiting for the last hour and a half. I need you to get on the wire to Mars. Tell Vance I need the fastest Deep Scan platform he's got. And have Butler muster me a platoon for Black Section. Ground Forces, light brawlers. Experienced."

Her voice sharpened instantly. "What's the job?"

"Should be just a bag and tag. I don't anticipate trouble. If Kliggerman has any apes with drop experience—great. But they have to know the business end of a rifle."

"Where are we going?"

"Little stroll in Red territory. We're looking for Black Thirteen."

There was an awkward pause. "Right. Sure. Do we have authorization for this?"

"Would I lead you on a mission three jumps into Tarka space without authorization?"

"Do you really want me to answer that question, sir?"

He almost smiled. "Get a move on, Lieutenant. I intend to get my money's worth before you leave us."

"Right. When's our ETD?"

"If they ask, tell them we left yesterday. And don't let Vance stick us with a slow boat. We have a very limited window. If we don't make it in time, there's going to be nothing left to see."

Her sigh was audible. "All right, boss. I'm on it."

"Excellent. TFC out."

✳ ✳ ✳

"It's safe now, sir. You can take off your helmet."

Cai Rui nodded silently and opened the keypad on the back of his left hand, entering the code. The recycler within his suit wheezed slowly to a halt; within a few seconds the helmet hissed and rose a quarter inch from his shoulders, breaking its seal with a sound like a wet kiss. He removed it and tucked it under his arm, his face expressionless. As always, there was a brief catch in his chest as he released the last of the canned air in his lungs, and a tiny squirming knot of panic before he could bring himself to breathe in the planetary atmosphere. He could never fully trust a new environment.

The rest of the team was already working in the quire of the cathedral. Three beam lamps had been arranged on the floor, pointing upward into the high arches above. The rood still hung from the ceiling, creaking in the wind that blew in through the shattered windows.

Looking up at the body, nailed to the elaborately carved cross in obscene imitation of a former crucifixion—at last he breathed in. It was cold on Ko'Grappa, but there was no masking the smell of death. The pale stone floor was black with blood.

"Cut him down." His quiet voice seemed to echo in the empty room.

The ensign beside him shifted, looking uncomfortable. "Gold Six told us not to touch—"

"Gold Five is telling you to cut him down." The voice, still soft and mild, cut through all objections like a cold scalpel. "That is my order."

"Yes sir." The boy turned away, triggering his radio and murmuring for back-up; it would take three men and a ladder to bring down the holy cross. Carved from Tarkasian ironwood and embossed with gold, the rood alone would weigh over 150 kilos in this gravity—and the man who had died there would easily weigh another 90.

Several feet away, Thatcher looked up and saw that he had arrived. She motioned him closer, indicating with a circular gesture that he should walk

52

around the blood rather than through it. He picked his way cautiously through the overturned pews and squatted beside her. Another victim here, Tarka rather than human, but wearing the same robe as the crucified deacon above.

"I do not understand it. Do you?"

"Starting to." She looked him in the eye, and he could see the strain of the past three days. Virtually none of the apes Butler had mustered had any medical or technical training; she had been forced to grid the site and lead the recon and survey teams herself. "You're not going to like it."

He shrugged. "That is a given. Tell me what you see."

"Well, we read the records. It really is a Roman Catholic Cathedral, apparently. Bishop's seat for the whole planet. There were over 30,000 Tarkasian converts on this ball—Christianity was apparently a big hit with the Crocs."

Despite himself, he almost smiled. "Well, that in itself is interesting. The Holy See has been busy making peace where others make war. One wonders what else they have got up to, when the high command was not looking."

She gave him a wry look. "Oh, one wonders." Her sarcasm was so edged and clear that he almost smiled.

He shook his head, dismissing the line of conversation. "Continue. Is it possible at all that the Tarka wiped out their own colony, for some reason?"

Her eyes were solemn. "I don't think so, sir. I'd agree with the original assessment—it's either Black Thirteen or the best damn imitation in history. The pattern has changed, but not the basic execution. And whatever did this?" She made a circular gesture, encompassing the cathedral and its martyrs. "I'm pretty sure it wasn't Tarka." She reached down with one gloved hand; the fingers of the Tarka victim were still clenched, thick sharp nails dark with blood. With a pair of tweezers, she plucked a shred of gore from under one of the cold claws and held it up to the light—a patch of skin sprouting dozens of pale brown hairs. "Tarkas don't have fur."

"Indeed. Neither do Hivers, to my knowledge."

"No sir."

"So...we are definitely dealing with something new." He tilted his head. "Interesting. This sect specifically taught non-violence. And yet...this one fought back."

Thatcher tilted her head to indicate the rest of the robed figures on the cathedral floor. "All five of them did. Definitely didn't surrender peacefully. Maybe they weren't as 'converted' as all that."

Cai Rui shook his head. "I wouldn't be too certain." He stood up, taking a few steps into the rubble, and bent to pick something up; when he turned back toward her, he held a long staff of gilt wood in his hand. The upper portion had once been carved into some kind of semi-circular shape; now it was a shattered mess, and clotted with dark blood. He held it out to her. "This is a crosier—a symbol of spiritual authority. No one would have dared to touch it but the bishop himself."

"Wow." She held the staff up to the light. "I should get this back to the trailer. These marks almost look like teeth—solid bar of ironwood, and I'd swear it's bitten half-way through."

"Indeed." He closed his eyes briefly, driving unbidden images from his mind. "It would appear that the holy father struck a few blows of his own, before the end. I think this was not the occasion for a quiet martyrdom."

She shrugged acquiescence. "I guess not."

"Have any other remains been found?"

"No." She lowered her eyes, and her voice dropped as well. "There aren't a lot of remains in general, sir. We're pretty sure the majority of the colonists weren't killed. Just…taken."

His eyes narrowed. "All of them?"

"We haven't searched any of the other sites on foot. If we take that Tark report at face value—they didn't find any survivors in the southern settlements, and those were much more heavily populated. This site was a city of over ten thousand, as near as I can tell, and…it's completely empty." She shivered. "We've been looking, believe me. We haven't found a single body. It's…truly uncanny."

"How many humans were here—do we know?"

"Not many. Just the missionaries, according to the records. And a few monks who were studying Urdu Kai. Apparently they wanted to make some kind of translation of the Bible in Croc."

"What about this human bishop? Any sign of him?"

"Taken too, probably. Kind of hard to tell. There was a good deal of killing, but…" Thatcher hesitated, glancing up at him before she finished. "We've lost most of the evidence, sir. It's obvious that there were deaths—there's no way a Tarka could have survived leaving a splash pattern like the ones we're seeing in the south. But local scavengers have been at the bodies. A lot of blood here and there, some extremities and bone splinters—but not a lot else. Not a big surprise. The local rats really seem to make short work of anything that's just lying around—they'll eat anything that resembles food or garbage." She shuddered. "Nasty things. Like weasels."

Another wordless chill went through him. "So you have not found...any sign that the bishop was killed."

"No. If he was, it wasn't in this building." She looked up at the hanging rood. "Those are the only human remains so far. This building has the only intact Tarka remains as well, of course—when they left, it seems like they deliberately sealed the place to keep out the vermin. I think...they wanted us to find it." She looked up again, her eyes drawn toward the dead man reluctantly. "They wanted us to see it just the way it is."

He felt and quickly suppressed the red flash of anger. "Agreed."

"Haven't found any enemy dead, either, although believe me—I was hoping. Just a few tufts of fur. I'm taking it home for analysis. I don't want to risk using the field lab."

"I see." He sighed heavily and closed his eyes. "Nothing else, then."

"I wouldn't say that. There's plenty of paperwork in the back—just no bodies." She pointed toward the sanctuary, the communion table still draped with embroidered fabric. "Behind that big altar we found more doors. There's some kind of personal chapel and office in there. That's where we found the records for the mission—those were in English. And there's some kind of personal diary in Latin. I figured you would want to see it, Commander." She avoided his eyes, her tone carefully neutral.

He nodded. "Thank you. I will have a look." There was a sound behind him, in the nave. "I have asked them to cut down the cross," he said. "You will assist them, please."

She nodded. "Sure. We need to examine the guy anyway. I was just putting it off until we had a chance to look at the evidence on the ground...."

"Of course." He turned away, cutting her off. "Thank you."

He paused for a moment, giving her time to look away. By now the scouts would have found a ladder in the empty city. They would cut Thomas down and remove him from the rood, but Cai would not watch—it would be impossible to hide his emotions if he was present.

For now he strode back toward the presbytery, looking for Father Tourneau's diary. Perhaps there at last there would be some clue, some hint as to what happened here—something he could take back to the Sol Force high command, and forward secretly to the Church, to tell them how all their years of work and faith had come to naught.

Because at this moment—he really had nothing. For seventy-two hours his team had been searching the winding streets and empty houses of Kolakaad, searching for survivors of this attack...anyone who might tell him who had come here, or why, or even how. No enemy force should have been able to approach this planet without ample warning; Ko'Grappa was equipped with the latest sensor equipment from the capital. They should have never been caught so unprepared.

And the mystery only grew more perplexing, the more closely it was examined. A ground assault on a city of this size had somehow swept every living thing from its streets—which was simply inconceivable. Over the years he had visited the sites of every colonial tragedy imaginable: plague, fire, famine, orbital bombardments and assault shuttle runs that killed thousands. But even when domes and bunkers were torn apart, when every man woman and child was ordered to abandon an installation, there would always be a few left behind, hiding in the cracks and crevices. Only when a whole world was reduced to smoldering, airless hell could you kill *every one*. In every other case, no matter how dire—life had a way of clinging to the rim.

And yet...they were gone. All gone. Not a single soul could be found. Males, females, children—snatched up as if by the hand of God Himself, by an enemy from whom none could hide.

The presbytery was silent. Cai ignored the written records on the table, and the little journal written in Latin; these were left for outsiders to find—Tourneau would never have revealed sensitive information there. Instead he went to the image of the Madonna in the corner, bending to whisper into her left ear: *"Ego sum nuntius Dei. Ostendete mihi solam veritatem."*

The hidden panel slowly lowered, and he quickly cycled through the last ten entries, looking for the final day.

The old man stood by the window. "They're coming." Cai winced at the quaver of fear in his voice. "I only have a few seconds of power. I won't describe them—I will try to kill one before we are taken. They may leave behind their dead. I do have time to give you this. Captured before the attack. I think you will know what to do." A sudden image flickered over the screen—it was the last of the entry.

"Redite," Cai said. The screen flickered; once again the bishop stood by the window. The entry played again.

"—I think you will know what to do," Tourneau said.

"Algete." The fleeting image froze, and he studied it quickly. Combat footage, captured by a Tarkasian orbital defense platform. The HUD gave the day and hour. Nearly four weeks ago.

Slowly he edged forward through the one split-second of crude footage—the shape of the enemy ship, the incoming fire, the flash and the ragged dissolution to snow as the camera was destroyed.

"Damn it," he muttered aloud. "We have all seen this before. Why, Father? Why would you waste your last moments with this?"

"*Iterum*," he told the machine. Dutifully it replayed the message. Cai's heart quickened—there in the upper right, what was that?

He bent close to the monitor, touching the dot with his fingertip. "*Maximus*," he said softly. The screen obliged, switching to maximum enlargement—and suddenly a second ship leaped out of the darkness.

For a moment, his eyes burned with tears. "I am sorry I doubted you, old man. You were right. That was worth mentioning."

"*Date mihi testimonium.*" The statue of the virgin spread her arms, revealing a red crystal heart. He plucked out the drive and the lectern slowly folded back into a seamless pillar.

Outside in the Cathedral he heard the ignition of the blowtorch. In moments, the heavy chain was cut; several men shouted as the weight of the Cross descended into their arms. Cai Rui closed his eyes, murmuring a brief prayer of thanks, and began to methodically gather all of the visible papers and storage media in the room. From the window, he could see a storm gathering over the sheltering crags of the city. The clouds were stained deep purple in the evening light.

7 | THE SNIPE HUNT

Two days after his return from Tarka space, Cai Rui sat in his office, waiting for the hatchet to fall. It arrived in the form of Conrad Vance, the Task Force Commander of Green Section, just an hour before the usual time for lunch. Cai Rui lowered his lids, watching the mechanized chair roll ominously toward his office on the display that Cicero had projected onto his corneas, and considered his options. Given the indignity of outright flight or of hiding under his desk like a schoolboy, he opted for Plan C: brazen it out.

Before Vance could breach the office door, however, the man posted at the greeting desk stopped the irate TFC at the door. "But Commander, you can't—" Sounds of a scuffle. "You haven't got an appointment—!"

"Out of my way, Ensign. That's an order." There was an ominous wheeze of machinery rolling forward, followed by the unmistakable sound of running footsteps.

"Sir, I have strict orders—!"

Cai Rui rose quickly from his desk and opened the door. Looking out, he saw that the Black Section adjutant had flung himself bodily in the path of the wheelchair, trying to hold back its beet-faced occupant with the both hands placed on either armrest. The sight made him wince; the boy could be seriously hurt if Vance chose to accelerate. His chair massed over 200 kilos.

Cai Rui cleared his throat deliberately; both participants in the struggle froze, looking up to meet his eyes.

"Quite all right, Singh," he said mildly. "In the future, a visit from Dr. Vance does not constitute 'being disturbed.'"

The adjutant removed his hands from the wheelchair, straightened stiffly and bowed, trying to recover his dignity. "Thank you sir." He turned to bow to his former opponent. "My apologies, Comman—"

The old man keyed his chair forward with a burst of speed, forcing the young Sikh to retreat with a distinctly rabbit-like hop or have the vehicle crush both his shins. Cai Rui smiled stiffly as the chair rolled past him, suddenly much less amused, and closed his own door quietly. He made a point of taking his time as he went through the motions of returning to his desk chair, sitting down, folding his fingers on the desktop, and looking across it at his visitor with an expression of polite expectation.

"What can I do for you, sir?"

Vance picked up the data pad on his lap and threw it onto the desk. "Start by telling me what the hell this is supposed to be!"

Cai Rui plastered the bland smile to his face and gently turned the data pad right-side up with one fingertip. "It would appear to be…a memo?"

Vance rolled directly into the desk, rocking the furniture and its various document stacks with an unsubtle thump. "Don't play games with me, boy. Where do you get the brass to release an All Points and call some kind of Snipe Hunt without going through the chain of command?"

Cai Rui looked down at the data pad again, glancing at the message on the viewscreen. A brief report and a single image from Ko'Grappa were accompanied by the bulletin he had written the previous morning. By now the memo had been broadcast to every ship and structure in the galaxy with access to a functioning Node array:

"Message begins. Intelligence reports from Deep Scan fleet suggest that Ripper ships have increased operations beyond random hits on colony worlds. Activity witnessed in allied systems indicates an attempt to set up fuelling depots at key points throughout the galaxy. In addition to the familiar cruiser and planetary attack shuttle, a new refueling-class vessel has also been spotted. Sol Force personnel are to be on the look-out for ships of this configuration – they are regarded as dangerous. Sol Force Command has issued a fire-on-sight order for all Black Thirteen vessels. A bounty of 10,000 credits is offered to the captain and crew of any ship able to bring down a Ripper refueling vessel. Intelligence is to be gathered post-combat. End message."

Looking up at the quivering face of his fellow TFC, Cai Rui chose his next words carefully. "We release a Black List memo every month, Commander. The Black List update has never been passed through the Legate—"

The chair crashed into his desk a second time; Vance's face had turned a deeper shade of red. "You offered a *reward!* Who's going to pay that money, Commander Rui—you? And how many of these mother-loving things do you think our boys are going to bag before they're done? Every damn ship in the fleet is gunning for them now! They're already calling 'em the Black Piñatas!"

Cai Rui raised his brows with mild surprise, and placed a protective hand on the stack of paper to his left. "That's…very colorful. I am touched by their enthusiasm."

"You're about to be *touched* with a bloody court martial, boy. Finance has been breathing down my neck for the last hour—thanks to you, I'm in this up to my eyeballs. And you can bet your cherries you'll be hearing from the Gnome King too, as soon as the Director is done chewing his ring."

Cai Rui stood, replacing his feigned surprise with friendly concern. "If that is the case, Commander, perhaps you should leave me. Naturally I will explain to the Legate that you had nothing to do with my memo. But if he should find you here when he arrives…" He let the words trail off for a moment. "Well. It might look as if we were somehow in collusion."

"Oh, I'm leaving." The old man's voice was a snarl. "I'd clean out your desk, if I was you. I give you another day. Two at the most."

Cai Rui smiled tightly and raised his left hand in a half-salute. "An honor serving with you, Commander."

The old man's eyes narrowed and his mouth hardened into a stubborn line of fury. The chair rolled out of the office, its bumpers leaving rubber scars on either side of the door as Vance exited in a high mechanical dudgeon. Sighing, Cai Rui picked up the data pad the Commander had thrown on the desk and set it aside, trying to reorder his thoughts. At last he reached for his comm switch.

"Singh, I will be out of my office for the remainder of the day. Please forward my messages to my quarters before you leave?"

"Yes, Commander."

He rose and tucked the data pad under his arm, sealing the office door behind him. As he exited the Section, he whispered, "*Cicero. Nollo hic esse.*"

His ears registered a brief high whine as his PDA processed the command. Immediately his scalp began to prickle with response as Cicero accessed the security network, erasing his master's body and voice from the monitoring equipment.

Head bowed, Cai Rui walked swiftly down the hall, listening to the successive pings as one camera after another was spoofed.

Thatcher looked up from her microscope as he entered the lab. "Ever hear of knocking?"

"Sorry." He closed the door behind him and put his back against it. "Need a place to lay low for a few hours."

Her mouth quirked at the corners, but she managed not to grin. "Finance?"

"No," he said solemnly. "The dome is under attack. By monsters."

She shook her head, rolling her eyes, and bent over her microscope again. "Sure, boss."

He walked toward the table, a broad flat surface covered in a sheet of sterile plastic. Several artifacts from Ko'Grappa had been laid out and tagged after analysis. "How goes the work?"

She sighed and straightened up again. "Faster without distractions, usually."

He shrugged. "Monsters. What can I say?"

She shook her head. "S'ok. My eyes are starting to cross anyway. Time for some more of that fine, fine BS coffee." She rose from her stool and stretched, tilting her neck to either side to loosen the muscles like a boxer, and stripped off her latex gloves. He noted with some concern that she immediately dropped them and her lab coat into the hazard box.

He walked up beside her as she turned on the faucet of the scrub sink. "Contamination?"

She nodded, wincing as she soaped and then rinsed her raw hands under the scalding jets. "Yep. Filthy buggers, whatever they are. Over three hundred strains of bacteria so far."

He cocked his head curiously. "Anything familiar?"

"Oh, hell yes. Hiver, Tark, Liir, Terra—it's like they've been rolling in the offal of the whole damn universe."

"Maybe they have." His tone was thoughtful. "Liir as well? That's interesting."

"Yep. No doubt about it. It's just a faint trace, but unmistakably Muurian."

"Interesting. Perhaps the Liir have not been as forthcoming as our other allies about Black Thirteen."

She dried her hands with a towel, nodding. "Would make sense. Probably touchy about looking weak to us, given their history."

"Possible. Regardless, there has been contact, whether they admit it or not. That in itself is … telling."

She sighed, reaching for the coffee pot. "If the sample is good? Sure. Dr. Kliggerman would have a stroke if I put this on a report. He'd shoot me full of holes in a heartbeat." She took a weary sip and made a face at the taste. "Sloppy collection method, my staff wasn't trained... and this lab is a joke by White Section standards. Hell, I've got random dirty apes wandering in at will. God only knows whose offal *you've* been rolling in." She eyed him sidelong, seasoning her cup with powdered cream.

"Point taken." He indicated the table with his free hand. "What about the macro-evidence?"

She sat down on the low billet couch she had dragged into the corner, setting the coffee down on the reading table beside her. "That would be a little harder to dispute. The hairs are mammaliform, for certain. They're oxygen breathers. And my, Grandma, what BIG teeth they have!"

His eyes narrowed. "The crosier?"

"Yep. That was a dental pattern, all right. And a damn nasty one. I can't extrapolate the whole skull from the bite, but we're talking 25 centimeters at the widest point from tooth to tooth."

Cai Rui held up his hands to approximate the width; she adjusted it, nudging his hands further apart with her coffee cup. He whistled.

"I scanned one of the impressions and had a reversal made." She reached into her breast pocket and handed him a lump of resin. "That's just one tooth, mind you. From the maxilla."

He held it up, turning the rough end toward the ceiling and letting the point hang downward, as if from a gaping jaw. It was a fang as thick as his thumb, curving down like a scimitar; the two rear-facing edges were sharp and serrated. "Good Lord. What would you use a tooth like that for, Lieutenant?"

"Just about anything I damn well pleased, I think." She took the model and dropped it back into her pocket. "Probably designed to saw through meat—that's not a Kliggerman answer, by the way, but I'm ninety percent on it. And I decided to run a few equations, just based on the depth of penetration. Those jaws were delivering at least a hundred kilos of pressure. Probably much more."

Cai Rui worked his own jaw thoughtfully, snapping his teeth shut in a mock bite. "How would you tell a thing like that?"

She shrugged. "It's a conservative estimate. The staff was made of Tarkasian ironwood—exceptionally dense and hard, once it cures. There's a reason that their carpenters tend to join it without using nails. You hit a knot and a steel point will mushroom like lead against it, or split outright."

"All right." He folded his arms thoughtfully. "Bottom line: what body size?"

"God. I have no idea. If it was Terran? If I had a mandible, or a set of lower molars? I could make an educated guess. As it is..."

"Give me a bare minimum."

She slapped the empty mug down on her side table with an angry thump. "I don't know. What part of 'I don't know' do you not understand?" Thatcher threw herself back on the couch in frustration. "The thing is not from *around* here, Commander. I've got damn little to go on. I can't make up a whole fairy tale based on a few hairs and a tooth mark!"

"All right, all right." He held up his hands soothingly. "Change of subject."

She put back her head and closed her eyes, massaging her temples with her fingertips. "Change of subject."

He put his hands behind his back, looking idly around the lab. "Have you given any thought to that promotion?" He spoke casually, bending to examine one of her computer screens.

She smiled, not opening her eyes. "In my copious spare time, you mean?"

"In your copious spare time."

"Yeah. I've been thinking about it quite a bit, actually. Especially that bit about being a target."

He indulged a lupine smile. "Reluctant to step into the reticule?"

"No, just want to have a flak jacket on." She sighed, running her fingers through her hair. "I decided to run a records search of those deaths before and after the armistice. I set Otomi as the endpoint, and ran the whole period."

He winced. "Did you do this on your own clearance?"

She cocked her head. "Why do you ask?"

He sighed. "Margaret, if you had arranged the murder of a fellow officer, wouldn't you want to know who was going through the death records?"

She sat silent for a moment. "Crap."

"What else did you do?"

"Ooooh, nothing," she said sheepishly.

"Tell me."

"I just...read a few reports and ran down a few system use logs. You know. To see what Otomi was up to, just before—"

"Margaret." He felt a wave of relief. "There's no way that you could have pulled Otomi's system log with a Lieutenant's security clearance. Whose number did you use?"

She looked down at her hands. "Promise you won't be mad?" Her voice was small.

"I make no such promises. Ever."

"Otomi's," she said, in an even smaller voice.

He cocked his head in disbelief. "What?"

"Her access number was still active." She shrugged, raising her palms helplessly. "It'll open just about anything…"

"How in the world did you guess Otomi's password? I've been trying to figure it out for months!"

She smiled. "It was easy. You just have to know who she loved best."

He raised an eyebrow. "You're not going to tell me?"

Her eyes twinkled. "It's a name and a date. That's all you're getting."

"Fine." He turned away, surprised by the strength of his own annoyance. "Tell me about these death records, then."

The brief spark of merriment died in her eyes. "Yeah. That. Well, you were right. A few big heads rolled… but a lot of small ones too. The last thing Otomi pulled up from the system was a 'suicide' report of some warrant in the Research and Development Corps. Funny—you wouldn't think a theoretical Node physicist would wire her own fillings to a comm terminal and 'electrocute herself'… would you?"

He took a deep breath. "No. That… doesn't seem probable."

"No. Otomi did a search for the woman's work in the database afterward, but apparently couldn't find anything. That was about… six hours before the shuttle crash."

Another chill went through his vitals. "A theoretical Node physicist? With nothing in the data base?"

"Yeah." She looked down at her hands. "They killed her, then erased her work from existence. That's like dying twice, for a scientist. Seems like a message. Maybe to the rest of her team."

He scowled. "Definitely." He paced across the floor. "Why would Otomi take an interest in Node physics? Was there a relationship between the two of them?"

"Jeez, boss, I don't know. I'm new to this game."

"Well, this isn't White Section, Margaret. We take wild guesses around here. Remember?" He gave her a sidelong grin. "How big is a Ripper, would you say?"

She threw up her hands. "I'd say it has three heads, and weighs about a thooooousand kilos." She rolled her eyes. "And on Fridays, it breathes fire," she added. "Happy now?"

"Yes. I think we should call in a render team and have them mock up a composite. I'll circulate it with my next memo."

He ducked the mug easily—she had deliberately thrown it high—and turned just in time to see it bounce off the chest of the MP standing silently in the doorway.

The tall man caught the cup as it fell with an effortless snap of his wrist, evincing no surprise. Without changing expression or taking his eyes from his target, he set it down on the file cabinet beside him.

"Task Force Commander Rui." The tone of his voice did not make it a question. "If you'd come with me, please."

Cai Rui turned back to Thatcher and handed her the data pad under his arm. "Belongs to Green Section. I was going to take it back, but it appears I am otherwise engaged. If you'd return it for me, Lieutenant?"

"Of course, Commander." As she bent forward to take it, she silently mouthed "good luck".

He nodded and turned briskly on his heel to meet his fate.

8 | A VISIT TO OLYMPUS

The empire's most commanding vista belonged to a hardened dome on the lip of the central caldera of Mons Olympus, looking out over the interplanetary starfield in the bowl below. At this hour of the day, the setting sun hung heavy in a haze of ferrous dust on the horizon, and the stars were beginning to pierce the thin atmosphere above like dagger points in a deep blue curtain. A constant parade of ships came and went from the level landing pads below, guided by the massive black glass control towers and tended by an army of busy service and fuel vehicles, all decked with warning beacons. It was a labyrinth of rainbow flashing lights and glowing engine trails, a constant, well-orchestrated flow of motion. From this height the field seemed a huge elaborate playground, populated by cunning mechanical toys.

Half of the Command dome was transparent, and in mild weather the blast shields could be rolled back to allow a one-hundred-and-eighty degree view of the starfield and the surrounding domes below. This space was dedicated to a single office, occupied by a single man: Edward Alton MacKenzie, the current Director of Sol Force. Now the MP was leading Cai Rui across a seemingly endless expanse of empty carpet toward that man—a massive dark silhouette standing against the blazing sunset, holding a glass of water in his hand.

"Task Force Commander Rui Cai. Black Section, Intelligence." The MP announced his delivery without emotion.

"Thanks, Paxton." The Director's voice was a mild, friendly baritone. "Any trouble finding him?"

"No sir," the MP replied. "He was just where you said he'd be."

"Excellent. That's all for now." The MP saluted MacKenzie's back and turned to go. Cai Rui stood frozen at attention, the bloody light of the Martian sun half-blinding him after the dim fluorescent strips in the corridors below. The sound of the MP's long retreating strides ended with the whoosh of a sealed door, and the Director took another small sip of water.

"Nice to see you again, Commander. How are you?"

He swallowed uneasily. "Fine, sir." MacKenzie still had not turned, but he still felt powerfully *watched* in the Director's presence.

Cai Rui had only met the man on two previous occasions. On the day that MacKenzie was made Director, Cai Rui had been one of a handful of junior officers in attendance at MarsDome, standing as an acting second to Commander Otomi. The second time was the day he had received his own promotion to TFC. MacKenzie himself had pinned the new tabs to his collar on that day, and Cai Rui had been struck then as now by how huge the man seemed in comparison to the majority of human beings.

MacKenzie's personnel file said that he was 193 centimeters tall, and weighed 112 kilograms—certainly on the far edge of the bell curve for human height and mass, but hardly impressive in comparison to the larger Hiver warriors or a bull Tarka. Somehow, though, he always seemed to loom much larger in person. His presence filled the room.

"Your name has come up four different times today, Rui Cai." The Director's tone was friendly. "I always find it interesting when that happens."

He could feel a bead of sweat rolling down the side of his neck. Keeping stride with the long-legged MP in the corridors between Intelligence and Command had raised his heart rate; now his uniform felt uncomfortably warm, and he was feeling a ridiculous urge to apologize for being "interesting".

"Are you a Catholic, Commander?" The question was posed placidly, but Cai Rui felt the keen edge of the guillotine against the back of his neck.

"Yes sir." The answer seemed to flow out of his mouth without volition. He had rehearsed for a line of questioning like this, countless times. Standing in this office now, the plan trickled away; he could not remember what he had so carefully planned to say. He had heard other officers speak of a similar effect, whenever they were brought into this room. It was almost physically impossible to lie to the Director.

"That's good." The Director took another sip from his glass. "I believe you're the highest ranking Catholic in the service at the moment, Rui. Since I received an interesting missive from Rome today, I was wondering if you and I might take a moment to discuss it."

Cai Rui blanched. "From Rome? You and I? But..."

"Who else, Commander?" The Director at last turned toward him, a black silhouette with the blood red light of Mars spilling over his broad shoulders. Ships rose and descended in bleeding sky behind him, their engine flares burning like torches. "I have a document here signed by the Holy Father himself, and penned by a Cardinal Amato, of the *Congregatio pro Doctrina Fidei.*" The Director's English was accented with the northeastern Americás, but his Latin was flawlessly European. "I would like you to read it, and tell me what you think."

He held out his left hand, and Cai Rui saw the scroll of precious vellum, tied with a black silk cord. Gingerly he stepped forward and leaned in to take it, unable to bring himself another step closer. As he plucked open the knot, a single beam lamp ignited in the ceiling above him, trained directly down onto his head and shoulders. The pen strokes leaped up at him, sharp and black against the creamy field as he unrolled the paper. The Director had turned toward the sunset once more.

When he was done reading, his hands were cold and numb. Feeling sick, Cai Rui rolled the scroll back up again, and fumbled clumsily with the tie. The Director took a last sip of his water. "Finished?"

"Yes sir," he said weakly. The light above his head went out suddenly, leaving the two of them in the gloom of impending dusk. The Martian sky had turned deep violet, the last light of the sun smeared in deep orange and crimson bands on the haze over the far mountains.

"*Latae sententiae.*" The Director's tone was sharply clipped. "I'm no Catholic, but Sol Force Legal tells me it's some sort of criminal term. It means that when a thing is done, the punishment is automatic. The Holy See isn't deciding it-they're merely announcing it." He moved in the darkness, and Cai Rui heard the whisper of his chair as he sat. "There's been a violation of canon law. It carries an automatic sentence. No deliberation or appeal."

"Yes sir." He tried to swallow again, and coughed instead; it felt as if there was a lump of cotton lodged in his throat.

The man at the desk was silent for a moment, his fingertips drumming gently on the tabletop. When at last he spoke, his voice was deadly soft. "I believe I'm being *threatened,* Commander. Personally and politically. Am I mistaken?"

Cai Rui clenched his fists. "No sir. In fact, I would say...it's a bit more than a threat."

"This sentence. 'Interdiction'. A punishment for political leaders—they tell me that it goes back to medieval times. In my case, the Church can't excommunicate me, because I'm not a member. But they can punish the people under my command."

Cai Rui licked his lips. "Yes. But...I'm afraid it's worse than that. Sir."

"Explain." The restrained anger in the Director's voice cut the darkness like a razor.

"The people under your command..." He hesitated, feeling the weight in his stomach drop a notch lower. "According to this ban, Catholics in uniform will be excommunicated *vitandus*—'to be shunned'. It means that other Catholics will have to avoid them. They won't have business or social contact with a member of Sol Force. Our own families aren't supposed to speak to us, unless we resign from the service—and no Catholic is supposed to buy or sell anything to any of us."

"I see." The soft patter of fingertips on the desktop continued. "Economic harassment. I suppose that might be annoying. Is there anything else to it?"

"Yes, sir. Definitely. A...spiritual component. The sentence of interdiction isn't confined to the people under your command. It..." He trailed off helplessly.

"Go on, Commander. Saying it out loud isn't going to make it worse."

"It covers the entire region under your authority, sir. While you and Sol Force are under interdiction, the sacraments cannot be celebrated. Anywhere."

The drumming stopped. "You're telling me that every Catholic in whole damn galaxy is going to stop praying while this sentence is in effect?"

"No sir. We can pray—but God may not hear us." He wanted to tug at his collar, suddenly desperate for air, but did not move. "There will be no baptism. No confirmation. No communion. No confession and absolution. No anointing of the sick. No ordination of new clerics. No marriage. Not even Last Rites. For anyone living under Sol Force protection."

The Director's voice remained quiet. "Everyone lives under Sol Force protection, Commander."

"Yes sir."

MacKenzie paused. "I'll admit that I'm a bit fuzzy about the doctrines of your faith, Rui Cai. Are you telling me that His Holiness the Pope is willing to deprive all the eight and a half *billion* Catholics living on thirteen worlds *of any and all spiritual comfort*—just to punish Sol Force?" There was a note of incredulity in his voice.

Cai Rui shifted uncomfortably. "I...I suppose that's one way of looking at it, sir."

The answer came briskly. "Well. I believe you're right, Commander. That is considerably worse than I thought." There was a moment of silence. "But of course, we have one alternative to this dire scenario."

"Yes, sir. The listed offenses were violence against an ordained bishop and the desecration of the Eucharist. But Sol Force was not the main offender. They're accusing the Tarka. Sol Force is named collectively as an accomplice to the act. So if you want to avoid the interdiction..."

"...all I have to do is break our treaty with Tarka, and declare them...what is the word he wants me to use?" The man's voice was harsh and flat.

Cai Rui swallowed bile silently. "Enemies of the Faith. Sir."

"Yes." All pretense of friendliness had dropped from MacKenzie's voice. "That's right. 'Enemies of the Faith.'"

Cai Rui fought the urge once more to reach up and loosen his collar.

"All right, Commander. I think we're almost done with this topic of conversation. Thank you for clarifying the matter. I appreciate your input."

"Yes sir."

MacKenzie shifted in his chair with a creak of leather. "Just for the sake of *information*, I believe I'll tell you what's going to happen next, Rui Cai. I think it's best that you know *exactly* what's on my mind." His pleasant baritone was relaxed and casual; the effect was thoroughly terrifying.

A cold bead of sweat crawled down Cai Rui's spine. *He knows.*

"Publicly, I'm going to disavow all knowledge of this bishop who was supposedly killed on Ko'Grappa. That's a Tarka colony. It's hell and gone from my territory, and I have no record of *authorized* human visitors to that planet. My deepest condolences to the Church in Her loss, of course. But any ape who sticks his nose that far out of my jurisdiction can't expect my protection. From anyone."

The chair creaked again, and the Director leaned forward, his voice dropping low. "Privately, you're going to tell your friends in the Vatican to drop this. Like a hot rock. Immediately. You're going to give them your personal assurances as a good Catholic, a loyal soldier, and the chief investigator of this affair, that the Tarka are not the guilty parties in this matter. That's what your report to *my* office said, and that will be our official line, Commander. *Even if you privately believe otherwise.* And you can tell them that I will never, regardless of how they threaten my people, help them frame my allies for a crime they didn't commit."

Cai Rui closed his eyes for a moment. "Yes sir."

"You might also want to tell them that I am not a man who takes threats lightly. And if they want to treat me like some kind of medieval monarch...I may just start to act like one. I've got a working calculator in my office; the current civilian population of Rome stands at about six million. The three colonies closest to the Tarkasian border have over ten million apiece, and growing. And here's a funny thing: I haven't received any threats from them lately. So you can sum up my position for them in five words: *don't ever make me choose.*"

Cai Rui opened his eyes and turned slightly to look out at the deepening darkness and the brightly lit starfield. "Yes sir."

"Good. That's settled then. Next order of business. My Finance Legate had a word with me this morning about a certain memo."

Reeling, Cai Rui could produce nothing more than another feeble, "Yes sir."

"Madsen seemed to think that ten thousand credits was an exorbitant bounty to place on a Black List sighting."

Cai Rui took a deep breath, bracing himself. "I acted on my own volition, sir. I take sole respons—"

"Personally, I thought it was a fine idea," the Director interrupted smoothly. His voice was once again friendly and mild. "I asked him why no one had thought of it earlier. It's amazing how short-sighted all these bean counters can be. False economy, really. Our battle fleets are basically idle at the moment. Not going to hurt them one bit to have something to shoot at. And we've never taken down a Black List vessel without netting substantial benefits."

Cai Rui took a deep breath. "Thank you sir."

"Not at all, Commander."

Fighting a surge of nausea, Cai Rui thought longingly of the door at the far end of the office, and the well-lit tunnels beyond. "Was there anything else, sir?"

"Oh, yes. One more little thing, Rui Cai."

The keen edge had returned to that friendly tone. Cai Rui felt a sinking sensation, as if the floor beneath his feet were rapidly descending.

"It's come to my attention that someone in your Section has taken an interest in a certain set of personnel files. Specifically, the records for a fifteen-month period surrounding the general armistice."

Cai Rui waited, but the Director said nothing further. The silence stretched; when it was obvious that some reply was respected, he offered a cautious, "Sir?"

"There was a certain amount of house-cleaning done during that period, Commander."

He clamped his teeth tight.

The Director went on. "I took the liberty of reviewing the data set that was delivered to your mobile terminal. I've resent that same information, after having removed a number of names from the list. These are the cases that do not need further investigation. Am I making myself clear?"

The sweat on the back of his neck was cold as ice. "Crystal. Sir."

"Excellent." There was a soft chime from the desk; the Director pressed a button. "MarsDome."

"There's an urgent call on the wire for Commander Rui, Director." It was the voice of the MP. "It's coded Ultra—shall I put it through?"

"Yes, Paxton. Thank you." A green light flashed. "This is MarsDome Actual," he said. "You are live."

There was a long silence, but finally Thatcher's hesitant voice trickled out of the speakers. "Message for Commander Rui, Black Section?"

Feeling a flood of gratitude, he took a step toward the desk. "TFC Rui speaking," he said aloud. "Proceed, Black Section."

"Commander, there's been an attack. There's a distress signal coming through. It's an NV tap—one of the rim colonies was hit."

The Director rose from his chair abruptly. "MarsDome speaking. Hit where and with what, Lieutenant?"

"Black Thirteen," she said simply. "At Colony N3.9.9. A place called Avalon."

"Thank you, Lieutenant." MacKenzie's voice was brisk. "I'll have the GF Cohort Commander raise a platoon for Commander Rui. As it so happens, the SFS Nanjing is in-system at the moment. Her skipper is TFC Wheelock. You'll be heading outbound with her to investigate."

"Yes sir. Black Section out."

He could picture Thatcher cutting the feed, and even the look on her face; this would have been the first time in her career that she made personal contact with the Director. For a moment he almost smiled, but now the man from MarsDome was turning back toward him, and his reprieve was close at hand.

"Number five," the Director said simply. "I believe that's a record, Commander. Nanjing is shipping out within the watch, so I won't keep you. But I would like you to pass on that message to His Holiness before you go. And have an informal chat with Wheelock at some point during your trip. She's seen some things that she doesn't care to put into a formal report. I think you're just the man to sort it all out."

"Yes sir." He raised his hand in a crisp salute.

The Director raised his forefinger to his temple and flicked it outward from the right brow, returning the salute in its mildest, most informal fashion. "Dismissed."

Cai Rui nearly reached the door before MacKenzie spoke again. Looking back, he saw the Director's silhouette once more at the glass window, a dark shadow surrounded by fiery engine trails and burning stars.

"By the way, Commander—Lieutenant Thatcher is a lovely woman, and not at all in the habit of talking to herself. If you ever want to remain hidden in the future, I'd keep that in mind." The man's teeth flashed white in the violet gloom. "Good hunting. I'll be seeing you."

9 | SPECTRES

The bridge was quiet at midnight, its stations manned by a skeleton crew. Cai Rui entered from the service corridor and offered a salute to the adjutant.

"Passenger on deck," the woman declared aloud. The rest of the deck looked up, a half dozen heads rising swiftly to see who had come into the command section; it was the work of a split second to size him up and return to task, eyes going back to their screens and displays.

Only the ship's captain sat facing the forward screen directly, her eyes fixed on the boiling clouds of Node Space. She glanced askance at him as he entered, but her gaze quickly returned to the depths, restlessly scanning the shifting blue tides. "Evening, Commander. Can't sleep?"

"No Ma'am. I was wondering if I might have a word."

"You may." She turned away from the viewscreen, visibly forcing herself to disengage, and rose from the command chair. "Helm, we'll be in the coffin."

The pilot turned her head toward the voice blindly, the navigational helm mounted over both eyes. "Yes Ma'am."

Wheelock was an older woman. She wore her rank in the form of a non-regulation hairstyle, with many years' growth of iron-gray hair bound into a single thick plait that ran down her back like the blade of a sword. As she led him into her map room, he noted her rolling spacer's stride, the heavily muscled shoulder and hip, the way she instinctively moved from one hardpoint to another in the room. It was a pattern he had seen before, in veterans of the Hiver War. She never left more than an arm's length from the nearest surface to use as a grip or a lever; if the ship's gravity failed she would be ready to launch herself like a cannonball in any direction. When atmosphere was screaming out of an open breach, those first into a suit lived to keep fighting.

She sat down at the map table, and gestured toward the corner. "I have tea, Commander, if you indulge."

He looked over to the kettle bolted to the wall. The smell of the brew was strong, a sweet powerful blend of tannins and spice. "Algolian?"

She nodded. "Help yourself."

"Thank you. I appreciate the hospitality." He picked a ship's mug off the magnetic board beside the kettle and thumbed open its iris lid. "The Director recommended that I try to meet with you while we were *en route* to Avalon. But over the past week, I couldn't seem to catch you at the right moment." He kept his tone carefully neutral; she had obviously been avoiding him, but there was no need to rub her nose in it now. Instead he filled the mug with steaming chai and removed his thumb from the button, letting the cup reseal itself as he turned toward the table. "I assume you know who I am?"

"Sure. You're the guy in charge of the BS." She winked, but there was a spark of challenge as well as humor in her hazel eye.

"Yes. And the Boogey List," he added, filling in the common Fleet pejorative for his monthly memoranda.

Her smile was wry. "Sorry. Otomi used to be good for a rise once in a while."

He shrugged. "I am a poor substitute in many respects. Did you have some 'BS' to report, Commander?"

Wheelock's eyes narrowed for a moment, and her mouth worked as if she had bitten down onto something hard. "If it was something I could report, I'd be a hell of a lot happier."

He opened the lid of his mug and breathed in the perfumed steam. When he looked up at her, his eyes were calm and curious, but he did not speak.

She sighed. "You ever hear of the Bermuda Triangle, Commander?"

"Can't say that I have."

"Old legend from before the Thaw. There was supposed be a special place in the Atlantic Ocean where strange things would happen to travelers. I guess it must have been somewhere around the old island of Bermuda, before it went under. Ships, boats, airplanes—didn't matter. Anything that carried people from one place to another could run afoul in the Bermuda Triangle."

He raised an eyebrow. "Run afoul?"

She looked down at the tabletop, embarrassed. "It was a spook story, basically. Navigation equipment would go crazy—compass needles spinning and the like. Boats and planes could lose their bearing and end up going in circles until they ran out of fuel and went down in the sea. And there were other stories. Disappearances, deaths. People would see strange things—ghost ships and phantom lights, foo fighters, little green men."

He smiled. "My kind of place?"

She snorted ruefully. "Yeah. BS all the way." Wheelock sighed and swirled the tea in her mug reflectively. "Anyway. I come from a Navy family. My Grandma used to tell us these stories to scare the bejaysus out of us before bedtime. Once I was old enough to stop having nightmares about my ship running wild and my bridge full of little green men, I forgot all about 'em." She paused.

"Until now," Cai Rui prompted. He blew across the surface of his chai and took a sip.

"Until now."

"And what brings this Bermuda Triangle to mind?"

"There's something wrong, Commander. I can't tie it all together—not yet. I haven't seen any foo fighters or little green men. But it all *feels* like Bermuda, somehow. If you catch my drift."

"Not yet, I'm afraid."

"Right. Little vague. The problem is...it *is* a little vague. A few anomalous sensor readings—who reports that? Suddenly our nav equipment is popping up Ghost Nodes all over the place, but people have always gotten those readings. Just...not quite so many."

"'Ghost Node'?" Seeing the look on her face, he offered an apologetic smile. "I'm sorry. I've never heard the term."

"The Node to Nowhere, Commander. It's a false reading from the Node Array. They're not that unusual, really. Navigators say it's the price you pay for performing complex quantum mathematics on the fly—sometimes you get a bad Node reading. No one knows exactly why. My old nav used to think they were Nodes that really existed in some other dimension or some such thing, but you know how navs are." She made a looping gesture beside her ear. "Anyway, no one takes a Ghost Node too seriously. Ghost Nodes and the Ghost lines between 'em are inaccessible. They have no effect on real ships. Whatever they are—you can't get there from here." She smiled grimly. "No matter how many of them you see."

Cai Rui frowned. "And you don't report these readings to Command?"

She shook her head. "No. Command isn't interested if it doesn't shoot at ya, for the most part. Navigators dump their data once in a while, when the ship is in drydock, but that's about it."

He squinted down at his chai mug. "And who reviews that data?"

She shrugged. "RDC, I guess. The people who design the equipment."

The hairs on the back of his neck had risen. "People who study Node physics, perhaps?"

"I suppose. Whoever does that kind of work. As I said, it's nothing to report to Command. They don't care about anomalous sensor readings, or strange accidents..."

"Accidents?"

"Deep scan ships. We lost two of 'em lately. Some kind of equipment malfunction, is what they're saying—atmospheric processors went out. People in the ship get to breathing bad air, without knowing it, and they go crazy. You listen to the tapes, all you can hear is someone on the bridge say something about a strange smell. And the next thing you know you're hearing screams, and guns firing at nothing. Next thing after that the reactor cooks off, and you're sweeping up the pieces. All hands lost."

His eyes narrowed thoughtfully. "And this has happened...twice?"

She shuddered. "Well, only once on my patrol. The boat was on my route—they went off the grid, so we stopped to investigate. Found a few of the bodies. They gave me a turn, lemme tell ya."

As the Commander turned her head, Cai Rui saw the web of scar tissue on the side of her throat. There was a matching net of ruined flesh on her right hand, as if she had been caught in a blast of flame. Considering the things this woman must have seen in battle, he wondered how horrendous a corpse would have to be, to *give her a turn.*

"Anyway, it's a serious enough issue that they're cycling the Deep Scan fleet back to the yard one at a time, to check their life support systems. They may swap out all the old ones just on general principles. The crews are nervous, and I can't blame them."

He paused for a moment, taking another sip of tea, looking for a way to phrase the question. "And do you think that a few simple repairs will solve this problem—?"

Her eyes shifted to the side. "Maybe. Maybe not."

He held out his open palms. "I'm listening."

She set down her mug, fixing him with an intense slit-eyed stare. "All right. But this is unofficial. Understand?"

He put his hand on his chest. "It goes no further than this room."

"It was the flight recording. The way the boy asked if anyone else could smell something...like he didn't really know what he was smelling. He had a tone. Little strange, little unfocused. The way you talk when you're trying to see something out of the corner of your eye, or make out a noise you can't quite hear. And I've heard that tone before." She crossed her arms, as if the room had suddenly grown colder.

"And where did you hear it?"

"Node Madness." Cai Rui looked at her in surprise, and she nodded grimly. "It doesn't happen much anymore, but—I've been in service a long time. Back in the old days, we had no clue that some people were sensitive to Node Space exposure." She looked down into her tea mug, speaking more softly. "We lost a gal on my first tour. I was just a warrant back then; she was one of my bunk mates. Little thing from Europa. Good spacer, good gunner, but...one jump, she lost it."

Cai Rui put down his mug. "What exactly happened?"

Wheelock shifted uncomfortably in her chair. "Second day down the pipe, she shakes me awake in the middle of the night. Says she's 'hearing' something outside the ship." She hesitated. "I figure she's having a bad dream and go straight back to bed. Didn't think much of it...until she went out the hatch a couple days later."

He winced. "I'm sorry."

"So was I. Happened again a few years later. My commanding officer caught the bug. Only he wasn't hearing things—he was seeing 'em. Or trying to. He kept staring out the portals, looking for something out in the pipe. You'd be talking to him about something or other, and then suddenly he'd turn his head, like he saw something out the corner of his eye. And he'd ask you if you saw it too." She shivered.

Cai Rui hesitated. "Did he—?"

"Take a Swim? No. Whatever it was, he didn't want to see it *that* bad. He died a few months later at Rigel...but it was Node Madness, all right. It just didn't kill him. He had to avoid the bridge during jumps, much as he could. He welded a sheet of deck plating over the portal in his quarters. That kind of thing." She shrugged. "Nowadays they'd take you off the line if you started showing symptoms like that, but back then we had other things to worry about. He was a good captain—that was all that mattered."

He nodded. "I see."

"At any rate." Her iron gray brows were knotted in a frown, and her mouth had hardened. "You don't see many people with the Jumps these days. Hell, I don't think they even call it 'Node Madness' any more—what is it these days, 'something-o-mania'?" She lifted one shoulder, eloquently dismissing the modern age. "We dim all the portals when we hop in the pipe, the hatches lock down automatically, and no one but the bridge crew can see a screen display of the Node lines while we're passing through 'em. Most captains switch to tactical view, and never look out at all. Everyone knows there isn't much to see. And if there *is* something to see—you wouldn't want to."

He kept his tone carefully casual. "I noticed that *you* were looking, Commander. And rather intently, at that."

She sat silent for a moment, avoiding his gaze. When she finally did look up, she looked straight into his eyes and he saw a battle-scarred she-wolf at bay, determined to go down fighting.

"I'm keeping my eyes open, Commander. Something's gone wrong with Node Space—hell, maybe there was *always* something wrong, and we just didn't know it. But whatever it is, it's getting worse. A lot worse. Twenty-five years on the line—my gut has never steered me wrong." She put a hand to her stomach and patted it, lips pressed stubbornly tight.

He hesitated. "And...err...your gut is telling you something?"

"It's singing me a goddamn opera. There's something living in Node Space, Commander. And it's found a way out. Something we can't quite see, or hear, or even smell, until it's right on top of us." Her eyes had gone unfocused, looking off into the distance in speculation. "Something...something that goes straight through a hull and three decks without leaving a mark. Maybe something like a Node itself—neither here nor there. Some kind of a spectre."

Despite himself, he shivered. "Whew. I think I've had enough, Gramma."

She laughed, and shook her head. "Crazy enough for you?"

"Not crazy, Commander." He gave her a look that he hoped was reassuring. "I don't know what will come of it, but I appreciate your confidence. I will follow up on everything you've told me. And your name will never come into it, of course."

She nodded, acknowledging the courtesy.

He rose from his seat, placing the empty mug in the wash rack beside the samovar. "If it's possible, I'd like to have a look at your navigational data. Perhaps there is a connection between the accidents and the Ghost Nodes you mentioned."

She stood up briskly. "Yours for the taking, Commander. Just bring up a data pad. You can pull it straight out of the nav."

He turned and offered his hand. "Thank you. I'll send my second. She'll be the one to do the analysis—she's a better science officer on her worst day than I am on my best."

She snorted and took his hand, giving it a firm shake. "I hear you. But do try to get some rest, Commander. We'll exit the Node in a few more hours, and I can't imagine those colonists will want us to dawdle to the rescue."

He gave her a tip-salute. "Of course. I'll give your regards to the little green men."

***

He tapped on the hatch, very lightly; Thatcher answered right away. "Yeah?"

"Can't sleep. May I come in?"

He heard the thud of the bar being lifted, and the hatch swung out toward him. "Sure."

He ducked through the circular portal into her quarters; it was a tight space, just a few inches between the dual bunks and the wall. The only luxury was a reading light, and the privilege of sleeping in the room alone. Cai Rui folded himself up and sat at the foot of the bottom bunk.

Thatcher sat cross-legged at the opposite end, back against the wall. She had already put on a skin-tight thermal layer to wear under her dropsuit, but her feet were still bare. Now she picked up the data pad she had casually tossed aside to answer the door. "What's up, boss?"

"I just had a very strange conversation with Commander Wheelock. I'll need you to go up to the bridge before we drop and download the readings off her nav."

She looked up at him with a lifted brow. "Nav data? What in the world do we need that for?"

"Node Space anomalies." He smiled thinly. "I thought they might be the sort of anomalies that would interest...a Node physicist. Or the TFC of Black Section."

Her eyes widened. "What kind of Node Space anomalies are we talking about?"

"They call them 'Ghost Nodes'. Apparently there are Nodes and Node Lines which can be detected with the navigational array, but which don't seem to exist when you engage the drive."

She frowned. "Well, sure. I've heard of a Ghost Node before. I didn't think they were really 'anomalies.'"

"Apparently they're becoming less anomalous with every passing year, which is what interests me. We haven't significantly changed the navigational array of the Node Drive for over thirty years. And the drive and navigational array receive more routine maintenance than any other ship system."

She pursed her lips. "Good point. If the array hasn't changed, there's no good reason for its rate of error to increase."

He shrugged. "It may be nothing. The Director personally asked me to interview Wheelock and follow up on anything she reported, so we'll take a look at this. The Commander also has a couple of accident reports that we'll need to investigate, deepscan vessels lost with all hands while on patrol."

"What happened to them?"

"No one knows, apparently, but Wheelock isn't sure these were really accidents. She recovered the black box recording from at least one of them. She says it sounded as if someone among the crew was suffering from Aortomania."

"Node Madness?" Thatcher looked skeptical. "That's impossible when you're outside the Node, isn't it?"

"Maybe." He looked down to the deck plate, thoughtful. "It isn't my job to discount the improbable." He tilted his head to glance at her. "Speaking of the improbable...I was wondering if you had made any progress."

"Not really." She held up her data pad. "I've been mapping those comm channels, but all it really does is confirm what you had already suspected. The whole network is pretty complex, but the only common point of transfer for all the traceable messages is MarsDome itself. All the Node communications are channeled through the command hub. And the delay between bursts is significant—up to seventy minutes minimum between reception and re-transmission. Sometimes more."

He nodded. "Did you manage to recover the message I sent to Rome?"

"I certainly recovered the message that Rome *received*. It wasn't exactly what you sent."

He sighed. "Yes. I suspected as much."

Her lips flattened with suppressed anger. "It's amazing the damage you can do by removal of one word. Especially when that word is 'not.'" She ran her long slim fingers through her hair, wearily pushing it out of her face. "You were right about where I'd find it, as well. It was planted in your deleted files as an Outgoing message, as if you'd tried to erase it."

He shook his head in disgust. "Bah. I knew it would have to be someplace relatively obvious."

Her deep blue eyes were dark with concern. "What are you going to do about this, Cai?"

"Nothing at the moment." He smiled. "We'll be out of the Pipe in less than an hour. Go get that nav data."

"Sure thing, boss." She immediately handed him the data pad, reaching for her socks.

Cai Rui took it from her casually. "Didn't I tell you to give this back to Dr. Vance, Margaret?"

She grimaced. "What does he need it for? Not like he has any trouble getting a new one." She pulled up a long black sock, sealing it just under the knee. "If he wanted it so bad, he shouldn't be throwing it at people."

He snorted. "I gather it's better than your old one."

"Much." She rolled up her other sock and pulled a boot up over it, grinning over her shoulder. "Twice the processing power, and it's hardened against EMP."

He shrugged. "They say it's how you use it..."

"They only say that to make you feel better when you have a crappy datapad." She held out her hand. "Gimme."

He chuckled as he handed it back. "All right. Magpie."

"Finders keepers, boss." She smiled, rising to her feet. "I'm off."

"Thank you." He paused. "For everything."

Her eyes softened for a moment, and she nodded. "No problem, boss. I'll see you on deck."

10 | INCIDENT AT AVALON

"Irony."

The word crackled softly in the earbuds, reception torn by electromagnetic winds. Cai Rui turned, and found Thatcher standing beside him on the crumbling lip of the bluff. "I'm sorry. I don't understand."

Behind the shining faceplate, she shook her head. "Only a human being could land on a rock like this and give it a name like 'Avalon.'"

He turned back toward the ruins. The shrieking winds of the sandstorm were only a faint whisper through the baffle of his helmet, but in his mind he could hear the screams. The sun was now rising through a clotted haze the color of iron, spilling down over the rim of the canyon and into the valley below. From the black well of shadow, the broken towers and shattered domes of the outpost rose stark and clear.

Raising his eyes again, looking out beyond the ruins to the sepia morning and the brutal mountains, he tried to see it. What had these peoples hoped for, when they gave this place a name so eloquent of sacred refuge…a world away from the world?

It was a peripheral system, off the direct trade routes from Terra and the Hiver front. A miserable hunk of stone, by most accounts, its water and oxygen bound mostly into polar ice and ferrous sand. But hidden beneath these wind-torn peaks were rich veins of metal and mineral deposits, including deep geologic evidence of earlier life; those with the skill could plumb the depths for a little profit, and bring in enough trade to keep the fledgling settlement in supply.

Over the years they had worked hard. With only a decade's labor they had achieved a summer thaw in both polar regions. Their population had grown steadily—despite a few setbacks, the outpost had been thriving. The aqueduct was still flowing even now, water bleeding from the broken reservoir and trickling away over black stone.

"*Deus misereatur,*" he murmured softly.

The earbuds crackled with Thatcher's voice. "Did you say something, sir? I think my receiver is breaking down."

"Nothing, Lieutenant. I believe we have enough light now. Let's have a look."

"Yes sir."

Cai launched himself from the hilltop, dropping the hundred meters to the valley floor in the drifting slow motion of reduced gravity. When he reached the talus slope below he bounded lightly from one massive boulder to the next, making his way toward the ruined dome nestled in the heart of the canyon. In the sheltered lee of the rock walls, the wind had dropped. It seemed almost peaceful.

"Black Nineteen reporting. Gold Five, do you read?"

"Gold Five," Cai said. "Affirmative."

"We're out at the beacon, sir. Something here you might want to see."

Cai planted his feet. "Affirmative, Black Nineteen. Gold Five, Gold Six receiving."

The faceplate of his helmet flickered, and the image washed over the screen. Despite the scattered black specks of missing data, the transmission was clear. He was looking out through the remote camera on Ensign Gardner's right shoulder, standing outside a small bunker—the guard shack for the colony's landing beacon.

The hatch to the bunker was still attached to one hinge, but it had been savagely torn from the other, the metal twisted and bent with force. Deep gouges were scored into the steel plate and the reinforced cement had crumbled under the onslaught.

The camera moved with Gardner into the bunker, tracking with his eyes as he stepped over the threshold. The action here was long over; the place was a gutted hulk, wires and circuits strewn obscenely over the torn remains of the monitoring equipment and the Node array. Against the far wall there was a broad, dark splash.

Thatcher's voice cut in coldly. "Nineteen, look above please."

The camera panned upward. The ceiling was streaked and speckled with black; the voice transmission sounded hesitant. "Did you want a … sample, G-Six?"

86

Thatcher sounded irritable. "That can wait. To your left, Nineteen. Ten o'clock high."

The camera turned obligingly, tracking to the corner—there was a box welded to the beam there, partially hidden from view. Three insulated cables still hung from the bottom, running toward the shattered consoles below.

"I believe that would be the relay box for their Node array," Thatcher said. "Looks to be intact."

"I read you. We'll patch it and see if we've got a ghost of the last transmission."

Cai Rui patched to Thatcher's private channel. "You're familiar with this type of equipment, Lieutenant?"

"Yes sir. It's an old system. These first-generation units used to need a big boost to get their signal through the Node—if you didn't have enough power, wouldn't go anywhere. Failed deliveries went to the relay box for automatic retransmission when the power returned to full." She paused. "I'm thinking in this case, it never did."

"I would not have known," he said quietly. "You're quite an asset, Lieutenant. Hidden depths."

She shrugged. "All these dustball colonies are the same, Commander. Secondhand equipment and expendable people."

He inclined his head politely. "Perhaps. Some might say the same of those living in a refugee camp on the outskirts of Chongqing. And yet a boy from such a place might rise to the rank of Commander, if he used his skills wisely."

Behind the glass, he saw her smile. "We all have to come from somewhere."

Gardner spoke up on the secondary channel. "Gold Five, I think we've got it. Would you like me to patch the signal through?"

"Black Nineteen, Affirmative. Private channel."

Cai's earbuds sizzled with static. "—Repeat! This Colony N3.9.9, Avalon station C, to all Sol Force vessels, do you read . . . ." It was a woman's voice, ragged with fear and desperation. "Please respond. We are under attack. The Rippers are back. God, they're everywhere..." The transmission rolled on, over a discordant babble of voices, as if several people had begun trying to shout over her at once. In the background, the hoarse wail of a crying baby pierced all other sounds, a descant of despair and exhaustion.

"It doesn't matter now. We're in the watch bunker, near the landing field. We've had to abandon the station. We had no idea what they were, until they started working together." A second explosion of babble. "It doesn't matter now, there are only six of us left. The rest are all dead or..." There was a reverberating thud in the background, followed by thin, high-pitched screams. The woman sobbed and her voice trailed away to a terrified thread. "Oh God...they've gotten so big..." Suddenly she gave an agonized shriek. "Jimmy, no! Don't touch the—"

Cai winced at the howl of feedback, and the transmission ended abruptly. Gardner's voice followed after a pause. "I'm sorry, sir. I-I didn't realize it was going to cut out at the end like that—"

Shaken, he broke the feed in mid-sentence. "Thank you, Black Nineteen. Hold your position."

He turned toward the east, trying to regain control; his heart rate had doubled. Cai faced the rising sun for several long moments, concentrating on the flow of breath, until the moment passed.

"Black Nineteen," he said at last. "Give me the date stamp for that last transmission."

The boy hesitated. "It...can't be right, sir. You said HQ got the distress signal from this place just a week ago. This thing reads out as hour twenty-three fifty-nine, two-two-twenty-four-fifty-three. That would have been over a year."

His skin crawled. "The signal we received was an NV tap, Black Nineteen. A non-verbal distress call."

Thatcher cut in. "You mean the colonists didn't send—?"

"All units, this is Gold Five. We are NOT alone. Launch motion tracking immediately. Fall back to the DV in pairs and prepare for launch." Cai drew his weapon; his tracking drones burst from the case like a cloud of angry steel hornets, sniffing for movement. Suddenly the HUD was alive with red shadows, closing in from the surrounding rocks.

"Thatcher—full burn. Get back to that shuttle. I'll cover your retreat." He bounded to the top of a boulder, looking for a firing angle on whatever was below.

"I...don't think...I can do that...sir." Her voice was strained, as if spoken through gritted teeth.

"Why the hell not?"

"Because...he...won't...let...go."

She stood frozen, her whole suit trembling; he could see her gun hand moving slowly. The trigger finger tightened spasmodically; he winced as a fusillade of flechette rounds spattered over the rocks around her.

Her breathing was hoarse and laboured. "Go...Cai..."

The gun roared again, and suddenly she shrieked in pain. Cai reeled, feeling the wave of agony—as if he had just blown off half his own leg. In the rocks there was an answering scream of pain and anger.

In a single motion he bent and lunged across the rocks. Thatcher had crumpled to her knees, air and blood hemorrhaging from the ruptured suit; he went down on one knee beside her, trying to put one of her arms over his shoulder for a carry.

"Can't..." She slumped onto her side, boneless. Looking down, he could see her jaw trembling with strain. The last word was forced out painfully, a last guttural growl of anger. "Goooooooooo...."

It happened so suddenly that his eye could barely follow it. Two hooks lashed up over the lip of the rock, attached to something like arms. One buried itself in her shoulder; another plunged into her abdomen. Her flesh parted in two separate directions.

His earbuds howled as her open comm line went dead. Cai reeled back, his face plate covered with a wet sheet of red; by instinct he uncoiled at once, leaping straight into the air—and sensed rather than saw the massive body that crossed the boulder where he had been just a split-second before.

"*Ignis!*" The jets of his suit roared to life, carrying him above the second leap. Several hundred feet above the valley floor, he paused to hover, passing the palm of his glove over his facemask; already the blood had begun to freeze.

"Whatever you are," he gritted to himself, "I will soon send you back to hell."

Why, this is hell, Cai Rui, a voice replied—cruel, insinuating, coiling like a serpent in his mind. *Nor are we out of it.*

Without hesitation, he turned and roared toward salvation in the west, his skin crawling with reaction. "Who are you?" he muttered. "What are you?"

My name is Legion, it teased, mocking. *For we are many. Oh but do come back, Cai Rui. For you have seen such things... and I am so very hungry.*

He let the pack roar at full burn for ninety seconds before he relented. The HUD said that he had traveled nearly two thousand meters. Slowly he throttled back on the fuel, letting himself sail in a low, pulsing arc over the ice-torn plateau. Scanning for a clearing in the rubble below, he finally let himself land on the curving lip of a lateral moraine with a view of the surrounding plain. He would have at least a few seconds to react, even if they encircled him—or so he hoped.

He toggled his microphone. "Barnswallow, this is Gold Five. We are under attack. Prepare for launch. All units: scramble for evac immediately."

The response was slow in coming, shredded by bursts of static, but it was still possible to make out the pilot's western hemisphere drawl. "Roger on sitrep, Gold Five," she said. "But that's a nega-tory on lift-off. Repeat, nega-tory on lift-off."

Cai Rui switched to the private channel irritably. "What do you mean, negative? We need to get the hell out of here!"

"Yep. *Xin loi* for us, chief. Barn is on fire. Been tryin' to get through to you for the last ten minutes, but our long-range comm is jammed from above. We've got two eagles in the sky, weapons hot. Judgin' by the fireworks I'd say they got gauss PD and grasslights at least."

Cai Rui looked up, sweeping the palms of his gloves over the smeared faceplate of his helmet, clearing the thin film of red ice. Through the turbulent morning sandstorm he could see the faint flicker of green and blue light as ships above exchanged fire. Two cruisers. Green lasers. "An orbital attack?" he said, incredulous. "But we had the latest scan. There were no other ships in this quadrant. No one could have reached us that fast. It's impossible—"

The pilot's voice broke in again, ironically amused. "I ain't sayin' what's possible, sir. Just what's happenin'. I got the message when our friends turned up. Two birds—they're NKC. Maybe some smaller support vessels, too. Don't know. That's all I got before they started jamming us." She paused. "Can't get a word back from the barn, but I don't think they can take that kind of punishment for—"

The fireball cut off her words, the unmistakable spreading lotus of oxygen-nitrogen aflame. For a long moment his earbuds hissed and moaned in silence. "Yeah," she said at last. "Guess that's it for Nanjing."

Cai Rui turned toward the east, throat tightening. In the distance he could see the dark shapes moving, indistinct but swift, loping around the boulders. They covered ground at appalling speed. There were at least a hundred, moving in clumps of five or six—squads, perhaps.

His mind moved swiftly, thoughts sliding into position like the beads of the abacus. Two cruisers of no known configuration. Employing either an unknown means of propulsion or an unknown method of avoiding detection—possibly both.

A distress signal sent as bait, drawing out the Black Section Commander to a distant, peripheral planet. "*Calling all Sol Force vessels. Black Thirteen attack at Avalon. Please assist.*" Not "Rippers", the colloquial name, but "Black Thirteen", an official designation.

Of course he had gone to check it out personally… and stepped into the waiting arms of a demon that knew his name.

It was falling into place quickly. Node array transmissions from Ko'Seth and Ko'Grappa—delayed at first, then blocked completely. A carefully worded report, sent from Mars to Rome—and arriving somehow with the details so garbled that the Holy See demanded war. A Node physicist murdered, her fellows cowed into silence, to cover the tracks of a hidden enemy.

Perhaps an old friend eliminated when she started to come too close to the truth?

There was only one answer, and it had rolled into his office under its own power just days ago: Vance. His flesh crawled as he remembered that data pad, tucked under his own arm as he left the room. How long had he carried it? Was it wired with a transmitter or a recording device? If so, how much had the old spider heard, brooding over his desk and its endless headphone jacks?

He toggled the comm. "Barnswallow, prepare for lift-off." He set his scope to maximum zoom, trying to make out the shape of the enemy approaching—at 500 meters they were still moving too fast from one patch of cover to the next to get a solid image. The one thing he could say for certain was that they ran on all fours, a predatory leaping gallop that sent a shiver down his spine.

Her voice carried the edge of angry frustration. "We got nowhere to go, sir. Soon as I fire up these engines, we're gonna be visible from orbit. We'll be the only duck in a great big empty shootin' gallery."

"Trust me, Lieutenant. We will all be much happier in the air. My ETA is three minutes." He turned and leaped from the moraine, augmenting his bounds with occasional bursts of the jetpack—trying to put as much distance as possible between himself and the voice that had crawled like a beetle within the folds of his brain.

Along the way, he muttered to his PDA. "*Cicero. Mappa strategia Avalonae.*" Obligingly, the suit laid a transparency over his view, assets marked in red. He had always been a careful man, but there were many worlds in the empire, and he had viewed so many schematics for so many missions that just this once, he had to re-check—if only to be certain that desperation had not supplied him with a false hope.

His last bound carried him to within twenty meters of the shuttle; his support platoon had taken up a circle of firing positions around the craft. "Good to see you in one piece, Gold Five." Gardner's voice, the young man rising from his crouch with a hand raised in greeting. "Thought we might lose you back there."

He looked into the boy's eyes and nodded. "Gold Six is gone." His voice was flat, quiet; it rang hollow in his own ears. He put his glove to his blood-spattered chest plate, trying to say something worthwhile. "She saved my life."

There was a hint of sadness in the eyes behind the faceplate. Gardner tapped his helmet in acknowledgment. *I hear you.*

"Fall out, Nineteen. Everyone into the shuttle." He stood on the ramp and waited until all twelve Marines had entered before he stepped inside and dropped the hatch.

The pilot was already strapped into her cockpit. She hadn't yet fired the engine. He dropped into the co-pilot's seat beside her, and she looked across at him. "You sure about this, Commander—?"

"Yes." He took the data line from the armrest beside him and plugged it into his suit, downloading his map into her console. The site he had selected was already tagged in red. "This is a strategic map of the planet. It is, of course, highly classified. We need to reach these coordinates." He tapped her navigation screen with his fingertip. "In one piece. We may be fired upon, from orbit and possibly from the ground. I assume you know the maximum elevation we can attain and still avoid laser lock from space."

She paled. "It's fifty meters. Maybe a hundred, in this storm?"

"Then I would suggest you fly the nap, unless you care to bet our lives on the weather."

She grinned, reaching for the ignition. "Saddle up, soldiers," she said, looking over her shoulder to those in the back. "We're in for a sporty flight!"

The men hurried into their flight webs, and Cai Rui quickly buckled himself into the seat. The woman was mad, of course, like all pilots. She looked forward to a potentially lethal rush at hundreds of klicks an hour over the skin of the planet's surface, buffeted by savage cross winds and blowing sand and ice, dodging unpredictable formations of rock and fusillades of gauss flack from above. This would be her idea of a "good time".

Cai Rui, although he preferred to err on the side of her madness, was not nearly so certain that all of these dangerous precautions were necessary. There were other, darker possibilities. As the shuttle rose from the ground, he switched his comm to ground channel and picked a random scramble. "All units. This is Gold Six. It is time for a debriefing. Acknowledge transmission NV."

He waited for all twelve lights on the HUD to blink affirmative. "Information on this mission is delivered on a Need-to-Know basis. Here are the things that you officially Need to Know.

"One: our support vessel in orbit has been attacked and probably destroyed. Long-range communications are being jammed at the system level. Even if the Nanjing managed to send out a distress call to Sol Force before they were jammed, reinforcements could not arrive here for several days. We have to assume that we are on our own.

"Two: We are about to become the first Sol Force personnel ever to survive contact with a new alien race. The creatures we are up against are not Hivers, Tarka or Liir. We don't know much about them—but today we've discovered that they don't need a spacesuit in ground conditions like these. And they have ships capable of taking down a Sol Force cruiser with all hands."

He let this sink in for a moment before he continued. "Those of you who have been with me on previous missions have probably already begun to put two and two together yourselves. We don't know what this race calls itself, but you have probably heard them called 'Rippers'. Today I found out why. Whatever they are, they've got huge claws. Very strong, very fast. And big."

One of the lights on the HUD flashed twice. "Yes, Black Fifteen?"

"How big is 'big', sir?" The Marine's voice had lifted half an octave with tension. "Are we talking bigger than a Daddy Croc or a Warbug?"

Cai Rui hesitated. "I didn't ask it to step onto the scales, private. It looked about the size of a Hiver Warrior or a Changed Tarka, yes. But I will admit that I couldn't see very well, with my helmet covered in blood."

The boat was accelerating now, spires of ice and rock flying by at terrifying speed. In the distance behind them, there was a series of deep, reverberating thuds.

"*Gāiside*," someone said. "What are they doing back there? Did you see those things hit? They were the size of a truck at lea—"

The only warning was the quick tilt of her helmet; suddenly the shuttle slammed into a bank. It shuddered with the nearness of the collision as something the size of a destroyer passed within inches of the stern.

"JEE-susmaryandjoe!"

The boom of impact rocked the shuttle. Cai Rui, his portside seat suddenly parallel to the ground, winced as his window was hammered by the upward plume of debris.

"What the HELL did they just throw at us!? What the HELL kind of weapon is that!?" The pilot continued her turning circle, engines screaming with strain.

Cai Rui looked down through the billowing sand, rapidly clearing before the onslaught of the wind. There was a significant impact crater below, but it was clear that the missile, whatever it was, had not hit at full terminal velocity. It had been some sort of ship or vessel, reduced now to a circular deposit of scrap—the colorful contents of the hold scattered over the icy plain.

Something within him seemed to go very still. "Lieutenant, make another pass."

"Why, so they can throw another damn building at me? Are you crazy?"

"Do as I say."

With an inarticulate cry of frustration, the pilot banked again, circling back over the impact crater.

"Hold steady. Camera on." The image panned over the interior of his face-plate, linked to the flight recorder of the shuttle. "Magnify."

There was silence for a few moments, finally broken by a horrified whisper. "My God. Look at all the people."

It was Gardner's voice; Cai Rui had forgotten that his suit was broadcasting. All twelve legionaries and the pilot were looking down on the strewn field of corpses—the naked dead of a dozen worlds.

Scattered among the wreckage there were Hivers, Humans and Tarka together—looking more closely, he could even see a few nude, pitiful Liir. The stunned pilot had slowed, without orders, pausing at a hover. The cameras panned over the carnage, slowly zooming in, clarifying, steadying the image. Even in death, these gaunt bodies and haunted faces were eloquent of a vast and prolonged suffering.

Slaves.

"*Deus misereatur,*" he murmured again softly.

Something stirred among the dead. "Follow motion," he said absently. The camera tracked a dark shape that feebly crawled among the broken flesh and steel. There in the wreckage was a twisted, shattered body, dragging itself by one heavy claw toward the shelter of a rock to die. Four limbs. Covered with hair. Broken jaws hanging wide in agony—jaws equipped with ferocious rending fangs. A large predator, born to kill.

"Behold the enemy," Cai Rui said. "We're not seeing him at his best, but—"

The creature rolled over onto its back, its body convulsing in pain. "Seeing *her* at her best, sir," one of the women said. "That one's a female."

The beast was now still, its massive chest no longer rising—and still the pilot hovered, her face rapt with horrified fascination. "Her belly is still movin,'" she croaked. "There's something inside her."

Cai Rui frowned. "Maximum magnification." Something indeed seemed to be stirring under the skin of the Ripper female—there was some kind of slit in her abdomen, filled with restless lumps.

"Gah!" The soldiers flinched as the worms burst forth, two bloody heads emerging from twin holes in the hairy carcass. They retreated rapidly into the bloody tunnels they had made, as if to flee the cold.

Cai Rui swallowed his gorge, nauseated. "I believe we've seen enough. Camera off. Move on, Lieutenant. We won't have much time."

The pilot leveled off, her face bathed with sweat. "They weren't really trying to hit us, were they. That wasn't about us at all."

"I don't think so, no," Cai Rui said—somewhat reluctantly. "I don't believe they would deliberately fire on this vessel."

She shuddered. "What the hell did they crash all those ships for? It must have been at least four went down—that can't have been an accident."

"I don't know, Lieutenant." But in his mind, the chorus of dead women was loud, words rising up in his consciousness and tumbling together.

The Rippers are back.

My God, they're everywhere.

We had no idea what they were, until they started working together.

The local rats really make short work of anything that's just lying around—they'll eat anything that resembles food or garbage.

Nasty things, like weasels.

My God, they've gotten so big…

Jimmy, no. Don't open the… hatch.

Because… he… won't… let… go.

11 | ESCAPE FROM AVALON

The hatch was covered with a layered blanket of ice. In the dark channel of this valley, periodic melts had brought successive flows of water down the face of the rock wall. Cai Rui tapped the surface again with his probe and then stepped back.

"Once more should do it. Very, very thin."

The soldier stepped forward again with the hot gun, re-tracing the same square with a quick, precise hand. His trigger finger was so delicate that only a pencil-slim line of the thermal foam was released. Within seconds of completion the lines began to smoke, scoring the ice even more deeply; when the reaction stopped, they had burned down to the metal. Cai Rui slipped the tip of his probe beneath the square cake and levered it away, revealing the old control panel.

Quickly he patched his suit into the lock. "Command override one-nine-nine-eight-zulu. Task Force Commander Cai Rui, authorization code Charlie-India-Charlie-Echo-Romeo-Oscar-four-three-Bravo-Charlie."

For a moment the mechanism was silent, and his stomach twisted in nauseating fear. Then, at last, the machinery within the mountain groaned. The ice trembled, and he hastily backed away, signaling the rest of the unit to retreat. There was a sharp *crack!* from the overhang above, followed by a burst of sound like small arms fire; the ice began to fall, dropping from the high cliffs to shatter on the stone floor of the cul-de-sac in massive sheets and chunks. The troops waited, tense and silent, until the tremor ceased, and then moved in quickly to clear a path through the debris.

Cai Rui placed his hand on the hatch and it rolled back, revealing a hole in the side of the mountain. "Black Twelve, Fourteen, take point. See if you can get the lights on." He switched to the secondary channel as the two legionaries moved in, stepping in through the hatch with pit-lamps on. "Barnswallow, how is the job coming?"

There was a moment's hesitation before the reply. "Doin' m'best, Gold Five. I just don't see how you're going to make this work. You won't be able to get a signal to this thing at all past 500 meters. Atmo is just too thick."

"The atmosphere will not be a problem, Lieutenant. Keep working."

He switched back to primary channel, turned and followed the second pair of soldiers into the hatch, leaving the rest to guard the entrance. "Twelve, is the generator functional?"

"Yes sir. It looks fine. We just need to juice it."

Cai Rui frowned—one of the two legionaries would be giving up a fuel cell from her suit. "Do it in one shot if you can."

"Roger, Gold Five."

His escort moved cautiously into the tunnels ahead, probing the darkness with their restless beams of light. "Looks like another hatch, sir." One of them held up a hand. "High security."

Cai Rui moved to the front and patched his suit into the second lock, repeating his command override and adding the code for Q clearance. The hatch slid aside, and he stepped through ahead of his companions. A niche had opened in the far wall; he walked to it swiftly and put the hand of his suit into it, fitting the fingers into the rough slots for a five-digit extremity. There was a brief sting at the tip of each finger as the system inserted its probes, connecting with his suit system and tasting him with its five needle tongues. A third hatch slid open in the far wall.

"Command override acknowledged." The smooth feminine voice sounded in his earbuds. "Task Force Commander Cai Rui, authorized to proceed."

He exhaled at last, feeling a wave of relief wash over him. "All right. We're in. We're going to have to move fast."

A second channel cut into his comm line. "Gold Five, we've powered the generator. Going to try to fire it up."

"Roger, B-Twelve. Proceed." A distant thrum reverberated through the cement floor, and the lighting system stuttered to life in a series of fitful flashes. The soldiers waited for several seconds to see if the glowing tubes in the ceiling would die and then flicked off their scope beams. Cai Rui smiled. "Well done, Twelve. We've gotten through here. Come on down."

He turned and loped into the curving labyrinth of tunnels, breaking a thick layer of red dust with every step. The last curve opened up into a bunker, its circular walls paneled by information screens and broken by five hatches.

Only one of the control boards was live, bleating its distress with a single flashing light. He forced a command through the circuits, trying to open the hatch doors. The mechanism would not respond.

He sighed. "Burn one. We have no time."

He paced restlessly as the team torched the hinges and the locks. After some struggle they at last managed to pull the heavy secondary blast door from one of the tunnels. He stepped in, looking for another security panel, and found another place to patch in.

"Cicero, *fulcrum totibus*." His scalp tingled as the PDA forced open the hatches all the way to the pit below. The HUD count-down gave him twenty minutes before they would enter the danger zone.

He turned to find all four soldiers standing behind him. "All right. We're going to have to do this right the first time—there won't be a second chance. Twelve, Sixteen—find us a gravbed and get it up to the top of the gantry. Fourteen, get down to the second level and hack the telemetry—I want to know where this thing was supposed to go, and whether it can be re-routed. Gardner—you're with me."

He turned and ran into the twisting stone tunnel, following a branch leading up a steep incline. The final hatch had only half-opened, its mechanism wheezing faintly in the dust; he gave it a push and stepped out onto a steel grate.

Even in a spacesuit he felt a tremor of reaction as he looked down. The walkway was suspended over a drop of nearly two hundred meters to the bottom of this massive stone tube, and the echoing clang of his footsteps vaulted down the length of the shaft as he clattered to a halt. The side of the rocket gleamed in the wan glow of the automatic lighting; he was now just a few feet away from many megatons of explosive force.

Gardner stepped in beside him. Cai Rui turned in time to see him grin. "Hello, beautiful." The boy reached out and stroked the panel almost sensuously with his glove, clearing a film of dust from the smooth heads of the magnetic screws. He glanced at the Commander. "Sorry. Looking forward to this—I've never seen one up close before."

"It's all right. Just be careful."

Gardner went to work immediately, releasing the seals to peel back an accordion of titanium steel. Cai Rui looked down again, hammering his brief spasm of vertigo into submission. "Fourteen, do you read?"

"Yes sir," came the voice from below. "Just pulling the coordinates. This thing is pointed at a planet in Tarka space—ninety-point twenty-one-sixty-point zero-zero-three."

"Ke'Vanthu." He closed his eyes. "Can it be re-routed?"

"Afraid not, Gold. The engine is just too primitive. It'll come up short if we point it anywhere else."

He hesitated. "All right. Get the launch sequence started."

"Roger, Gold." The woman switched to broadcast. "All units—look alive. I'm going to fire the charges to clear the silo doors. Acknowledge transmission NV."

Cai Rui sent his silent acknowledgment and braced himself on the gantry; Gardner paused and took a firm grip on the panel he was working on. Seconds later a series of deep percussive thumps sounded overhead, as the clearing charges went off on the mountaintop above.

It was an old silo, built more than a decade before the founding of the colony on Avalon. Secret installations like this were hidden on a number of obscure rocks in open space, during a period when the limited range of Node drives made it difficult to get within throwing distance of enemy systems. A base like this would house up to six of the deadly old drones, ready to be launched by heavy lifters into orbit and targeted on strategic systems nearby. Modern advances had rendered the old fission-based drives obsolete, and in key positions throughout the empire they had been replaced. But many of the hidden silos were simply decommissioned. Sol Force never really "decommissioned" a weapons system, however. The security codes were kept up to date, even when other types of maintenance were allowed to slide.

Some lessons are impossible to forget, Cai Rui thought. *Even a rusting sword can save your life.*

Overhead the doors slid back. Ice and grit showered down into the pit. The shrieking wind was immediately audible above, and the silo moaned with resonance like the hollow body of a massive flute. When at last the roof above was clear, the stormy steel-gray sky of Avalon boiled above. Two legionaries rose from the floor of the silo, standing on a gravbed; Cai Rui tossed them the hooks from the gantry and helped them tie up the levitating platform.

The two women worked swiftly. They helped Gardner remove the protective paneling from the rocket's payload and disconnected the massive warhead and liquid boosters from the missile. By the end of the job, all five suits and the gravbed itself were groaning from overstrain. The team rode together to the entrance and navigated the platform carefully over the broken ice and stone of the chasm. The pilot and her shuttle were waiting, along with the guards he had left.

"Load as much as you can," he said tersely. "The warhead is the priority."

The pilot looked over his shoulder at the payload he had brought; behind the glass of her helmet, she paled visibly. "That's a whole lotta boom, sir."

"Yes it is. If the extra fuel tanks are too heavy, drop them there." He pointed to a notch in the rocks, the last narrow point before the chasm opened into a broader canyon. "They may come in handy."

Cai Rui recorded a crystal as the soldiers went to work. When it was finished he ducked back into the shuttle. The pilot was still there, sitting in the cockpit—watching the screens for any sign of movement.

"Upload this to the comm." He handed her the crystal. "I'll program the lift-off myself, if you don't mind."

With a silent nod she slotted the crystal into the communications array, transferring command to the co-pilot's seat in the process. Quickly he programmed the auto-pilot sequence—a simple lift-off, followed by rapid rise as quickly as possible into orbit. The message he had recorded would be broadcast repeatedly...for as long as the shuttle was intact.

"All right, people." The door of the shuttle sealed behind him, the thrum of its warming engines blending with the howl of the storm. "Let's fall back. We need to get into the silo and—"

My, my. What a merry chase you lead, Cai Rui.

He reached for his weapon, dropping into a silent crouch and searching the surrounding rocks. All of the legionaries reacted instantly to his movement, assuming defensive positions, guns at the ready.

His broadcast was brief. "Fall back in pairs. Get back inside the entrance. Now."

No, no, no. That will never do.

The flicker of a shadow was the only warning. The Rippers dropped from above: only one of the two soldiers to the rear managed to dodge, throwing himself to the side just an instant before his attacker struck. The other man had time only for a brief bark of fright before he was crushed beneath the weight of his opponent.

She landed on all fours, her two huge foreclaws buried in his torso. There was a horrendous crunch as she dropped her head and quickly crushed his helmet in her jaws.

The squad turned and opened fire, pouring a torrent of steel into the two massive bodies. One of the Rippers collapsed, her flattened skull riddled with holes; the other staggered forward, snarling, fangs still festooned with torn cloth and rags of flesh. Cai Rui spared only a single backward glance before turning the other direction—in time to see a second pair slinking through the narrow entrance.

There was only a moment to react. The shuttle was already rising from the valley floor, its maneuvering thrusters firing to maintain safe distance from the jagged rock walls. Cai Rui fired a short burst into the nearest target, eliciting a shriek of rage as it fell writhing to the ice, to bite at the stinging wounds in its side. The pilot dropped to one knee beside him, ready to fire—but the second attacker had taken cover behind an outcropping.

Cai Rui looked up as the fifth Ripper sprang, high above. Without hesitation he fired, a quick precise burst of three shots into the torso. It screamed, body twisting in midair, and missed its leap onto the wing of the shuttle; instead it thudded into the cliff face and tumbled helpless to the rocks below, landing with an audible snap of shattering bone.

The shuttle cleared the cliff tops, rising steadily into the turbulent sky. Its recorded message began to play—his own voice torn apart by bursts of howling static. "Attention...—mander Cai Rui...mber 4320...."

Fight all you like, little ape, the sinuous voice snarled in his mind. *I will take you in the end.*

Cai Rui smiled coldly. *Tu et quis exercitus, canicula?*

What army? The rage in the voice was unmistakable. *Yours, slave.*

The sudden roar of gunfire was nearly deafening; the pilot's rifle blazed only inches from his helmet. Cai Rui reeled, his earbuds shrieking with feedback for the split second before they mercifully died. He threw himself to the side, seeking cover, and looked back just in time to see her body jump and shiver as a dozen rounds ripped into her. Her chest an open ruin, the woman was dead on her feet several seconds before she hit the ground.

Cai Rui rolled, putting his faceplate to the ground and wrapping his arms around the helmet protectively. The rocks and ice all around him had come alive, ricochets of shattered stone and steel bounding from every surface. His HUD lit up in a dozen places, red flashes to signal the breaches in his environment suit.

At last the hail of death stopped and he rolled over, looking back into the valley behind. The last soldier was still standing, blood and air leaking from a dozen holes. His gun still chattered, hammer falling over and over on the last chamber of an empty clip, his finger still locked tight on the trigger.

The rest of the squad lay still, torn apart by the guns that they had turned upon each other.

Cai Rui crawled toward the man who stood alone, his blood steaming and freezing black in the deep shade. Suddenly the soldier stiffened and dropped, falling to his knees and collapsing onto his side like a puppet with its strings cut. Cai Rui reached him just as he rolled painfully onto his back.

It was Gardner. His eyes were wide, pupils reduced to pinpricks, his breath coming in swift shallow pants of shock and imminent death. The faceplate of his helmet was already cracked, the warmth of his breath staining the cold glass with pink frost.

The wide green eyes blinked, and somehow seemed to sharpen; the boy's lips moved. Cai Rui tapped the side of his helm to indicate the broken earbuds. He lowered his head, letting his faceplate kiss the glass of the boy's helmet so that the sound of his last words would carry.

"Wha'd I do that for, boss?" Gardner said, his dying voice high and plaintive. "Wha'd I do...?"

"It wasn't your fault." The Commander closed his eyes for a moment, fighting down a surge of grief. When he opened them again, the soldier's chest had stopped moving.

You are alone now, the voice said. *Surrender.*

Cai Rui dropped onto his belly, sighting down the barrel of his rifle. *Never.*

Even as he thought the word, the first fuel tank exploded. The second tank ignited a split second later. A tower of flame rose at the mouth of the valley, shrapnel whistling in every direction at the speed of sound. Cai Rui screamed with the fire, letting the blast of heat and light wash over him. It would have been meaningless, if the suit was intact; as it was he was burned through every breach. The pain on the left side was particularly intense. When he turned his head, he saw a shred of twisted steel buried in his blackened shoulder.

Ice and stone crashed into the canyon, the walls on either side of the valley mouth collapsing inward with a roar. Cai Rui forced himself up to his feet and staggered back the way he had come through clouds of dust and ice, moving toward the hatch in the side of the mountain. His HUD was a mass of red lights—the breaches in his armor, the movement of his foes. Heavy bodies dropped into the canyon behind him, moving forward cautiously in case he had set some other trap.

He stepped in through the hatch and closed it behind him. There was no time to jam it shut.

The voice came again—amused, though less vibrant through several feet of rock and steel. *Where are you going, Cai Rui? You cannot hide in the mountain. My Hands will dig you out like a grub if they must.*

Bracing himself on the wall, he bent and opened the emergency repair kit on his left calf. *Dominus pascit me, et nihil mihi deerit.* In his mind the words were chanted aloud, echoing in the space of a humble chapel on Luna. *The Lord is my shepherd, and nothing shall I want...*

I am your Lord, Cai Rui. The voice deepened, and a slow chill crept down his spine, spreading into his limbs. *You will obey me.*

He remembered Thatcher's scream. Fighting the icy grip closing slowly to crush his mind, Cai Rui reached up to the metal shard in his shoulder. Gritting his teeth, exerting the full force of his will, he gave the jagged spear of steel a quick, hard twist. The pain was astonishing, so intense that it burst behind his eyes as an explosion of light. For a moment, everything went black—but when the light returned, the cold invisible hand on his soul was gone.

For that you will suffer, the voice snarled.

Cai Rui smiled. The first heavy thump sounded on the door behind him: his hands shook as he peeled the backing from a patch and fitted it over an ugly gash in the chest of the suit.

In pascuis virentibus me collocavit... One of the HUD lights stopped blinking, and he clumsily peeled the backing from a second patch. *Super aquas quietis eduxit me.*

A second impact hit the door, deeper and more confident. Cai Rui limped down the tunnel, seeking the second hatch. With every step he recited another word of the psalm—using it as a rope to drag himself through the dimly lit hall. "He restoreth my soul," he gasped aloud, in English. *Animam meam refecit. Deduxit me super semitas iustitiae propter nomen suum...*

You cannot hide from me, Cai Rui, the voice said. Its touch upon his mind was light, caressing. *I feel your pain. You will not last long, with such an injury. I will find you wher—.*

When the second hatch slid shut, the voice was abruptly cut short. Some part of him noted the range, even as he stumbled toward the emergency flood room and opened the storage compartment. The atmosphere leaking steadily from his suit was making him increasingly lightheaded—even with the two largest holes covered, there was no way to maintain the pressure.

He nearly wept with frustration when he pulled out the spare suit—a clumsy old monstrosity nearly thirty years out of date, impossible to mate with the modern command and control of his own. It was only when he looked at the name and the height/mass tolerance label that he grinned.

Guard Commander Shoney, saints be praised, had been a fat man. Cai Rui pulled the body of the old suit over the leaking remains of his own, and quickly mated the collar to his own helmet with a ring of sticky patches. He stumbled the rest of the way to the gantry holding a spare tank in his arms, loading it into the empty missile tube before he crawled inside.

The accordion panels folded back into place, magnetic screws spinning in the suddenly dark chamber. "Commander Cai Rui," he said aloud. "Emergency command override. Activate launch sequence."

He closed his eyes and lay down on his side, arms wrapped tight around his spare oxygen in the dark. There was no other way to secure or brace himself; as the rocket began first to rumble and then to roar, he simply tried to tighten every possible muscle to avoid losing consciousness.

The sound was unbelievably loud, all-consuming, thunderous. The acceleration crushed him to the curving floor of the chamber. A single line of verse echoed in his mind, over and over, as the booster soared toward the roof of the sky: *Nam et si ambulavero in valle umbrae mortis, no timebo mala, quoniam tu mecum es.*

For though I may walk in the valley of the shadow of death, I will fear no evil, for Thou art with me.

At last the divine fire slowed and then stopped, the empty booster dropping away into endless night. He heard and felt rather than saw the protective panels peeling back from the drone all around him, releasing the missile for its secondary stage. His body rose from the floor of the chamber in freefall, his suit expanding and inflating in vacuum.

His temples were pounding as he clumsily opened the channel to the shuttle. The recording he had made sounded tinny in his ears as he activated the flight cameras.

"Attention enemy vessel," his recorded voice said. "This is Sol Force Commander Cai Rui..."

The Ripper ship loomed closer than he had expected. It was an ugly thing, a massive conglomeration of mismatching parts, its engines massive and red hot.

"...returning from the surface of Avalon. Please hold your fire. Repeat: please hold your fire."

As he watched, the enemy launched a grappling hook toward the shuttle. The camera rocked with the impact of the heavy claw, listing to the side as the larger ship reeled it in.

"My shuttle is not armed. My crew and I wish to surrender."

The engines of the missile thrummed beneath him as the Node drive engaged.

Cai Rui smiled.

"*Acalanthis,*" he said. "*Ignis.*"

His camera view disappeared in a final flash of light as the warhead aboard the shuttle detonated. Cai Rui closed his eyes. *Eripuit me de inimicis meis fortissimis, et ab his qui oderunt me: quoniam confortati sunt super me.*

He delivered me from my strongest enemies, and from those who hated me: because they had power over me. "Thank you," he whispered, and finally lost consciousness.

12 | RENDEZVOUS AT KE'VANTHU

The touch was gentle, a palm with the nap of heavy silk passing over his brow. Still only semi-conscious, the old impulse remained: he tried to reach up, to take that delicate hand and bring the perfumed wrist to his lips. The attempt to move brought an answering stab in his shoulder. The pain shocked his eyes open; he winced at the sudden brightness of the cool, trembling blue light.

She was looking down into his face, her eyes wide with emotion. As he watched, her pupils expanded and changed shape, forming the crimped ovals of deep pleasure. "Caido," she mouthed—but her husky voice was muffled, so soft he could barely hear.

"Sara." His own voice was a painful rasp. For a moment he could not tear his eyes away from her face: the huge shimmering leaf-green jewels of her eyes, the golden mask of tiny scales stretched taut over her cheeks and chin. A crest of glossy obsidian framed her face like a crown of braids. *My Iron Lotus.*

He closed his eyes again, trying to orient himself—but when he reached for recent memory, it was somehow elusive. Bright flashes of fire and blood slipped between his fingers, to scatter like fish vanishing into dark water. He opened his eyes again, speaking in Urdu Kai, forcing his gaze away from her to try and take in the rest of his surroundings. "Where am I?"

The room was bare, well-lit. A smell of antiseptic and ozone hung in the air. Somewhere behind and above him, there were machines. A tangle of tubes running various fluids were attached to his body. Hospital, he thought. Something has happened to me.

"Aboard my personal ship," she replied, in English. "You were recovered from the tube of an empty node missile in orbit around Ke'Vanthu." Her eyes flashed with tender amusement. "Needless to say, when I saw the report, I told the Supreme I would handle the matter personally." She switched to Latin. "*Scivi te futurum esse. Non alius in mundo tam insanus est qui in tali loco inveniretur.*" Her scarlet tongue flickered laughter. "I have missed you, Caido."

She was talking nonsense. "In the tube of a what—?" He frowned, struggling. His mind was slow, leaden. He could not remember. "That's...not possible."

Her pupils narrowed. She looked to the side. "Something is wrong. He does not understand me."

"He will." The voice was soft and pitched high, a light, feminine electronic trill. "He is not yet healed."

But there was also a voice in his mind, speaking other words—a sound both soft and yet somehow huge, like the whisper of a giant. *I have not yet given back all of his pain.*

Cai Rui snapped to the side, hurling himself violently from the bed. It was a brute instinct, an act of pure adrenaline. A dozen patches and tubes wrenched from his body in that instant, falling in a tangle as he dove from the mattress—away from the voice.

Stop. His body hovered just inches above the floor, caught in an invisible field. The force lifted him, turning his body gently, holding his limbs immobile as if the air had somehow thickened like amber. *Do not be afraid,* the massive voice whispered. *You will not be harmed.*

His heart was pounding. Every word that echoed in his mind seemed to magnify the fear. "Let me go!"

Sara had pounced up onto the bed; she scrambled nimbly aside now as he was returned to it. "Cai, please—!"

The musical voice sounded again from the corner of the room. "Do not be distressed," it said in Tarka. "He is...confused. He has been...harmed...in many ways."

Leaking from a dozen re-opened wounds, Cai Rui snarled defiance. "Show yourself, monster."

Steel slithered over the bulkhead. A hulking shape moved into view from the right, walking on a forest of metal tentacles. The faceplate of the helm was a curving dog's snout of clear glass, framed and braced by shining red and gold enamel. The large streamlined body was encased in silvery plates, its fins and flukes set off by scarlet fletching.

Behind the mask, the cetacean's head was serene, cool grey, its large liquid eyes black and unblinking in a fluid medium.

"You are Liir."

It dipped its body, as if to bow. The speaker in its chest trilled softly in Urdu Kai. "Remorse. This one did not mean to cause alarm."

Cai Rui relaxed somewhat, and instantly the grip on his trembling body eased. "I expected... something else." He frowned once again at the darkness in his mind. "I don't know what."

"Ishii is not the enemy. He is a healer." Sara stepped back, clearing the path. "Let him help you, Caido. *Amabo te.*"

Despite himself, he smiled slightly at the caressing tone of her voice, pleading in Latin. She manipulates as others breathe—so natural. Still lying amid the stained and rumpled sheets, he glanced at the Liir and nodded. "Yes. On one condition."

The Liir stopped. "Condition?"

"My pain. You will give it back." He met the liquid eyes. "All of it."

Once again the Liir bowed. Cai Rui took a deep breath, suppressing a shiver of apprehension, and closed his eyes.

It was not a gentle transition. The numb darkness of his mind flooded with a torrent of memory, so suddenly that his body rebelled. He heaved upward, a strangled sound torn from his throat, wrenching his shoulder with a bolt of agony, and turned to empty his stomach over the side of the bed. His abdomen clenched painfully, several times. Nothing came up but clear, bitter bile.

Dead. All dead.

When he was finished he was pale and trembling, covered with a sheen of cold sweat. The physical pain came on more slowly, as the burned skin and trickling holes in his flesh came alive in symphonic succession. Soon his whole body was a map of misery—but he was once again in full possession of it.

Sara sensed immediately when the first storm of reaction had passed. With a flick of her finger she motioned in two orderlies to attend him, swiftly and silently changing the soiled sheets of his bed and replacing them with new lengths of clean fabric.

When the sheets had been changed, the two young Tarka put on new gloves and each picked up a tray of shining instruments. They held the trays at arm's length as the apparatus came alive around him, twisting like a nest of living vines. He watched in disbelief as the glittering needles, scissors and clamps rose from the trays on their own and darted like bright steel insects around the bed to snip and refit his various catheters, shunts and intravenous tubes.

Perfectly sterile. He watched as the cetacean's invisible hands changed his dressings and re-closed his wounds, bracing himself against successive waves of nausea as the needles pierced his far-too-lively flesh.

He glanced at the Liir's face. Behind the muzzle of thick glass its eyes were deep, unblinking, infinitely calm.

Remorse. The word bloomed in his mind like a bouquet. In a split-second he felt all the emotions accompanying the thought: the desire to take back a poor decision; sheepish recognition of one's foolishness, and blindness; sorrow for another's pain and loss. For a moment it was impossible to disentangle his own mind from that of the other. *This one did not know that you could hear.*

"I can't," he said aloud.

"Can't?" Sara cocked her head quizzically. "Can't what, Caido?"

The other remains deaf, the whisper said. *She cannot hear us unless we—* "—use fleetsong," the Liir trilled aloud.

Cai Rui frowned and turned to Sara. "*Massaaku.* I found them on Avalon. They are like this one." He tilted his head toward the Liir. "They talk by thinking."

"They are nothing like 'this one.'" The mechanical voice had deepened, icy with disdain. "Nothing." It turned toward Sara. "Work is finished. With permission, Ishii the Drowned will depart."

She reached toward it, touching a steel fluke with her speckled golden hand. "Please do not be offended, my friend. He does not know you as I do."

"He will learn." The Liir's voice was cold.

Cai Rui watched the creature leave with narrowed eyes, listening as the rasp and squeal of its mechanical tentacles retreated. Sara gave a silent flick of her tail to the two attendants and they followed after, sealing the room behind them. She crossed her arms over her chest as she turned toward him and thrust out the supple curve of one hip—a practiced human gesture. He remembered the days she had spent watching the women of his species, mimicking every movement and expression like a dancer learning new steps. "Well?"

He sighed, lifting one arm feebly. "God help me. Come closer."

Her eyes smiled and her tongue flickered. "You are in no shape for *kokari*, my dearest. Even if it were not a sin." Nevertheless she moved forward, coming to the edge of the bed.

He smiled sadly, reaching for her hand. "I can look at you, at least." He closed his eyes, nauseated and weary. "And if I must go to hell, I fear it will hold few surprises. I have lost six *saal*'s worth of soldiers, including a woman who loved me. My father has been taken. My friend was crucified. My Church and my Supreme are threatening to destroy one another." He closed his eyes, passing the ball of his thumb over the warm rough silk of her palm. "It has not been a good month."

"I am sorry." She knelt on a chair beside him, and tenderly the tip of her tail stroked the arch of his foot. For a long time, she simply sat beside him, and he let his body relax. Despite everything, it was good to be beside her, if only for a moment. *If life could end here*, he thought, *it would be all right*.

His breathing eventually became more smooth and even; she stirred before he could drift off to sleep. "Caido... we must talk, if you are able."

Reluctantly he lifted his eyelids, looking up into the intricate agate eyes, now golden yellow with concern. "I am able."

"Forgive me. You were close to death when they found you. The colonial authorities here nearly killed you with kindness—gave you too much oxygen as you were coming out of suspension. If I had not summoned Ishii, you surely would have died." She touched his face again. "You must tell me what happened; I will avenge you. A hundred ships now answer to my command."

"Ah." He hesitated, and then squeezed her hand. "I am sorry. Demoted to *Lac Tar*?"

She turned her head away, dropping her eyelids, lifting one slim shoulder in an eloquent shrug. "I am content." Her voice was soft. "Politics is a dull game. It is more exciting to lead warriors."

He snorted. "Lie to everyone but me, Saradora."

She turned back to him, and her eyes smiled merrily. "The rest of the Council have been suspicious for years. They had the chance to move against me and took it; it was as simple as that. I could not leave His side to come to Ke'Vanthu, unless I was willing to return to the ranks." Her tail tip caressed him with its soft pad. "Given the circumstances, I made the choice that seemed best to me."

He nodded. "You received my message before I left for Avalon, I hope."

"It was not delivered. Fortunately, I have other sources of information."

"It was a trap." His fingers tightened once more. "I was betrayed. One of my fellow officers helped the Rippers to lay an ambush for me—I believe it was Conrad Vance, although I cannot confirm that as yet. There was a creature on Avalon who knew my name—or tore it from my mind. The enemy is telepathic. And they have other tricks..."

"I know." She lowered her eyelids gently and breathed a sigh. "Ishii and I have learned much already. You have been unconscious for longer than you know, beloved." Her eyes turned serious, pupils slitted. "We were able to guess at the home coordinates of your missile. My fleet has already been to Avalon. The Rippers fled into a hole in space, as your own ships do—we lost them there. But my soldiers found what they had left behind."

"And what was that?"

She hesitated. "Perhaps when you are stronger."

His grip on her fingers grew tighter, despite the pain. "Tell me, Sara."

"Better to show." She freed herself from his grip and activated her wrist cuff, tickling a combination of its colorful jewels with her fingernail. "Screen," she said, speaking Kona Kai. "View holding cell ten. No sound."

The far wall of the room hummed as thousands of tiny photocells were activated. Its featureless blue surface dissolved, as if the wall had vanished between his own room and another. Only the occasional sparkle of a lost bit of information revealed that it was an illusion.

The little room was dark, the far wall broken by a single window, a sunbeam slanting down through its bars. A messy cot had been shoved into the corner. A shining pool of water had spread across the stone floor from a spilled Tarkasian drinking bowl. The room's only decoration was a crucifix, the plaster image of the Savior looking down sorrowfully upon the man who knelt weeping before Him.

He recognized the cell immediately; he had occupied one very much like it as a novice. Even the scuffs in the plaster were familiar—he could swear there was one in the corner he had made himself.

The man wore a black robe and a belt of rough rope, his feet bare. Sitting with his back to the screen, his head deeply bowed, his whole body shaking with tears, nonetheless there was something in the shape of his bald pate and pink ear tips that was unmistakable. His left hand was folded, the arm held tight against his ribs—the other fist jerked repeatedly, slapping first one bony collarbone and then the other. With every motion his body jumped in response—as if he had been struck.

Despite himself, his eyes filled with tears. "*Deus misereatur.*" He turned to her. "Where did you find him?"

"In a foul lair underground, among the gnawed bones of many." Her eyes were grim, burning a deep orange. "They were keeping him. Or rather...one of them was keeping him."

His jaw clenched. "Yes. I believe...I know which one that would be."

She folded her hands together, her eyes full of sadness. "They have broken him, beloved. Ishii has done what she can, but you see him now at his best. She made this room to match a place in his memory—a place which gave him comfort."

His throat tightened with a lump that could not be swallowed. "I know it. It is a cell from the House of Studies in Rangoon. He was the abbot there when I was a child."

She pointed to the screen, and then repeated the old man's gesture herself, touching her fist to each collarbone. "She has given him an illusion to hold in his hand—a whip with many tongues. He believes that he is..." She winced, shivering. "Striking himself with the lash. Over and over." Her tail twitched with agitation. "If it were real, he would have whipped himself to death."

He closed his eyes. "It is a scourge, Sara. To whip himself is an act of penitence." He looked at the screen again, forcing himself to face the image. "For some great sin has been committed. He is trying to make amends to God."

She lowered her head and her eyelids again. "There are some things I will never understand, Caido. Much as I try." She gestured toward the screen. "Ishii has worked very hard. He could not speak at all when we found him. I still cannot understand what he is saying—he speaks only Latin, it is not my best language..."

"I must speak to him."

She flinched. "He is...quite mad, beloved."

"Nevertheless." He pointed toward the screen. "Can we exchange words from here?"

Reluctantly she blinked assent. "Are you sure you wish it? He is not the man you knew."

His voice hardened. "He most certainly is. And I must speak to him."

She took a deep breath and reached for the cuff again. "As you say."

The sound of the old man's weeping filled the room, echoing as if through a chamber of stone. "*Mea culpa*," he sobbed. "*Mea maxima culpa*..."

Cai Rui spoke, reluctant to interrupt. "Father?"

Tourneau gasped and froze, turning toward the screen with a wide-eyed, hunted look. Cai Rui flinched at the sight of his face, gaunt and hollow-eyed, scarred and beaten. He had lost a great deal of weight in a very short time—they had fed him little, if anything at all.

It was nearly impossible to connect this man to the one he had seen just a few weeks before, bravely recording a message for others to find in the presbytery on Ko'Grappa. He might not have guessed even that the two were brothers.

"Who's there?" The voice was a hushed whisper. "Who speaks?"

"It's me, Excellency. Cai Rui, your Archdeacon. Your godson."

The old man frowned. "Cai Rui? Where are you, boy?" His eyes darted about nervously, searching the room.

"In the next room, Excellency. I…I heard you praying."

"Why do you keep calling me that? I am no 'Excellency.'" He made a peevish face.

"He remembers little," Sara murmured in Tarkasian. "They have taken most of his memory…"

Cai Rui held up his hand, warning her to silence. "You have forgotten, Excellency. You were made the metropolitan of a new diocese four years ago. You are a bishop now."

The old man seemed confused. He licked his lips nervously. "I do not remember."

"You have brought the Faith to a new race of beings," Cai Rui coaxed gently. "Made many converts. Won many to the light of God."

He blinked. "I…did?"

"Yes. On Ko'Grappa."

Tears began to flow down the old man's cheeks. "Ko'Grappa…"

"Do you remember?"

The bishop put his face in his hands. "May God forgive me…"

"He can," Cai Rui said warmly. "He does. His love and His mercy are infinite. This you taught me yourself, years ago. And you have only to confess, and all can be forgiven…"

The bony shoulders heaved, and the old man's body wracked with sobs. "He was strong," he whispered hoarsely. "So strong. He moved me about like a puppet. I was helpless to resist." He looked up to the ceiling, his face raw with agony. "I could not save them, Lord. Benedict and Antony died trying to defend us. And Thomas…" His face crumbled. "My poor Thomas…"

Cai Rui winced. "I know." He remembered the deacon hanging from the rood. "I saw…"

The old man looked down into the palms of his open hands, his gnarled fingers curled into claws. "With my own hands, I drove the nails." He took his robe in his hands and clutched at himself, his head bent, convulsed by emotion.

Cai Rui recoiled. "Dear God."

The old man threw his head back suddenly, his whole body locked into a wordless howl. Cai Rui grimaced; Sara curled into a ball, all three of her eyelids clapped shut, both hands clasped over her ears.

It went on and on, impossibly, as if all the pain and rage and loss and guilt and shame in the universe cried out at once. When the old man fell to the floor, pounding his withered fists against the stone, Cai Rui turned to the Tarka woman at last.

"Enough," he said. "Please. Help him. Make it stop."

"Ishii." She spoke firmly to the screen. "Enough."

Bishop Tourneau suddenly went still. The image of the monastic cell dissolved, its holographic illusions broken to reveal a simple berth somewhere in the ship. The Liir stood in the corner, its serene gray face bent in silent contemplation. "He will rest now," it trilled.

Lightly the old man rose, as if gathered into the arms of an invisible angel, and floated toward the bed. A new pair of Tarka attendants hurried into the room to tend the fragile old ape, nestling him on the bunk into a cocoon of restraints.

Cai Rui squeezed his eyes shut, fighting tears. Sara touched his arm lightly. "He will die soon, despite everything." Her eyes were saturated with sorrow. "Ishii cannot repair the damage that has been done, and the fits...they come often, and do more harm each time."

Cai Rui trembled. "Has he said more? About his imprisonment?"

"Yes, Caido. Ishii has learned much." Her fists clenched. "These 'Rippers', as you call them—they tear more than flesh, and steel, and even space. They also rend the minds of those they take captive."

Her tail flicked, the rapid staccato of rage. "What they rip free, they make their own." She turned toward the screen, indicating the old man now dying in his silken bonds, wrapped like a fly in a spider's web. "The one that took Tourneau—all that he once was, all that he knew—has learned to call himself 'The Deacon.'"

Her eyes whirled with swift emotions. "And this 'Deacon' wants you, Cai Rui. He wants you very much." Her tongue flickered nervously. "He means to make you a part of himself."

13 | THE QUICK AND THE DROWNED

In the beginning, the tide was black, and the Song was the pulse of a great drum. The drum was Love, the sea was blood, and the warmth of his mother's womb held him safe from all things. Father came near, in the dark, and sang; the People came near, in the dark, and sang. Quiet, clinging tightly to Mother-soul, he listened and he learned, and he waited to be born.

As a child he hunted, quick and slim among the rocks, chasing the sweet fish in the shallows and straining to lift himself from the water to chase his friends over the sand. When Mother called he came, nuzzling her soft belly for milk and her gentle mind for love. When Father called he came, and father tossed him high, singing, into the bright sun, and Father caught him again. And with the other young ones he played the games of stronger-smarter-louder-faster, and they all tried to keep their secrets. But no one could.

When he was old enough Mother and Father called to him, and he followed them out of the spiral city and into the blue beyond, where the emptiness asked its own questions and hunger sharpened his body and mind. In the darkness of the depths he listened, and far from the radiant noise of the teeming spiral he heard at last the Voice that beckoned, the ancient thunder of the abyss and its wisdom, waiting to shape him into a man.

And as a man the cool sea streamed over his skin, a living wind full of Song. And Cai Rui soared through the water, surging along at speed in pursuit of his prey. She fled forever before him, darting this way and that, diving low to pass through graceful arches and hide her white shape in reefs where only a child should be able to pass. With a joyous shout he smashed stone and brought the old ruins down, driving her up into the open once more to fly again and leave a corkscrew trail of bubbles to tickle his chin. Younger and swifter she laughed, teasing him with the promise of pleasure and slipping always from his grasp, and when at last she turned toward the sun he followed, to catch the exquisite flexing curve of her body as she burst from the water. And he held her there, naked in the air, a Song of glistening light upon supple skin, salt droplets turning to crystal ice in her hair, until she begged for mercy and promised, ever so sweetly, that she would never run from him again.

Mind and body he flowed into her, enfolding her in his embrace, turning her gently onto her side so that they could drift together in the warm shallows. He made love to her deeply, passionately, constantly, penetrating deeply her body and soul, and letting her delicate loving tendrils flow into him, to drink in his spirit and know him utterly.

And then he sank and found himself in the cold, circling deep with the heavy water on his back. The dead warrior stayed beyond his reach, a ghostly presence behind his armor of frozen steel. *The way is here*, the Drowned said. *Take your last breath.*

And he turned and leaped toward the light and thought of her, of the sun on her dappled body and the sound of her laughter and the exquisite sheathe of warmth that enveloped him and all that he had been. And the moment he held her cupped tenderly in his mind, the thought twisted like a savage blade deep in his flesh, and suddenly he felt her soft skin burning and broken with bleeding sores in a sea gone black with poison, and heard her lilting sweet song whipped to silence, her laughter turned to tears, and then, worst of all, the tiny pulsing light of new life within her snuffed out in pain... a new Song choked from existence before it could swim.

He turned from this anguish and plunged deep into the cold and dark. For her, he could do anything, suffer anything. Dive deeper than death, fly farther than pain, pass into the mouth of the inconceivable.

For her he would Drown.

And when he passed into the House of Steel they seized him in the darkness, with the terrible implacable strength of the Dead. They gripped him, dreadful in their patience, waiting until the breath within him turned stale. And crazed with the terror of the moment, he half-changed his mind, thrashed in his frenzy, begged for mercy and fought for life...held fast by their grimly silent unison, until at last the final gush of true air came bubbling out of his lungs in agony and the sea...cold, black...flowed into him and through him, drowning out all the warmth, light, and life he had known.

Cai Rui opened his eyes and sat bolt upright, his belly heaving to hurl water up out of his lungs. New air whooped into him, filling his body with a desperate cry, and he had the dizzying sense of having held his breath for much, much too long.

The ceiling above was dim and blue, soft patterns of light trickling from the machines around his bed. He raised his hands in front of his face, still panting, and for a moment he recoiled from the wrongness of the bandaged arms, the hands and fingers, the tiny body lying feeble in this thin, lifeless medium that left him gasping and heavy, crushed by his own weight and barely able to—

"No." He said it aloud. He felt the pressure of rejection building within him, forcing the other out of his mind. "I am not...you."

The whispering voice answered, sly with amusement. *No, you are not,* it agreed. *Ishii does not wander in the dark.*

Cai Rui sat silent, instinctively forcing body and mind to be still. When he was ready, he reached out again tentatively. *Can you hear me?*

The answer came gently. The tone was amused and indulgent, an adult speaking to a child. *Yes. Always.*

He hesitated. *Was that your—? Did I—?* He stopped, unable to fully formulate the questions, even as thoughts.

Yes. Those were true-life-things-of-mine.

Cai Rui tried to pat his puzzlement into a shape, to send it to the Liir's mind, but discovered that words were easier. *Why did you allow it?*

More amusement. *Curious to see what you could do. You are not like others-of-the-same-kind. And I thought you might learn.*

He closed his eyes and frowned. It was becoming easier to speak without speaking, but somehow he still had a sense of being clumsy and weak. *Learn?*

Sharing is not taking. The Liir paused, and he felt the gentle tug in his mind, as it searched for a pattern to fit its thought. *Every hand is not a fist.*

Shaking, Cai Rui forced himself to relax, releasing the defensive control that had never before been fully conscious. He suddenly realized that he had been feeling the Liir's presence all along, a constant shadow in the back of his mind for days. Ishii watched over his dreams as he slept—and the Liir was an active force within his body, forcing skin and flesh to knit so fast that he could practically track the changes hour by hour.

He took a deep, cleansing breath now, in through the nose and out through the mouth, pleasantly reminded that both nose and mouth were in good working order. *What do you want?*

The Liir's whisper was soft, but somewhere beneath the surface there was a glint of steel. *What do you want?* it asked. *Father-yours is dying. The Suul'ka has torn his mind. His wound...flows.*

Suddenly Cai Rui could feel it, the sense of life draining away—a chill stealing over his extremities as he bled out slow, alone and helpless in the dark. The sensation slowly evolved into a sense that a human mind could do the same, and for a moment he lived the reality—hope, thought and memory dripping slowly from his own rent soul until he was left gaping into emptiness, hollow and bereft.

This was Tourneau's dying.

Cai Rui wrapped his arms around himself, shivering in horror. *What can I do?*

The current of cold, black rage welled upward from the depths, rushing over his skin. *Suul'ka must be destroyed.*

He felt the meaning of the word rather than intellectually understanding it. Suul'ka was the voice that had spoken in the dark, on Avalon: the voice of hate, of lust, of murder. Cai Rui drew up his knees in the hospital bed, lowering his forehead to meet them. *Yes,* he agreed at last. *It must be destroyed. Show me how.*

Soon. The Liir's massive voice retreated, and he had the sense of something huge moving away in deep water, leaving turbulence in its wake. *You are not ready. Rest.*

The whisper was soft, its sibilance blending into the hiss of waves on a quiet shore. Cai Rui felt his muscles cool, relax and slacken. Looking up, he saw the needle drifting down like an autumn leaf from the venous feed to his arm. A single drop of narcotic dew was still clinging to the point.

"Wait." But already he was falling, and the invisible angel caught him in its arms and lowered his body, a feather on a puff of wind, into the bed.

Sleep. I will make you strong.

* * *

When he woke again, another full day had passed. Cai Rui opened his eyes and found the bed already tilting upward to allow him to sit up. He was lying on his back, dressed only in bandages. As he watched, a tube attached to the shunt in his wrist silently disengaged, pulled free by an invisible hand, and coiled itself neatly on the hook next to a bag of pale blue fluid hanging on a rod above his head.

Where are you? He spoke instinctively with a combination of word and intention, reaching clumsily for Ishii with his mind.

A brief spark of bright joy flared in his chest, and despite himself, Cai Rui jumped. In a split-second he realized that this was a standard greeting between Liir—the telepathic equivalent to a wave or a nod. Ishii moved into his peripheral vision with a metallic squeal, steel tentacles easing him forward across the deck. Calm, unblinking black eyes looked down at him; it was odd that he felt that he could detect a humorous twinkle in the Liir's expression.

"Hello." His own voice sounded a bit rusty; he tried to clear his throat.

"Greetings." The Liir's mechanical voice was a soft high trill in Urdu Kai, a sound entirely unlike the deep soft whisper of its telepathic sending. "Food has been prepared."

Prompted by a sense of expectation, he took a deeper breath through his nose. When the rich aroma reached him, the effect was nearly explosive. His mouth suddenly flooded and a ravenous craving for sustenance ripped through him. He was starving. "Yes. Please. I need to eat."

The massive invisible hand cupped him lightly, holding him steady as he lowered the retaining rail of the bed and swung his legs over the side. A pair of black *t'mao* had been left for him, folded neatly on a stool beside the bed. He picked them up and shook them out. The fabric was deeply dyed and woven from soft, thick Tarkasian silk. He gritted his teeth against the pain in his shoulder and leg as he limped into the loose Tarka trousers, leaning heavily on Ishii's invisible presence as he worked his uninjured leg into a voluminous sleeve of cloth.

A mirror bolted to the wall reflected his battered body. He looked up as he closed the traditional tail-flap of the split skirt at his hip and belted the garment at his waist. He was wearing them sideways, but the cut of *t'mao* was blessedly forgiving—not unlike Japanese *hakama*, and one of the few Tarka garments a man without a tail could wear without looking and feeling too painfully ridiculous. Bare-chested, bandages bound around his shoulder and arm, he still felt somewhat exposed, but he was more than respectably dressed from the Tarka point of view, and this would have to do.

Cai Rui turned to the iris port of the room and moved slowly toward it. The Liir followed silently, his own massive body drifting a few centimeters above the floor, carefully supporting every step as his patient took it. Despite everything, the occasional stab of pain from his healing body was astonishing. By the time he could step into the adjoining room of his hospital suite, he had broken a sweat.

Sara was already seated at the table, wearing a simple sleeveless tunic over her body. In the corner behind her, her sleeping hammock still hung from its hooks. "*Kala d'oyo!*" Her pupils danced merrily. "You are looking well."

"I look like the Devil's leftovers." Cai crippled over to the table and took the edge in one hand. "Which is just what I am." A place had been set for him opposite her. There was a square bowl with a high vertical rim, divided into four sections and the usual Tarkasian flatware—thick-handled knife, long spearing fork and a small personal ladle. He lowered himself onto the bench, summoning all the brittle dignity he could.

Sara's tongue flickered amusement. "As you say. I am glad to see you nonetheless. I could not wait another minute!" She reached out and pressed the button on the top of a domed lid, her eyes brilliant green with pleasure. "My chef makes the best *po'goru* in the fleet."

Cai Rui looked into the bowl with some trepidation. The smell was rich and aromatic, and he noted with some relief that there did not appear to be anything still swimming in the broth. He had learned from experience that Tarka cooks could not be trusted—they would include a few native touches in even the most traditional human dishes. "What's in it?"

Sara picked up her long-fork and stabbed it into the soup, plucking out a prize: a dumpling, its thin pastry shell cleverly wrapped around the filling in origami folds. She held it out proudly, baring her white teeth. "What do you think? *Dumplenu* is what civilized people eat in their soup, *ne?*"

"I cannot argue with that." He smiled and reached for his ladle as she triumphantly popped the dumpling into her mouth. He had scooped half the soup into his own bowl before he remembered the Liir, now resting quietly in the corner. He turned, gesturing vaguely with his own spoon. "Ishii? Do you...eat—?"

"Thank you," the voice-box on the suit chirped politely. The face behind the plate of glass was implacable. "This one's needs are met."

"Ishii has her own food." Sara's voice was complacent. She had taken the serving dish and emptied the remainder of the soup into her own bowl, taking care to scoop out the tasty tidbits which had sunk to the bottom. "She doesn't eat as we do."

Cai Rui turned back and looked down into his own bowl, feeling strangely conflicted. Intellectually he knew that it was ridiculous to think of Ishii as "male"—he was every bit as wrong as Sara, when she spoke of the Liir warrior as "female". Liir were a hermaphroditic species, and these gender concepts would never have the same meaning to Ishii as they naturally would to a human or a Tarka.

Nonetheless he could not help but feel that Ishii really was far more male than female, by human standards—and had been for most of his life. And Cai Rui also had a sense of poignant loneliness, even of bereavement, on the Liir's behalf. All brought on by a dumpling. A thing as simple, as good, as ordinary as a meal was denied to the Drowned, along with all the other ordinary pleasures of being alive.

At the moment he turned to ask, he had received a single vivid image of the feeding tube from which Ishii took nourishment. Ishii drank a rich bland liquid from a dead hose to sustain his life. But the contrasting image of an adult Liir's natural food was still equally clear in Cai Rui's mind; he retained those memories from the shared dream. The joyous snap of a fresh fish between his jaws, the sweet wriggling explosion of a live jelly on the tongue, the piquant crunch of kelp pods—all these things were still in the back of his mind. The strange flavors and sensations of that other life were vividly real...but for Ishii they were dead. Willingly sacrificed for the sake of military service. Cai Rui raised the ladle to his lips and felt a stab of sadness as he let the savory liquid spill over his tongue.

Thank you. The internal voice was gentle. *But this one is not the only Drowned.*

Thatcher's face suddenly bloomed in his memory like a flower—cheeks flushed, eyes closed, lips parted with the sensual gasp of pleasure. Cai Rui nearly choked on his dumpling. Of course. To the Liir, a vow of celibacy was just another death...

Please. Don't do that again.

Apologies. This one is too close to you. Must withdraw.

A wave of energy seemed to flow out of him. In a split second the Liir departed utterly, leaving his mind clear, sharp and strangely empty. At the same moment the full weight of gravity descended on him. The return was so sudden that the ladle dropped out of Cai Rui's fingers, ripped from his grip as if the object had transformed instantly into a heavier element. It dropped with an embarrassing splash into his bowl. Cai Rui reeled, dizzy, gripping the table-top to keep from falling off the bench entirely.

Sara lowered her own fork, concerned. "Cai?"

"Sorry." He looked up with a wan smile. "Weaker than I thought."

She tilted her head. "Can you not yet eat?" She cast a sidelong glance at Ishii. "Perhaps you should lie down again?"

"No, thank you." He steadied himself, forcing his shoulders and spine to stiffen. "When I have finished, please."

"As you say." She looked away from him, hiding the shape of her pupils, and toyed with a floating pink vegetable in her bowl. "Perhaps some talk?"

"Yes." He picked up the long-fork, battling the tremor in his hand as he did so, and speared an elaborate dumpling. Despite his cavernous hunger, he took a moment to admire the delicately pleated dough before he bit it in half. The filling was typically Tarka, a finely minced white meat. Doubtless it was made from one of Kao'Kona's native insects, standing in here for Terran lobster and nearly indistinguishable in flavor. The chef had mercifully relented on the spice.

"I have spoken to my *kegenu* about this man you mentioned—Vance. They have assembled what we know of him." Her eyes had kindled to a business-like, thoughtful amber. "A very dangerous foe. And he has reason to hate the Tarka."

Cai Rui looked up, curious. "Does he?" He was familiar with the basic details of Vance's dossier—he had investigated every Intelligence officer of TFC rank. It would be interesting to see how much the Tarka intelligence community would know, however.

"*Ne.* His son was one of the very first to die in battle against my people, many years ago. A task force of your ships stumbled upon a battle between Tarka and Liir. The Amtara of that battle group had been given strict orders to challenge all ships entering that *lolo'kaad*. If they would not depart, he was to attack."

Cai Rui nodded. "I am familiar with the incident. It was our first contact with your people. We did not expect to encounter another alien species. We were hunting Hivers at the time."

Sara raised her cocked arm and entered a command into her bracer. A panel on the wall beside the table flickered and came to life, displaying combat footage from the Tarka perspective—a long narrow band display from the gun cameras, edited to cut from ship to ship as a Sol Force cruiser group was first accosted and then attacked. His eyes narrowed as he watched the first of two armored support destroyers destroyed by a missile barrage.

"Times past," she reminded him softly, reading his face.

The tanker went up in a spectacular explosion, and he suppressed a wince. The command cruiser moved to screen the remaining complement, and the surviving destroyer and deepscan vessel fled for the Node point. The Tarka footage ended with the destruction of the destroyer Von Bek, caught and obliterated just seconds before reaching the safety of Node Space. The deepscan vessel disappeared.

"This vessel was called 'Koparnicao'—named for one of your great scientists."

"Copernicus." He corrected her pronunciation absently. "A deepscan vessel. *Laogena.*"

124

"Copernicusss." She repeated the word under her breath softly, reaching for its unfamiliar sounds and emphasis. "*Ne*. What is important is that the young commander of this ship was also named Vance. He was William Vance, the son of Conrad Vance, who commands the *Laogenu* of your entire fleet."

Cai Rui nodded.

Sara's display shifted subtly, the dimensions of the screen changing from rectangular to square. The image resolved itself quickly to become a second clip of the SFS Copernicus. The deepscan vessel tumbled helpless in space, its hull scorched and battered, its tail section bleeding sparks and debris. He recognized the footage immediately—it was shot by the first crew to approach the vessel when it was finally found.

"This ship appeared to escape unharmed from our attack at Kam'Kir. In fact, the detonation of the destroyer Von Bek had badly damaged this 'Copernicus.'" She pronounced the word perfectly on her third try, and playfully showed him the tip of her tongue when he looked up from his bowl, surprised. "Its fission engine was badly hit. The crew died within hours, overcome by the radiation poison. In the end, Lieutenant Vance was the last left alive. He piloted the ship out of Node Space and recorded a message for your people, warning them not to attempt to board his ship. His father...chose to ignore that warning."

The display shifted once more, and Cai Rui made a face. Somehow the Tarkasian agents had obtained copies of Sol Force medical records; now he was looking at a preoperative photo of Conrad Vance. The man's wasted torso was covered with bleeding sores, the flesh of his arms and legs reduced to cancerous rags. The eyes looking up into the camera were feverishly bright with pain and defiance.

"Vance went into the ruined ship alone to recover the body. He paid a predictable price for this folly. Despite his protective gear, he absorbed so much radiation in the few minutes he was aboard Copernicus that he could not be held in the crew compartments on the return trip to Earth. He had to remain in the cargo bay for nearly a week, with no company but his son's corpse."

Cai Rui raised the bowl to his lips and drank a warm gulp of the fragrant broth, offering no response. He had reviewed the data available on Vance in the man's formal dossier; this material was not there. Whoever was working for the Tarka had penetrated Sol Force Intelligence very deeply. Nuanced information about a high-ranking Intelligence officer would probably come from another Commander, or a close staff officer. Odds were that the leak was in Red Section, obviously.

Sara went on, blithely ignoring his contemplative silence. "Vance did not wish to live. His body was crumbling around him like a tower of mud, but he refused to agree to the surgery which was proposed to save him."

Cai Rui put down his bowl. "Your source is well-placed."

Her eyes sparked green merriment, and her pupils flexed with pleasure, as if the two of them were playing a game. "Indeed."

"This part of the story, I do not know." He reached for the domed lid of another serving dish, and found it filled with fresh, thin-skinned fruit. The tureen brimmed with small pale pink spheres, deeply crimson berries, and astonishingly bright yellow heart-shaped drupes with a flat seed inside. He smiled. He had no allergies to any of these, and the yellow hearts were special favorites.

"It was simple enough. In every empire, there are a few persons who are not easily dispensable." She plucked a berry from the bowl casually. "Vance was such a man. Commander of your watcher-fleet, he had also designed and built the majority of your faster-than-light communications. He had intricate knowledge of the Node arrays and he was one of only three persons in your empire who possessed all of your codes for encryption and decryption of messages."

"I see." Cai Rui frowned. He bit into yellow skin; the fruit within was paler yellow, firm and sweet. "The Director had few options."

"*Ne.* Nonetheless she made an effort to spread the blame. His fellow officers were summoned, and put to a vote. Collectively they declared him unfit to decide his own fate." Sara's eyes darkened. "Vance was not permitted to follow his son into death. The surgeons performed many operations. In the end they saved his skull and spinal column, a few vital organs. The remainder of his body was replaced with machinery."

"This was wrong." The trill of Ishii's mechanical voice sounded from the corner, and Cai Rui started. The Liir had been silent and motionless as a stone throughout the meal—but clearly he had been listening. "They stole his death from him."

"Perhaps so." Sara's eyes were dark and golden with thought. "Certainly there have been unforeseen consequences." The final image of Vance was relatively recent. The Green Section Commander sat in his mechanical chair, his lower torso and legs hidden in the chassis. "Vance seemed to recover, and returned to work. As the technology has improved, his body has been upgraded. Yet he remains seated in this mechanical chair year after year, as if to protest."

"That is certainly possible. At this point, I wonder if he does not remain in the chair to avert suspicion."

126

Sara cocked her head curiously. "Avert suspicion? How would a chair accomplish this?"

Cai Rui put down his spoon, fighting his unsteady hand. "If what I suspect is true, he is a traitor. Perhaps the most dangerous traitor in the history of Sol Force. But my culture has a number of blind spots where the disabled are concerned. Even if the high command were searching for a saboteur within the ranks, they might pass over him as an unlikely suspect."

Sara waved her fork in a circle, urging him to continue.

"When a human has received some profound injury, fellow humans see him differently. We regard the disabled as powerless. There is an unstated assumption that they cannot harm us. An irrational prejudice—one which Vance may cultivate deliberately, to lower our defenses." He shook his head with bitter self-disgust. "It works quite well. Even I did not suspect that he was plotting my death until it was far too late."

Her pupils flexed with consternation.

He dropped his eyes, suddenly exhausted by the magnitude of the problem. "He will not be easy to combat, nor to remove. Vance has been with Sol Force for decades. He helped to build the Nova Maria. He has designed the majority of our communications equipment. He has many friends...and even his enemies may consider him above suspicion." Cai Rui sighed. "Meanwhile, he sits at the heart of Sol Force communications like a spider. He can pull the strings as he pleases. There is no way to communicate with Mars without having the message pass through his hands—and all messages going in or coming out of his web can be tailored to his agenda before he passes them along."

"He is also in direct communication with the *masaaku*," Sara said. "Or at least, with one of them. Whatever he wishes the Deacon to know, Vance is able to pass on. He must have given the creature its own Node array." Sara's eyes had shifted to a dangerous deep orange. "It is a clever net they have woven. We must find a way to tangle the two of them in it."

He looked up at her again, searching his heart for the spark of fire that would match the burning light he saw in her eyes. At the moment he could not find it. He was just...tired. The strain of sitting up unassisted was beginning to wear on him. He could feel the weight of his body pulling at the thin tissues that held his half-healed wounds shut.

"I trust that you will think of something," he said at last. "I can see that you have a plan." She tilted her head at him again, and he gave her a sad smile. "I have known you long enough to know when you are scheming."

She opened her mouth as if to speak, and he held up a hand to forestall her. "I will do it." Exhausted by pain and grief, he closed his fingers as if to crush her unspoken protest in his hand. "Whatever it is. I am sure that once I know the details, I will not like it at all. But I will do it, so long as you will first do something for me."

She regarded him quietly for a long moment. "And what must I do for you, Caido?"

"Call the mission in Ko'Seth. Bring someone to perform the Last Rites for Father Tourneau."

"But that might take days, beloved." She tried to speak gently, but her tail flicked with agitation. "Tourneau is very weak. He may not live—"

Cai Rui turned to the Liir. "He will live long enough. The ritual is important, to him and to me." *You can keep him alive for a little longer*, he thought.

"Yes," the Liir trilled. Silently it added, *We can prevent his departure for now.*

"Very well," Sara said. "I will send word immediately. And when this is done—"

"Then we will return to Avalon."

Her eyes flashed a spark of red irritation. "What? Why would we return to that gods-forsaken place?"

"I have my reasons." He put his hands on the table and struggled to his feet. When Ishii's invisible arm steadied him, he felt only a numb sense of gratitude. "These are my terms, Sara. Take them or leave them."

"I will take them," she said to his retreating back. "But you are right, Caido. You will not like my plan."

14 | LAST RITES

The door slid open; the orderlies stood in the open arch without entering. They tilted their heads to either side. "Var Cai-ri," one of them said pleadingly. "Are you sure there is nothing that we—?"

"No." His tone was firm. "I will be ready in a moment."

He turned back toward the bed, looking down at the wasted body. Tourneau's ribs rose and fell steadily, but his skin was only a thin tent over bare bones. Gently, Cai Rui lifted one of the old man's gnarled hands and used the rag to clean it, carefully dabbing the torn fingers and wiping the battered palm. He worked swiftly, cleansing the bishop's hands and feet; when he had finished he tenderly replaced the thin sheet and blanket and picked up his basin and rag.

The Liir remained in its corner, unblinking and inscrutable. He turned toward it now. *Will he be ready?*

Assent.

He turned and left the room, sealing it behind him. Outside, he found the two Tarka waiting; they exchanged an awkward glance and then one of them hesitantly held out his hands to take the basin and washrag. Cai Rui surrendered it, and saw them relax visibly as he untied the sleeves of his robe. His insistence upon cleaning the chamber and its occupant himself had disturbed them. They retreated now, backing away without turning, their heads lowered respectfully. He turned to see that two groups were converging at this intersection of corridors.

Sara had returned from the right with her command staff. Like the ship itself, her officers had been prepared for the occasion. He had told her simply "everything must be clean", when he began preparation for the Sacrament; she had taken this to mean that her ship must be ritually purified, and the entire interior of the cruiser had received a mirror polish, down to the last scale of every hand aboard. By stint of salt, perfumed sand and vigorous oiling her crew had given themselves a gloss from crown to tail: Now all five of her officers had donned their dress uniforms, ventral armor rising at the shoulders into jeweled epaulets, their crests decked with swirling bands of iron and creamy jade. The massive bulk of the Amtara filled the corridor, casting a shadow over the four females who commanded the support vessels of his *fane*.

The Lac Tar herself wore a gown of clinging white film, split over each sinuous hip and over the base of her tail, and a sleeveless tunic of shining golden mail. Her fingertips and toes were sheathed in enameled steel razors, bound by red cords which criss-crossed to her elbows and knees. Her coronet was simple and regal, also of gold, and her blades hung over both shoulders.

Glancing the other direction, he saw the delegation from Ko'Seth. The contrast could not have been more extreme; their pale feet were bare, their bodies cloaked in rough robes of coarse brown cloth, their faces covered by low hoods. Each one wore a large pectoral cross on a rope about his neck, and each of the three carried in his hands a wooden chest as beautifully carved and elaborate as his own clothes were plain.

Cai Rui stepped back as the two groups came together, half of him marveling at the orchestration of the moment, the other half wishing it were done. Sara stepped forward, leaving her officers behind, and turned to face the leading member of the opposing trio.

"Respect." She spoke the simple, traditional greeting in Kona.

The leading male raised his chin, and the hood of his robe fell back, revealing his face. "Respect." He turned, and his pupils bent into a kindly curve. "*Vale*, Rui Cai," he said, offering the Latin greeting softly.

Cai Rui's throat tightened. "*Vale*, Mateo. Thank you for coming."

The Tarka inclined his head, dropping his eyelids graciously. "*Habas yan*." He turned toward Sara, returning to the clipped cadence of Kona. "Your mother sends her regards."

"Mine to her also."

Mateo inclined his head in obedience. "She wonders if you are well?"

Sara's eyes stirred with annoyance. "Very." Changing the subject, she added, "You have clipped your crest, cousin Mat. It pleases me." Her tongue flickered. "Modesty becomes you."

He stiffened. "I have taken the tonsure. I am a priest."

"Oh, eh?" Her tone was negligent. "How interesting. You are here to perform this ritual, then?"

His eyes flashed red, and then went cool yellow. "We are." He turned back to Cai Rui. "Is he ready?" He spoke in Latin. "We were told that this was very urgent—I was afraid we would come too late."

"He is ready." He fought down a surge of heartache. "I have done what I could to prepare him."

"Then we will begin." Without another word, the priest offered him the carved chest. "If you would be so kind, brother."

Cai Rui took the casque reverently and followed the three Tarka into the room, watching as they quickly set about their tasks. In one chest, they had packed the thurible, the chrism, the wine, water and candles; in another there were incense, linens and candlesticks neatly placed beneath a white branch of Tarkasian willow.

Mateo reached into the folds of his robe and removed a small paper book, bound with a thin slip of recycled leather. Seeing Cai Rui's expression, his eyes smiled.

"A gift. The bishop gave it to me when I became a Porter. I had hoped he would remember..."

Seized with sudden anxiety, Cai Rui raised a hand to interrupt. "He...barely remembers himself, Mateo. Lately he has been...very rude to the Tarka he has seen. Please do not be offended if he—"

The priest raised his hands. "Be at peace." His voice was soft and kind. "We were warned of this madness. He has mistaken us for the Adversary, I am told." He clucked his tongue, pupils crimping sadly. "We will try to set him at ease." With a silent signal, he had his deacons light the candles and incense; the overhead lights in the room were extinguished, and all three raised their hoods to cover their faces. Cai Rui handed over the Host and went to the bed, bending to gather the old man in his arms.

He took a deep breath, closing his eyes. *It is time.*

Assent. Ishii opened to him, and he felt the web surrounding the old man's mind, binding its fragments together with an intricate net of will. Now he watched as a few strands of the web slipped, and felt Father Tourneau's body shiver as he awakened for the first time in two days.

He looked down as the bishop stirred, and held the frail body close as it began to shake. The blue eyes opened, sunken into deep pits of suffering, and the lips parted. "Cai," the man creaked.

"Yes Father," he said softly. "I am here."

"*Pythona...*" The voice was faint. "*Pythona videram...*"

His eyes stinging with shame and grief, Cai Rui passed a soothing hand over the old man's brow. "He is gone, Father. It is time to take the Sacrament...do you understand?"

"*Nollo me dare Serpenti,*" the old man said, clutching at Cai Rui's robe urgently. "*Conserva me...mi filii...*" The bleak eyes filled with tears, and the bishop began to weep.

Cai Rui held him close, feeling the sick heart beating desperately against the old man's ribs. He looked up, and met the eyes of the Tarka shining luminous beneath the hood. "Please," he said. "He...fears the Serpent. As quick as you can."

The Tarka bent, placing his soft palm over the old man's eyes, gently urging them shut. "Antonius Pious Tourneau," he said, "you are a child of God. Do you have anything to confess?"

Tears flowed down the old man's cheeks. "With my own hands," he said hoarsely, "I drove the nails..." His chest shook with a painful sob.

The pale eyes flickered, and the priest hesitated, waiting to see if Tourneau would speak again. "Do you repent your sins—mortal, grave and venial?" he said at last.

"*Mea culpa,*" the bishop moaned weakly.

"And do you offer to God your sincere contrition?"

The old man reached up weakly, taking the Tarka priest's hand. Blindly he pressed it to his lips, breathing in deeply.

"Then receive the grace of God and His forgiveness," the priest said quickly. "And vow to sin no more." He took the willow branch and dipped it into Holy Water, sprinkling the old man with a reminder of baptism. "By His love you are cleansed."

A deacon came and knelt beside the bed, opening the final chest; Father Mateo removed the Viaticum wafer and a slip cloth, stiffly embroidered white-on-white.

"The body of Christ," Mateo murmured. As if by instinct, Father Tourneau opened his mouth, and the priest placed the Eucharist wafer upon his tongue. Firmly he held the white cloth beneath the old man's chin, careful not to let a single fragment of the Host fall as the wafer was painfully swallowed.

A tremor passed through Tourneau's body. In Cai Rui's mind, the whisper of the Liir was urgent. *He slips away.*

The Tarka priest stood and took up his oil, pouring out the golden chrism into his left palm. He bent, a robed shadow in a cloud of perfumed smoke, and swiftly dipped the thumb of his right hand into the oil and drew the shape of the cross over each of Father Tourneau's eyes.

"Through this holy unction and His own most tender mercy may the Lord pardon thee whatever sins or faults thou hast committed by sight." He made a second cross over the old man's nose. "By smell." Repeating the same over the ears and mouth: "By hearing, by speaking, by tasting."

He moved nimbly to the foot of the bed. "Through this holy unction and His own most tender mercy may the Lord pardon thee whatever sins or faults thou hast committed by walking." Mateo drew the cruciform over each foot, and returned to the bishop's side to sit beside him on the bed and complete the blessing.

He took the old man's hand in both of his own, and bathed the withered, battered skin generously with oil: when he had done this, he made the sign of the Cross over the palm. "Through this holy unction and His most tender mercy may the Lord pardon thee whatever sins or faults thou hast committed with this hand."

Tourneau wept freely, bringing up his anointed hand to his own lips to kiss the crossed palm. Matthew took up the second hand from the opposite side of the bed, and completed the blessing. "And with this one."

The bishop's body was now shaken by a more powerful tremor. Mateo put his anointed palm over the old man's eyes once more, and bent his head in prayer. "My eyes are ever upon the Lord, who frees my feet from the snare," he said. "Look upon me, have pity on me, for I am alone and afflicted. Relieve the troubles of my heart; bring me out of my distress. Put an end to my affliction and suffering; take away all my sins..."

The golden eyes opened and met Cai Rui's serenely. "See how many are my enemies," the Tarka said. "See how fiercely they hate me. Preserve my life and rescue me; do not let me be disgraced, for I trust in You."

Cai Rui closed his eyes.

He passes, Ishii said. *I can hold him no longer.*

"Let honesty and virtue preserve me; I wait for You, O Lord...redeem the universe, God, from all its distress."

He returned to Ishii's web, the binding tendrils woven around the fragments of a shattered soul. He felt the Liir withdraw, felt Tourneau's body seize and convulse as the death rattle rose in his throat. The flow outward was sudden, forceful, as if a tourniquet was removed from a dreadful wound.

When he opened his eyes again, the bishop of Grappa was dead.

❋ ❋ ❋

He moved clumsily in the improvised suit, and the temperature gauge did not seem to believe that he was warm enough until his body was dripping sweat. Nonetheless he doggedly continued, toiling over the rocks slowly, until at last he came to the last low rise above the ruins of the Avalon.

The stain was nearly invisible against the black stone, but he knelt and touched it with his gloved fingertips, silently mouthing the syllables of her name. Rising, he took out the wristband Sara had given him. He held it up awkwardly, twisting it this way and that, watching the light blink until he had a directional reading.

Carefully he picked his way down among the jagged boulders, pausing occasionally to consult the wristband. Finally he found it, torn and bloody beside a pool of standing melt-water in the black scree.

The suit was just a torn rag, the upper torso shredded and the glass of the helmet long gone. The wristband was more interested in the discarded slab of plastic further up the ravine, lying where it had finally slipped from her pack after her body had been dragged over a hundred meters. He walked toward it, feeling the bile rise in the back of his throat.

Vance's datapad was still intact. Looking down at it, he fought down a wave of hatred so intense it was nauseating.

If he wanted it so bad, he shouldn't be throwing it at people.

Sickened, he turned away and went back to Thatcher's suit. He knelt on the sharp rocks beside it and gently turned it over, laying it out as if it were the body itself. The name patch still clung to a tatter on the left breast; he activated his own suit's cutting claw and snipped it free, putting the scrap of cloth in his collection pouch. When he was finished he folded the arms over the chest and prayed.

It took hours to collect the stones and lay a cairn in the valley. It was a black oval mound, as high as his waist and as long as a colonial girl, raised on powdered milk and bittersweet dreams on a desolate frontier. By the time he finished he was gasping, the recycler of the suit wheezing on the verge of collapse. The Tarkasian wristband had long since been blinking a never-ending string of curses and imprecations, as its mistress demanded, via the Egg Knock code, why he did not return to the shuttle.

At last he went to the data pad and forced himself to pick it up. He would return it to its rightful owner soon enough; first he had other debts to pay. As night fell on Avalon, he walked slowly back to the shuttle. The cold winds around him began to scream.

15 | THE COUNCIL OF CHOZANTI

The Tarka shuttle descended in a deep indigo twilight, the stars above blazing through the thin atmosphere with feverish clarity. Cai Rui folded his hands over his abdomen as a few wisps of cloud trailed by; his seat was locked into the sleeping position, tilted all the way back to face the night sky. He had to roll nearly all the way over to see the sparkling domes of the city below, swarming with hundreds of lights—a dozen glass bells filled with fireflies.

It was Sara's plan. True to her word as ever, he did not like it a bit. She insisted that there was a Hiver prince, a former Strategist of the imperial navy, who was willing and eager to help with her scheme. He and his sons would provide them with a bait-ship, to draw the enemy out into the open.

But I will be the bait.

He sighed and shifted awkwardly, trying to find a comfortable position. Neither the hastily re-tailored suit nor the cradle seat were specifically designed for his anatomy. As the bird set its skids down on the landing pad, his position rocked back and forth like a hammock. He found himself looking enviously at the Tarka pilot seated beside him, sitting up and holding herself serenely steady with a securely wrapped tail.

The shuttle set its skids on the landing pad, and the landing lights all around them went from blue to red. Cai Rui unbuckled himself from the rig and the young Tarka helped him out of the chair. She remained at his side solicitously as he walked to the door of the shuttle. The hydraulic elevator slowly lowered them into the base.

The final set of blast doors sealed above and sounded a triple klaxon. The pilot opened her shuttle doors, dropped the ramp to the blackened steel pad, and walked to the sealed entrance. She entered the code and spoke to the receiver mounted on the wall. "Kala Konak'Orr arriving," she said. "With a guest."

The doors slid back instantly. Cai Rui flinched and took a step back, despite his best intentions. Two towering Hiver warriors stood just on the opposite side of the door, the nearest heavily plated thorax just inches from his face.

Damned Hivers. No sense of personal space.

The creature's armor was mottled gray and black, colors flowing in a camouflage pattern over his carapace. He wore bandoliers of ammunition wrapped around the chest and abdomen, over a black flak jacket. Red leather sheathes were strapped over the lower portion of each forelimb, from the joint to the wrist— they covered the jutting steel fighting blades bolted to his body. The tooled leather bore a silver hexagon of rank, and had been worked into a complex, seemingly abstract geometric pattern. One mitt was wrapped around the shaft of a nasty-looking spear.

Cai Rui looked up into its eyes, shining behind the barred visor of its helm, and suppressed an inward shiver. There had been a ceasefire in effect for nearly two years, but the pit of his stomach still went cold at the sight of a Hiver.

Its voice was low and metallic, speaking *Urdu Kai* with a thick Hiver accent—a buzzing slur of any sound which required a tongue. "You will be escorted to the council chamber. Follow, please."

The warrior turned and clashed down the hallway, marching on his four lower limbs at a ceremonial pace which was, coincidentally, as fast as his charges could walk without breaking into a run. Glancing to the side, Cai Rui saw that the Tarka girl seemed happy. She took off her helmet as they walked and drew a few deep, deliberate breaths of the canned air. When she noticed he was watching, she turned to him with smiling eyes and gave him a very human thumb's up of encouragement.

So much like her mother. There was a pang in his chest as he smiled back. The girl owed much to Sara in manner and grace, and she had her mother's enormous eyes—but her markings were more like her father's, bands of deep violet and black. It was easy to see why she had been named "Kala"—she was beautiful even to a human eye. He was amused that she still gave her surname as "Konak'Orr", announcing her mother's former rank and her father's clan.

Still declares herself a daughter of the Supreme, he thought. *She must love to fight. Perhaps this one will join the Council herself someday.*

Following her lead, he removed his own helmet. She was right—the air was fine, and if anything rather sweet. Nothing at all like the dead canned stuff he would expect in a Human or Tarka dome. He had heard that Hiver air recyclers were much in demand—the trade ships couldn't ever carry enough of them. Walking through these halls, it was easy to see why.

As he walked he carried the helm in his left hand, favoring the right shoulder. Ishii had managed to close the wound completely, but the cracked bone was still not fully knitted. Despite Sara's assurances, a few interesting days in Ishii's company had revealed that the Liir was not primarily a healer.

The Hiver led them around a curve and thumped the butt of his spear in a syncopated rhythm on the echoing floor. The double blast doors opened, revealing a vast hexagonal room with a large hexagonal table placed in the center. Instantly there was a hush, as when a great deal of murmured talk is silenced at once.

"Kala Konak'Orr," the Hiver warrior buzzed, announcing them to the assembly. "And her guest."

Around the table a number of chairs and sitting platforms had been placed, built to accommodate various species. Sara was already seated on one side, along with several other members of a Tarka delegation—beside her there was a massive male, but Cai Rui did not recognize him. Kala winked and went to sit with the rest of the Tarka, leaving him standing alone.

Already the talk had resumed, a low murmur of many voices speaking softly in more than one language. Cai Rui looked around the room, trying to take in as much detail as possible. The walls were honeycombed with niche chambers, each one planted with some kind of orchid; the blooms were large, opulent in red and gold, and they filled the air with a smell like roasting honey and cinnamon. A large Hiver faction sat on the far side of the table, workers and warriors separated into two groups and seated around two sides of the hexagon. A wide space was left open between them.

Ishii had been given a full side of the hexagon, the bulk of his battlesuit resting on its nest of steel tentacles. A single lonely chair was set along the other empty edge of the table. His Hiver escort indicated the seat and Cai Rui walked to it, feeling very awkward and exposed. He sat down, placing his helmet on the table beside him.

The warrior thumped his spear again. Again the room hushed. The Hivers at the table turned expectantly. On the far side of the chamber, two more warriors opened a second set of doors. Everyone in the room rose, including the Tarka faction; Cai Rui hastily followed suit.

The blast doors of the chamber were massive, over three meters high and twice as wide. Nonetheless their host had to duck his head as he entered the room, so as not to brush the top of his horns on the lintel. He was a Hiver Prince, his body the color of swirling, opalescent gray smoke, his armor dappled with black. His wore an intricate breastplate of shining steel over his thorax. The floor rang beneath his steel-shod feet as he strode into the chamber, moving with the swift and deceptively light grace of a thoroughbred. As he approached the table he spread his wings and arms; the shining refractive membranes broke the light into prismatic rainbows on the chamber floor, and when they rattled they made a sound like a hard rain on a dozen tin roofs. All of his assembled people answered him with four decisive, percussive thumps over the armor of the chest—including the Tarka. Even Ishii had balled one of his tentacles into a fist and used it to pound the floor.

An entourage of Hiver workers followed quietly behind him, rolling along a wheeled cart draped with bright brocade. As the massive Hiver reached the table, the warrior behind Cai Rui buzzed out his title: "Behold His Majesty, son of the High Queen Radiant Frost, patriarch of the Burning Sun Clan, Protector and Regent to the nest of Chozanti, former Strategist of the Imperial Fleet, our Lord Father Prince Chezokin the Twice-Born."

A single massive thump of greeting followed—uncertain, Cai Rui stamped his foot along with the others. The Prince inclined his head graciously and folded his wings, reclining in the space that had been left for him at the table. His entourage rolled his hidden cart into place at the table at his right side and then stepped back soundlessly, taking an unobtrusive place behind him.

Chezokin made a long liquid stream of clicks and chatter, and Cai Rui lowered his eyes. He had never learned to speak *ri'kap-ken*, although some members of his team had been more proficient. His chest ached for Thatcher at that moment. She had been so good with Hiver transmissions...

Ishii's voice sounded in his brain, terminating his line of thought. *Apologies.* The word was couched in a bed of emotion—the Liir's mildly embarrassed remorse, along with a sense of pity. *Your mind is bleeding again.*

It still took a conscious act of will not to look at Ishii when the Liir spoke telepathically. Cai Rui kept his eyes focused on the Prince. *I forget that you hear.*

Ishii's presence in his mind went cooler and darker, murky with the sense of impending threat. *Others will hear as well, when the enemy is near. You must learn to bleed...selectively.* Then, changing the subject, it added: *If you wish to know, the Prince thanks his Children for their respect. He offers sympathy and remorse for their pain. He promises that there is hope.*

Pain? Cai Rui stared blandly ahead, but in his mind he frowned. *What pain? What hope?*

This room is filled with rage. Ishii's mental voice was quiet. *Reach out and you will feel it.*

Curious, Cai Rui attempted the exercise, opening his mind to the atmosphere of the room. Instantly he felt it wash over him, like a wave of terrible heat from a great fire—rage and more rage, hatred so deep and intense that it was all-consuming, agonies of humiliation and shame, grief that went beyond speaking. He recoiled instantly and slammed his mind shut, but not before he had seen himself through Hiver eyes: a weak, flabby, freakish thing, soft and squirming and unclean. How could such a creature be of any help—?

The Prince extended one of his limbs toward Cai Rui and another toward Ishii, speaking in Tarkasian. His voice was deeper even than that of the warrior, but strangely smooth and pleasant, like a bow drawn across the strings of a great cello. As he spoke, one of the workers present softly echoed his speech in Hiver for the rest of the clan's leaders. "Welcome, new friends. We thank you for coming." Turning to Sara, he said, "We have enriched the air for your visit. We hope it pleases."

"Very much so. Thank you, Great Prince."

"Will you translate words for our other guest?" he asked. "We regret we have not learned the speaking of his language."

Sara hesitated and glanced at Cai Rui.

"That will not be necessary," Cai Rui said, taking the cue. "I speak Tarkasian languages well enough."

The Prince turned toward him. "We are pleased. There is much to say and little time."

"I understand."

"Sara Mak'Kona has informed us of your situation. We have invited you here to explain our terms."

Cai Rui stiffened. "Terms? I thought these were already agreed."

Sara spoke up. On the floor behind her, her tail gave a single twitch of agitation. "You said nothing of new 'terms' when I contacted you."

Chezokin inclined his head. "We regret to say that our own circumstances have changed."

Two young Tarka half-rose from their seats, but the Changed male at Sara's side waved them down. Sara glanced at him and then looked back to Cai Rui. She shrugged, as if to say, *it's up to you.*

Cai Rui showed the Prince his palms. "We are listening, Majesty."

Chezokin spread his wings. "It is only a small change. All will proceed as we had previously agreed. With one exception: I wish to participate directly."

A silence followed, and Cai Rui waited for the Prince to continue. When it was awkwardly clear that Chezokin was waiting for a response, he said at last, "I'm afraid I don't understand."

"My sons and I will do as you ask. But I wish to accompany you on the mission. When we reach the ship, I will take command in battle. Regardless of the outcome, in the end I will be there."

A rattle of voices suddenly rose from the Hiver faction, as several workers and warriors spoke up at once. The Prince turned and silenced them with a thunderous rattle of his wings and a harsh, throaty command.

Cai Rui spoke quietly in Tarka. "Your people are concerned, of course. They see no need for a person of your stature to risk his own safety."

As the words he had spoken were echoed in Hiver, the room went deadly silent. All eyes turned toward him, and the Prince lowered his head. Cai Rui remained very still; the posture was eerily similar to the stance a Hiver warrior would assume directly before the charge.

"Forgive me if I have spoken out of turn, Prince Chezokin." He kept his voice soft and even. "This plan is highly dangerous and may lead, at best, to the deaths of many. I would not wish my own father to accompany me. I can only assume that your own sons feel the same."

A murmur passed through the crowd, and he saw Sara's eyes flash joyfully across the table. He had said the right thing, apparently. The Prince visibly relaxed, letting his wings half-fold. "You are not mistaken. They fear for my life."

"As do I."

There is more, Ishii warned. *He holds back the rest. The Queen has expressly forbidden this thing; if he leaves this planet, he will act against direct orders.*

Chezokin cocked his head curiously, and Cai Rui continued. "The peace between our people is very fragile, Prince. You are a son of the High Queen. Has Her Majesty given Her blessing to this venture? If not, what price will my people pay if you are killed?"

The silence in the council chamber was deafening. When at last the Prince spoke, his voice had lowered an octave. "Lan Mak'Kona is the son of an Empress. His sister is a mate of the Supreme. Do you fear reprisal from the Tarkasian Empire, should they fall in battle?"

Cai Rui's gaze was level. "I did not intend to have them with me, aboard the ship."

The Prince spread his wings wide, and they trembled as he spoke—a silvery whisper of growing anger. "And what of this one?" He indicated Ishii with a swift flick of the forelimb. "Does your Liirian ally have no value to the Liir? And what of you? Will your own leader smile at your demise?" He crossed his forelimbs, his naked blades gleaming in the golden light.

Cai Rui lowered his eyes. "I cannot speak for Ishii. But I am a person of no consequence, Prince."

The wings rattled, and a soft murmur passed through the Hivers at the table. "Nor was I, when my life began. I am called Chezokin—He Who Is Faithful. It is not the name of a born Prince. These wings were my reward, for service to my people."

The Prince rose from the table, standing to his full height. "Let us speak plainly," he said. "None of us wish to die. None of us are expendable. And neither were the thousands who were taken from us while our empires raged uselessly against one another. We have warred until our people are exhausted—and all the while, we ignored an enemy that hid in the darkness, striking from the shadows to plunder every undefended nest."

The Prince lowered his head. "You ask what will Our Mother will say, if Her son is lost in battle? I do not know. She said nothing when a thousand other sons were taken. She said nothing when I asked for the ships to seek this new foe and root them out. She said nothing when Her own sister was taken from this planet, and I asked for the funds to pay her ransom to these ones you call 'masaaku'. She said nothing when I begged Her to return me to the fleet, so that I might seek the devils who had taken my mate and enslaved my children. And She says nothing when the remains of our beloved Princess are returned to us in this charming box."

He turned and yanked the brocade drapery from the cart beside him. It was a crystal tank, filled with clear fluid, lit softly with a blue ultraviolet glow. Inside floated the unmistakable skull of a female Hiver, every inch of flesh picked from the beautifully intricate skull. Only the golden filigree of metal attached to her crest remained.

A soft keen went through the Hiver faction, a high-pitched sigh of pain. Cai Rui needed no tricks to feel the mood in the room.

"You ask what Greatmother will say? Perhaps it is time for Her not to speak, but to listen. Let Her receive this message, before we depart: Chezokin remains faithful, but he is no longer a Prince."

Once again the Hiver crossed his forelimbs, placing blade on blade. This time, the embrace of his own slender body was much tighter. Hugging his chest, he reached behind himself and grasped the roots of his massive wings.

Cai Rui rose from his chair, horrified. Around him several Hivers had done the same. The sound of breaking chitin and rending flesh was terrible, like a tree being ripped from the ground. Horribly, one of the wings was more stubborn than the other—the Prince wrestled with it for several seconds before it finally tore free.

Reeling, Chezokin hurled his wings onto the table. "I have spoken. Let my clan brothers send this gift to my Mother, before we depart. Tell Her that I have gone to war—that I will drag Her enemies into the light whether She wills it or not."

"Tell Her I will love Her always. But I am Chezokin—a person of no consequence."

Despite himself, Cai Rui's eyes filled tears. He bowed low. "Your terms are more than fair."

Sara and her brother rose.

"Let us depart."

16 | ABOARD THE JADE MIRROR

The Hiver bent over the table, the curving lens of its visor gleaming. The mouthparts moved thoughtfully as it worked, as if it were silently speaking or nibbling at something particularly delicious. In three of its four hands it held tiny instruments, using them to probe, tweeze and snip with refined skill. The data pad was quickly dissected into three layers, each one consisting of circuit boards, insulated wires and micro-components.

It looked up, sapphire eyes magnified hugely by the visor, and trilled appreciatively to Cai Rui. When he did not answer, it tilted its chin up to address a second, softer trill to Chezokin; the massive Prince loomed behind his son, watching over his shoulder.

The Prince turned to Cai Rui. "He says it is a wonderful thing. He has never seen a Node array reduced to such a tiny size."

Cai Rui nodded, his teeth clamped tightly shut. "Yes. Quite wonderful." He clenched his fists under the table top. "Please ask if it is still broadcasting."

The Prince relayed the question, his head cocked to hear the soft twitter of response. "He says that the damage is very slight. He believes it can be repaired." Chezokin inclined his head. "If you wish it."

He shook his head. "No. Not yet. Can the data be recovered from storage?"

Another musical exchange followed, and the Prince once again spoke in Urdu Kai. "Ezz'in says, this is very easy." The Prince seemed amused. "He is able to do much more."

Cai Rui shook his head. "The data is sufficient."

Receiving instructions, the worker tilted its head to the side—a gesture he had learned to recognize as the equivalent to a shrug. Its hands worked swiftly, plucking a series of black spheres from the eviscerated data pad and placing them one by one into an adapter. When it had finished, it swiftly connected the resulting matrix to the table. The embedded screen in the table top lit up, forming a display of *ri'kap-ken* characters and images.

Prince Chezokin bent over the table, speaking to his son in low tones. The smaller Hiver—Cai Rui realized to his dismay that he had begun to think of it as a "boy"—pointed to a red character, set beneath a pink blob with two tiny black dots. As Chezokin reached for it, Cai Rui snorted suddenly; the image was a caricature of a human face.

"These are the files you requested." The Prince activated a second display. Cai Rui looked at the red characters, trying to make sense of the display, and finally reached out tentatively and tapped one with a fingertip.

He smiled. The Hiver was a clever boy indeed. It had included the operating system of the data pad as a mechanism to open its own files; a second, nested display appeared, a miniature version of the data pad's own viewscreen. "Cicero," Cai Rui said softly. "*Tangi interfaciem.*"

His scalp prickled as the PDA reached out, seeking the nearest interface. He felt the surge as it found the familiar configuration within the Hiver system and flowed into it, connecting to the virtual data pad. He bent over the table top, navigating through the menus until he found the navigation data she had stored for analysis.

"*Praebe,*" he said. Cicero opened the Node map, bringing up a flattened view of the navigator's display from the Nanjing. "*Praebe...*" He trailed off, searching for a description of the anomalies that would not confuse the PDA. "*Praebe portas sinistras,*" he said at last. *Display the sinister doorways.*

The complex jumble of Node Lines receded, leaving behind a chain of the anomalous Ghost Nodes. They pulsed red against the black field, and his intuition leaped at the pattern. He touched a coordinate at random, zooming in to confirm his suspicion.

The display listed its map code: N2.4.8. Spica.

Orienting himself swiftly, he touched another Ghost Node. The map zoomed in to identify N5.0.1, Etos'che. He lit up the rest of the Ghosts in Hiver space: Xheketch'is, Zozoris...Chozanti.

He winced and reached for Tarka space. N.6.3.5 was Ku'Van. Nearby, a second pulsing wound proved to be Ko'Rorkor. A third and fourth had opened at Ko'Seth and Ke'Raath...and of course Ko'Grappa.

His gut twisted at the site of the Ghost Nodes in human space. He had already seen the breach at Spica; he could easily predict the Node at Avalon. But there were three more that he could see, at Fort, Hynek and Rigel, and more opening everywhere, including Liir territory and unclaimed systems.

Chezokin spoke suddenly. "Where is the star of Chis'ka-tet?"

Cai Rui started; in the silence he had forgotten that the Prince was watching. Now the former Strategist lowered the long fingers of his silvery hand to the screen.

"Should it not be there?" Delicately, he tapped one of the greyed-out systems.

Cai Rui frowned. "Yes...that should be the map coordinate." Mentally he ran through his timeline, squinting at the starfield, and then suddenly tapped the screen with his own finger. "Ka'Saak is also missing!"

Chezokin's head tilted from side to side in agreement, and the worker trilled excitedly. "Do your own star-holes perish, with the passage of time?" He crossed his blades reflectively. "We do not think so."

Cai Rui looked down at the map, feeling the gathering force of a hunch. "Cicero," he said. "*Praebe malafortunas.*"

The accident reports appeared on the map, twin green splashes to indicate the loss of two assets from the Deep Scan category. The first had occurred at Mjolnir system—the nearest adjacent star to Kepler. The second was at Biter, the jump closest to Avalon.

There's something living in Node Space. And it's found a way out.

He looked up at Chezokin. "Prince, the time has come to speak very plainly." He touched the screen. "You and I both have eyes."

The Hiver tilted his twisted horns in silent agreement.

"Your people and mine are at peace. But we do not love one another."

Chezokin tilted his assent in the opposite direction, keeping his blades crossed.

"We were not told of the attack at Chozanti. I will not question that decision now—done is done. I cannot say that things would have ended differently for your...wife, had we known. But I think we can agree that every lie and omission has cost us dearly."

The Prince spoke, his voice low and sweet. "Truth."

He tapped the screen again. "Please tell me, if you can—has there been a Ripper attack at Zozoris?"

Chezokin's jaws clashed negation. "No. Not to my knowledge. We have battled Tarka there, and your own ships, many years ago. But not slavers."

The Hiver's mouth could not form the word, but Cai Rui nodded comprehension. "Does this ship have a reliable channel of communication to Tcho'to'pre?"

The Prince lowered his head. "No. I am sorry. It is only a trade ship; a vessel of this class cannot command the attention of the Queen."

Cai Rui nodded grimly. "I thought so. Very well." He turned to the smaller Hiver and offered a respectful bend of his head. "Please tell your son Ezz'in that I would like to have the Node Array repaired."

Chezokin touched the worker's shoulder with his long hand, speaking in a low tone. Ezz'in chirped a happy assent and went to work, merrily unravelling a complex nest of hair-fine wires.

Cai Rui bowed to the Prince. "Thank you, Majesty," he said. "I must speak to Sara Mak'Kona before she departs."

The Prince crossed his blades and mimicked Cai Rui's gesture, bowing his crest. "You are welcome, Task Force Commander," he said. His pearlescent eyes spun golden and full of humor. "But a 'person of no consequence' is not 'His Majesty.'" The giant mouthparts slid across one another with a sound like sharpening knives. "Such a one is only 'Chezokin.'"

✳ ✳ ✳

He found her in the rear section, speaking to the larger male Tarka in low clipped Kona Kai. As he entered the two of them stepped apart, turning to confront him simultaneously as an intruder.

He held up his hand. "Respect." He kept his tone cool and formal, body courteously stiff. "May I have a word, Lac Tar?"

Her eyes smiled. "You may." She glanced at the hulking male beside her; he stepped back and turned away, taking a sudden interest in the Hiver engine and its three diminutive worker attendants.

"We may have to adjust the plan. There is new information." He quickly reviewed the navigational data from the Nanjing. "I think you can see why this should be relayed immediately."

She had crossed her arms to listen, a gesture that reminded him curiously of Chezokin; it occurred to him that she mimicked the prince's body language as easily as she had acquired human gestures. "I agree. Someone must take this information to Kao'Kona quickly, and the garrisons at those planets must be warned. If what you say is true, Raath and Rorkor are very much at risk."

He suppressed a roll of his eyes. "Human and Hiver worlds are in danger as well. Someone must send word to MarsDome, and the Queen."

Her eyes whirled. "Ayo. And the Black as well."

"I'm glad we agree. I need you to open a channel in broadband and—"

She shook her head human-style, eyes turned a pale shade of lilac. "I cannot do that, Caido."

"Why in the nine hells not?" he snapped. "Can't you see that—?"

Her tongue quivered amusement. "I see much, Cai Rui. I see that the enemy has penetrated the Ko' in ways that you have not considered. It is useless to fight at the walls if you have surrendered the keep."

He took a deep breath. "Explain," he said at last.

"Think, my dearest. The *massaaku* have corrupted one of your own *taru*, a Sol Force officer—oath-bound and close to the seat of the Director. It was he who betrayed you to the Deacon; he sold you to your death, and we do not yet know what coin he was paid."

"I am...quite aware of that," he gritted. "I do not see what that has to do with—"

"This man was in charge of your fleet communications, was he not?" she asked pointedly.

"Yes," he admitted reluctantly.

"Clean water does not flow from a poisoned pipe, beloved. We are very distant from your home world. This man's ships will be the first to receive any message we send. Sar only knows what message would reach the Director's eyes and ears—"

He cut her off with a slashing gesture. "All right. You win. But we could still send word to the other worlds. Tcho'to'pre, Kao-Kona, and Muur—"

Her eyes smiled. "Tell Ishii what you know, and the Black will hear of it. Of this I am certain. As for the others...I will send word to them, and to your Director, without fail. There is a way. But I will not use the broadband channel."

He shook his head. "But why?"

Her tail flicked, and her eyes glinted crimson. "Do you think that humans invented betrayal, Cai Rui? Ne. There are traitors of every race. It is time to pull our tail knives. The only messages we should send in the open are those to lure our enemies to their deaths."

He stood and regarded her thoughtfully. "I take it this means we will proceed as planned?"

"No." She lowered her lids, thinking. "I will have to send one of my ships back to Kao'Kona immediately. I had planned to place her *tar* aboard this ship—I have few that speak *ri'kap-ken* among my complement—but I will alter that plan. My brother will replace her, and travel with you aboard the Jade Mirror."

Cai Rui looked uneasily over her shoulder at the broad-backed male. "Are you sure—?"

Her eyes flashed. "I trust Chezokin and his sons, but not completely. They have had personal contact with the *massaaku*, to be sure—but who is to say what parts of the story are true? You do not speak their tongue—Lando does, and he is strong. If they think to betray us, he can fight. And I will not leave you undefended among them."

He hesitated for a long moment. "You are willing to use me as bait," he said at last. "I am surprised to hear that you are … concerned with my fate."

"You wound me, Caido." Her eyes flashed pale blue. "There is a difference between risking a life, and throwing it away."

He spread his hands. "You win again."

"Two falls out of three?" she said, teasing. "Go back to the Prince and record your message. I will explain things to Lan." She tilted her head toward her brother, now engaged in a stream of clicks and chatter with the Hiver engineers. "He is young. I think he will be glad for a chance to win honor."

"As you wish." Cai Rui looked into her eyes, and switched to Latin. "Goodbye, Sara. *Si vales, valeo.*"

Her pupils smiled, eyes emerald with emotion. "'If you are strong, I am strong,'" she said, translating the words into Kona. "*Kala du kai*, my dearest. And *bona fortuna*—good luck."

17 | BETRAYAL

C ai Rui and his playmates sat in a circle on the cold cement floor, the three of them so close that their knees were touching. A beam of dirty winter sunlight surrounded them, filtered through a sheet of plastic nailed over the window-hole. The aluminum roof of the shack occasionally creaked with frost, and the wind beating on the walls made the plastic sheeting hum. The only other sound was the soft, continuous sigh of the rice pot steaming in the corner, filling the single-room dwelling with the smell of survival.

Steam rose to the ceiling and rolled along the corrugated metal roof, condensing on the cold surface. Occasionally a single drop of rice-scented rain fell into the center of the children's circle, joining the previous drop to form a tiny pool.

Cai turned to Sara, sitting to his right with her tail neatly wrapped around her feet. He had never known her at this age, her creamy scales still the color of milk, her patterns pale pastel. She held her pale golden hands cupped to cover her eyes.

"Ok," he said. "You can look." He held up his own two hands, curled up into fists of mystery for the ancient guessing game. "Which one is it?"

Her green eyes narrowed, and for a moment her tongue flickered uncertainly. Finally she tapped the back of his left hand with her nail. "That one."

He smiled and turned his hands over and opened his palm. The piece of candy, the very special prize, was in his right. "Sorry."

"Bugger." She rose gracefully, unfurling and stretching like a cat. "I hate this game. I'm going to go play outside." She backed out of the circle of light and vanished, dissolving into the shadows of the room.

Cai Rui hid a smile. Even in his dreams, she was the same. If she couldn't win the game, she would declare it pointless and refuse to play. He turned to his second playmate, a child with no face or features—instead the body was cut from the cloth of deep space, formed from black darkness scattered with distant stars.

"It is my turn." Ishii spoke with the soft, vast voice of the waters. Black hands rose to cover the place where a child's eyes would be.

Cai Rui put his hands behind his back and juggled the candy back and forth. He frowned with concern; this was the abbot's very special gift. He did not want Ishii to have it. "Ok."

When he brought his closed fists to the front, Ishii pointed to the left. Cai Rui opened his hands. The candy was in the left.

"Again," he said, and Ishii obligingly covered his eyes. He juggled the candy again, and on the next try Ishii correctly guessed the right.

Cai Rui frowned. "Again."

Ishii covered his eyes. Somehow, Cai Rui felt him smiling.

He juggled the candy behind his back, looking at Ishii through narrowed lids. Feeling oddly triumphant, he brought his fists back to the fore. Ishii looked down at them briefly and then back up into Cai Rui's eyes.

"The candy is on the floor behind your back."

Cai Rui flushed. "You're cheating."

"Yes," Ishii said. "And so are you. Would you like to try again?"

Moved by the stubbornness that comes only in dreams, Cai Rui soldiered on. He tried everything. Once he hid the candy in the rice pot. Once under a broken brick. He hid the candy in the pocket of his mother's ragged jacket, as she lay sleeping on the floor. Nothing he did would fool Ishii. Every time, the dark child simply pointed to the place where the bright circle of sugar was hidden.

Finally, in desperation, he tried one last gambit. He held out his two fists, suppressing a grim smile. "Again."

Ishii lowered his hands and looked at Cai Rui. He shook his head sadly. "You have swallowed the candy. A dangerous ploy—what if I did this?"

He raised one dark hand, and suddenly his black fingers had become four gleaming obsidian knives. So swiftly that it was nearly impossible to follow, his hand darted toward Cai Rui's stomach.

Cai Rui fell back, a cry of alarm and anticipated pain on his lips, but the blades did not penetrate. Instead Ishii squatted over him, letting the light of the sunbeam slide over the black metal just inches from vulnerable flesh.

He looked down at Cai Rui, the stars in the depths of his face shimmering like a dozen eyes. "The enemy will not be so gentle. To him, this is not a game. And he has weapons more terrible than mine."

The tears of a defeated child sprang up in Cai Rui's eyes. "Then how can I win? Where can I hide it?"

Ishii smiled. He gave his wrist a little flick and made his appendage a small human hand once more. Then he opened the hand; the striped disk of candy lay in the cup of his black palm. "Watch."

Cai Rui stood, and suddenly the walls of his childhood home fell away, collapsing outward and vanishing. The two of them stood in a region of strange rolling dunes. As he focused on them more closely, he could see that they were mountains of candy, made up of billions of pieces identical to the one that he had tried to hide from Ishii.

Ishii climbed to the top of a pile, the candies crunching and sliding like scree beneath his feet. When he finally achieved the summit, he cocked his arm and threw the single piece out into the rolling white sea. It vanished into anonymity, one among billions.

In the blink of an eye, the two of them sat once more on the cold cement floor, facing one another cross-legged in a beam of winter sunlight. A drop of rice water fell in a silvery flash between them and joined the small undisturbed pool in the center of their circle.

Despite himself, Cai Rui smiled. "That was good," he admitted. "What was that place?"

"The night sea in which your people swim." Ishii shrugged. "I have no word for it. It is the treasure trove of your life, where all you have known and experienced falls into the birthgrave. My people have no such refuge."

Cai Rui frowned. "Is the candy lost?" he asked. "Will I ever see it again?"

Ishii held up his two open palms. "What candy?"

* * *

He woke up abruptly, sitting up with a start. As usual, his forehead smacked solidly into the bulkhead above him. This had happened so many times that now the impact was cushioned by a pad of soft insulation foam—he had taped one to the spot days ago, to spare himself more bruises.

Now he lay back with a sigh of irritation, rearranging himself in time and space, dreams fleeing in the wake of pain. The headache had been with him since he boarded, a constant drumbeat of pulsing pain. Drugs, light adjustments, tinkering with the atmospheric mix—nothing seemed to work. Life aboard a Hiver ship was a never-ending migraine. The most he could do was drive the throb of discomfort into the background for a while, with the help of a fistful of pills.

A fistful of pills which had now run their course.

He pinched the bridge of his nose savagely, driving the hurt back into the rear of his skull, and then opened his eyes in the dark. Something was wrong. In the six days he had been aboard the Jade Mirror, he had developed a sense of the rhythms and routines of the weary freighter. Instinct told him he had not slept long enough for this much darkness.

Wordless, he craned his head to look down from his topmost bunk. The ship was oddly silent—and curiously loud at the same time. He recognized the sound, a sweetly resonant high-pitched chirrup that seemed to issue from several places throughout the room. It was the old song of summer, the one he would hear as a child when he crept out of bed at night to sit on the cool stone steps and listen to the crickets singing.

It was the sound of Hivers snoring. And it came from everywhere.

With gradually building dread, he chinned himself down from the high shallow storage compartment which had been converted to make him a bunk. His bare feet touched the floor soundlessly and he crept to the side of a bulky shadow. As he bent, he saw the sleeper was a warrior called Yzeket, sprawled ungracefully half in, half out of the doorway.

Cautiously he touched the warrior's carapace. The massive chest moved slowly, the chirring song emerging in long musical sighs from the wingpits in his back as he slept. But the eyes were not covered by their protective lids—instead they seemed to be open, staring blind and sightless into the dark.

A cold dread washed over him. He looked down, and saw the customary weapons holstered in the *chez-rek*'s bandoliers were missing. With a sudden premonition he turned back to the place where his own clothes and weapons should have been, hanging in a sac beside his makeshift bunk.

Gone.

Something in the bowels of the ship rattled, followed by a thud of heavy impact. Cai Rui looked up suddenly, eyes wide.

"No," he said softly—more in disbelief than command.

The pain in his skull suddenly intensified, surging back into the space behind his eyes with a vengeance. He staggered and fell to his knees, clutching his temples. Beneath him the floor begin to vibrate, a rising thrum that spread from the depths of the Mirror and into his bones, his blood and brain, threatening to spin his body into fragments. The song of the engine whipped through him like a thousand burning wires, cradling him in agony.

The sense of penetration was palpable, as if the surface tension of a liquid were suddenly broken. He fell heavily onto his side, head spinning, retching silently as the universe turned itself slowly, painfully inside out.

Lungs, heart, stomach lurched to a halt, in the interminable choking interval as the ship traveled through the skin of the universe. Its emergence was just as palpable, a slow revolution from the gut-wrenching realm of tortured amber to a place of torturous confusion, of wheezing gasps and gagging stomach rebellion. Cai Rui squirmed, holding his skull, trying with all his might to keep it from flying apart. His mouth was full of blood... he had bitten his tongue. Fresh sweat bathed his body.

The Jade Mirror had made another jump through the Queen's Gates.

He tottered to his feet and staggered into the hall, half-stumbling over the bodies of several massive Hiver warriors. They lay where they had fallen, as if sleep had suddenly overtaken them all at once: between one bite and another of a ration bar, standing at a guard post, in mid-step while exiting the head...

A gangway traveled the length of the ship's spine. As he padded barefoot along it he turned, listening. Somewhere in the command section he could hear a new sound, a trilling cascade of keystrokes. Even as he opened the control room hatch, some part of him recognized it—all Tarkasian computers made those eager little sounds as they accepted a command.

The massive male turned toward him. His pupils had folded into a complex origami of amusement and surprise.

"Why... hello, stump. What's the matter? Not sleepy?"

For days Lan Mak'Kona had spoken every word in this same tone—the contemptuous sneer of a bully who issues a challenge that others are too weak to answer. Cai Rui registered the insult without speaking, meeting the eyes of Sara's younger brother without changing expression. Slowly he wiped the blood from his mouth, and then just as slowly and deliberately raised his eyes to the viewscreens, to take in the rolling tapestry of space.

In the course of his work he had studied spy footage from two dozen Hiver worlds, keeping track of every planet on their Gate network. This one, however, would never have needed such an introduction. Any human spacer would have recognized it at a glance.

Outside, the void was awash with wrecked ships. The scattered remains of a hundred broken hulls tumbled, silent and black. Here the cavernous, gaunt ribs of a sundered Hiver dreadnaught gleamed, rolling slowly up into the light as the ship completed a ponderous pirouette in the darkness. There the melted command section of a Tarkasian cruiser tumbled in slow somersaults through the night, trailing a glittering necklace of wreckage from the Sol Force destroyers that had smashed into either side, dragging it with them into death. It was a glittering field of devastation, extending as far as the eye could see, the remains of a battle so massive that its litter had left a permanent ring of debris in orbit around the tiny yellow star. Now this ring had become its own monument to the dead—a frozen, hallowed cemetery for the three races who had once fought and died to call this system their own.

Durendal's Drift.

He closed his eyes, letting the old plan slip away. He was light years away from that rendezvous, and the carefully-laid ambush that had once seemed so clever. Here and now, the future yawned before him like an abyss.

When he opened his eyes again a moment later, he discovered that there was only one question left to ask. "Sara's plan? Or yours?"

Lan Mak'Kona rattled his tongue with laughter. "You give my sister too much credit. Even now she rages at the helm, watching her precious pet disappear into my coils. No, her great scheme was only to help you capture your enemy and avenge your father-ape." He bared his tusks in disgust. "Pathetic."

"Ah." Looking down at his hands, Cai Rui could not hide his smile. She had not betrayed him. It was strange, in the worst moments of life, how such a small thing could matter.

The son of the emperor looked at his face and made a harsh bark of disbelief. "*Grak.* The pet is happy now, is it? Still has his lady's love? And much good that will do him."

Cai Rui looked up and raised his eyebrows. "And yet it is always a pleasure to be chosen. By a woman of quality."

Even as he spoke, he knew that the bolt would strike true. Lan Mak'Kona stiffened visibly, his pupils tightening to pinpricks of fury. Cai Rui cocked his head, feigning mild interest as the boy battled with rage. The spoiled scion of a wealthy family, a male like Lan Mak'Kona made the Change by means of wealth—not glory. But son of an emperor or not, he was not likely to impress a woman of his sister's rank.

Looking at him now, Cai Rui could almost see the yoke around that massive neck. The boy would never go far on his name alone. He would not have fathered many children among the elite, as yet; at best he might have hired himself out as a stud service to his inferiors—if his family would allow even that. How it must rankle him, that golden cage: to have the appearance of status, of power, of manhood—and not the reality. He would be little more than a plaything until he could distinguish himself in politics or battle.

Cai Rui shook his head, poisonously amused. All this trouble and pain—to be betrayed, in the end, by a two hundred kilogram teenager.

"Well then," he said mildly. "I suppose we have a new plan."

The Tarka bared his massive tusks. "Not really. Only a few details have been changed." His golden eyes gleamed savagely. "We still try to lure the Deacon in to snatch a prized captive. We still meet the *massaaku* in a pre-arranged location, pretending that we will make the exchange." His tongue rattled again. "But we do not lead him to an ambush of Hiver vessels pouring through an empty gate."

The young Tarka rose from the pilot's chair, advancing on Cai Rui with the slow, weaving predatory dance of a snake. "Instead, we see how deep his pockets go, this Ripper," he rumbled softly. His head cocked to the side. "If he is willing to go to such lengths for one paltry stump-tailed ape—what will he give for a Hiver Prince?"

Cai Rui took a step backward, but the hand shot out too quickly, snapping shut around the bones of his arm in an eye blink, with a grip like iron.

"Would he attack on my command, perhaps?" Lan Mak'Kona leaned close, bringing his ivory tusks within inches. "With a few well-placed blows, I might raise a full rebellion against this Son of Orr," he hissed softly. "There are many who would prefer to see a son of the Kona sit in the Temple of Steel."

Cai Rui bared his teeth in return. "The only child of the Kona fit to sit in that throne is your sister," he said sharply. "As for you—I suspect that you are about to discover how our friends treat royalty." He lifted his chin, indicating the viewscreen.

Lan Mak'Kona turned just as the proximity warning of the old freighter began to pulse. Frozen, he watched as the fabric of space ruptured, and the massive nose of the enemy ship hove into view.

It was eerily at home against the backdrop of the drifting graveyard, a nightmare vessel bolted together from the dismembered remains of a dozen derelicts. The curving prow of the disk loomed over them, and every portal bristled with guns. From this distance it seemed that every one of those guns was trained on the vulnerable flanks of the Hiver freighter, helpless in the dark.

"Well done, Lan Mak'Kona." Cai Rui laughed bitterly. "Your plan is without flaw. Even the Supreme cannot say that He has ever been where you stand now—standing alone at the helm of a rusting freighter in the face of an enemy cruiser. You have cleverly arranged a bad death for yourself and all aboard, by delivering three prizes to an enemy of your people—a Hiver Prince, a paltry ape, and a Tarka fool." He shook his head. "What will you do for an encore, I wonder? Kill yourself before the Deacon can tear out your soul and make you his catamite—?"

The boy turned to him with a snarl of terror and fury. Cai Rui smiled—even as he registered the moment he had gone too far. He had only a split-second to regret his choice of words before the massive fist was in motion, hammering him back down into the black.

18 | THE BATTLE OF THE JADE MIRROR

"**S**weet Bleeding Gods of the Abyss." The Amtara shook his head. "I do believe that is the *ugliest* damned thing I've ever seen."

She tapped her wrist-guard, zooming the camera view in tighter on the alien cruiser. "If there are gods in the abyss," she agreed drily, "That ship was built in their harbour."

As they watched, a pair of heavy hooks deployed from the belly of the strange patchwork vessel to grapple the Hiver freighter. The ship was held in a parasitic grip and reeled closer to the enemy's ventral hull; Sara winced as glowing plasma torches emerged on mechanical arms and began to slice, cutting cleanly through the bulkhead fore of the engine like a surgeon's scalpel.

In the forward sections of the Jade Mirror, the lights went dead—she could almost hear the life support systems grind to a halt. *Take a deep breath, Caido,* she thought. *And pray that all of Ishii's tricks will work.*

"They are good at what they do. And whatever they are—they are growing bolder." He turned slightly in his chair. "That is no raider. It is a ship of the line. If they are building vessels of such a size, they mean to use them soon. In the open."

"I believe you are right." The Iron Lotus stood on the command deck of the Tarkasian cruiser *Habas'ku,* her hand placed in the ceremonial position upon the back of the Amtara's chair. She favoured the old man with a pupil-smile, never taking her eyes from the viewscreen before them. Only her tail betrayed any agitation... rolling in a slow, lazy circle upon the bulkhead. It could lash out in a strike or draw the blade sheathed at her calf in a split-second.

"So these are the things that attacked the House of Grappa." He flexed his fist and turned back to the screen, crest bristling with menace. "Say the word, my Lady. We are ready to send them back to hell."

"*Ne.*" She spoke quietly. "Patience, *Amtarado.* Stay hidden. Let them take our bait. Then we will move in—to cripple, not to kill." She bared her teeth. "We will take them as they have taken us. Alive."

He growled in the back of his throat, a low deep rumble of impending aggression that thrummed through her fingertips and into the room like a crack of thunder. Every woman on the bridge could feel it—that surging thrill of masculine power. A moment later the navigator threw a quick, appraising glance over one shoulder, her pupils rounded with desire.

Sara's tongue flickered. Seeing her force commander's silent laughter, the pilot turned abruptly back to her console and became urgently interested in scanning the debris field. "Holding position, Amtara." She spoke crisply, and pointedly addressed her immediate superior. "They have not detected our presence."

Sara answered almost musingly. "They cannot penetrate the cloak. This we learned at Avalon." She watched with disgusted fascination as the strange alien ship extended a boarding chute toward the freighter, now helpless in its grip. Her tail resumed its restless coiling dance. "We should be safe for now. Maintain radio silence."

"'Safe'? We are more than 'safe', surely." The Amtara swept out a hand to indicate the ships under his command. "I do not understand why we wait, my Lady. We outnumber them four to one." There was a hint of petulance in his tone. "And yet we cower and skulk among the corpses?"

"We do as we must," she said sharply. "We have allies aboard that ship, Amtara. Oath brothers who risk their lives in an act of subterfuge. They depend upon our ability to carry out this plan." Her voice was laden with a deadly chill. "If you are incapable of subtlety, say the word. I am sure I can find someone to command this *fane* with more finesse."

The old man stiffened. "You will find me quite capable of anything you require, Lac Tar. If the details of your plan had been shared with me…"

She resisted the urge to cut him off impatiently, letting his words trail off into silence without reply. Rather than speak, she watched the Ripper ship nose through the debris field aimlessly, dragging the smaller Hiver vessel along in its arms like a *jin-fly* winging aloft with its prey. He was watching her from the corner of his eye; she permitted herself a womanly shiver.

After a brief, awkward pause, he spoke again. "I apologize. Your sibling is a brave lad."

She let her eyelids close briefly in agreement. *Too brave*, she thought. *Too brave, too young, too willing. I should never have permitted this. I should have used someone else's brother.*

She could still see the way he had caressed the mound of eggs with his slender hand, the way his fingertips trembled—wanting, but afraid to take. "But shouldn't I earn these, *Saradora*?" His expression was painfully open. He had not so much as tasted a woman before, much less her favour. A boy's longing to be a man now warred with his sense of rightness, and everything hung upon his heart-breaking faith that Big Sister would know what was best.

Big Sister would never lead him astray.

"You will, *Landomo*. Believe me, you will." She caressed his crest lovingly, and drew him close. "You are a clever boy, my brother." She embraced him, letting him feel the steady beat of her heart against his chest. "And someday, you will be a brilliant man. But for now, Ishii says that you must be something in between. You must meet this enemy neither before nor after the Change... but during."

She released him and reached to the bowl, heaped with the pearlescent treasure. It had taken less than a day to gather this prize; she had only to send the message to her list of contacts. Upon receiving those four words—*"I need a favour"*—her friends and allies had sent enough of these to Change a dozen men.

Carefully she selected the one she had marked with a drop of blood.

"This one is mine." She offered it to him, holding the creamy golden oval in her palm. "I ask you to take it, my brother. It is the greatest honour I have to bestow. It will hurl you into the teeth of my enemies. It will bring you pain, and madness, and an early death. If there was any other I could trust—"

"*Habas y'an.*" He cut her off, his young voice surprisingly firm. Without hesitation, he took the egg and placed it between his incisors. Her heart clenched with fierce love as he tilted his head back and split the egg between his teeth. Like a true Kona, he savoured every drop of the rich yolk, letting it bleed over his tongue and down his throat slowly—and then crushed the shell and swallowed it, eyes lidded with sensual pleasure.

When he lowered his head and looked at her again, his eyes blazed red—but his smile was still a boy's. "Wonderful. Are they all so sweet—?"

She shook her head. "I have been told that every woman is different." She reached to the bowl again, playfully. "Perhaps you should try another?"

He hesitated. "How many should I have? Do I need to eat them all? And all in one day?" He took the egg gingerly, a small round favour with a brilliant emerald hue. "I have never read the Books of Change. I thought it would be years before I needed them..."

And again she felt that pang of shame and regret. *It should have been. Poor, poor Landomo. My sweet little kinsman. It should have been years.*

Her heart went out to him, alone now in the dark bowels of the Hiver ship. It must be cold, waiting in the silence of his armour for the enemy to find him. He would have dragged as many of the sleeping Hivers as possible into position, placing the majority of bodies on the bridge and in the engine room. Command staff and engineers would not be killed immediately when the Rippers boarded— this much they knew.

Her reverie was interrupted by the voice of the navigator. "A second ship, Amtara." Her voice was tense. "Coming from the void."

Sara's eyes flew open just in time to see the grim silhouette sliding from its unholy tear in the universe. As before, the arrival of a Ripper ship reminded her uncomfortably of the way a blade punched through an enemy's back might look as it emerged from her chest.

This one was even uglier than its sister, a hammer-headed monstrosity bristling with guns. Even on its midsection it carried more heavy turrets than two comparable Tarkasian cruisers combined. And now a third ship was coming, sliding from the void like a shark—twinned in the egg from the other escort vessel, a mirror in every way.

Bitterly she turned to the commander. "Well, Amtara? What do you think? *Does this even up the odds to your satisfaction?*"

✳ ✳ ✳

Lan Mak'Kona crouched in the dark. He was afraid, and he was alone. And he was the only being awake aboard the Jade Mirror.

With every passing moment, some new thought or feeling assailed him. Now his lips peeled back over his fangs, fear suddenly passing into a spasm of nearly unbearable rage. All five chambers of his heart were pounding; the wine of violence pumped steadily into his blood as if some hidden spigot in his breast had broken. Unbidden, his hand went to the handle of his war hammer, and for a full second there was nothing but the red haze of slaughter in his field of vision. Every beat of his heart seemed to whisper: *kill, kill, kill.*

"*Ne.*" He spoke aloud. Exerting every iota of his strength, he forced his grip to loosen. He was Lan Mak'Kona. He must do as he had sworn.

No sooner had he conquered one storm, but another tore through him. Thwarted in its drive to anger, his body suddenly shook him with a furious surge of *vanuu*. He closed his eyes, desperately trying to reign in his rebellious mind. Every woman he had ever known, seen or imagined crawled out from the recesses of his brain and tore away her clothes. Thousands of them writhed, cooing and purring and promising all, entwined into an endless labyrinth of muscular thighs, wicked tails, flickering tongues. Every beat of his heart seemed to whisper: *kokari, kokari, kokari.*

"*Ne!*" he cried aloud, resisting a sudden urge to beat his own helmet with his fists to make it stop. Instead he mentally chanted his own name, throttling the madness with an iron will: *I am Lan Mak'Kona. Lan Mak'Kona. Lan Mak'Kona. I will do as I have sworn.*

The darkened ship rocked, and he felt the booming impact of the boarding chute striking the upper plating of the hull. He looked up, as the ceiling first began to hum and then to glow. A slow drip of molten steel rained down from the burning circle slowly forming above, and finally rubble crashed down into the cargo bay, leaving a gaping hole.

The hot steel congealed and froze in the chill dead air of the ship, forming strange stalactites of metal. The ramp slowly descended into the room, finding purchase on the floor surface below and embedding itself with a fusillade of explosive bolts driven into the deck plate. For a moment all was still.

The first beast leaped down in a single bound, landing on all fours with a boom of massive impact. The Tarka flinched, seeing the flat feral head moving slowly from side to side, nosing the air. A second Ripper padded down the gangway to join the first, striding further into the room.

Slowly he straightened, letting them see him rise from his crouch behind the crates. The first animal stalked a step toward him, hackles rising: she planted her feet, parted her jaws and roared defiance.

Instinctively he felt his own lips draw back to answer the challenge, and he fought the urge to leap forward and split the beast's skull. More Rippers were coming, rapidly leaping and loping down the ramp into the cargo bay, and as they entered they turned toward him and kept their distance, slowly circling with the slow gait of predators surrounding a potentially dangerous prey.

There was a pause, and a sudden ripple seemed to pass through the monsters. They roared together, a massive wall of sound that buffeted him even within the confines of his suit. And now another was coming, and the beasts around him sank down on their haunches, jaws gaping, their dark tongues lolling as they panted steam in the dark.

Lan Mak'Kona could feel the Presence flow into the room, coming closer with every step. Another animal sauntered down the ramp, nearly half again as big as the others, its shoulders rolling with ursine grace and its back humped upward to support the weight of an ornate saddle.

A slim figure sat astride the beast, its body pale as sand and covered with a short velvety coat of hair. It held a staff in one long-fingered paw, the end capped with a smouldering, glowing barb of hot metal. Lan felt his crest expand, the red tide creeping in at the corners of his field of vision. Every instinct told him this thing was an enemy, and male—a monster come to burn the *ko'* and trample the children to death.

Massaaku. Kill it, kill it, kill it now.

As he entered the room, the Slaver's bottomless black eyes found the Tarka prince waiting. A cold wind seemed to blow through Lan Mak'Kona's space suit as the long, lean snout turned toward him.

It is here, Dominus. A snarl revealed twin rows of needle-like fangs. *We await your pleasure.*

The second beast moved faster, bearing its rider down the ramp at a light-footed trot that made the Tarka's stomach clench. This Slaver had a brindled hide, his flesh speckled with white and black, his eyes ruby red. He did not speak immediately, fixing Lan instead with an intent stare.

He felt the impact like a physical blow, as if someone had suddenly slapped the back of his crest with an open palm. Despite himself Lan opened his jaws and bellowed rage at the brindled rider, throwing back his arms to expand his chest to full capacity. The sound within his own helmet was deafening. The beasts on the floor before him crouched lower, cringing away.

Leave him for me.

Lan looked up to see the velvety black steed descend in a bound, her huge foreclaws gouging the deck as she landed. Her master sat light in the saddle, his body black as midnight, his throat encircled by a natural band of pure white hairs. He carried no staff or tools of any kind. The high arching dome of his forehead was encircled by a band of rusting red iron. In the center of that band the Tarka recognized a human cruciform symbol. He had never been more powerfully reminded that this Cross was an implement of torture, the scaffold upon which a god had died.

Here the emblem was inverted, the crossbar low instead of high.

The two henchmen eased back, their mounts sinking into a crouch as the master of the ship rode forward. Eyes as cold as the lightless void turned upon the Tarka. Lan Mak'Kona flinched from those bottomless depths, words shriveling on his tongue.

Hello, lizard. The voice was elegant, cruel—amused. *I have come for my gift.*

Lan pointed to the packing crate in the far corner. "There," he said aloud—fighting the urge to run to it. "I sealed him in." He thrust out his chest. "To keep him safe."

Ah, yesssss. It was a long, satisfied sigh of relief and satisfaction. *Yes, very good.* The slaver leaped lightly from the saddle, landing beside the box. Long, splayed black fingers passed over the metal surface, caressing it with naked avarice. The lips rose in a twin sneer of feral satisfaction.

Five of the beasts surrounding the Tarka broke off, joining the Deacon beside his prize. As if in sudden, silently unanimous agreement all five of them moved together, bodies shifting into position around the heavy crate; two on either side lifted the corners with their massive paws, while the fifth slid beneath the box and pressed upward, taking the center of the burden onto her back.

He turned and swung back into his saddle, following the five as they carried his prisoner up the ramp into his ship. Boldly Lan Mak'Kona stepped forward.

"What of my payment, *massaako*?" he demanded. "What of the ransom I was promised?"

The black master did not turn.

Kill this thing, the Deacon said—addressing his underlings with a casually broadcast thought. *Its brain is too jumbled to penetrate. Strip the ship of slaves and salvage—what you find is yours.*

Lan Mak'Kona shivered at the note of delectation that crept into the voice. That voice held the tone of a keenly and long-anticipated pleasure soon to come as it said: *I am not to be disturbed.*

I will be...reading.

✳ ✳ ✳

Hurry, little one. The whisper was low and urgent. *We must make haste.*

Ezz'in turned his head, looking away from the shoal of broken ships with a start. "I am sorry. I have never...been outside before." He spoke into the tinny

163

confines of his suit, not daring to broadcast the words. The Liir had his own ways of hearing. "I am not really a spacer."

Ishii cruised past him in the dark, regarding him with a gelid eye. The Liir was in his element here, a graceful and deadly aquatic predator finally freed from the chains of artificial gravity. Ezz'in tilted his head, marvelling at this mechanical beauty, even as he quailed at the destructive power of the suit—here in the void it flowed and pulsed like a sea blossom, spreading its poisonous tendrils in the tide. Now the Liir hovered beside him, tentacles entwining his body to gather him up, and the Hiver locked his mouth tight against a rising squeal of terror.

Like a bundle of dry twigs, he thought helplessly, feeling those coils close around him. He would break me just like a—

Do not be afraid. The words were both a reassurance and a command; the imperative flowed into his body like narcotic smoke. Ezz'in gasped, limbs going lax; he lost his grip on the hull of the Mirror and the Liir reeled him in close.

The Hiver stared goggle-eyed out through the slit of his visor as Ishii flexed his powerful body, the manoeuvring jets of his battlesuit giving him thrust; the two of them swooped silently through the void, heading for the upper hull. As they cleared the prow of the Mirror, Ezz'in felt his hearts grow icy with dread.

He tilted his head back and politely tapped the Liir's chest with one digit. "Excuse me? Please?" he asked. "Forgive me if I am mistaken, but—is that not a second cruiser?" He hesitated. "And a third?"

Yes. There are more Suul'ka than we had planned. The Liir's mental voice was grim.

Ezz'in was silent for a moment. Hanging in the void, he turned and deliberately looked over the ship which now clung parasitically to the remains of the Jade Mirror, appraising it quickly with an expert eye.

"Could we—go in up there?" He extended his forepaw tentatively.

You know best, steelsinger.

The Liir turned and slid like a shadow over the enemy hull, keeping to the darkness and casually avoiding its portals as he moved. As they flowed over the surface, the Hiver found himself making a mental catalogue of the bits and pieces. The ship's thorax was armed with Tarkasian weapons, taken from some derelict ship. Seeing the nose of a gamma warhead protruding from a tube of a missile launcher, Ezz'in shook his head—the arms might have been taken from this very battlefield. Despite himself he clucked disapprovingly at the poorly joined seams where the weapons had been welded into place. Brutal in battle, perhaps—but it would never hold.

"Garbage," he said primly, to no one.

The Liir's mental whisper was amused. *Quiet, steelsinger. There are others who hear.*

Ezz'in laid back his antenna apologetically.

Ishii slowed. *This is a place that opens.*

The small Hiver twisted, turning to confront the assault shuttle of the enemy ship. It was an ugly thing, a saucer-disk girded round with massive thorns of rusting steel, mounted on a flimsy gantry above the command center. He scanned the surface for a grip and reached out, seeking a purchase. At last he hooked his forelimbs through a pair of rounded rungs. The Liir's tentacles withdrew slowly, releasing him to find his footholds. Ezz'in locked himself down, clinging with all four lower limbs.

Father needs me, he said, steadying himself. *My brothers need me.* He reached for his chest pack, taking out his tools. The design of the hatch was very simple. It was meant to be dropped open when the disk entered a planetary atmosphere. The hinged gate would form a protective sheath, and allow the warheads within to be fired clear of the vessel. There could be three or four of them aboard, perhaps a few kilotons a piece. Of little use against an enemy ship, but devastating to a domed city.

The engineer within him shook his head in grudging respect for the ugly efficiency of the device. He placed the end of his pry bar beneath a poorly fitted plate of metal and gave the Liir a signal. Invisible hands took the lever and peeled the panel free silently, sending the old rivets adrift. Ezz'in cocked his head, looking into the black pit of the exposed crawlspace, and quickly levered himself into it.

Wriggling, he thrust his narrow shoulders into the nest of wires, his chelae quivering with disgust. All of it was dead, useless, connected to nothing—this whole hull section had been torn like the armour from a dead warrior and welded in place, its old functions lost in the process. He had to use all his strength to force his way through the mess, hauling himself limb over limb into the rapidly narrowing gap with nothing but his helmet light to guide him.

At last he expelled his breath, flattening his abdomen, and gave himself a final push. He was wedged solid now into the gap between inner and outer hull, and finally he could see the cables, bound with red insulation and humming with life. They coiled just inches beyond the farthest reach of his forelimbs, running through a hole in the curving wall below him to the control panel within.

Hissing frustration, he thought longingly of the pry-bar he had left with the Liir. No time to return for it now. He would have to improvise. He looked down at his chest, swiftly running through the inventory of tools, and finally pulled out the one solution he liked the least.

At least it would be quick.

He polarized his visor and took a deep breath. The torch ignited in his hand, a long blue tongue of liquid oxygen and fuel mingling into a jet of flame; instantly a nest of old wires wilted and melted into a blackened clump at its touch, retreating from the heat. Ezz'in winced and turned the torch toward the live cables, increasing the feed. A silent cyclone of blue fire whirled into the narrow gap. The cables twisted like snakes in the blast and swiftly parted, the live ends arcing for a moment with a fat white pop of electricity.

He cut the torch, wriggling desperately to back out of the breech. All around him the wires had begun to smoulder. The clumsy seal of the lower hull plate had burned through, and the ship's atmosphere was leaking into the crawlspace. The dead plastic and rubber came alive with the touch of oxygen, writhing as it blistered and burned.

Trapped and struggling in the smouldering nest, he nevertheless held silent as the melted mass of copper and steel began to eat its way through his suit. *Open the doors*, he thought, desperately hoping the Liir would hear him...

He felt the shock go through the wall, the thudding impact as the hatches were torn open, warheads tumbling free into vacuum, and the disk's atmosphere vented into space. Instantly the conflagration around him died, and Ezz'in yanked his limbs free of the charred tangle. He extricated himself quickly, wriggling and tugging against a thousand snags, and thinking with every one: *dead. Dead. This would have been my tomb.*

At last he emerged into the refreshingly wholesome danger of the open void, and found the Liir waiting, holding the hatch plate in its coils. Wordlessly Ezz'in crept past the last of the old warheads, with a superstitious shiver of disgust as his belly brushed the curving surface. He sidled through the ruptured deck cautiously and into the interior of the disk. Ishii followed, drawing the gate closed behind them.

After the narrow space between walls, the interior of the shuttle seemed almost cavernous, a black yawning pit. Ezz'in clung to the wall, searching for the control panel, and finally found it along the curving wall. He braced his hind legs and worked swiftly to re-route the power, patching the cable to seal the old hatch and restore the atmosphere.

A flickering red glow appeared in the ceiling above, and a surge of artificial gravity suddenly seized him; Ezz'in stumbled and fell, toppling over before he could adjust his legs. Something heavy crashed into the deck beside him, and he turned to find himself facing an open maw, jaws spread wide to crush his face.

The Hiver shrilled in terror and rolled to the side. A second crash followed the first, and then a fusillade of momentous thuds, as if someone had fired a heavy gun—he cringed as the remaining five corpses rained down around him, tumbling from freefall and slamming into the reactivated deck.

The Liir settled to the ground more gracefully, descending onto its steel tentacles slowly. *Do not be afraid,* it whispered. *They cannot harm you.*

Ezz'in picked himself up carefully and looked down at the Ripper on the floor at his feet. The hairy limbs had locked in the moment of its death agony, and the jaws gaped wide for a breath that would never come. Its eyes had burst from the sockets and frozen solid.

Fighting the urge to empty his thorax, he turned and stumbled toward the control panel. He had never killed an enemy before—not even by decompression. It was not as pleasant as he had hoped.

I must leave you now, steelsinger. The Liir was moving through the far side of the shuttle. With an invisible touch it opened the seal and flowed soundlessly into the narrow chute beyond; the hulking steel shape slipped down the corridor and disappeared into darkness. *I am needed elsewhere.*

Ezz'in tilted his head in acknowledgment. "I will seal the door behind you," he said aloud. He took up his instruments, looking over the hodgepodge mess of soldered wire and cross-routed controls, and shook his head in revulsion.

Garbage.

There was much work to do.

* * *

He did not use his Hand to open the box. They were too clumsy for the task. He would not risk his treasure to a crude claw. Dismissed, the women ambled to their respective corners. He removed the saddle from his Alpha, and freed her to tend to animal concerns. She marked his thighs with her velvet muzzle and stretched luxuriantly, extending her punchclaws and flexing her spine in a long, low curve. The others rose and moved aside as she nosed among them, searching the offal for an adequate bone. When at last she flung herself to the deck, taking her accustomed place nearest to him, she held a gnawed pelvis between her paws.

He turned away, suppressing a snarl of irritation. He was not a woman, to be content with trifles. Life was short—too short to gnaw bare bones while others stripped the meat. Increasingly his duties chafed him. He no longer cared to harvest and salvage. He was weary of the void, and of serving as an errand boy. But his weariness went far deeper than this: he had grown impatient with life itself. With the Vigil. With Greatfather—even with Communion.

He was past the fourth season, and soon he would end. He wanted some treasure of his own, to take with him into the dark. He was too old to drink all he knew from Greatfather's teat. Too old for common knowledge, and narcotic rites. Let his sons dream of serving the Great Masters. He was an old Zuul. He had given all his years serving the lesser master. He was done.

For years he had possessed nothing that was hidden. No secret, no riches but the shreds left to glean from exhausted slaves. He had lost his taste for worthless scrap, thrown to the troops when they were ripped to the core. He had been weak, stupid to wait.

The strong do not wait for plunder to be given. They take what is theirs by right of strength, he thought. He clenched his fists: he was no longer such a fool. He had found this strange and precious jewel in the wild lands, a mystery shared by a very rare and special breed of slaves. And against all orders, in defiance of Greatfather himself, he had taken their secret, and kept it for his own.

He nudged a switch with one of his wives, casually flicking it upward with her claw. Light spilled over his shoulders. He turned toward the sheet of shining metal he had mounted on the wall, regarding himself in the polished surface.

"*Daaaaay-khoen,*" he growled aloud, shaping the foreign sound with his tongue. His lips peeled back over his teeth, smiling, and he caressed the creature in the mirror with his paws. No, he could not speak it properly. The word in his mind could not be pronounced by his own mouth. But in this autumn year, he had become what no other Zuul had been before: a creature with a name.

Let the others drag their captives to the chamber hunting for trifles. A shield, a circuit, a weapon, a word for "master"—what were these things to him? The Inquisitors searched tirelessly for power. In the end, who was made stronger? Only Greatfather. What little they could keep for themselves was only what He deemed of no worth. Never would He permit them such riches as the Deacon called his own.

Deus misereatur. He heard the slave in the box stir, its mind rousing from a painful slumber. The Deacon licked his teeth at the unfamiliar words in that delicious mind. He let them trickle through his trove of secrets, sifting them over the pretty pebbles until he understood. "*May God have mercy,*" the slave said.

The Zuul smiled and turned toward the crate. He never tired of this game. *Noli timere, Cai Rui. Do not be afraid.*

God is dead—but I am here.

* * *

Lan Mak'Kona moved slowly, and kept the crates behind him. The thick-bodied females followed, slinking forward in the dim light. As he edged toward the exit, he felt the tremor of the deck beneath his feet and turned in time to see that two of them had circled around behind. Now they moved in, shoulder to shoulder, to block his retreat, panting steam between laughing jaws.

He whirled quickly, and dodged the first tentative paw as one of the beasts batted at his swinging tail. The riders moved in closer, radiating cruel amusement. The Tarka's own tongue flickered, as he looked back one last time. His hand closed on the hilt of the war hammer as the beasts crouched low, gathering their muscles into a set of massive springs.

They came in high, twin leaps timed together to rend his body between their outstretched claws. Fast as they came, the Tarka was faster; his powerful legs carried him over the assault in a single bound. With his free hand he caught the lip of the highest crate in the stack above him, and with one heave he had pulled his whole body into a turn, flipping tail over heels to land lightly at the top of the pile.

The two Rippers crashed chest and chest, colliding with an angry snarl on the floor below. In that moment of graceless confusion Lan Mak'Kona hurled the hammer sidearm, with all his strength, into the low dome of an ursine skull. It connected with a low *crak!* of kinetic impact and a bright splash of blood; the creature dropped, paws twitching. He double-tapped his fingertips and the hammer whistled back toward him, circling in the gloom to find his grip in the space of a second.

Mak'Kona's tongue rattled laughter as the pale rider gave an angry squall of pain. Swiftly he threw his weapon to his tail grip and launched himself further into the rafters, brachiating palm over palm through the pipes and cables to the far wall. He took shelter in a high niche and raised his wristband, keying the jewels in rapid sequence with a whispered prayer: "*Sardomo*, don't fail me now!"

The last key flashed rapidly, and he heard a faint crackle of electricity. He looked down; the Rippers crouched hungrily beneath him, eyes shimmering in the low light. Lan whirled on the ledge and tail-whipped the hammer into their midst viciously; the beasts scattered in avoidance, and he leaped down into the circle, catching the hilt as it rebounded.

The enemy roared outrage. Three of them moved together, coordinating a strike high and low. The Tarka bounced over the dual lower assault and met the single upper charge in mid-air, bringing up his legs and tail to grapple. The female wrapped her forelegs around his body, jaws snapping at the faceplate of his helm. Lan drove his fist repeatedly into her throat, searching for a vulnerable windpipe beneath the shaggy coat. As the two of them rolled, shrieking and kicking, the other females snarled and snapped and tried to catch a stray piece of him in their jaws.

His opponent broke free and leaped away. In that moment he was open, trapped on his back; he turned swiftly and made a breaking roll to the left, dodging just a split second before the pale rider stabbed his glowing iron staff down into the place where his face had been.

With uncanny grace his roll evolved into a handstand flip, and the Tarka gained his feet at a run, hammer still in hand. Looking toward the exit, he found the brindled rider and its mount waiting to intercept him, their red eyes gleaming.

The slaver put a paw to his forehead, his mount kneeling low. Lan Mak'Kona stumbled to the side, struck as if by a physical blow. But even as the Imperator snarled triumph, his Tarka foe unwound his steely haunches in a final leap. Lan rose high into the air, whirling his heavy weapon overhead. The slaver's triumph turned to terror as the Tarka descended with the hammer held high. The rider turned and threw himself clear just an instant before a savage two-handed blow split his saddle, and snapped the spine of his steed like a rotten bough.

Lan stood on the mound of the fallen corpse and turned toward the oncoming *masaaku*, spreading his arms wide. As the remaining ten beasts crept nearer, ears flattened in rage and fear, he filled his lungs and bellowed out a saurian roar of challenge.

The creatures shuddered in reaction and shrank back for a moment. When they came on they came slowly, edging toward him in a low defensive crouch. He backed away, letting them come, until he felt the bulkhead looming behind him.

He was trapped now. They approached him cautiously, looking for an opening. Lan gathered himself and roared one last time, filling the hold with the thunder of his bellow as the two slavers and their women closed in for the kill.

All in all, he felt he had done well. They were all very far from their ramp at this moment...and he had provided more than enough noise and distraction to cover the stealthy rattle of deck plates, and the gentle click of ignition.

The slavers had only a split second to turn before the Hivers opened fire, and the hold was awash in a sea of flame.

* * *

"What is your order, *Kaan Dai*? We await your command."

"Wait for a sign. There is time." With a herculean act of will, Sara Mak'Kona held her stance on the bridge. She stood tall, one hand on the back of the Amtara's chair, the other at her side, and studied the new enemy cruiser with cold deliberation. "The point defence is likely gauss," she said lightly, inviting speculation.

The old man dipped his crest. "*Y'an*. Probably the best they have."

"Nonetheless, a great many guns." Her eyes were cool yellow, pupils narrow with thought. "And many turrets of mid-size, as well. Even a Hiver does not have such terrible jaws."

"At least four on the command section alone, Lac Tar—there may be six, but it is difficult to see." The tactical officer provided the count dispassionately, looking up from her display. "Another two amidships, perhaps a third on the tail."

"The largest turrets also concern me." Her tail flicked irritably. "Their engines have a fusion signature, *ne*?"

"Yes, Lac Tar."

"Perhaps some old cannons," the Amtara offered. "Plasma. Such guns would keep good company with the rest of their arms. These ships are cobbled together out of flotsam, *Lac Tar*."

"So it seems." Her pale yellow eyes slowly began to tinge with red. "Well, we shall roll the dice. Helm—maintain cloak. Calculate the maximum range of such a weapon—we will stay well beyond it." Her tongue flickered. "We will let our missiles do their work. When we break silence, tell the *Kal War'ko* to cripple our main target. All other ships will target the escort exclusively. All turrets." Her pupils shifted to daggers, fixed on the hammerhead cruisers. "I want those ugly *doku* dead."

* * *

Ishii slid into the dark passage, narrow and cramped. The ship was an iron reef, a winding labyrinth of tunnels and empty hollows. All around him, it pulsed with obscene life. He pulsed with it, imitating the sound and shape of its united mind with effortless horror.

They were made of hunger and pain, these *Suul'ka*. He could feel the cold current of their lives tearing through him, the constant dagger-stab of empty belly and the shrieking, never-ending howl of hate-love-fear. Within his suit he shivered.

So alone, he thought. *All together, all alone.*

A bright flare of energy moved toward him in the maze, a seething cauldron of anger embedded in the red spiral flow of primal, feral need. Its mind sent a savage growl of command toward him as it came, hostile and cold. *You have left your post. Dominus will be angry. There will be pain for ALL.*

Ishii flinched—the thought carried with it a bolt of remembered agony, inflicted casually by one stronger-than-self. He struck back without thinking, without warning, lashing out with the rod that the little steelsinger had given him. The pry bar whistled around the corner and speared the enemy through the brain pan, putting a merciful end to its life of anger, fear, and pain.

Even as the bright hot star of the thing's rage-mind went dark, its red body-mind rushed toward him with a roar. They rounded the corner and came for him together, snapping and snarling, enraged and grieving for their father, lover, master, food-giver. Shaking with pity and revulsion, he seized each of them one by one and crushed them to death, trying to silence their dying yips and howls before others could hear. By the time he had finished both his suit and his mind were leaking. He keened into the last thimble of empty space within himself as the last body dropped to the bulkhead, its red heat slowly slipping away into cold darkness.

Within those mounds of empty flesh, bright quick lights were already stirring. Swiftly and ruthlessly he extinguished them, pinching out every pinprick of greedy light. With chilly efficiency he poured his body next into the bridge compartment, leaving the master there nailed to his chair with the hunting rod, his mother-slaves broken in pools of blood.

Ishii lifted the spear of steel and turned to swim deeper into the labyrinth, although every part of him longed to flee. The song of hate and fear was rising, spinning in the belly of this ship to a fever-pitched, symphonic hurricane. He must move through those winds and into the eye of the storm, toward that glistening pearl of cold black that lay at the heart of this maze.

The others were merely symptoms. Their leader was the disease. And with every life he devoured, he grew stronger. Even now Ishii could feel the cancerous tendrils of his mind sinking into new flesh, cutting into the living tissue of memory like razor-lipped remoras.

Somewhere in the darkness, a soul began to bleed.

19 | THE DEACON

Pitch black. Cai Rui stirred and fought his way back to consciousness, trying to straighten his body. He was folded in half, his knees drawn up to his chest, in a confined space. He raised a hand, exploring his prison. A cube of vacuum insulation. Perhaps a meter and a half square. The distinctive hexagonal nap of Hiver manufacture.

Deus misereatur, he thought. *They've put me in a damn packing crate.*

The cold mind sliced into his thoughts effortlessly. *Do not be afraid, Cai Rui,* it said. *God is dead—but I am here.*

Instantly his hand went to his throbbing temple, as if to fend off that touch. It was close. Very close.

Hello, monster, he offered, forcing the words into a conversational tone. *We meet again.*

The clunk and rattle of the hasps sounded, and he cringed from the sudden light that poured down into the box. Blinded, numb with hampered circulation, he felt the crate tip over and tumble him unceremoniously out onto a metal deck.

The creature stood over him, a silhouette against the light. It bent down, obsidian eyes gleaming with the reflective sheen of a nocturnal predator, and regarded him with luminous curiosity. The wiry frame was laced with ropes of whipcord muscle and covered with a coat of short, glossy black hair; its breath was hot and fetid with corruption. The skull bulged high over beetled brows, and on its forehead it wore an iron crown.

"Demon." Cai Rui choked out the word in disbelief.

Yesss. The muzzle wrinkled in cruel amusement, revealing twin rows of gleaming teeth. The black hand descended, its spidery fingers spread wide. *Welcome to Hell.*

For a desperate split second he tried to escape, turning to grind his aching cheek against the foul, sticky floor. But the beast had him in its iron grip, one paw wrapped tight around his throat, the other clamped palm-down over his temple, and the pain lanced deep into his skull.

"Demons are the servants of the Adversary, Cai Rui." Father Tourneau stood at the window, looking out into the gardens; sun and tropical heat poured into the room through the open shutters. "They are the angels who were cast from heaven, along with Lucifer, at the beginning of time."

"But why did God create *angelus malos*?" His own voice rang tinny in his ears, thin and high.

"'*Diabolus enim et alii daemones a Deo quidem natura create sunt boni, sed ipsi per se facti sunt mali.*'" The old man quoted the decree effortlessly, and the boys in the room looked down at their data pads to see the link. "The Devil and the other demons were created by God with a nature that was good, my son—as we ourselves were created with a nature that was good. But they have made themselves evil, as we too stain ourselves with evil at their urging: 'by the envy of the Devil, death came into the world.'"

Cai Rui looked down at his tablet, and used the stylus to bring up a link to Isaiah. *"How are you fallen from heaven, Lucifer who rose in the morning? How have you fallen to the earth, who wounded all the nations? You said in your heart, 'I will ascend into heaven, I will exalt my throne above the stars of God, I will sit in the mountain of the covenant...I will be like the most High.'..."*

For a moment it was there, and it seemed that he understood something very important and deeply true. Then the thought was torn away, with a brutal yank and a gush of pain and confusion, and Cai Rui cried out aloud.

"No!" His fingers curled in a useless spasm, as if they could somehow clutch the fleeing thought. With a hollow sense of despair, he searched his own mind, trying to find the wounded place and the memory now missing. It was impossible; he could only feel a raw sense of violation.

Fallen from heaven, the Deacon mused. The gaunt hand tightened around his throat. *Yes. I will know...more of this.*

* * *

The creatures were tough. Yzeket had to admit that much. This one would not lay still and be done. Her body was a scorched wreck; her sisters and mate lay dead or dying. Still she crawled, claw over claw, to escape the flames. He put the barrel of his scattergun to her skull and destroyed her, the shot echoing through the burning cargo bay.

"That was the last, Father." He turned. "All clear."

Chezokin churred a low thrum of acceptance. "Regroup. This one was easy." He turned to the Tarka. "Thanks to Lan Mak'Kona."

The young Prince straightened and took up his weapon. Here and there his suit was blackened by a gust of fire, but for the most part he had kept well clear. "I will go first," he said boldly. "Their slaver tricks do not work on me."

Chezokin inclined his head and offered the ramp with his extended hand. "As you wish, Var Lando." As the Tarka bounded lightly up the ramp, Chezokin peeled the sheathes from his shining blades. When he turned to Ykezet, his voice was warm and conspiratorial. "We have a few tricks of our own, *ru-rek*. Do we not?"

The warrior rasped laughter and raised the barrel of his flamethrower. The hold of the Mirror was awash with choking clouds of ash, the stink of charred hair and meat. "Yes, my Prince."

There was a cry from above; Chezokin turned without a word and charged, galloping up the ramp and bursting up into the enemy hold. Yzeket followed, the rest of his *rek* following close behind in a clattering mass.

It was a large compartment, lit with haphazard beam lamps bolted to the walls in strange places. Even as the warrior oriented himself in the room, he turned to see that the Tarka was already down. They had fallen upon the young Prince instantly, like a pack of beasts. A snarling, tearing clot of animals held his four limbs fast, and another mounted slaver had speared him through the shoulder of his suit with a long barb of iron.

Chezokin did not hesitate. As he achieved the top of the ramp he hurtled forward in a thundering steel-shod rush. He closed the distance in the space of a second, and lashed out with a savage twin strike. The rider fell in two halves upon the deck in an explosion of blood; his mount stood a moment longer, jetting ichor from the stump of her neck, before she dropped beside him.

Chezokin waded in further, catching a third beast on the backswing to cut a deep gash in her flank; she howled and leaped aside, releasing her grip on the Tarka's arm. The blood-spattered blades turned and darted forward, stabbing toward the unprotected eyes of a fourth foe and slashing at the muzzle of the fifth. As the Rippers flinched back, the Prince whirled and struck out with a double kick of his rear legs. He caught one a heavy blow to the head. As she lay stunned on the deck he trampled her, pulping flesh and bone beneath his heels.

Yzeket turned away and scanned the room carefully. It was an open cargo bay, crammed with the broken remnants of many ships. Hull plating and armour had been cut into sections and stacked against the walls. Turrets and tubes were strewn over the floor and standing in tall, unstable piles around the room. In the blink of an eye he recognized the red lasers ripped from the point defence array of a Kherz'a cruiser. There were engine parts as well, and other things he could not recognize.

He clashed annoyance. It was a claustrophobic, untidy warren of theft and destruction; it would be a nightmare to dig their enemies out of this mess. He whistled to his *rek*, urging them to form a defensive phalanx.

A flicker of movement caught the corner of his eye. Yzeket turned and opened the cocks of his thrower, sending a long plume of flame down a twisting corridor of jagged debris. Something shrank back into the darkness.

It was an eerie feeling when he lost control of his limbs. He shut off the valve, letting the plume die down to a guttering tongue at the weapon's muzzle. The creatures were slinking toward him quietly, their mirror eyes shining in the light of his flame. For some reason he no longer thought that this was a bad thing. The rider had become a russet prince, astride a fine and loyal steed. He held out an imperious hand, and the *ru-rek* turned back toward his Father.

The Hiver warriors opened their throwers full bore, bathing Chezokin in a sudden torrent of screeching flame. The white Prince straightened, his body a dim shadow in the midst of a hellish inferno, and turned to face them.

Some part of Yzeket quailed as the great body turned and surged back across the deck. Chezokin strode without pause through the screaming firestorm, moving with purpose through a white-hot wall. He emerged on the far side, his whole body glowing the incandescent pale yellow of hot coals, striding easily as if the firestorm were no more than a summer breeze.

Yzeket felt the Slaver's will crumble at the sight. A surge of the creature's fear rolled through him, and he lifted his gun to fire a shot into his Father's back, a broad useless cough of flechette ammunition that rebounded from Chezokin's armour like rain on a stone.

At last his hands and ears were his own, and hastily Yzeket lowered his weapons. He threw his head back and keened a long howl of grief and shame. Only years of training kept his weapons in his hands; he had an almost unbearable urge to cast them aside and throw himself onto his own blades.

My Prince. My own Prince. They made me—

Chezokin struck, spearing his enemy through the belly and lifting him from his woman's back like a fish on a gaff. The low vibration of his voice set the floor to shaking in his rage.

"I am the *Father* of the *Burning Sun.*" With every other word he gave the Slaver a sadistic shake for emphasis. The little monster yowled in pain, its women cowering as Chezokin loomed over them. "My sons cannot *hurt* me, *massaaku*. But I? I can hurt *you.*"

Yzeket reopened the bore of his flamethrower. Beside him his brothers did the same, setting the Rippers to the torch in an ecstasy of loathing. The vermin scrambled away, turning to leap and scrabble into the mountains of trash; he lifted the scattergun and fired, knocking them back to the floor to be burned alive.

He would offer no mercy cut to any that he killed. For the present...it pleased him to hear them scream.

* * *

"*Daiko!*" The woman's voice was thick with excitement. "There is fire aboard the Jade Mirror!"

Sara raised her fist with a shout of joy. "There is our sign. Attack!"

The Amtara rose from his chair, and his command reverberated across the decks of all four vessels like a crack of thunder. Hundreds of hearts began to pound, galvanized by the rumble of his voice into battle fury. "Strike group *Thagroku*, drop cloak! *Kal War'ko*—target the first cruiser with your torpedoes. *Garanu*, *Ao'thaak*—missiles on the two guardians. All guns. FIRE!"

The warning drum sounded, a single reverberating beat as the cloak disengaged. Sara's heart stopped as the two sleek Tarka assault cruisers materialized in battle formation, poised at the outside limit of plasma range. *Habas'ku* fired her own long-range missile, sending a fusion-tipped arrow streaking off through the dark. *Garanu* and *Ao'thaak* turned their tubes onto the pair of *masaaku* strike ships, unleashing a missile to either side. *Kal War'ko* lumbered between them, its belly heavy with torpedoes; the first pulsar torp launched toward its quarry, soaring through the void toward the salvage vessel. A pair of missiles followed within seconds, leaving a propulsion trail as they flew.

For a seemingly endless moment, the weapons winged toward their targets unimpeded. The four Tarka cruisers moved in slowly, engines at lowest power. Then the distant barrels began to flicker as enemy gunners engaged the incoming fire. There was a sudden bright flash of fusion as one of the missiles detonated well short of the target, and then a second. Sara hissed frustration—one of the two Slaver ships was completely untouched.

"*Massaaku* returning fire, *daiko!*" the pilot shouted.

A bright hot explosion suddenly lit up the darkness; two warheads had struck the enemy amidships. The cruiser's belly section exploded, the innards of the ship blasted into vacuum. Only a bare spine of steel held the bridge and engine together.

Sara pumped her fist with brutal satisfaction. "Yes! *Kala du'maas!*"

"Ha!" The Amtara's snarl was contemptuous. "They are nothing but rust."

"Enemy firing turrets, *Kaan Dai!* They've turned their guns on *Ao'thaak!*"

Golden yellow bolts tore through the darkness, a nine-fold pulse of energy from each of the two enemy ships. Sara's eyes widened, joy vanishing in the space of a heartbeat. *Too fast! Much too fast!* By some trick of fate both *massaaku* cruisers had fired their large turrets at once, the one unleashing its salvo just an instant before the section was lost. Now a double barrage of amber death crossed the battlefield in the space of an instant, converging on the forward sections of *Ao'thaak.*

The cruiser staggered as the first bolts struck, one after the other punching through her armoured hull like fists through paper. From the bridge Sara watched in horror as the second trio of shots followed into the cavernous hole the first had made; with the third the bridge exploded.

The decapitated ship shuddered in the void, trembling with impact and bleeding energy and gas into space. Helpless, it keeled over onto its side, and took the second incoming salvo in its belly. Another fireball bloomed as the ship's magazine cooked off, taking all sections fore of the engine with it; *Kal War'ko* veered away, her armoured flank licked by the burning cloud of debris.

Sara whirled on the tactical officer. "What the suffering hell was that?"

The woman shook her head helplessly. "Better than our best, daiko! And by far. I have never seen the like. It must be a new heavy fusion cannon—we have no weapon of such power!"

Swearing savagely, Sara wheeling on her Amtara. "Don't just stand there, fool! Get these ships moving! We must close quickly—those guns will tear us apart!"

The old man tilted his head with a wink. "Why yes, Lac Tar," he said mildly. "Of course." He engaged his wristband, sending out his command roar to the remaining fleet. "*Garanu, Kal War'ko*—full speed! Finish off the Slavers with a slashing charge. That is an order!"

"Yes, *Kaan Dai!*" The voices of both captains answered in chorus as their engines engaged. Sara clung tightly to the Amtara's chair as the ship suddenly accelerated, hurtling through space into the open jaws of the enemy. As they approached, she saw *Kal War'ko's* tracking torpedo strike its target, crashing into the *massaaku* salvage ship with a crippling flash. The engine and the lights of the bridge went dead as the torp's EMP went through the hull.

Do not worry, my friends, she thought silently. *We are coming. We will not leave you alone in the dark.*

* * *

Cai Rui felt the impact, a rolling shock that trembled through the bulkhead beneath his body. The overhead light flickered and went out.

The Deacon growled, a low canine sound of uncertainty. He looked away, over his shoulder, and a heavy shape moved in the darkness. Cai Rui heard the slow click of claws over the floor, and the sound of a machine engaged. A mangled confusion of guttural sounds poured from a hidden speaker somewhere in the room. Distracted, the black Ripper barked answer to the chorus of howling voices.

Cai Rui closed his eyes, feeling the blood run from his nostril down the side of his face. Weak and tentative, nonetheless he reached out gently with his mind, touching the shadow that hung over him with its talons at his throat.

"—cannot move, *Dominus*," the voice was saying. Filtered through the Deacon's consciousness, the strange words were clear. "Our claw-ships have been attacked; one fortress is burning. The heretics have lost but one cruiser, and they are coming in for a kill..."

"Launch our boarding pods," the Deacon snarled. "We will take them with imperators."

"We cannot, *Dominus!* The slaves have broken free—did you not hear? We are being boarded ourselves. There is fire in the stomach of the ship. The bridge does not respond. We have sealed the engine room to hold them off. We await your—"

Suddenly the long snout whipped back toward him, eyes blazing bright in the dark. *You DARE!?*

Pain ripped through him, a lancing flash that shot through his skull and into his body like lightning. Cai Rui caught at the bony wrist at his throat, his body locked into a helpless galvanic arc of agony, his mouth opened into a silent scream. For an endless moment the pain rocketed through him, tearing at his body and mind; when at last it stopped he sobbed for breath, his skin dripping with cold sweat. His flesh was trembling uncontrollably, jumping on his bones as if an electric current were passing through it.

Never, never touch me, slave. The voice was saturated with rage. *Never.*

Cai Rui opened his eyes and let the tears of reaction roll down his cheeks, licking the blood from his own cheek. "Never," he gasped.

The skeletal hand tightened, and the black palm slapped down onto his temple again. The enemy mind plunged into him like a jagged knife, twisting back and forth, seeking.

Ambush, the black voice whispered. *Sneak attack. Secret. Plans.* The Ripper dropped the words like depth charges into Cai Rui's consciousness, sniffing for the answering flash of guilt. *Where is it, slave? What have you done?*

Face ground flat into the reeking filth of the deck, his temples pounding with steady pain, bleeding and shaking...Cai Rui began to laugh. His chest shook. The breath hissed between his torn lips with a taste of copper.

"Wouldn't you like to know?" he gasped aloud, helpless with laughter. "Wouldn't you *love* to know?"

A sudden surge of emotion rose in him, a bittersweet cocktail of pride, anger, and loving admiration. *Whatever she is doing,* he thought, *I hope she wins...*

The Deacon snapped angrily at the thought, sinking its icy claw into his brain. *Oh? And who is "she"?*

✳ ✳ ✳

"Very good," Ezz'in chirped softly to himself, covering the spliced wires with a twist of sealant tape. He tapped the keys; the docking array responded with a heavy crunch of vacuum bolts and a squeal of metal. The shuttle trembled in its cradle, floor shaking beneath his feet.

He looked up through the viewport, examining the enemy cruisers with a critical eye. The thorax of the first was still burning; its massive cannons were lost, but the hideous head still bristled with light gauss point defence and medium mass drivers. It limped into position, turning to face the oncoming Tarka, and he saw a fourth cannon mounted on the engine.

The second was intact, unscratched after the first pass and preparing to fire again. He laid back his antenna in dismay, torn by uncertainty. Which ship? Where should he strike? He was no warrior. He could not decide.

He hesitated, hands at the helm. Perhaps it would be best to wait and see. The Tarka might yet prevail. Perhaps...perhaps he would only harm his friends with clumsy interference.

Perhaps it would be best to wait and see.

***

The Hiver bent and offered its forepaw; Lan Mak'Kona reached up and took it, letting the warrior haul him to his feet. "Hurt," it said, speaking Urdu Kai, indicating his shoulder.

"Yes," he gritted. He spoke in *ri'kap-ken*. "Thank you."

"Welcome." The warrior made a circling gesture with its hand, asking him to turn. "Hold still."

Mak'Kona dropped his lids protectively as the blade rose and came down in a swift cut. The barbed staff parted with a snap, its cumbersome end clattering to the deck. The heavy iron head remained buried in the meat of his shoulder—pierced through suit, flesh and bone.

The Hiver turned his body back around and clapped his good shoulder. "Good," it said. "Cannot fix it now. Understand?"

Lan tilted his head to the side, *Hiver-yes*.

The warrior wheeled, reaching into its carry sack for a second tank of ammunition. At that moment, Lan saw the gleaming eyes in the dark.

"No!" he shouted. Vainly he reached for his hammer, but already the two beasts struck. Their heavy bodies crashed into the Hiver from the side in eerie unison, their legs moving like the gears of a strange machine. The warrior toppled under their combined mass, lashing out with his free blade to try and throw one off before he went down. Jaws closed with a crunch, rending his armour, and the massive claws rose and fell like pistons, perforating his head and thorax in an instant.

Lan hurled his hammer, dropping one of the two with a wet spatter of brains and bone. The other lifted her muzzle, festooned with phosphorescent Hiver blood. She barked a cough of animal defiance as the hilt slapped back into his open palm.

Some instinct made him half-turn at that moment, seeking a foe. A shadow flickered in his peripheral vision; he hurled himself to the side, dodging the thick body of the Ripper as she dropped from the tower of parts overhead. He barked pain at the impact as he fell, feeling the heavy iron grind in his shoulder. Bleeding afresh and hurting, he struggled clumsily to his feet.

The squat beast had risen onto its hind legs, massive paws wrapped around the length of a heavy pole-arm of her own. She shuffled toward him sidewise, shoulder first, holding the weapon at the ready; he backed away, seeking a defensive position among the wreckage.

He never saw the fourth, crouching in the shadows and waiting her chance. She attacked silently, lashing out with a low cutting swipe at his vulnerable legs in the dark. Suddenly his feet were struck out from under him by a thick paw and he crashed again onto his side, knocking a stack of scorched semiconductor coils onto himself in a tangle.

Lan rolled, trying to regain his feet. The Ripper sprang. She landed on all fours, her two forepaws driving the wind out of his chest. Her fangs descended; he brought up the hammer defensively, jamming the handle sideways between her jaws before they could close on his helm. With a cry of anguish he tried to hold her off, but his right arm had no strength. She felt the weakness and whipped her head in the same direction, forcing the handle out of his shaking grip. He twisted, trying to free the hammer for a one-handed blow, and her savage teeth snapped shut on his bad arm.

Lan Mak'Kona howled as she wrenched back and forth with the powerful muscles of her neck, tearing scale and sinew with every predatory shake of her head. He heard and felt the wet wrench and pop as bone dislocated at the shoulder. A hot gout of fluid suddenly splashed down his side; the force of her final yank sent her tumbling and scrambling off his chest, taking his arm with her.

He rolled away feebly, the hammer forgotten, reaching with a free hand toward the wound. Blood pumped over the fingers of his suit, black in the dim light. A wave of cold nausea swept over him. His head rolled back and he found himself staring up at the distant ceiling, darkness swallowing the edges of his vision in a rising tide of pain and shock.

I am sorry, Sara, he thought. Heavy lids dropped over his pupils. *I did my best.*

The last sound he heard as consciousness slipped away was the ominous creak of deck plates underfoot. The remaining Rippers were moving in for their share of a royal feast.

* * *

"Give up, stump," she hissed, tickling his ear with the tip of her tongue. "Once again, you underestimate a woman with a tail."

She held him tight, his legs pinned between her thighs and bound fast by her iron coils, his neck hyper-extended backward by a sharp-nailed grip under the jaw. Cai Rui gritted his teeth in frustration as his bones and tendons creaked under the pressure, sending shooting pain into his shoulder and back.

"Yield," he said angrily.

The Tarka girl held him for another half-second, as if to grind his nose in defeat. He heard the amused flutter of her tongue and surged up out of her clutches, his cheeks burning with emotion. She gained her feet before he could, nimble body flipping upright into a heel squat on the mat.

"Best two of three?" she said, speaking Mandarin with her strange low voice. "I never tire of beating you."

He clamped his lips shut, turning away. There was no disputing the matter. She had won fairly. To the extent that forcing him to combat her freakish body could be called fair! She wanted to learn the martial arts of his people; the abbot had commanded him to make her welcome and teach her what they studied at the school. Now she had grown fond of the Brazilian jujitsu. The style suited her. She brought down her fellow students daily, and delighted in winding humans into submission holds. Her muscular limbs had conquered him in one humiliating wrestling match after another.

In three weeks, she had become completely insufferable. Enough was enough.

"Best two out of three," he agreed grimly. "But you must catch me first."

She cocked her head, eyes gleaming green amusement. "Catch you? How hard could that be? You move like a—" She paused, searching for a word, but could not find it. "You are slow as a go'ma," she said, choosing a beast from her own planet. She imitated its sluggish crawl with her rippling hand.

He smiled. "We will see. Ready?"

She lifted her chin. "Always, human. Go on and run!"

He turned and bolted, so quick that even she was surprised. He took the court-yard steps in three bounds and shot out through the back gate, diving headfirst into the jungle. She followed swiftly, leaping up onto the high wall and launching herself into the treetops overhead. She pursued him like a gibbon, her body gliding swiftly from branch to branch as he pounded down the path on foot, leaping over tumbled stone and fallen logs on his way to the old ruins in the valley below.

In the end he burst out into a clearing, a wide plaza of old granite, its blocks heaved upward by the roots of the jungle. A dozen serene stone faces surrounded him, the ancient idols half-toppled in the mud, their vacant eyes draped with lianas and vines. She hurtled down from the high branches and landed lightly in his path, tail extended and arms spread in her combat stance.

"I have you," she said. "Fight."

He raised his fist. The first stone whistled past her shoulder, a near miss. The whoop of a second sling followed; a rock struck her shoulder with a stinging snap. A third and a fourth followed instantly, sharp impacts to the chest and hip. The Tarka dropped swiftly into a defensive crouch, bringing her forearms up to protect her head. The stones flew thick and fast, rebounding from her creamy scales like a punishing rain.

All around them the jungle was alive with the rhythmic whoop of whirling slings, a beat as steady and quick as the blades of a fan. Cai Rui held up his open hand again. The others held their fire and emerged from cover among the ruins, the slings still whirling, stones at the ready.

Sara Mak'Kona peeked out from between her hands, green eyes gleaming merriment. "Well, well. At last you show some teeth! *Kala du'maas,*" she said. "You win, human. From now on, I will speak to you with more respect."

He nodded, and offered her his hand. "Never underestimate a man without a tail."

✳ ✳ ✳

The Deacon hissed annoyance. He pushed the old memory aside impatiently, disdaining even to destroy it. *Useless,* he snarled. *That is nothing.*

Dominus. The call was muted. *Do you hear?*

He turned his head, reaching for the joined minds in the hold below. *Yes, my sons. I hear.*

Help us, Lord, they pleaded. *We are trapped. The slaves are strong.*

In one swift surge he plunged into their minds, receiving the torrent of information in the space of a second. *Yes, I see,* he mused. *A clever ploy. They have brought their own Lords into our midst.*

What shall we do? We cannot remain hidden long. The bug-things pursue us by scent...

The old Zuul reached out, extending his power to the bowels of the engine room. Unbidden, all Hands turned toward the view ports. He looked through their eyes out into the void, thinking quickly.

You must abandon the hold, he replied at last. *Move as one. One Hand at least must reach the helm and man the forward guns.*

Yes, Dominus. The wave of their relief rippled through him as they received permission to flee from the fire. *We hear and obey.*

* * *

Somewhere in the dark, metal clattered to the floor. A Hiver voice cried out. "My Prince! The enemy is escaping!"

Chezokin wheeled. "Where, my son? Do you see them?"

"There!"

The last of the Slavers skulked through a gap in the warren of rusting steel, looking back over its shoulder with eyes shining. Chezokin clattered to a halt, looking at the narrow crack. Even a warrior would never fit through such a narrow space. He shrilled in frustration and clashed his chelae in anger.

"Not so easily," he hissed. "Not this day." He turned to the warriors. "Back away. Be prepared to fire."

Obediently the *rek* danced backward, scuttling down the twisting corridor. Chezokin crossed his blades protectively and took a few steps back. He lowered his head as he ran, compacting his body, bending forward at the thorax. By the time he reached the wall he was moving at ferocious speed, and his shoulder struck the mountain of metal like a ram.

The towering stack trembled, the whole pile tilting dangerously from the blow. For a moment it rocked, raining parts from the top of the stack into the aisles below; Chezokin dug in his heels and shoved hard, then stepped back to watch it tumble over into the hold.

The toppling stack went down like a felled tree, crashing over into the next. The weight and momentum tipped the next stack over, and as those two crashed down together they caught a third, and a fourth, until half the cargo bay was falling, an ignominious landslide of garbage.

Chezokin scrambled to the top of a sliding hillock of debris, searching for his prey in the wreckage. The golden rider lay trapped under the barrel of a half demolished turret, struggling feebly to free itself from the weight that held it

187

pinned. Throughout the pile, other Rippers stirred, trying to wriggle out from under the crushing debris.

The Prince danced over the dunes of steel, stabbing and slicing the female things with his vengeful blades. The rider yowled and snarled with every blow, struggling with increasing desperation to tear himself free.

At last Chezokin stood over him, his pearl-golden eyes shining, pale armour stained with gore. "That was for my Princess," he said, bowing low over his prey. "This is for me."

The heavy blade descended, spearing the slaver's head like a melon.

Another voice rang out. "My Prince—the Tarka bleeds!"

Chezokin shook his head, scenting the air quickly. The warriors were not mistaken. Somewhere close, Lan Mak'Kona had spilled a great deal of blood.

He turned and scrambled back through the darkness, trying to find his ally in the tangle of trash. For the space of another few heartbeats, the last two survivors waited; then, safe at last, they rose and slipped quietly into the corridor, heading for the bridge.

* * *

"*Garanu*—take the lead and open fire!"

The Amtara's voice rolled over the decks. Ahead of them in the rush, the remaining assault cruiser unleashed the fury of her dumbfire missiles on approach, spitting them out rapid-fire toward her target. Within seconds the speeding swarm was closing in on the wounded enemy cruiser, and the darkness lit up with a furious chain of explosions as the slavers engaged their point defence.

Sara flinched as the *Habas'ku* passed into the range of the medium turrets. The comm howled as the close range jamming struck, the enemy ships roaring into the void to spoof the auto-tracking of weapons. The bridge gunners lifted their heads from the targeting lenses and turned toward the portals, putting the guns on manual.

From this range, the sweeping claws of the Slaver command sections were clearly visible, sporting a horrendous array of medium turrets in their open arms. Each horn of both bridges carried twin banks of three mass drivers; now they opened fire, filling the void with a bludgeoning hail of super-dense alloy spheres.

Habas'ku rang like a bell under the impact, shuddering and heeling as the onslaught tore at her armour and guns. A bright flash on the port side and the howl of decompression signalled the loss of a light turret on the nose of her ship. Sara was nearly wrenched from her feet in the two seconds it took for the Amtara to drop the vacuum shield. Life support groaned; she dropped the visor of her helm and sealed it shut. Still the *fane* burned at maximum speed, never hesitating, passing now within meters of the enemy.

The golden pulses flashed again, triple bolts of fire ripping from the heavy turrets. *Kal War'ko* in the rear took the brunt of the blow; several shots flew wide and tore long gouges into her slanting hull, but two slammed into her dorsal surface. The barrage section torpedo tube crumpled under the onslaught, useless.

"*Sar'du saak,*" Sara hissed. "Is there a single scale on the damn things which isn't made of guns!?"

Habas'ku launched her second missile as she passed through the gauntlet, the rocket-driven warhead soaring in a wide circle. *Garanu*'s close-range attack bore fruit at last, her dumbfire barrage peppering the nose of her gutted foe.

"Ha! *Kala du'maas, Garanu-da!*" The Amtara's triumphant roar rang through her helm as ugly muzzle of the Slaver vessel erupted under the onslaught, its savage banks pounded by one explosion after another. *Garanu* had now passed through the gauntlet, out of range of the forward facing turrets. She fired her rear gun, a savage tail whip of armour piercing missile, and burned for the distance.

Sara's heart leaped up into her throat as the Slaver vessels returned fire. Golden death belched from the large rear turrets, an ugly cross-fire. The crippled enemy struck hardest, all nine of her bolts ripping into *Garanu*'s vulnerable gut. The mission section went up in a gout of flame; the engine followed, a spectacular double detonation that blinded the bridge of *Habas'ku*.

The rattle of hard rain on a thin roof sounded as *Habas'ku* flew through the remains of her slain sister, but *Garanu* had not died in vain. Sara turned in time to see the wounded *massaaku* cruiser perish. *Garanu*'s armour piercing missile had been the decisive blow; the enemy's command section exploded, and *Kal War'ko*'s fusion missile soared through the fire and rocked the engine section, obliterating its ugly rear gun to add glorious insult to injury.

Sara snarled wordlessly, baring her fangs in defiance. *Die, go'rada. Die.*

"Rear section—fire!" Still holding to his grips at the helm, the Amtara's voice rang out, cutting through the cacophony of alarm like an axe. Now *Habas'ku* made her own tail-strike, launching twin fusion missiles toward the enemy. They soared through the void and converged in an instant, slamming into the remaining *massaaku*'s tail section with savage impact.

"*Daiko!* Enemy returning fire!" The tactical officer's voice was shrill. "The salvage cruiser, Amtara! The forward guns—they are live!"

Sara wheeled in disbelief, her eyes widening in shock. The Slaver salvage ship had somehow regained control of its bridge; a torpedo slid from the massive tube on its chin, speeding toward the bulk of the oncoming *Kal War'ko*.

"No," she said softly. "Ishii...no!"

The torpedo struck the barrage cruiser dead on, plunging into her already-vulnerable mission section with deadly accuracy. A crippling storm of lightning passed over *Kal War'ko*'s hull.

"An EMP pulsar, *Kaan Dai!*" The tactical officer looked up. "It has disrupted her systems—*Kal War'ko* is dead in space!"

And yet the cruiser drifted on, helpless, driven by her own forward momentum into a close pass with the enemy ship. As *Kal War'ko* slowed, engines dying, the *massaaku* moved in tight. From its midsection a pair of hideous hooks shot forward, plunging into the Tarka cruiser like huge harpoons of rusting steel. Now it held her, bound in its coils, as the ugly guns on the midsection tore *Kal War'ko* apart.

"No!" Sara clutched at the rungs for support. *Habas'ku* had passed out of range of the escort's medium turrets; there might still be a chance. "We must come about. We can fire another round of missiles, surely!"

"Amtara....the third cruiser has fired its tail. A missile." The tactical officer looked up, her eyes pale with fear.

"Brace for impact!" the old man roared. "Engine, begin bank. Now!"

Habas'ku veered into her final manoeuvre, turning to face her enemy with the strongest armour of the prow in the path of its deadly rear cannon. In the arms of the enemy, *Kal War'ko* died in a triple welter of fireworks, leaving the ugly hooks empty of all but shattered debris. The salvage ship's missile struck *Habas'ku* in the engine, rocking the ship with its impact.

"Tail section! Answer and report!" The Amtara's voice was firm and calm, a stone of authority in the stormy sea.

The response trickled feebly from the speakers of her helm. "Point defence has taken down the missile, *daiko*. But the warhead has released—a green cloud!—it burns—"

The scream of lost signal and the explosion were simultaneous. *Habas'ku* shuddered as her engine went up. Sara was thrown from her feet at last, hurled to the deck as the ship rocked in the void.

The Slaver ships hung in space, decks burning with a dozen fires, the turrets torn from their sides by Tarka gunners as they passed. Sara Mak'Kona rose to her feet, looking down the barrel of the heavy fusion cannon. Silently, she shook her head.

It was not how she had planned to die.

* * *

Ezz'in sighed, a faint wheeze from his wing-pits in the confines of his suit. No, no, no. This would never do.

He cocked his head, looking up again at the surviving enemy cruiser. The head and thorax were heavily damaged. A few good blows would shatter it for certain. From a mathematical perspective, he thought, the Tarka had done rather well. Had their barrage vessel survived its pass, this enemy would have been destroyed. It was no fault of theirs that the Liir had failed to fully disable the bridge of this vessel. This was the madness of battle, or so his brothers said. There was much left to chance, and no plan would survive contact with the enemy.

His slim fingers danced over the keys of his control pad, and the assault shuttle responded with a hum as its engine engaged. Without hesitation he lifted off from the docking array, freeing himself from the gantry and clearing the upper bow of the Slaver ship with a single surge.

His many options had narrowed now, and silently he thanked the Goddess that he had waited. Without hesitation he flew toward the tail section of the escort cruiser, wheeling in a long soaring arc to come in low and fast, straight into the barrel of its massive rear gun. This cannon was their strongest blade. It must be destroyed.

Ezz'in kept his hands at the helm for as long as possible. He had always enjoyed flying, and the operation of machines. In the final moments, however, he armed the warhead in his hold and released the helm to automatic. As the open bore of the heavy cannon loomed, he lowered his head and folded his arms protectively over his eyes. It was nothing he wished to see.

He had never died in battle with an enemy before...but it was not as pleasurable as he had hoped.

* * *

Dominus, we are hit. Our brothers aboard Amnach have betrayed us.

In the flash of an instant he saw it with his own eyes—the razor-edged disk sailing into his engine, detonating in a low pulse as it obliterated the barrel of his rear gun. His Hand roared aloud, echoing their master's mental snarl of outrage. With a flex of his will he kept them at the turrets as his own anger roared up within him like a tower of flame.

Idiot, he snarled. *Amnach is overrun with rebel slaves.* The master's voice was low and deadly. *Our Lord has driven himself mad with his meddling. Now he throws away our lives. I will tear out the old fool's heart with my own claws when this is done! Helm, bring this ship about.*

His mind struck out like a lash, and the Hand on the bridge leaped into spasmodic action. The cruiser heeled about, turning its vicious head. The crippled engine groaned, the reverberating moan of its pain echoing through the hull. The Imperator bared his fangs in a grimace as his beloved Hammerclaw slowly, painfully brought its fangs to bear. He would finish his foes face to face, and board his master's ship for good measure. It was time for a reckoning with Father, and a change of command. A Lord too weak to lead must die.

***

The razor disk sailed in over *Habas'ku's* shoulder, winging into view like a shuriken hurled by the Divine. Sara leaped into the air, incredulous, a full somersault of amazement and joy as the shuttle rammed into the *massaaku's* engine with a boiling white flash of fission.

"Ahai!" she cried. "*Sar* is on our side today!"

The Amtara's eyes turned emerald green with laughter. "All guns," he growled into the comm. "Target those cannons. Disarm this butchering fiend before she comes about, or she will have us on a spit."

The remaining light gunner on the prow opened up his turret, firing precise bursts of gauss into the enemy vessel. The missile crew had finally reloaded the tube; they launched the fusion warhead, the slim rocket sailing through the darkness toward the exposed *massaaku* flank.

Sara held her breath, heart hammering in her chest. The missile struck true, slamming into the massive cannons of the Slaver's midsection in a bright flash. For a moment the enemy ship seemed to shudder with the impact, shaking like a wounded beast as the sacrificial blade tears free. Then its entrails burst wide, the great energy turrets detonating in a spasm of murderous flame.

Gutted, its ventral section gaping in space, still the *massaaku* turned, struggling to bring its hideous head to bear. Sara's eyes paled, seeing that angry muzzle come about. Even in death, this razor-fanged brute would lunge for an enemy's throat.

* * *

Yzeket pulled the trigger of his thrower; the barrel coughed and spluttered, yielding nothing more than a faint lick of flame. Empty. He was dry.

He raised his scattergun he charged across the deck, firing a thundering shot over the heads of the three Rippers as they crouched over their prey. They froze, heads jerking about to confront him, and then fled like rats in the light. He fired again, catching one in the hind leg before she could slip away back into the shadows. He paused as he stepped over her to blow her head from her shoulders.

Mak'Kona lay in a spreading dark lake of fluid, missing one of his limbs. The Hiver knelt beside him. The Tarka was alive. But judging by the smell alone, he would not last for long.

"Father!" Yzeket whistled across the hold, forcing his voice to its highest pitch in the thin foul air. "I have found him!"

Chezokin scrambled through the wreckage, using all four hind limbs to maintain his balance in the sliding debris. "He lives?"

Yzeket chattered uncertainty. Chezokin slid to a halt beside him, descending to gather the broken Tarka into his arms. "Well done," he churred softly. "There may yet be time." He lifted his head. "Who still has a burst left in his thrower?"

Another warrior stepped forward. "My Prince."

"Good. Yzeket, Xhozek—hold the Tarka. He may waken—pain makes them strong." The Prince placed his burden in their arms, showing them where to grip the strange body. "Tak'axin—bring me the fire."

Tak'axin laid back his antenna, distressed. "Father?"

"Trust me, my son. I have seen the Tarka close such wounds in battle. We may yet save him, if we can stop the flow."

The warrior held up his thrower in obedience.

"A short flame. But very hot."

The thrower opened its bore, the warrior turning the cock to bring it down to a narrow hot point of white-hot flame. Chezokin held up the flat of his blade, bathing the steel in the torch until it glowed cherry red. "Hold him," he warned again.

The blade descended, slicing away torn shreds of flesh and hide with a hiss of roasting meat. Lan Mak'Kona woke with a shriek, his body thrashing in reaction; Yzeket hung on with all his strength, fighting to keep the Tarka in place as Chezokin patiently burned the wound shut.

At last it was done. Yzeket looked down into the strange eyes, silvery with shock and pain in the light of the thrower's flame. Suddenly the pinprick pupils expanded, unfolding into a circle of recognition. The thick limbs shivered.

"All right," the Tarka rasped. "Let go."

Yzeket tilted a nod and slowly released his grip. Chezokin stepped back silently as the young prince was lowered to the ground.

"I am sorry," the Tarka said. His free hand had gone to his wounded shoulder, bracing but not touching the charred stump where his arm had been.

Chezokin's head rocked back in confusion. "Sorry?"

"About your son." Lan Mak'Kona pointed to the fallen Hiver corpse. "I could not save him."

The Hiver Prince lowered his head silently. The warriors exchanged a scent of wonderment between them.

"Will you live?" Chezokin asked at last.

Mak'Kona turned to look at his wound with a shudder. "Thanks to you— perhaps." The pale eyes flashed a spark of green. "At least I will see what comes next."

"Trouble." Chezokin turned, indicating the far side of the cargo hold with his blade. "We are trapped. My sons and I cannot open the blast doors to the engine room. The guns there are still in operation—we have heard one missile launched already. We must find a way to assault that compartment, Lan Mak'Kona. If not—all may be lost."

The Tarka dropped to his knee, wearily wrapping his tail around the hilt of his war hammer. "Surely we can think of something, Prince. In all this mass of guns and gear—is there nothing that could breach that door?"

Chezokin clashed negation. "It is all dead, my friend. My sons and I do not know these weapons, or how to repair—"

Politely, Yzeket raised his antenna. His father turned toward him, curious.

"Forgive me, father." His antennae drooped in abject apology. "But that is not entirely true." He hesitated, embarrassed to contradict his betters.

"Go on, child."

"I was the gunner of a Kher'za destroyer—I know my own weapon. They have the turrets here, my Prince. Give me a live cable—I can make them fire."

The Tarka's eyes brightened. "That is possible?"

Yzeket tilted assent. "Yes. But we must have power." He shrugged. "We have none."

"Gather your weapons. I will bring the power." The lizard prince looked up, examining the ceiling above, and his lids closed briefly in pained resignation. "Just...give me a moment. I cannot climb so well in this condition."

Chezokin tilted his head back. "Perhaps you will not have to climb. Show me where to stand, Prince Van. I will raise you high."

The Tarka pointed. "The cables are there," he said, indicating the massive yellow serpents twining along the roof of the bay. "I have seen them before. They are a Tarka design. Such arteries lead to a fusion core—they must be feeding this section of the ship." He took a deep breath. "Bring them down, you will have all the power you need. Perhaps more."

The Hiver Prince chittered amusement. "Let us try. If we live...it will make a fine tale." He turned to Yzeket. "Gather the turrets, child. You have work to do."

Yzeket thumped his chest. "As you command, my Prince." He turned away, quickly scanning the wreckage. There were many turrets aboard a Kher'za—he needed only one. The trick would be finding a needle...in a stack of needles.

***

Fire flickered at the viewport, an eerie staccato strobe of muzzle flash and detonation. The skinny beast crouched in the corner, snarling and barking his commands to his servants elsewhere in the ship. Cai Rui moved cautiously. Ever so slowly, he lifted his head.

He could not see the animals in the dark. Instead he could hear them, the deep rapid pant of carrion breath, the sodden crunch and rasp of teeth on bone. He opened his eyes wide, trying to force his pupils to adjust to the low light, and saw the yellow mirror flash in the corner as one bulky shadow turned toward him.

A low warning growl rumbled in her throat. Curious, Cai Rui reached out toward her, and gently touched her mind.

The beast cringed, the sound of aggression turning upward into a high whine. *No hurt!* it cried. *No hurt no hurt no hurt*—.

Cai Rui restrained a gasp, lying very still. *No hurt*, he agreed hastily. Hesitantly he shaped a warm intention, trying to remember an animal that he had known. He closed his eyes, bringing back the feeling: fingers sliding into thick fur. Massaging silky ears. Scratching that one spot that a paw could never reach...

The beast rose from its seat and padded across the floor, moving toward him with a slow, measured tread. He flinched as the thick claws clicked on the bulkhead beside his cheek, his heart thudding in his chest and temples like a drum.

The hot breath gusted over his skin, and he felt the long snout sniffing him over.

No hurt, he thought softly. His hand twitched as he mentally formed the caress.

The muzzle nudged him, rank and wet. Tentatively his hand moved, lifting from the floor. She bent and rubbed the side of her head against him aggressively, and his fingers lightly stroked the clotted fur. He reached in, restraining her rumble of pleasure.

The golden eyes opened and he looked out into the room, the darkness dispelled. To her the world was black on gray, a realm of shapes and movement, dominated by the languor of safe-lair-home and the rich, pleasant smell of death.

Cai Rui turned her head gently with his will, looking around the room. The other four beasts lay idle around the room, grooming their coats and chewing their heavy claws clean. He cast a fearful look at the diminutive figure in the corner, barking into its talk-machine. The Ripper woman whined softly, and he felt her rising anxiety as he used her eyes to gaze directly at the Deacon.

No look master. The thought was only half-coherent, bestial and strong. Cai Rui felt the wave of dread roll through him, the memory of pain.

Dominance, he thought. A pack hunter with a hierarchy of strongest to weakest—a direct gaze into the eyes was a challenge.

He turned her head away, taking advantage of her relief to examine the rest of the room more closely. Struck by a sudden thought, he breathed in deeply, through her nose as well as his own. To him the reek was overwhelming, a sweet-rotten stench of rotting corpse; to her it was simply the smell of food, and family, and home. More importantly, however, was the smell that was missing. No urea, no tang of dung.

He closed his eyes, searching his mind for a familiar sensation; a full bladder. He sent it outward, pushing slightly as he drove it into her brain.

The beast turned and ambled away, moving toward the far wall. As she reached the portal she rose onto her hind legs and batted at an iron ring with her punch claw. The door slid open, and she dropped to move out into the hall.

Cai Rui was on his feet instantly, moving at speed through the portal. He felt as well as heard the animal cough of alarm in the room behind him, the sudden scramble of heavy bodies rising and rushing toward the door. He walled off his mind and ran down the twisting corridor, following the trail of dim red emergency lights through the bowels of the ship.

The Rippers galloped after him, their bulky bodies clattering over the deck like a pack of rabid bears on his heels. The black presence followed at his leisure, pursuing the human's fleeing mind with chuckling amusement.

Very good, Cai Rui. My pets seldom get to play. The Deacon snarled encouragement. *Run, slave, run!*

Blindly he crashed into the bulkhead, the corridor turning in a hairpin. Cai Rui rebounded, barely keeping his feet, and continued around the corner in a rush.

He crashed again into steel, a cold curving plate of shining metal and glass. Ishii regarded him with liquid eyes.

Took you long enough, Cai Rui snapped mentally. He did not restrain his wave of relief—so powerful that he nearly fell to his knees. He scrambled over the Liir's coils and into the corridor behind. *What the hell were you waiting for?*

Remorse. This one did hurry. Ishii turned toward the oncoming rush, his thought flavoured with sorrow and shame. *But he was afraid.*

20 | A MAN WITHOUT A TAIL

Lan Mak'Kona hooked the thick cable with his hammer. "I have it," he said. His body curled upward, and he reached for holds with his feet and tail. "Give me a moment."

Chezokin waited anxiously below. "You will not fall?"

The Tarka clacked his tongue irritably. "The least of my worries." He eyed the thick cable. It was anchored to the ceiling clumsily, nailed to the bulkhead with a series of rusting eyebolts. "This ship is a nightmare."

Chezokin whistled agreement.

Lan took the hammer grip with his tail and braced himself; it took only a single blow to snap the bolt, letting a fat length of the cable droop into the cargo hold. Moving along the length of the conduit, he repeated the process, dropping the heavy coils into the waiting arms of the Hivers below.

"*Sardo,*" he muttered. "Look at all this. Where does it all go?"

Chezokin called out below. "We have it, Prince Lan. Will you come down?"

"Just...just a moment." Curious, he handed himself along the path of the cable. It split and branched in two directions; he chose the left hand path and followed it, shuffling awkwardly hand-and-foot along the ceiling.

The cable was routed through a hole in the bulkhead; there was a hatch here, hidden from view from the main floor. Looking down, he saw a path of heavy round iron rungs leading down to the floor far below.

"Well well," he muttered. "What have we here?" He hooked his hammer into the handle and twisted, turning the crank and dropping it open on its hinges.

Then he tossed the hammer up over the lip of the bulkhead and hauled himself up after it.

Lan Mak'Kona bared his fangs in a savage smile, eyes shining green as he looked up through the scarred bulkhead at the stars. The gunner's cradle sat empty, controls at the ready; the missile was already loaded into its rack. The black cone of an *Umol* gamma warhead gleamed in the muzzle flash of distant guns.

"Prince Lan?" Chezokin's voice echoed dimly through the hatch.

"Just a moment," he called, settling himself into the gunner's chair. He leaned forward, activating the controls. "This won't take long."

***

The guns of the enemy cruiser pounded without mercy, riddling the bridge with a flood of deadly iron spheres. Sara Mak'Kona signalled the Amtara on the far side of the compartment, pointing to her wristband. She had taken cover beneath the dead navigator's console.

Urgently she tapped her wristband in EK code. *Is there nothing we can do?*

The Amtara looked down at his own band and tapped out his terse reply. *Gauss gone. Missile crew dead. What?*

She paused and then rattled out a second response, flinching as another round ripped through the panel beside her, leaving a series of holes the size of her head. *Turret intact?*

The Amtara looked over his shoulder. *Don't know. Will look.*

She watched as he crawled elbow over elbow across the deck, pausing occasionally to avoid a shower of sparks and shrapnel from above. Achieving the far side of the section he rolled over onto his back and looked up into the gunner's cradle.

Turret intact. Empty rack, he said.

Coming. She followed after him swiftly, slithering over the rubble-strewn deck with sinuous grace. Arriving, she rolled over beside him and looked up at the missile turret. *Habas'ku* had heeled over with the loss of her engine, turning her underbelly toward the enemy—the medium turret was partially shielded from the onslaught of the *massaaku's* mass driver rounds.

She rolled into the old man's embrace, putting the glass of her helm against his to shout through it. "Can you lift a fusion missile?"

His eyes flashed silver, and then sparkled green. He dipped his crest silently, reaching up to remove her.

The old man rose, leaping up into the turret bay through a hail of sparks. Sara slithered up after him; as she pulled up the last length of her tail the deck below her erupted, a gout of flame rising as the deck they had been lying on just moments before collapsed.

The Amtara bent his knees and thrust his arms under the weight of the missile. Sara squatted beside him, guiding the nose of the warhead into the rack. She saw the strain in his eyes, the pale green iris dotted with starbursts of blood. He dropped the load at last, toppling onto his side, and she saw the hole through the back of his suit—a shrapnel wound leaking blood and air into the void.

Sara Mak'Kona squatted and slapped a patch onto the hole of his suit. "Live, old man," she whispered. "That's an order." She turned back toward the gunner's cradle, flinching as another salvo of steel ripped through the ship. Light as a feather, she leaped up into the cradle. Her fingers danced as she activated its controls. Wheezing on reserve power, the turret spun slowly, the missile rising into position as it turned.

She put her eye to the targeting reticule, waiting patiently until the Slaver entered her sights. Taking a deep breath, she pulled both triggers.

There was a long moment of silence, and in that endless span of time her heart quailed. Then, at last, the rack trembled; the propellant had finally ignited. The last fusion warhead of the *Habas'ku* sped toward the enemy, twisting on its path through a hail of misdirected steel to burst on the port side of the slaver's bridge.

The enemy vessel shuddered as the banks of its left claw exploded, leaving a jagged stump where half its head should be. And still the turrets of the right claw were live, pumping out their streams of magnetic steel.

A second missile struck the *massaaku* vessel from behind, plunging into the rear of its hammerhead bridge with a bright explosion. The blast was blinding at this distance, a hot golden fireball that filled half the void with its glare. Sara threw herself down beside the Amtara, dazed. The bridge of the enemy was destroyed.

At last the mass drivers of the Slaver ship were gone.

✳ ✳ ✳

Lan descended the rungs to the cargo bay swiftly, dropping the last few meters to floor lightly. Chezokin and his sons had completed their make-shift turret, a pair of battered red lasers braced in the center of a bank of rusting iron. The yellow cable had been diverted through an ancient coupler; the light beside the barrels blinked a steady pulse of warning green.

Chezokin inclined his head; Lan Mak'Kona did the same.

"Are you ready, brother?" the Prince said.

"Yes." Mak'Kona's eyes shimmered brilliant green. "I have done what I could."

The Hiver turned. "Yzeket—fire when ready."

The mottled gray warrior nodded silently and dropped to his knees, thrusting all four of his arms into the firing sleeves of the old turrets. The warning lights flickered one last time, changing from green to red. Lan Mak'Kona dropped his lids, protecting his pupils.

The laser screamed suddenly, an unbearable stuttering howl of energy ripping through the atmosphere of the hold as it poured into the blast doors. Lan Mak'Kona roared in anguish, trying to cover his ears with the one arm he had remaining. The Hivers folded themselves defensively, protecting their heads from noise and light. The plate steel glowed under the barrage of fat red needles; it softened rapidly under the tattoo of hot light. In seconds it began to melt and blister, bubbling and dimpling under the luminous assault like fat in a fire.

Yzeket adjusted his turrets, guiding the dual stream of red flashes to cut the bulkhead open. Lan Mak'Kona squinted against the glare of molten steel, and saw a score of leaping shapes move in the engine compartment beyond, scrambling uselessly to escape the barrage of incoming fire.

Chezokin bent low, his huge hand descending to Yzeket's shoulder. Lan Mak'Kona saw his mouthparts move, and the warrior's head tilt in acknowledgment, but he could not hear what was said. The barrage of laser fire continued, ripping into the engine compartment to obliterate its crew.

"Wait!" The Tarka roared into his own helmet, his echoing shout lost in the shriek of the turret. He leaped to his feet, waving, trying to catch Chezokin's eye. "Wait! Please! Did you not say that there was a—"

The explosion threw him backward suddenly, hurling his body into the bulkhead behind him at the speed of sound. Barely conscious, Lan Mak'Kona watched as a slow cloud of green gas billowed out of the ruptured engine compartment, swallowing the Hivers and their barricade whole.

The Tarka tottered to his feet and staggered away, seeking the safety of the narrow corridor to the bridge. He reeled around the claustrophobic hairpin corner and out of the path of the cloud, his body aching with impact. Behind him the wreckage of the cargo bay hissed and groaned, dissolving and settling in the corrosive cloud.

The low thrum of the ship's engine went silent. The vessel was dead in space.

*＊＊

Ishii let the human retreat into the reef behind him and turned to face the enemy. The black vortex whirled with monstrous energy, a torrential maw of power and greed. The winds ripped through him, chilling his blood to ice.

Suul'ka.

The response was a razor-edged snarl, slicing his thought to ribbons. *Do not dare!* The pain ripped through him in retribution, an ancient memory of the knife and the lash. *NEVER dare to speak the Holy, slave!*

The Liir spread his tentacles in the dark, fanning them out into the arms of Shiva. *Come then. Silence my song, paingiver. If you can.*

The mad body-mind surged forward, thundering toward him in a wall of flesh. Ishii hurled his spear, driving the metal bar into the chest of the nearest to burst her beating heart. She dropped in her tracks, the light of her life winking out in an instant. Her sisters charged over her empty shell and surged onto him in a wave, tumbling him helpless with their combined weight.

Claws hammered into his body, piercing steel and flesh alike. Ishii barrel-rolled beneath them, hurling them off in a mass. He retreated, lashing out with a loop, twining it around the closest throat. The beast struggled ferociously, all four feet fighting for purchase on the deck plates as he drew the noose tight. He twisted the steel garrotte into fur, meat and bone, spinning it until the arm of the suit snapped at the casing, and backed away as the creature struggled in bewildering pain.

The master weathered her agony without flinching. As he passed he flicked a paw in her direction. *Silence,* he said, and crushed the bleating mind with a single deadly command. At his word she died, the red heat of life extinguished like a candle in the dark.

Ishii trembled with loathing and tail-slapped the deck, wrenching up a shower of bolts and rusting shards of metal. Summoning all his strength he began to form the whirlpool, a spinning corona of whistling, singing steel.

The human hurried forward, crouching beside the dead *Suul'ka* to wrench the hunting rod from her chest. One of the remaining beasts snarled, hurling her body into the path of his retreat. He danced aside lightly, swift as lightning, and drove his weapon into her eye.

The beast shrieked agony, rearing onto her hind legs to bat at the rod of steel wedged into the socket of her skull. The Deacon snarled, one paw rising inadvertently toward his own face. Ishii seized the bar and thrust it home savagely, shattering the final wall of bone to penetrate the creature's brain. The human ducked under her outstretched claw and flattened himself against the hull as she crashed to the deck.

Ishii advanced slowly, rising up onto the nest of his tentacles, framed by a cyclone of steel in the darkness. Behind him there was a liquid trail, his own life bleeding away.

What are you, the voice demanded. *You are not like others of your kind.*

The Liir answered with a barrage of piercing metal.

✳ ✳ ✳

Chezokin rose in the cargo hold, rearing high to see above the roiling sea of poison gas. His body burned, every joint and seam of his armour giving way in painful lesions as the acid ate into his flesh. Half blind with agony he reeled toward the engine compartment, forcing his legs to move through the maiming current to reach the distant fire hatch in the wall.

His hand crumbled as he caught the rung, the great fingers shattering into a bleeding stump as the delicate plates of shell gave way. Trumpeting pain, he bore down with his shoulder instead, forcing the handle down. The emergency vent burst open with a howl, venting the corrosive atmosphere into space.

His hind leg snapped suddenly, dropping him to the deck as the joint parted under his weight. The Hiver Prince caught himself with a weakened blade, half tearing his arm from the socket as he struggled to hold himself upright. For a long moment he stood, fighting to remain on his feet as the flesh slowly sloughed from his body, and the wind screamed through the vent. Finally, turning his burned eyes back to the cargo hold, he forced the rung back up and sealed the breach.

The Prince dropped, all four legs giving way, his steel blades splitting from his arms in a welter of blood. His breastplate crashed to the bulkhead as he fell. The warriors in the hold unfolded, rising from their defensive positions against the barricade. Armour smoking with the poison, bleeding from acid burns over their backs and blades, they rushed to their Father's side.

The scent of his precious blood hung in the last wisps of poisoned air. Chezokin made a low loving sound, raising his burned limbs toward them, and then lay still. The Hivers keened, a high ululating cry of distress, as his fluids emptied onto the bulkhead.

Once again, the Queen's most faithful son was dead.

***

Lan Mak'Kona stumbled through the narrow halls, his vision blurred with shock and concussion. The Slaver ship was a twisted madhouse, full of doors that opened onto blank walls and corridors that crossed and re-crossed themselves in useless circles. Only by listening for the groan of tortured metal could he keep his bearings, moving away from the ruined hold and toward the nose of the ship.

At last he rounded a final corner and saw the bridge compartment, a deep open drop leading down to a gunnery pit and a command center below. He flinched back, seeing the *massaaku* and his animal bent intently at their tasks, the rider seated with his paws to his temples in deep concentration, the beast seated with her obedient claws hooked into the triggers of the gun.

The Tarka's eyes burned with red hatred as he saw the beast that had taken his arm, her flank still scored by the sweep of Chezokin's blade. Silently he retreated, backing up a few steps for momentum, and then launched himself over the ledge.

He landed feet-first on the Slaver's shoulders, shattering both the frail collarbones with the impact of his massive weight; as the beast shrieked in pain Lan Mak'Kona brought down his clenched fist, battering his foe unconscious with a single rocking blow to the temple.

The Slaver roared in sudden pain and confusion, struggling to free her claws from the hampering gunnery cradle. The Tarka lunged forward, leaping up onto her shoulders, whipping his tail around her neck. As she flailed and struggled he flung himself off again, pulling the coil tight from a distance of over a meter. Bracing himself with both arm and legs, it still took every ounce of his remaining strength to choke the struggling beast until she went limp.

Lan Mak'Kona dropped to the deck, exhausted.

"Sara," he said aloud. "I must remember to tell you." His lids dropped slowly. "It is a hard thing, to be a male."

***

Cai Rui hung against the wall, watching as Ishii and the Deacon joined battle, a rapid exchange of invisible blows too fast and deadly for the human eye to see. The hurricane of whirling metal howled, tearing the bodies of the two female Rippers to shreds. Black blades plunged into the Liir's mind, wrenching and tearing up great bleeding geysers of memory and pain.

His head was throbbing in nightmarish agony. Cai Rui put his hands to his temples, fighting the steady pulse of red pain which seemed to balloon larger with every heartbeat, filling his skull with the crash of blood.

Now, a voice within him whispered softly. *Strike. I cannot hold for long.*

The pain erupted, a volcanic surge unfolding behind his eyes. Red and white spun into a candy spiral as Cai Rui staggered forward, and threw his arms around the Ripper's neck.

"Something for you," he gritted. His wrath unfurled, plunging like a sword into the unprotected recesses of the Ripper's mind. "Something you left behind."

No! the voice shrieked. *No! Out—! OUT!*

Take it. Cai Rui's mind belched forth its hidden cargo, streams of suffering that poured into the Deacon like venom into a helpless vein. *You wanted Tourneau—I have him. Take him all.*

Cai Rui shuddered as the emotions flowed out of him, tears streaming down his filthy cheeks in the dark. *Take his love,* he commanded, ramming the ache of longing into the darkness—the desire to make someone's life better. *Take his pity. Take his shame. Take his fear.*

The Deacon thrashed, howling, tearing at his human assailant with ragged claws. Cai Rui clung, grim as death, determined to maintain contact as Ishii closed the trap. Deep within the domed skull the pattern took hold, the network of connections blossoming through dormant tissue as the shrivelled capacity for empathy awakened.

With one last desperate effort the Zuul lashed out, lancing into the depths of the Liir's brain to take control of his telekinetic power. The battlesuit suddenly went mad, flailing wildly, slamming repeatedly into the deck, battering the cetacean's body into the bulkhead with crushing impact.

Through it all, the cool mind did not waver. *It does not matter, Suul'ka,* it whispered. *Kill me. I am already dead.*

Cai Rui tightened his grip.

Stop, the voice begged. *Please. I will do anything. Please. I will serve you. I will be your son. Do not...do not make me this mother-thing. Do not take my strength.*

"What strength? You are nothing," Cai Rui said aloud. The trembling body in his arms collapsed, shivering with reaction; contemptuously he let the Ripper fall to the deck.

Not true. The Liir's whisper was gentle. *He is not 'nothing'. He is Zuul.*

Cai Rui turned, feeling rather than seeing the broken body in the dark. He dropped to his knees beside the Black Swimmer, reaching out to touch its face; the glass over the Liir's snout was shattered, and his suit had emptied a pool onto the filthy floor.

"Ishii..." He trailed off. The Liir's emotions surged through him, a tide of regret and sorrow.

Dying. Hurry. Bring him to me.

Cai Rui turned wordlessly and picked up the Deacon by the scruff of the neck. Limp and whimpering, the slave master was surprisingly light to carry. Cai Rui dumped the creature beside Ishii in the dark, resisting the urge to wipe his hands on the nearest surface—touching the thing gave him a spasm of almost unbearable loathing.

"Kill it if you want," he said. "You've earned the right."

Silence. He is newly Drowned. Show him respect. There was a faint note of contempt in the Liir's voice. *Not every hand is a fist.* Ishii reached out, tentacles stirring, drawing the Deacon's twisted form into his embrace. *I have something for you,* he said gently. *To carry with you into the dark.*

Cai Rui staggered back as the Liir's mind crashed open in the room, the floodgates bursting into a thunderous song. Somewhere in the deep, a great heart was beating; with every pulse, the heart poured out its love. That love flowed like a red tide through an eternity of arteries and veins, firing them with light and beauty, until at last it returned in a final aching burst to the center and poured out joyously once more.

The Deacon's voice was small. *What is this, Dominus?* he asked. *I do not understand.*

Mother, the voice whispered. *It is mother. Her name...was Heart's Joy.*

The massive sides heaved, and fluid gushed from Ishii's lungs. The Black Swimmer opened his coils, releasing the bewildered Deacon from his grasp. With a final effort he forced the last of the stale fluid from his body. Then he shuttered his mind, and quietly died.

***

Sara Mak'Kona tapped at the hatch with a shard of metal, rapping out a warning for the crew. The mission section commander tapped back the "all clear" and turned the handle, opening the port; Sara turned in the void and let the younger Tarka take the awkward mass of the Amtara's body from her shoulders, then turned and slid into the last surviving section of Habas'ku.

Atmosphere restored, she lifted the visor of her helm. "He is injured," she said. "Shrapnel wound. Have the medic see to him." Wearily she turned to the section commander and lowered herself to the deck. "Anything to report?"

"Your sibling, Lac Tar." The woman's eyes flashed green triumph. "He has the helm of the slaver vessel—he lives."

"And the others? What of them?"

"Ten Hiver survivors, Kaan Dai. And three *massaaku*, taken alive. The rest are all dead."

Sara dropped her lids. "The human and the Liir?"

"He did not say, Lac Tar."

"Ask." She turned away.

The woman turned and went to the comm, tapping out a message to the enemy bridge. Sara waited, eyes closed, head bowed, listening to the series of clicks as the answer came.

Liir. Dead. Friend. Says. Never. Underestimate. Man. Without. Tail.

Despite herself, her pupils smiled.

"Humans," she said aloud. "Bloody things are indestructible."

21 | IN THE GARDEN OF MA'AK

A few months later, Cai Rui took his place at the rear of the human delegation, pausing to straighten the cuffs of his spotless black uniform. The amphitheatre was built in the shape of a huge flat-bottomed bowl, with forty layers of nested steps and benches arrayed around a circular stage in the center. Overhead the dome soared skyward, filtering the tropical sun of Kao'Kona and scattering its rays to saturate the marble and the towering trees below with rich golden light.

He looked down and saw the Director enter, flanked by his Legators and an assortment of human dignitaries. With some amusement he recognized the scarlet robes of the Cardinals, one of which could only be Amato, sternly refusing to look around at their surroundings or be impressed as they strode in behind the military officials. The Consortium ministers behind them were more shameless, smiling and nudging one another to murmur a comment whenever some new wonder caught the eye. Trailing at the rear came a pair of extremely nervous-looking colonial governors, who looked around them as if they expected to be barbecued and devoured before the end of the day.

Glancing to the side, he saw Commander Carroll step down to take her place beside him, taking advantage of their position at the back of the crowd to loosen the high collar around her dark neck. Her blood red uniform had a russet cast in the garden light, and a layer of shining sweat covered her ebon cheeks. "Commander Rui," she muttered by way of greeting, keeping her eyes forward.

He nodded silently, taking her cue.

She pointed her chin almost imperceptibly down into the bowl, indicating the gathered crowd of alien dignitaries. "That'd be a hell of a place to drop a bomb, wouldn't it?"

Cai Rui nodded grimly; all four factions had placed their most powerful dreadnaughts in orbit to prevent just such an eventuality. Nonetheless it made him nervous to see them gathered together, and obviously the Red Section Commander agreed. The Hiver Queen glittered in the yellow light, her sparkling crown of chitin rising high in a sweeping spread of diamond filigree. Her sedan was flanked by four Princes and her snow white ceremonial guard. The three Liir battlesuits to her left were so highly polished that they were nearly blinding, tentacles arranged into spiral blossoms beneath the occupants. The Supreme Commander had arrived on the scene a few minutes before, carried by forty of his soldiers in a combination of litter and throne. Now he sat opposite the Hiver faction, his Council of Nine arrayed in their ceremonial positions behind his massive steel chair—each woman with a hand on one of the elaborate jewelled staves that circled behind him, the powers behind his throne.

A familiar figure stood beside him, in the position nearest his left hand and closest to the fore. Her tall lean body was sheathed in golden chain, the hilt of her curving *sar* jutting above her left shoulder, her crest adorned with the golden tiara of her mother's house. Her brother stood beside her, his chest covered with black matte plate; he carried no weapon, but his left arm shimmered in the amber light with the sheen of new steel.

Carroll followed his gaze. "Those two are Mak'Kona," she said, speaking so low that it was audible to no one else. "Children of the El Empress. Boy's a recent Var—lost his arm in a fight, apparently."

Cai Rui suppressed a smile. "Interesting."

"Very. RDC would love to get their hands on that prosthetic. Liir-made. Like their battlesuits." She took a handkerchief from her pocket and patted her brow casually. "He's bought a commission in the Navy. Rank of Sippa. The troops are calling him *Lan Liir'doma* now."

He raised an eyebrow. "'Lan the Liir-handed'?"

"Yep." Carroll's voice was flat. "Gives me an ulcer just looking at him. Kid's going to be trouble. I guarantee it."

Cai Rui offered a tiny shrug. The final players had arrived, a second Tarkasian litter modestly carried by a mere dozen bearers. It was settled into a cradle beside the raised podium, the bearers dropping to one knee and lowering their heads.

The occupant emerged from black brocade curtains, densely embroidered with designs of fruit, flowers and birds in shimmering golden thread.

It had been many years since he had seen Ma'ak, Empress of the Lokor and by far the most active Tarkasian diplomat of her generation. She had aged well; her creamy scales still had their pearlescent sheen, only one shade lighter in the fifteen years that had passed. Like her daughter, her build was delicate by the Tarka standard—a body straight and slim as a sword.

She was dressed in a simple black gown, her pale arms sheathed to the wrist with bronze guards inlaid with black gems. She touched one of the gemstones lightly as she ascended the stairs with slow dignity, her train trailing down the stairs behind her to conceal her tail. When she spoke, her low voice was broadcast over the crowd, the words translated with a slight delay by speakers placed within hearing of each faction.

"Esteemed guests. We thank you for this gracious visit." She paused, allowing the translators to finish, and opened her arms to all present. "I welcome you to Kao'Kona, and to my home. I hope that you will stay to refresh yourselves and to enjoy my garden."

"Better believe it, lady," Carroll mumbled beside him. "You drag us fourteen jumps to Kona—we wanna see a buffet."

"Before we move on to more pleasant things, however, we must speak of the common threat that brings us together on this day." The Empress lowered her arms, her eyes shimmering with violet sorrow. "I speak of the *massaaku* fleets now massing upon our border, and striking deep into territory held by your people as well."

Carroll stole a side-long glance at him, to see his reaction; Cai Rui's face was a grim mask.

"There is a saying among my people: 'Many hands make light work.' It is my hope that this common enemy will prove to be a common cause. For too long we have quarrelled, my friends and my neighbours! And none can deny that our quarrels have cost us much."

Radiant Frost tilted her head to the side, ever so gently. In the golden light her wings shimmered, refracting the solar energy in a rainbow.

"We must put our backs together now, and fight for our common survival. For in our struggles and our warring, we have created a common foe."

The Supreme crossed his arms impatiently, his crest bristling with irritation; Sara turned toward him, and Cai Rui saw her delicate hand fall upon his shoulder with a feather touch. His eyes flicked toward her for a moment, cooling to amber; his tail tip tapped the ground, once, the last visible signal of his irritation.

"It is difficult to explain the nature of these creatures who call themselves 'Zuul.'" Ma'ak was unable to pronounce the word properly, catching its first consonant between her teeth. "There is much yet to learn from the prisoners we have taken at Durendal, and the vessels captured by our combined fleet."

Carroll snorted softly, muttering out the side of her mouth. "Oh, she is *good*. One Liir battlesuit and a Bug freighter, four Tark cruisers—that's a *combined fleet*."

Cai Rui did not smile.

"What we have gleaned thus far is both saddening and disturbing. It would appear, esteemed guests, that we have a new enemy—and this enemy is ourselves."

The Garden was deadly silent as the Empress turned to face the Hiver Queen, opening her hands in sorrow and apology. "From you, Great Mother, the *massaaku* have taken the name of their own leader—he is called the Great Father, and he leads their legions as the patriarch of man clans." She brought her palms together, turning her body with effortless grace toward the human delegation. "From you, my human friends, they have learned the language of the sacred, and the tongue spoken by your Roman faith."

Cai Rui winced at the poor translation, even as he saw Amato and his fellow bishop stiffen in offense.

Ma'ak flowed toward the Liir, seated silent in their shining armour in the sun. "From you, Liiranu, the slavers have taken their most terrible weapons, and the knowledge to build cannons beyond the power of anything we have seen before."

The Empress crossed her arms in the ensuing silence and turned to the Supreme Commander. She bowed low, seeking his permission to speak further, and with a flick of his fingers he granted leave to proceed.

"But what, you ask, have the slavers learned from the Tarka? Well may you ask. It is in the dark glass we sometimes see ourselves most clearly, and some things are easier to show than to tell." She turned toward her curtained litter, bending and holding open her arms. "Come to me, my son. It is time."

The Red Section Commander craned her neck to see what would emerge from the litter. A ripple of reaction went through the human delegation as the child stepped bravely from the litter. Dressed in scaled leathers and bearing a miniature sword, he marched up the steps with the curious sway-backed stride of a Tarka—which was quite eerie, given that he was clearly human.

The strange boy ascended to the top step and took his place beside the Empress, just a half step ahead of her left hip—the position of favour and deepest trust. He crossed his small arms, brow creased in a frown. His head had been shaved, and he wore a circlet of gold, rising into a sheaf of hammered leaves at the back of his skull, in clear imitation of a Tarka's crest.

Ma'ak put her hand upon his shoulder. "This is my godson, Tor. We met four years ago, when he was quite young." The boy lifted his chin, his black eyes calm and proud. "Tor'do was sold in the marketplace, here on Kao'Kona. He was purchased by an acquaintance, who thought that I might find him...an amusing pet."

The men and women in the front row reacted strongly, a sudden burst of sound. The Director, arms crossed, turned toward them. Cai Rui could not hear what he said, but silence followed, and the Empress continued.

"Naturally I was appalled to find that the ancient laws against this practice had been broken. My people, I assure you, have not permitted the sale of slaves for a thousand years. As an executor of the Supreme Law I took the matter quite seriously." The Tarka woman's eyes flashed crimson, and she raised her free hand in a fist. "The trader who had turned *massaaku* was found. He was thoroughly questioned, and claimed innocence by letter of the law. The Supreme Law states that the sale of persons is forbidden, but by his reasoning only Tarka could be defined as 'persons'. The people of other races might be bought and sold."

The Liir reacted strongly, the tentacles of their battlesuits rising defensively; the sons of the Queen took a half step forward, as if to defend their sovereign. Ma'ak held up her hands to forestall them, her eyes golden orange and cold.

"Needless to say, I am sure, I explained to him that he was...in error. When he had revealed all, he and his clan received my sentence."

Cai Rui stole a glance at Carroll and lifted an eyebrow, curious. She gave her head a tiny shake and winced. "You don't want to know."

The Empress lowered her hand. "I have since requested a re-wording of our ancient writings, in light of recent change. I believe generations of the future will thank us if we allow no further...confusion."

Looking down at the child beside her, she cupped her hand stroked the back of his neck a single time. He smiled, receiving her affection, and glanced up briefly to meet the eyes violet with regret.

"Punishing the slaver did not comfort the boy, of course," Ma'ak said. "I resolved to return him to his people. An expedition was sent to the place where he was taken. The trader had revealed the location of a human settlement, a hidden world beyond the borders of your present domain."

She inclined her head toward the Director, and he lowered his chin, avoiding her eyes—two of the Legators exchanged looks, but said nothing. "We tried to return the boy to his clan...but his people were gone. All taken...by *massaaku-Zuul*."

Cai Rui winced, mentally putting a time signature on the attack.

"These slaver-Zuul did not learn all of their cruelty from my people." She spoke firmly, straightening to regard the assembly. "But as you all can see—we too have contributed a share of what they are."

Overcome by emotion, Cardinal Amato broke ranks with the delegation, moving toward the Empress. "Barbarians!" he cried.

Startled but unmoved, Ma'ak looked down at him as he strode up in his crimson robes to the very base of the podium. Her Tarka bearers rose in unison, reaching for their swords—she held up her hand silently to forestall them. It was the boy that finally stopped Amato, leaping down into his path with his knees bent, arms open, one palm extended and the other elbow bent—a fighting stance. When the Cardinal met his eyes, the child opened his mouth and voiced a perfectly credible warning hiss.

Amato halted, looking down at the boy in disbelief, and then raising his chin and his voice to confront the Empress. "Barbarians," he said aloud, firmly. "You have kidnapped this child from his people! And held him captive—for years!"

Ma'ak tilted her head at him curiously, and then turned for help to the Director. "Excuse," she said in English. "What is this word, 'kidnep'?"

"To take a person by force," the Director replied, his voice clipped with anger. "Away from family and friends." He glared at the Cardinal's back, as if wishing his pale eyes could bore through him.

The Empress looked down at the man standing before her, her eyes gently green. "I am sorry you misunderstand." She stepped down to join the boy on the bottom step, gently taking the child's raised fist in her hand. He looked up at her, seeking guidance, and she inclined her head *no*, eyes smiling. "Tordo, we do not strike a guest."

"Do you deny that the boy was stolen?" the bishop said. His voice echoed throughout the amphitheatre. "Do you deny that he was kept against his will?"

The eyes of the Empress shifted sadly. "I do deny it." She turned to the child. "Tordo, were you stolen from your people? Taken by force, *kidnepu*?"

The boy inclined his head solemnly. "No, Auntie," he said aloud—speaking Kona.

"Why did you go with the trader, my dearest?"

"I was sold."

The Empress paused, and then asked, "And what did your clan receive, Tordomo? What payment did they wish, for a boy child of their people?"

"Water, Auntie." The boy turned and looked the Cardinal in the eye. "They sold me to the trader for food and water."

* * *

Cai Rui stood alone at the edge of the garden, looking through the glass at the expanse of the city below. The Garden was built at the top of the mountain, and from this height the concentric layers of the city led down into the depths, over a thousand feet and through thousands of years of urban history to the valley below.

"Beats mine all to hell, doesn't it." The man in the plain blue uniform raised his glass, moving in beside him to share the panorama—the great city spread out for miles, its rooftops and gardens glittering like a box of jewels in the setting sun. "Gonna be a long time before the MarsDome has this kind of view."

"Good evening, sir." Cai Rui did not turn.

"Good evening to you, Commander." The Director took another sip of his water. "Saw you slip away from the festivities, and thought we might have a word."

He took a deep breath. "Yes sir."

"I wanted to ask if you'd considered my offer."

Cai Rui nodded. The Director's voice was casual, but he could feel the weight descend onto his shoulders. "I have."

"And?"

"Sir. I must respectfully decline."

Silence followed, for a few awkward seconds. Finally the Director sighed. "It's a good jump, Commander. Better pay, better hours. Take it. If you do...you never know. You could be looking down from Olympus yourself, someday."

Cai Rui lowered his lashes for a moment, shutting out the blinding sun. "Again, I must respectfully decline."

The Director pursed his lips, but nodded. "All right. Nguy Sen will take the job and he'll do it well, so I'm not going to force the issue. I can't afford to lose key personnel at a time like this. If you won't take the promotion—we still need you."

"Yes sir. I would be happy to continue my work, and I have much to report. First, however, there is another matter that I have to discuss with you."

The Director's eyes twinkled. "Wondering how I smoothed things out with His Holiness?"

Cai Rui hesitated. "That...wasn't what I had in mind, sir, but I admit that I am curious. I was surprised to see the Cardinals here—"

"Two words, Commander: Pope-Mobile."

He halted in puzzlement over the unfamiliar word. "Pope...mobile?"

"Personal luxury destroyer, training for a professional Swiss guard crew, and unlimited refuelling at all Sol Force colonies." The Director's smile was cynical. "His Holiness likes to visit the Faithful once in a while."

"I see." Unable to completely restrain his laughter, Cai Rui bent and transformed it into a polite cough. "Well, I'm...glad to hear that the situation has been resolved...constructively."

"Indeed." The Director took another sip from his glass. "What was it that you really wanted to talk about, Rui?"

"Vance."

"Lost him." The Director looked away, but Cai Rui could feel the rolling thunder of rage under the surface, a bottomless fury. "We've tracked every lead. The bodies of the crew have all been identified; they were spaced a few Nodes from Junction. He's disabled all the locating devices on the ship, of course. Not surprising, given that he designed most of them." He turned to look at Cai Rui directly. "You received the list I sent to your terminal?"

"Yes sir. I did. Commander Otomi's name was still on it."

"Otomi was loyal." He shrugged. "To the species and the office, not the man or the woman sitting in it. I suspect it was not a personal thing." He sighed. "I don't believe she ever would have been party to something that would hurt the Force or the human cause."

Cai Rui's throat tightened. "No sir. I would agree."

"Then why are we still discussing it, Commander?" The blue eyes turned toward him—it was a demand, not a question.

"Because I believe that Vance took her life." Cai Rui removed the crystal from his breast pocket. "This is all the evidence I have been able to gather thus far. She

216

had begun to suspect that the Ripper drive system was Node based. After having seen their ships in action, I think this is a certainty."

The Director took the crystal and slipped it into his own pocket. "Are you coming back to work, TFC?"

Cai Rui offered a clipped nod of assent. "Yes sir. I have some concerns for my safety, of course. Commander Otomi was killed by a fellow officer. I have no desire to follow in her footsteps."

"Understandable." The Director turned away, looking out as the city kindled deep red in the last rays of the sun. "I'll watch your back, Commander, if you'll watch mine."

Despite everything, Cai Rui smiled. "Thank you, sir."

The man from MarsDome shook his head. "Don't mention it."

22 | THE MAN IN BLACK

C ai Rui looked up from his desk, putting on his mild-mannered smile like a mask. "Doctor."

Commander Kliggerman pointed to the guest chair. "Commander. Good to see you back. May I sit?"

He nodded graciously. "Of course." As the old man wearily dropped into the seat, he stood and went to his samovar. "Green tea?"

"Please." The White Section Commander accepted the cup with visible gratitude. "*Schönen Dank.* Thank you, Rui."

Cai Rui inclined his head pleasantly and resumed his seat. "How was the trip to Irridia?"

One of the bushy eyebrows rose. "Highly productive. You have read my report?"

"Of course. Excellent work, as always." Cai Rui folded his hands. "And our 'friend' was helpful, apparently."

"Oh...very." The Doctor's tone was dry. "Exuberantly so. I had to assign a special technician to write it all down."

"I see." Cai Rui sipped his tea. "Any more suicide attempts?"

The scientist shrugged. "A few. Nothing catastrophic. I sew him back together. He heals. Quite alarmingly fast." He sighed. "The self-mutilation continues, of course. There is nothing we can do to prevent it. If he is not restrained, he will always find some way." He shrugged. "He seems to find the pain...comforting?"

"I see."

"I must admit, Commander—I am a bit overwhelmed by all this." Kliggerman rubbed his palm over his balding pate. "Just a simple man, really. Blood-and-bones biologist. Jobs like this...?" He trailed off helplessly. "To do it properly, I must be a sociologist, linguist, psychologist—bah." He shook his head. "There should be a department."

Cai Rui smiled; it was one of Kliggerman's favourite rants. "I believe we've discussed this before. Some sort of...task force to investigate alien culture." He shrugged. "Of course, some would say that we already have Red, Yellow, and Blue Sections of Intelligence..."

"*Ja, ja, ja,*" the man said irritably. "And soon we will have another for Zuul. What, Section Purple? *Meshugas.*" He made a gesture with his hands, as if to press several things together. "Put all of them together, is what I say. All the language, culture, psychology. Make them coordinate."

Cai Rui shook his head. "Those three Sections are already unwieldy. To combine them into one Section..."

"Not a Section, Commander! A Corps. Separate, like the Research and Development, or Intelligence—they should have their own dome." He rolled his eyes. "Trust me boy. It's the only way to get rid of them."

Cai Rui chuckled. "You may have a point."

The older man took a sip of his tea. "They tell me you refused a promotion." He looked up from under his bushy brows. "This is true?"

"This is true."

"You do not want to be a Legator?"

"Call me crazy."

"All right, you are crazy." The White Section Commander winked. "But I wondered if there was a reason."

"At least one compelling reason, yes."

"Afraid of Vance? His people, maybe?" the Commander's gaze was frank. "I heard...things."

Cai Rui regarded him coldly. "There was a good deal to hear."

The old scientist held up a hand to forestall him. "Please. We were not friends. I only pitied him. He was never the same after his son died."

The Black Section Commander sat silent, hands folded.

Dr. Kliggerman looked down into his teacup. "Well. I should thank you, really. Otomi and I..." He trailed off awkwardly. "Things happen, of course. One continues to care for a person."

Cai Rui relaxed somewhat. "I believe I understand."

In the ensuing silence, the old man returned to the previous topic of conversation. "Perhaps you were not quite ready to move on, then. For personal reasons."

Cai Rui looked up from his desktop. "Personal?"

The old man's eyes were touched with his genuine sorrow. "She was...a special woman."

"Ah." He paused. "Margaret."

"It was not your fault, you know."

"Perhaps." Cai Rui's voice was quiet. "But she was not the reason."

"Anyway. So long as you are not...flagellating yourself." The old man sighed. "I get enough of that these days."

Cai Rui looked down again, allowing himself a moment to restore his composure. "No."

Commander Kliggerman sat back in his chair, bringing the teacup to his lips. "Then why?"

Cai Rui's smile returned—the old scientist's straight-forward approach was sometimes refreshing. "Some things are easier to tell than to show." He put a hand to his throat. "*Cicero—tenebrae. Praebe cornices.*"

The PDA obligingly turned down the lights in the room, reducing it to near darkness, and activated his desktop holo display. A convoy of ships materialized in the camera view—a stream of Liirian colony vessels, decelerating in-system as they moved toward the surface of a pristine world.

Dr. Kliggerman cocked his head. "One of your files?"

"The latest. This footage is just thirteen days old." Cai Rui sipped his tea. "Watch."

The Doctor nodded, putting the cup to his lip to watch the Liir ships make their approach. As the sleek vessels touched the upper stratosphere, a strange ship darted from the clouds to intercept them, a flattened, aerodynamic wedge of bronze shaped for atmospheric flight.

Dr. Kliggerman spit out his tea in a spray as the darting wedge of metal was joined by a second, a third, and a fourth. In seconds, the entire flotilla was under attack, seized in tractor beams and dragged into the clouds.

"*Mein Gott.*" The White Section Commander turned to him in amazement. "What the devil is that?

Cai Rui smiled. "A mystery."

"Was it—Zuul? Is that possible?"

He shook his head. "Definitely not. I've showed the footage to our friend—he went into hysterics immediately. Wouldn't look at it. He said that it was 'Mother.'"

Dr. Kliggerman turned to the hologram with renewed interest. "That's very... suggestive, no? Race X from Irridia? Is that possible—?"

"I have no idea." Cai Rui shrugged. "I've been analyzing the footage extensively, of course. But unless you found hard evidence of their technology—?" Kliggerman shook his head in the negative, and he sighed. "Then I am afraid at the moment, I cannot call it anything but 'Black Fourteen.'"

The White Section Commander shook his head. "Another one."

"Yes. Whatever it is, we have not seen it before. Neither had the Liir. They contacted me instantly. They seem to have decided that I am the 'go to' sentient of reference for things of this kind."

"Perhaps you are." The Doctor's eyes were bright. "Perhaps that is why you remain only a Task Force Commander. Perhaps in truth, you are only interested in one Section of Intelligence."

Cai Rui winked. "It's the uniform," he said. "I can't resist being a Man in Black."

APPENDICES

These appendices may not be of interest to all readers, and I sincerely hope that the audience will be able to read and enjoy *The Deacon's Tale* without referring to the appendices at all. After years of daily interaction with fans of the *Sword of the Stars* series, however, I know that there are some who have an inexhaustible appetite for the fine details of this imagined world. They want it all, and delight in being the academic experts of an alternate universe. It was for them that so many thousands of words of Lore have been created over the years, and it is for them that I include a small part of that corpus here. They are meant to entertain.

As an additional note, I should probably say that the appendices that follow are focused mainly on the historical events, people and places which are mentioned in passing in this particular novel. Readers who want information on other aspects of the Sword of the Stars universe can ask the author any question they wish on the forums at Kerberos Productions, the makers of *Sword of the Stars*. They can also search the in-game Encyclopedia of our latest release, *Sword of the Stars 2: Lords of Winter*, and the free, fan-created on-line Wikis which players of the game have filled with information over the last six years.

APPENDIX ONE: TERRA, SOL FORCE AND *HOMO SAPIENS* IN THE 25ᵀᴴ CENTURY

Newcomers to the *Sword of the Stars* universe are often curious about the future history of humankind, and where their own species stood in the 24th or 25th centuries. This brief overview focuses primarily on Terra (the human home world), Sol (the human home system), and on aspects of human life in the future which have changed radically from the norms of the present day.

The planet Earth of the 25th century has very little in common with the Earth as we know it today. The events of *The Deacon's Tale* are set in the year 2438, at the beginning of the Zuul War, but prior to this point the human race had already experienced a series of environmental, political, and social catastrophes which set the stage for the rise of Sol Force and the events of this novel.

The Thaw

Many of the projections for the future of humankind in the Sword of the Stars universe are based on "worst-case scenarios", in which the direst of many possible futures was taken as a given. The first of these dire possibilities was environmental catastrophe: Cai Rui's home world has witnessed a massive global climate change, leading to the complete dissolution of the polar ice caps and a hundred-meter rise in sea levels around the world.

This change took many decades from 1970-2200 CE. The event as a whole is popularly known as the Thaw. By the 25th century the process was long complete, and many generations of humans had already inherited a landscape barely recognizable to many of us today. Many hectares of the eastern United States, northern Europe, South America, and eastern China are now beneath several meters of salt water. The cities, nations and peoples that once occupied those coastal regions have had to adapt or disappear.

Citizens of the USA might be interested to know that in the future, Memphis, Tennessee is a thriving sea port, which presides over the bustling fishing and aquaculture industries of the Mississippi Islands. Houston, New Orleans, Miami, Savannah, Richmond, Washington D.C., Philadelphia, New York and Boston are all drowned cities.

In Canada, the Hudson Bay has expanded to swallow all of the major settlements of the coast and Southampton Island, including Churchill and Coal Harbor. Of the remaining population centers of the former eastern seaboard of North America, Quebec and Toronto are the most ancient and powerful that remain standing.

Further to the south, many islands of the Caribbean have disappeared, including the majority of Cuba. The eastern coast of Mesoamerica has seen a radical change in its coastline. Miles of coastal lowlands in southern Mexico are under water, most of the Yucatan is now under water, as are low-lying areas of Belize and the Mosquito Coast. The Panama Canal is no longer necessary, as an open sea lane exists in the Strait of Nicaragua.

The South American continent has been invaded by the sea. The Amazon Basin has become the Amazonas Bay, the inundation of salt water destroying 1.4 billion acres of tropical jungle which had been the oldest surviving forest on the planet, standing for 56 million years. 40,000 plant species, 3000 species of freshwater fish, and thousands of unique reptiles, birds and mammals have become extinct in the process, and 30 million human beings from 350 different indigenous cultures have died or been displaced. Further to the south, the former basin of the Rio de la Plata is also completely flooded, Buenos Aires is drowned and Ascunción and Santa Cruz are now the largest ports on the Gran Chaco Sound, which divides the southern tip of the continent into two peninsulas.

The continent of Africa has also seen profound changes in its topography. On the western side of the continent, the rising Atlantic has swallowed the Guinea Coast, inundating southwestern Mauritania and drowning all of Gambia, Guinea Bissau, and most of Senegal. Sierra Leone has lost over half its landmass and the rising Gulf of Guinea has claimed the coastal capitols of many former African nations in the region. South of Gabon, the western coast of Africa has been less effected. The major losses to the eastern coast of Africa have been the coastal forests of Mozambique, Tanzania and Kenya, lost to the Indian Ocean. The rising waters have created a natural sea lane between the Red Sea and the Mediterranean, severing at last the land bridge between Africa and the Near East.

The rising Mediterranean has affected all nations which once bordered upon that sea. The Nile Delta is inundated, and in northern Egypt and Libya the sea has claimed thousands of square kilometers of the northern Sahara, leaving the Libyan Plateau a peninsula still connected to the rest of North Africa by a delicate land bridge. Tunisia has been split in two by inundation, and south of Carthage the former Great Eastern Erg is now the Gulf of Algeria. Annual rainfall to all of North Africa has increased enormously, and much of the Sahara has shifted from desert to grassland.

Radical changes have taken place in the low-lying areas of western Europe. Barcelona and the French Riviera are lost to the sea and the Italian coastline has changed dramatically, its coastal lowlands completely engulfed. The heel of the world's most famous boot is now the island of Puglia, and the Adriatic has claimed all of the former Po Valley, which is now flooded to the foothills of the Alps. Even Rome has survived only at the costs of billions of dollars' worth of sea walls, which have been maintained for the last three hundred years.

Northern and Western Europe have both been devastated by inundation. Western France, Ireland, England and Scotland have all been reduced to chains of scattered islands. Half of Belgium is under water, and Denmark, the Netherlands, and all of northern Germany are lost to the sea. Most of eastern Poland, Lithuania, Latvia and Estonia have been reduced to scattered islands in the Baltic. The Gulf of Finland has risen to drown not only Helsinki but all of northwestern Russia, leaving a complex but navigable channel between the Baltic and the White Sea to the northeast. In Southern Russia, the Black Sea and the Caspian Sea have become a single body of water, and expanded to claim the lowlands of southern Romania and the Ukraine as far north as Kiev. It is possible to sail all the way from Istanbul to Kazhakstan.

The Middle East has also been reshaped by the Thaw. On the western coast of Saudi Arabia, many miles of temperate coastline have been lost to the Red Sea. In the east the Persian Gulf has risen to claim even more territory. Qatar is under water, Oman has lost its lowlands, and much of fertile Ash Shariqiyah region of Saudi Arabia has given way to salt marshes. All of the lowlands of Mesopotamia, Kuwait and southern Iran are under the sea; the city of Mosul has become a sea port.

All of southern Pakistan and the Gujarat region of India have surrendered to the Arabian Sea. Karachi and the coastal cities of India, including Mumbai, Kolkata and Chennai, are all drowned. On the eastern side of the Indian subcontinent, all of Bangladesh and the Orissa and Bihar regions of India have been swallowed by the Bay of Bengal, leaving India with a horn very similar in shape to the Horn of Africa.

In Southeast Asia, the Andaman Sea has claimed all of southern Myanmar and the Malay Peninsula is now an island chain. Indonesia has lost all of its low-lying territory on the east coasts, and the thriving cities of Jakarta, Singapore and Surabaya are gone. All of southern Thailand, southern Vietnam and Cambodia are inundated by the South China Sea including the great cities of Bangkok, Phnom Penh and Saigon. The northern regions of Vietnam have not fared much better; the fertile coastal regions are underwater, along with the cities of Da Nang, Hue and Hanoi. Only the stony spine and foothills of the Annamite Range have survived.

China has been catastrophically altered by the Thaw, its southern provinces radically reshaped by the rising sea, the famous ports of Macao and Hong Kong long drowned. The north eastern provinces if anything have been even more devastated by inundation, with the Yellow Sea sweeping in to claim all the lowlands south of the Mongolian Plateau, including the great city of Beijing. Eastern Japan has suffered similar losses to the Pacific Ocean, and the city of Tokyo is under many meters of water.

In the South Pacific, many of the former islands of Micronesia, Melanesia and Polynesia are now beneath the waves, and southern New Guinea is inundated. Australia has suffered heavy losses of arable land along the entire circumference of the continent, with a total loss of all the coastal settlements of the Northern Territories and Queensland and a massive inundation of formerly arable lands in Victoria and New South Wales. The cities of Adelaide, Melbourne and Sydney have been saved by billions of dollars' worth of high tech engineering and sea walls which hold the Pacific Ocean at bay.

The Conflagration

By the 23rd century, daily life on Earth had become extremely difficult, for a number of reasons. The industrial excesses of the 20th and 21st centuries left many parts of the globe stripped of natural resources, deforested, and/or saturated with dangerous toxins. As the rising waters and torrential storms of the Thaw swept over these blighted landscapes, hundreds of millions of human beings were displaced, and millions of acres of arable land and potable water resources were lost. Rising seas washed over the industrial titans of the 20th and 21st centuries. The legacy of industry and waste disposal in Southeastern North America, eastern China, west Africa and the former Soviet Union poisoned the seas that had engulfed their former coastlines.

All sea life which could survive in the resulting soup of leaching poison was so saturated with heavy metals and other pollutants that it became impossible for humans to rely on marine resources for food. By the mid 22nd century and for generations after it was a fatal risk to eat salt water fish, sea weeds, mollusks or invertebrates in many parts of the world. Even in allegedly "safe catch" environments, all marine comestibles were highly suspect, and in any region without rigid and vigilant regulation, sale and consumption of toxic sea foods were common. Even when a meal did not lead to immediate and painful death for the diner, the accumulated toxins of several such meals might kill the victim over time.

The combination of diminishing land for agricultural use and toxic marine resources created a dire shortage of food in many parts of the world. Many human populations, already dispossessed and impoverished by loss of their homes, were trapped between the rock and the hard place of starvation or self-administered contamination. The consequences of choosing the latter could include hair loss, lesions, loss of teeth and bone degeneration, as well as horrific birth defects.

Tensions had predictably increased over the decades as this process continued, and by the early 23rd century wars were erupting with fair regularity throughout the world. In 2216, the first limited nuclear exchanges began to accompany more conventional clashes of arms in Africa, Eurasia, and the Western hemisphere. The first use of nuclear weapons took place in the Kashmir region of the Indian sub-continent, but North America, Eastern Asia, Europe, and Australia would also suffer major strikes over the course of the next 20 years. Each of the individual conflicts during this period has its own name: the Kashmir War, the Megiddo War, the 16 Minutes' War, the Sino-Australian War, the Arctic War, etc.. In the end, however, the entire period is best remembered and is commonly taught by its collective name, the Conflagration.

The wars of the Conflagration are widely regarded as wars of Reformation. In 2239, Rome was one of many European cities badly damaged by factional strife. Wildfires burning during the bombing of Rome killed thousands, destroyed many of the city's priceless antiquities, and nearly breached the city's sea wall. This catastrophic loss of heritage and life provoked Pope Theodore IV to throw the full weight of the Church behind the world-wide peace movement of the period. The war in western Eurasia ended with the signing of the Pactum Consortio Europae (Consortium of Europa Agreement) in Rome in 2245, and Europa thus became the world's first Consortium government.

The Consortia

Terra in the 25th century is ruled by eight geopolitical conglomerates, each laying claim to a large geographic territory and millions or billions of citizens. The Europa Consortium was the first to form, but the Arctic, Australarctic, African, Ērānshahr, Han and Américas Consortia quickly followed.

The Consortia are divided into states and provinces, which occasionally correspond to pre-existing national boundaries and administrative units. The overall system is parliamentary and ostensibly representative, although in many Consortia there is little social mobility, and access to education and influence for all social groups is not always equal. Incomes and rations of food, energy and space for individuals, families and communal groups are set by unanimous votes by parliamentary committees which include the elected representatives of all regions, the leaders of the Consortium's Security Forces, and a Science and Ethics Advisory Board.

In the 23rd century and for the next two hundred years, Consortia governments cracked down sharply on their citizenry, and exerted heavy controls on consumption of resources and energy, non-sustainable industry, human reproduction, travel, and freedom of information. Protests, civil disobedience and rioting were common responses to the pressure on the general population. When the first human colonies were established in the early 25th century, Sol Force received millions of applications to emigrate, despite the dangers and the risks. As many colonists put it, "Life on the frontier is hard—but life on Earth was hell."

Religion in the 25th century

Although there are hundreds of surviving sects and faiths still commonly practiced by humankind in the Sword of the Stars future, this novel touches upon only two. Roman Catholicism will be familiar to most readers, but in the 25th century the numbers of the Faithful have grown from a mere one billion souls in the present to nearly eight billion human adherents Empire-wide. The first missions to proselytize a non-human population have also been founded upon two Tarka worlds, Ko'Seth and Ko'Grappa.

The other faith group mentioned in The Deacon's Tale is the Utilitarian Church, which formed in the 22nd century in the aftermath of the Thaw and the rise of the Consortia. The tenets of the modern Utilitarian Church are derived from ancient and contemporary Utilitarian philosophy, which once upheld the principle of the Greatest Good as an abstract ethical goal. This religion is now practiced by billions of human beings, and modern Utilitarians speak of the Greatest Good and the Divine, or "God", interchangeably. The faith has been increasingly popular since the life and times of the famous 23rd century Utilitarian saint and evangelist known as the Comedian, whose history and thoughts are chronicled in a gospel called the "Quotations". Typically printed or re-printed on recycled waste paper, the Comedian's gospel is popularly known as "The Little Brown Book".

Utilitarians are dedicated pacifists and do not believe that any war can serve a Greater Good, and thus be sanctioned as a morally correct course. Accordingly, modern Utilitarians have forbidden all members of the Church from joining Sol Force in any capacity since the beginning of the Hiver War, and relations between military servicemen and Utilitarian authorities are always somewhat strained.

The symbol known as the Tertium, or "Three Arrows", is familiar to many in the modern world. It is stamped on the collection bins that we use for recyclable materials. The most widespread religious symbol of the Utilitarian Church, the symbol of the Tertium represents the cycle of change and renewal for all existence: matter, energy, and spirit. The arrangement of arrows into a triangle serves as a reminder that the Universe is a closed system, and that all we do returns to us, good and bad.

Sol Force in the Year 2438

The following is not at all a comprehensive history of Sol Force and its achievements as an institution. These are simply a few miscellaneous definitions, biographies and notes which may help to place the events of *The Deacon's Tale* in context.

Sol Force Intelligence Corps (a.k.a. "SIC" or "the SICkness")

The smallest of the five Corps divisions of Sol Force in 2438, the Intelligence Corps made up less than 10% of all Sol Force personnel. The majority of men and women employed by Sol Force were assigned to its Ground Forces, Space Forces, Research and Development and Administrative Corps.

PDA

Personal Data Assistant. Cicero, Cai Rui's often-invoked electronic adjutant, is a wireless command and control system, including an artificially intelligent component. Only thirteen fully intelligent PDA systems are known to have been designed and installed into Sol Force personnel before the death of the cybernetic systems savant, Otomi Sayoko. Cicero was one of the thirteen.

Sol Force possessions

The "Thirteen Worlds" officially chartered by Sol Force in 2438 were Terra, Isis (2410), Spica (2415), Junction (2412), Midway (2412), Mjolnir (2413), Arcadia (2416), Nova Roma (2417), Hynek (2420), Vision (2421), Nemesis (2423), Fort (2428) and Kepler (2433). Sol Force control of the region designated as "Human Space" extended considerably further and included many outposts, listening posts, refueling stations and garrisons located in systems unsuitable for significant human occupation. In addition, many human-occupied worlds defended and supplied by Sol Force had not yet been granted the legal status of a colonial charter by the United Consortia.

Remembrance Day

The United Consortia of Terra established this holiday as a day of planetary mourning and reflection, not only for the crew of the Nova Maria, but the millions of Terran citizens killed when a Hiver fleet led by Obsidian Crown attacked the Earth on January 10, 2408.

Starfield on Mars

Construction on the MarsDome command center began in 2436 under the Directorate of Edward Alton MacKenzie III.

Data pad

The standard office and field computer of the 25th century, a data pad is a thin wedge of electronic components, covered by a light protective case of shock- and shatter-proof plastic.

Commander Otomi

Task Force Commander Otomi Sayoko. Born in 2332, Otomi Sayoko had received degrees and honors from the Han Consortium Institute of Technology, the Massachusetts Institute of Technology and the Europa Institute by the year 2356. Recruited as a member of Sol Force in 2366, Otomi was a member of the Sol Prima research project and a colleague to the pioneering physicist Blasky Yao Hsiang. In the years following the Sol Prima accident, she helped to develop the navigational computers of the first Node-capable starship, the Nova Maria, and many of the core information systems of the early military starships developed by Sol Force during the Hiver War. She assumed duties as a Task Force Commander in the Intelligence branch in 2412, and remained in command of Black Section until her untimely death in a shuttle accident on the surface of Luna on December 30, 2436.

Hiver Armistice

Signed on April 13, 2436 by Queen Radiant Frost, Director of Sol Force Edward Alton MacKenzie, Supreme Commander Var Ishi Thok'Orr and representatives of the Liir, this peace treaty was the first of four diplomatic agreements to secure a general peace among the known races.

Director Edward Alton MacKenzie

Born September 11, 2386 in the northeastern mountains of the Américas Consortium, Edward MacKenzie began his service career in 2401 as a member of Américas Security Forces. Transfer application to join Sol Force was accepted in 2407: placed in the new Ground Forces Corps, MacKenzie's service during the Hiver War earned him a series of field promotions and commendations. He was posted to Davos in 2412 for Officer Training, promoted to the rank of Tennant and thereafter assigned to the defense of the newly formed colony of Isis in 2414.

Promoted to Centurion in 2415, he acted as planetary Tribune after the death of his commanding officer during heavy fighting during the Tarka siege of Isis and was taken prisoner when the defensive satellites of the colony were destroyed in 2417. Deported to the infamous prison planet Ke'Trath by his captors, in 2419 MacKenzie led the general insurrection and eventual overthrow of staff assigned to guard the prison camp. Promoted to Primus of the Tarkasian theater in 2421 and Cohort Commander of Spinward Operations in 2428, he was eventually made Legator of Ground Forces in 2430 and assumed the Directorate in 2434. By 2438 he had received the Crimson Star and ten additional wound bands, the Terran Cross, five Meritorious Service Medals and the Platinum Star for Extraordinary Valor in the course of his Sol Force career.

Latin in the 25ᵗʰ Century

New Latin is the official language of the Europa Consortium, and has been since 2245. Although many regions and principalities within the Consortium speak other languages in common parlance, Latin is used for all official documents and is the primary language taught in schools. After over 300 years of use by Church, Consortium and common people, it has evolved into a vibrant spoken and written language, and it is often used by Sol Force and its personnel. The official motto of the service is *Per Ardua ad Astra*, "Through Hardship, the Stars", but the unofficial motto often scrawled on warheads and hulls after the Hiver attack was *Repensum est Canicula*—"Payback is a Bitch".

A brief glossary of Latin terms and phrases follow, in their order of appearance in the text of *The Deacon's Tale*. For convenience they are organized by chapter heading.

Chapter One:
Sorora: "Sister".
Lux: "Light".

Chapter Two:
Cicero. Praebe gladium Damoclitis.: "Cicero, display the sword of Damocles."
Cicero. Procede per tempora.: "Cicero, proceed through the ages." (Note: Cicero is an Artificial Intelligence, programmed to respond only to commands and requests issued in Latin.)
Cicero. Insignum maximum: "Symbol enhanced to largest size."

Insignum Hiveris maximum: "Hiver symbol enhanced to largest size." The Latin neologism *"Hiver, Hiveris"* is a simple third declension noun of the masculine gender.

Chapter Three:
Congelat'elevator: Caecus surdusque.: Literally "Freeze elevator. Blind and deaf."
Cicero, restit'elevator: "Cicero, restore the elevator."

Chapter Four:
Praebete crucem, si placuit. Arma reliquenda sunt. "Present the cross, sir, if you please. Weapons must be left behind."
Nomen? "Name?"
Do't detes, non? "Keep an eye on it, no?"
Congregatio pro Doctrina Fidei. The Congregation for the Doctrine of the Faith.
Dei semper gratia. "Always by the grace of God." Matthew 6:26: "Behold the birds of the air, for they sow not, nor reap, nor gather corn into the granary, and yet your heavenly Father provides for them. Are you not of greater value by far than they are?"
Gratia, gratia. "Thank you, thank you."
Cupietis aut biber'aut cenare? Num carebitis quoquam? "Will you desire anything to drink or to eat? Is there anything you lack?"
Ut Deus vult. "As God wills."
Ferte cenam ad studium, Johanne. Amabo te. "Bring dinner to the study, John. Please."
Pax Tarkana. Literally, "the Tarkasian Peace". A non-aggression treaty had been signed by Tarkasian and human ambassadors in 2434, orchestrated in part by Pope Caius III and the Tarkasian Empress Ma'ak.

Chapter Six
Ego sum nuntius Dei. Ostendete mihi solam veritatem: "I am the messenger of God. Reveal to me the only truth."
Date mihi testimonium. "Give me the recording."

Chapter Seven
Nollo hic esse: "I don't want to be here."

Chapter Ten
Deus misereatur. "May God have mercy,"
Ignis! "Fire!"
Mappa strategia Avalonae: "Strategic map of Avalon."

Non-Latin foreign languages and jargon used by Sol Force military personnel in this chapter:

Xin loi: Literally "I'm sorry"—in this case "too bad" or "tough luck".
Eagles: ships of the Cruiser class.
Gauss PD and grasslights: gauss cannon point defense and green lasers.
NKC: "No Known Configuration."
Gāiside: "Holy crap."

Chapter Eleven
Fulcrum totibus: "A lever to all."
Tu et quis exercitus, canicula? "You and what army, bitch?"
Acanthis: "Barnswallow."

Chapter Twelve
Scivi te futurum esse. Non alius in mundo tam insanus est qui in tali loco inveni-retur. "I knew it would be you. No other man in the universe is insane enough to be found in such a place."
Amabo te. "Please." Idiomatic. Literally, "I will love you."
Mea culpa, mea maxima culpa: "Through my error, through my greatest error." It is part of a traditional Latin prayer called Confiteor—"I confess."

Chapter Fourteen:
Vale: "Greetings". Idiomatic, literally it is a command. "Be well".
Pythona... Pythona videram..: "The Serpent... I have seen the Serpent."
Nollo me dare Serpenti. Conserva me...mi filii..: "Do not give me to the Serpent....save me, my son."

Chapter Sixteen:
Tangi interfaciem.: "Touch the interface."
Praebe malafortunas.: "Display the accidents."

Si vales, valeo.: "If you are strong, I am strong." Idiomatic, a standard greeting or goodbye between close friends.

Chapter Nineteen:
angelus malos: "Evil Angels".
Diabolus enim et alii daemones a Deo quidem natura create sunt boni, sed ipsi per se facti sunt mali.: "The Devil and the other demons were created by God with a nature that was good, but through their own fault became evil." Declared by the 4th Lateran Council in 1215 CE.

Chapter Twenty-Two;
Cicero—tenebrae. Praebe cornices.: "Cicero—darkness. Display the crows."

APPENDIX TWO: *TARKA SAPIENS*

For obvious reasons, this appendix cannot be an exhaustive account of the Tarka people and their Empire. I have included only a few notes to set the scene of this novel from a Tarka perspective: a few details on the Empire in 2438, its relevant cultural traditions, and a glossary of the Tarka language terms used in this book.

Setting the scene

In the year 2438, the territory controlled by the Tarkasian Empire and its Supreme Commander, Var Ish Thok'Orr, included six core worlds and twenty newly founded colonies which were still in the very early phases of development. The home world of Tarka sapiens and capitol of this expanding Empire is *Kao'Kona* (literally "Fortress of the Gods").

Kao'Kona is a warm, heavily vegetated planet, its biosphere thick and fertile, its topography dominated by primeval wetlands and old growth forests. It is surrounded by nine small moons, the "Nine Sisters". These relatively tiny satellites are universally characterized as female and divine in Tarka culture, although on different continents there are different names and myth cycles associated with the lunar goddesses.

Tarka planet names

In the Tarka language, the word *ko* has a rich abundance of connotative meanings. The most basic translation of the word is often "fortress" or "citadel", as the *ko* is always a protected space. But the word also means "home", and thus can be used to describe any personal residence, from a great palace to a cardboard box in the gutter. *Ko* doubles as "household" and serves as the metonym for the family as well. It is used by Tarka sociologists to describe the fundamental social unit of their species: one or more adults and the children that they collectively raise.

It is for this reason that the majority of Tarka planets and colonies are always named with the prefix "Ko" (or the same word in other dialects, with a vowel shift to "Ke", "Kao", "Ku", etc.). Literally these would translate as "the cherished home of the people" or "the fortress of the people". The six core colonies of the Tarkasian Empire in 2438 were Ko'Seth, Ku'Van, Ko'Rorkor, Ko'Grappa, Ke'Vanthu, and Ke'Raath.

Tarka castes

Tarka civilization is splintered into many hierarchies, each with its own chain of rank from highest to lowest. In general, the broadest divisions of Tarka society are those of caste, followed by those of clan and family. There are three traditional castes in Tarka society, and these three castes have been kept separate for long enough to begin the formation of some sub-species traits.

The military and professional castes are the *Urduku*, the Common Folk, and serve as a middle class. Physically speaking, *Urduku* can be picked out by their size and the range of their scale colors and patterns, which give them excellent camouflage in an arboreal environment.

By far the largest and most varied population group is the so-called Gutter Caste, the working classes of Tarka society. Gutter Caste members practice the majority of trades and represent over sixty percent of the general population. Physically speaking, Gutter Tarka are notable for robust health and the brilliance and beauty of their scales, which have much brighter and more highly contrasting hues than Tarka of other castes.

The smallest caste group among the Tarka is the *Kona*, "the Exalted Ones", the ancient ruling elite. Members of the Kona caste were once god-kings analogous to an Egyptian pharaoh or a Chinese Emperor; they are said to be descended from specific gods of the Tarka pantheon, and the leading member of a Kona family is also the officiating cleric of that god's highest temple. The Kona are the traditional royal families of the nine continents of Kao'Kona, the so-called "Nine Emperors" of the Tarka race, and even in the modern age they have significant power and influence. Physically speaking, members of the Kona caste are adapted for life at higher elevations than common Tarka, and have slightly different physiology and metabolism than *Urduku* and Gutter Tarka. They tend to be physically smaller, especially the females, and of all Tarka they are the only caste which suffers any deleterious side effects from inbreeding. Traditional Kona have a relatively small range of scale colors and patterns; each clan of the Nine Emperors is named for the dominant color of the clan'sir scales.

The Nine Emperors

The nine surviving clans of the Kona caste are all named for the dominant color of their scales; among the Tarka, this biological feature was traditionally imbued with symbolic meaning. As an example, centuries ago the *Pon Kona* ("White Emperors") claimed descent from the Tarka God of Death, whose epithet was *Var Ponu*, "He Who Whitens". When a Tarka dies, the color drains from the anterior portion of the eye and the inner lids often close, leaving the eyes of the corpse white; Tarka representations of ghosts, monsters and demons have the white eyes of the dead; statues and paintings of death deities, male or female, nearly always depict them as white-scaled from head to foot.

The white scales of the Pon Emperors therefore invoked powerful associations with Death, and the majority of heroic legends and myth cycles among the Tarka will include a visit to the White Mountain, the traditional seat of the Pon Emperor's court. If a mortal hero or heroine lost a loved one, or had to travel to the Land of the Dead for some other reason, he or she could petition the Pon Emperor to "intercede with his Father", the White God. More often than not the Emperor would refuse, of course, but this was seldom the end of the story. Typically there was a White Lad or a White Maiden who would take pity on the protagonist and find a way to sneak past the clan leader and into the underworld. For thousands of years the Pon Kona were said to guard one of the portals into Hell.

Similar associations exist for all of the Kona clans. The *Bak Kona* ("Black Emperors") were said to be children of *Koka*, "She Who Burns", a Goddess of Fire. The Kona characters of *The Deacon's Tale* are children of the *El Kona*, the Golden Emperors. The Empress Ma'ak, their clan leader, is the high priestess and living avatar of the Goddess *Nura*, the Dawn.

241

Tarka languages

Kona Kai is literally "the High Speech" or "the language of the gods". This dialect is spoken and written by the ruling caste and their functionaries, and is common in religious liturgy and courts of law. The Tarkasian military and its imperial bureaucracy commonly use *Urdu Kai*, "fleet speech" or "the common tongue". Alien races typically encounter the Tarkasian military and its Empire long before coming into contact with Tarkasian civilians and any other aspect of traditional Tarka culture, and so the majority of humans and Hivers who speak "Tarka" will be speaking the language of the military, the Empire and the middle caste in general: this language is called *Urdu Kai*, "Common Speech". The vast majority of the civilian population on Tarka worlds will speak one or more of the lower caste languages collectively known as *Horodu Kai*, "the gutter dialects". There are thirteen languages spoken by the Gutter Caste, but these are all members of a single language family; in different regions and trades it has diversified, but the majority of dialects are mutually intelligible.

The only language universal to all living Tarka is the Egg Knock Code, a rhythmic sempahore which Tarkas learn to speak even before they are hatched.

Tarka names

The conventions of Tarka naming are relatively simple to discern by context, but a formal review helps to illuminate the language in general. The formal name of any Tarka will have three components: a personal name, a family name, and a clan name. Thus the current Supreme Commander's name, *Ish Thok'Orr*, indicates that his personal name is Ish ("quick, lively"), the head of his natal household was *Thok* or *Thoka* ("superior", in this case a military rank corresponding to Major) and his clan name is *Orr* (literally the Tarka equivalent to "smith", a worker in steel).

Personal names for males are simple and usually end in a consonant. The female variant of the same name will end in a vowel. The male version of the name may double as an adjective, while the female will be used as an adverb. The common name *Kal* connotes "beauty" in Urdu Kai, but a ship called the *Kal War'ko* is "The Beautiful Jade Castle", while adding the feminine *kala* to a verb means that the thing has been done "beautifully, extremely well, in a way most attractive".

Tarka personal names are modified by means of title, suffix and infix to indicate relationships and social status. Adding the word *Var* ("father") to a male's name indicates that he is a Changed male, capable of fathering children. To add a suffix to a male or female personal name indicates intimacy, at minimum a friendly personal relationship; Tarka who consider Rui Cai a personal friend call him *Caido*, "dear Cai", and in especially tender moments one might call a woman *Saradora*, "my beloved Sara".

A further evolution of a Tarka's name takes place when he or she becomes a clan leader or head-of-household. The personal name is modified to reflect the role. If female, the gendered ending of the name is dropped, and the central vowel is doubled as an infix. The connotations of any word's meaning can be enlarged by a similar process. For example, a Tarkasian *kum* is a small kingdom or province, but the word for "empire" is *ku'um*. The word *bhut* is used for tiny figurines and statuettes, but a life-size or monumental statue of a god or hero is a *bhu'ut*. And while a person might be irritated by a spot of *khak* ("dirt") on a freshly cleaned floor, the word *kha'ak* is analogous to Latin *terra*, and describes a whole landscape; Tarkasian farmers are *kha'aku*, "those who work the land".

In this novel, a woman who was once called *Maka*, "She Is Fair-Minded", becomes upon her ascension to clan leader *Ma'ak*, "Justice". One or both of her children may eventually serve in the same role after her death, and their names would be modified accordingly. If *Sara* ("She Is Sharp") becomes Empress, she will become *Sa'ar*, "Military Genius". If the ascending child were *Lan*, "the Large One", he would become *La'an*, "Immensity".

Lac Tar

The highest rank of the Tarkasian military. In theory, the Lac Tar is a war-leader of 100,000 souls, but in practice the *lactaru* generally command whole theaters of war rather than a single army of any particular size. The numbers under their command vary according to the situation.

Daiko! Yan'-sara, dai.

Literally: "Boss! To be like a sword, sir." *Yan'sara*, "to be sharp", is an idiomatic turn of phrase for the Tarkasian warrior, indicating the "sharpness" which makes a person quick-thinking, well-informed, or otherwise ahead of the competition. The *sar* is both a swift, light curved blade commonly carried by warriors and also the personal name of the Tarkasian god of war, *Sardo Kal*, "Our Friend, the Sharp Son of Beauty".

Masaaku

Literally, "The ones who strike without warning". Slavers.

Habas yan.

"I am honored."

Humaanu

This is the polite term which Tarka use to refer to the human race as a whole.

ko'di

In the Tarkasian language, the diminutive suffix can also distinguish between large collectives, such as a major urban center, a colony or a whole planet, versus single cities, towns or outposts. A *ko'di* is smaller than a *ko'*.

kokari

Literally, "to be aflame", but most commonly used for sexual desire. In many Tarkasian dialects, *kokari dok* ("entwining in flames") is a euphemism for playful, non-reproductive sex.

"Six saal's worth of soldiers"

A *saal* is the smallest command unit of the Tarkasian military, consisting of ten warriors. The crew complement of the S.F.S. Nanjing, a detached platoon of Ground Forces legionnaires and a Black Section operative lost in a single mission, would add up to 59 apes, which would equate roughly to six *saalu*.

t'mao

Tarkasian garments for the lower body are typically divided into two types. The *mao* is an undivided skirt or sarong, generally worn only on formal occasions, by priests or by the elderly. *T'mao* is the general term for "trousers", and typically refers to a traditional split skirt for men, cut to accommodate the tail in the back.

Kala d'oyo

Literally, "Beautiful of you (plural)". An idiomatic greeting for those who have accepted an invitation or arrived to a meeting place.

po'goru

Po is a soup or stew which includes meat. *Po'goru*, literally, is "foreigner's stew", and the term is all-inclusive of many dishes adopted from an alien race.

dumplenu

Adapted from the English "dumplings", what Tarkas called *dumplenu* are actually Asian *shuǐjiǎo*, "boiled dumplings".

kegenu

Literally "Listeners". A term for professional spies.

lolo'kaad

The military of the early Tarkasian Empire divided its holdings into these units. A lolo'kaad usually contains six or seven star systems.

Kal War'ko

Literally "Beautiful Jade Castle". A Tarkasian Cruiser.

Habas'ku

"House of Honor". A Tarkasian Cruiser.

Garanu

Literally, "They Will Shed Blood." A Tarkasian Cruiser.

Ao'Thaak

"Blue Thunder". A Tarkasian Cruiser.

Kala du'maas

"Beautifully struck", an excellent blow.

Go'ma

A miniature tree sloth common to the Tarka home world.

Sar'du saak

An unprintable reference to the war god's genitalia.

Lan Liir'doma

"Lan the Liir-handed".

Tordo, Tordomo

Endearment variants of the masculine name *Tor*, "Made of Stone".

Kidnepu

A neologism formed by giving the English "kidnap" a common Tarka declension.

APPENDIX THREE: *HIVER SAPIENS*

Hivers are a rare phenomenon, a fully sentient eusocial species. Like the simple mole rat and many insects of old Terra, their biological strategy includes division of reproductive labor, overlapping generations, and cooperative care of young. They are not at all a telepathically linked "hive mind", however, nor are individual members of the species less than fully-formed personalities. No Hiver is less than fully sentient unless physically damaged or suffering from a chromosomal birth defect.

Hivers have three biological castes: the Worker, the Warrior and the Royal. Workers and Warriors are sterile males, and the Royals are viable males and females. Morphology, psychology and lifespan of the three castes are all very different.

Warriors have the shortest lifespans and the widest range of physical body types; socially they are relegated to military service or high-risk, high-stress industrial labor. Their bodies are often adapted to the tasks they are assigned, and a Warrior`s metabolism, respiration, armor, size and mass can all be tailored to suit local conditions or a specific task. Warriors can range in size and mass from small, hyper-light individuals adapted to flight to heavy, massively armored hulks suitable for mining and security forces. In general they produce a stew of aggression hormones and are subject to stronger emotions, especially anger, than other Hivers. Warriors seldom have a natural lifespan over 60 years.

Workers are smaller than Warriors in general, with lower mass than the average human. They are the rank and file in the majority of all skilled and unskilled professions, including sciences and engineering, the arts and priesthood, manufacturing, agricultural labor, and service industries. Workers are sensitive and intelligent as a rule, but they can be as stubbornly loyal as Warriors when tested. Their expected life span ranges from 50-90 years.

Royal Hivers fall into three categories. Prince and Princess Hivers are the most common Royals. Socially speaking, biologically viable males and females are both highly valued and hold a great deal of political and social power, but Hiver society is both matriarchal and matrilineal overall. The core unit of Hiver society is the clan, which consists of a Princess and her sons. In some cases a Hiver clan will also have a Prince Consort, a male breeding partner who is father to one or more generations of children. The lifespans of Hiver Royals are very long, in comparison to the sterile castes. Princes live over six centuries on average, and Princess Hivers live for over a thousand, barring accident and illness.

This long potential lifespan is extended further in a Hiver Queen. The Queen is essentially a third class of Royal, a Princess who achieves full sexual maturity. Typically a Princess can only produce male offspring; the Queen is able to create new female offspring, and is thus the creatrix of new clans, the Mother of Mothers. At this juncture in Hiver history, it had been normal for thousands of years for the entire Hiver race to have only one Queen. The Queen's biological and political power was sacralized for the sake of social and political stability; the majority of Hivers in any walk of life would bow to the authority of a Queen, and the "Greatmother" of the Hiver race was both biologically and politically supreme.

Hiver characters in The Deacon's Tale

The Hiver characters in *The Deacon's Tale* are members of a single extended biological family. Chezokin is a Royal male, a Prince, formerly a Strategist (a rank equivalent to Admiral) in the Hiver fleet and now the Prince Consort to the Burning Smoke Clan, which specializes in manufacturing and shipping. The other Hiver characters in the novel are Chezokin's biological and adoptive sons, the children of his murdered wife, Divine Smoke, who was their mother. Ykezet and other Warrior characters in the book are members of an elite personal guard, sworn to defend and fight beside their father, Prince Chezokin. The only Worker character in the novel is Ezz'in, who accompanies his father and brothers for an adventure aboard the Jade Mirror.

Hiver languages

Full literacy for Hivers requires the mastery of three written languages: *K'en-k'en*, *Ri'kap-ken*, and *Tcho'to-ken*. The majority of Hivers can read and write only in *K'en-k'en*, a phonetic language which represents sounds with symbols, while colors and smells are represented with punctuation marks.

Military Hivers, imperial bureaucrats, historians and scholars must also learn *Ri'kap-ken*, derived from the oldest surviving Hiver language group. In *Ri'kap-ken*, whole words are represented by complex symbols, and combinations of symbols render sentences or whole thoughts. The arrangement of different symbols into different configurations can change the meaning drastically, as when the word "ally" becomes "enemy" by placing a single stroke in a different position.

By contrast, the *Tcho'to-ken* written language is an art form, analogous to calligraphy painting; Hiver royals often write poetry, personal letters and diaries in *Tcho'to-ken* form, using perfumed scrolls and inks which add to the meaning of the finished piece. *Tcho'to-ken* pieces are considered works of fine art, and even other races have been known to try to collect them when they can. Director Edward A. MacKenzie was given the gift of a folding screen made from Hiver papyrus and painted by a royal artist with a *Tcho'to-ken* poem when the Human-Hiver peace treaty was signed in 2436, for example. In the two years that followed, the slow curing of the inks and dyes released a different fragrance every day.

Hiver names

Hiver naming conventions are relatively simple. A Worker or a Warrior generally has a full name consisting of a personal name and a clan designation, or a mother's name. The pool of names for Workers and Warriors tends to be limited, and many personal names are so common as to be almost generic. The most common name for a Hiver Worker, for example, is *Chekin*, "Faithful" or "Humble". One of the most common names for a Warrior is *Yket*, "Brave". Either the Worker or the Warrior would introduce himself as "*Chekin* son of (insert mother's name)" or "*Yket* of the (insert clan name)". Literally such a name would translate as "A humble son of the Princess" or "a brave son of the clan". Close associates might have a nickname for this Hiver, but this would never be known outside his intimate circle unless he became a literary figure.

Royal Hivers are usually given more elaborate names at birth, in an attempt to invoke connotations of beauty, power, and strength. Since royal markings are often dramatic, the names may reflect the appearance of the new-born Royal infant; the infamous black Princess of the Interregnum was named Obsidian Crown, for example, while her aunt's white chitin was acknowledged with the name Radiant Frost. Other Royal names may invoke a desirable connection with nature; the two Queens prior to Radiant Frost's ascension were Iron Tempest and Immaculate Pearl, and the Princess Regent was called Autumn Twilight.

The names of Princes reflect similar aspirations to those of Princess Hivers, but they can also invoke masculine beauty, martial skill, and death, as well as a connection to powerful, elemental and potentially destructive forces in the natural world. Iron Razor, Silent Forest and Storm of Bones are well-known and recognizably "princely" names. The name Chezokin, however, is not at all Royal, and requires a brief explanation.

Reincarnation among the Hivers

Due to the quirks of Hiver physiology, death is not necessarily the end of a Hiver's life. A great deal of short and long-term memory is stored in crystalline form in a Hiver's brain case, and these chemicals can be extracted intact for days, months or years after death. With the help of a Princess or Queen, who passes these crystallized chemicals through her digestive tract, the memory of the fallen Hiver can be re-born in a freshly laid egg. The result is a new Hiver which has many of the memories, skills and experiences of the Hiver who died.

Such a Hiver is called a *zok'an*, "a Beloved". The word carries connotations of immortality and re-birth. Once reincarnated, a Hiver is entitled to add the infix *zok* to his or her name. Examples include the legendary Hiver warrior *Rizokis*, "Beloved Blades", or the Hiver Prince *Chezokin*, who has taken the most common and least impressive Worker's name, *Chekin*, and added the infix to become "the Humble Son Re-born".

Hiver Imperium in 2438

In the year 2438 (Hiver Year 4044), the Hiver Imperium was much diminished from its maximum territorial extent. Hiver-controlled space consisted of eight core systems and a number of badly damaged or newly settled worlds. The Hiver home world, Tcho'to'pre, remained intact, and the surviving core systems of the Hiver race were Chis'ka-tet, Etos'che, Chozanti, Zozoris, Xhezek, and Chyprek.

The Hiver Imperium had been reunified in 2435 under Queen Radiant Frost, who assumed the throne and put an end to a long Interregnum. Prior to this event, the Hiver race had been without a Queen for many centuries, and fallen into disorder; many factions and individual clans were fighting for control of Hiver space, as Cai Rui observes in his Commencement Address.

The "Hiver War"

The brief and bloody conflict between the newly emergent Human race and the Hiver clans during their Interregnum raged from 2408 to 2436. The war began when a nesting fleet led by renegade Princess Obsidian Crown attempted to subdue Terra, the human home world, via orbital bombardment. Enraged by the unprovoked attack, Sol Force responded by exploring and colonizing all neighboring systems in force, destroying any pre-existing Hiver population in any system they were found. Formerly Hiver-held systems lost to the human race during this period included Rychopre, Tisketis, and Rizdet.

A taste for cheese

Hiver gourmands have a deep love of human cheeses, yogurts, alcoholic beverages, vinegars, and sourdough breads. They take great pleasure in the variation of flavors and fragrances offered by Terra's native microorganisms. Cultures of lactose and a few other random sugars are also able to intoxicate a Hiver; the standard alcohol molecule that Humans enjoy, although it registers as tasty and interesting, does not affect their brain chemistry the way it does a Human's.

metz'ekqua

Literally "infinite hatred", "revenge without numbers". The morality of Hiver clans can be feudal at times, and the life of each Hiver can be weighed and given a value in blood or coin. The lives of Warriors are not often counted when one clan demands reparations from another, but the lives of Workers and Princes killed unjustly or without cause can be weighed and a "blood price" for their deaths can be demanded as the price of peace. The phrase metz'ekqua, however, indicates a crime so enormous and abominable that it is impossible to place a number or value upon it. Reparations are therefore impossible to calculate, and peace cannot be bought at any price. The only possible solution is the absolute extermination of the enemy.

Hiver air recyclers...

The Hiver sense of smell is far more developed than that of other sentients, and Hivers are extremely adept in arts and sciences which make use of their enhanced faculties. They excel in chemistry and delight in cooking and blending of perfumes and incense; their air filters and pollution control measures are second to none.

"These wings were my reward for service to my people"...

All Hivers are naturally equipped with wings, but in the Worker and Warrior they are generally clipped at birth and are reduced to the wing cases in adult life. Royal Hivers, however, take great pride in their wings, and they are carefully groomed and pampered to enhance the beauty of both males and females. When Chezokin says "These wings were my reward", he is referring to his rebirth as a Hiver Prince, an honor granted to him upon his death as a former Worker.

Greatmother

The Hiver Queen is known as *Tcho Zok'anin*, Holy Mother of All.

Another jump through the Queen's Gates...

The Jade Mirror is a Hiver freighter, and it travels via a network of instantaneous matter-transmission Gates. Traveling by Gate is not congenial to the constitution of non-Hivers, and can cause serious physical problems due to the stresses of temporary ischemia. Common symptoms of Gate sickness include nausea, vomiting, palpitations, sweating, acute anxiety or fatigue. Repeated Gate transport is not recommended for non-Hivers and in rare cases may cause death by cardiac infarction, ischemic or hemorrhagic stroke, as thrombosis and aneurysms may appear anywhere in the victim's body.

ru-rek

A commander of a force of twelve to twenty-four Hivers, a rank equivalent to Lieutenant.

rek

A force of twelve to twenty-four Hivers, equivalent to a platoon.

"I am the Father of the Burning Sun … ".

Chezokin's chitin is highly resistant to both small arms fire and open flame. All Hiver chitin is defensive, a composite substance similar in structure to modern composites of ceramic and carbon filaments. The Burning Sun clan specialized in manufacturing, however, and the Prince, like his wife and sons, is especially resistant to heat and sparks.

APPENDIX FOUR: *LIIR SAPIENS*

*T*he Deacon's Tale, like the majority of background fiction for the *Sword of the Stars* universe, is told from a predominantly human viewpoint. In the year 2438, the contact between *Homo sapiens* and *Liir sapiens* was extremely limited. Only one human being had ever visited Muur, the Liirian home world, and no Liir had ever visited Terra. Sol Force had no diplomatic ties with the Liir species beyond a non-aggression pact which bound Hivers, Tarka and Liir as well as Humans with a promise not to fire on one another's ships.

The Tarkasian Empire shared a disputed border with the Liir in the early decades of the 25th century, and it was along that chain of systems that the majority of Tarka-Liir battles took place, including the skirmish witnessed by the SFS Copernicus and its battle group after their disastrous first contact with the Tarka at the Battle of Kam'Kir.

Nonetheless, humans had developed the Blue Section team of Sol Force Intelligence to learn more about the Liir and their empire, and White Section had acquired a few Liir cadavers to find out what they could about Liir biology. What follows is a few of the details available to Sol Force personnel like Cai Rui in the opening months of the Zuul War—in particular those which help to illuminate the words and actions of Ishii, the book's Liir character.

Prehistory and recent events

The Liir are an air-breathing aquatic species, and bear a limited physical resemblance to the extinct cetaceans of Old Earth. They are the result of a long-term process of environmental change: an ice age lasting millions of years initially allowed for the development of mammalian species on the isolated tropical islands and huge ice shields of their home world, but eventually an extended warming period resulted in a planet with less than 10% of its surface above water. The vast majority of land-dwelling species returned to the sea—including the early ancestors of the Liir.

The Liir have not been a star-faring species for long. Up until 2200 CE, they were a peaceful race with limited technology. Various agrarian and nomadic cultures operated within the rich waters of their home world, and war was virtually unknown to them. Although they had not developed far in the sciences of architecture or ballistics, some Liir groups were extremely advanced in bio-engineering, aquatic horticulture, volcanic engineering and metallurgy.

The first human being to have personal contact with the Liir reported what he gleaned from interviews with Liir spacers and Liir citizens on Muur, the Liir home world. The story they told at the time was that their people had been enslaved by star-farers called the Suul'ka. The Suul'ka established a powerful industrial base on Muur and force-marched the Liir through the Industrial Revolution by employing them as slaves in mining operations, factories and manufacturing facilities.

After several decades of abuse, realizing that the greed and rapacity of the Suul'ka would destroy the aquatic environment of their home world completely, the Liir rebelled against their space-faring masters. The war was remarkably bloody in its early stages, but finally ended when the Liir unleashed a "living weapon" which could attack the Suul'ka in space. It was impossible to say what biological agent the Liir may have used, or what vectors it followed. Sol Force Intelligence assumed that a plague weapon had been deployed, one so virulent and lethal that it quickly spread beyond the colony and completely eradicated the Suul'ka, at least from that sector of space.

In 2438, the state of Liirian culture and technology was a result of this successful rebellion. The former slaves of the Suul'ka quickly absorbed the abandoned technology of their masters, and adapted the old drives, guns and orbital elevators to their own use. Driven by natural curiosity and the desire to pre-empt any further assaults from the stars, the Liir began exploring and colonizing space. By the year 2438, they had established a presence in four core systems surrounding their home world: Biima, Shuulsi, Moshu and Tuumen.

Physical and Social Characteristics

The Liir are an unusual species in more ways than one. Their bodies are sleek and dynamic, allowing for fast movement in water. Although they appear completely smooth, their skins are in fact coated with a layer of dense, fine fur, patterns and colors of which will vary with the individual. They bear live young, and all members of the species are hermaphroditic, possessing both male and female sex organs. The majority of Liir are capable of both fertilizing as a male or bearing young as a female, but only the very oldest Liir can do both at once—it is normally impossible for a Liir to impregnate as a male while carrying an offspring itself.

Liir take on gendral pronouns to indicate the dominant pursuits of the phase of existence through which they are passing. A Liir who is gestating, birthing and nursing young, for example, considers herself a "she" since her existence is devoted to her feminine side. An Elder who has ceased to function as a female is usually a "he", although there are rare exceptions to this rule.

A newborn Liir is very small, less than half a meter in length and weighing only 8-10 kilograms. By the time they reach the age of majority, after a period of roughly fifty years, a standard Liir will be around three meters long and weigh approximate 120 kilograms. There seems to be no natural end to the potential life span of any given Liir, and throughout their lives the Liir never stop growing: some observers have reported sightings of elder Liir over 60 meters long, massing many tons.

The most unusual feature of the Liirian race is not the shape of their bodies, however, but the power of their minds. The Liir communicate largely by telepathic means, although they do have some very rudimentary sound-signals that convey strong but simple emotions—being startled, amused, frightened, angry, etc. In addition to their highly evolved telepathy, they have developed a refined and instinctive use of telekinesis.

Liir do not have opposable digits to manipulate objects. Although they are equipped with small and highly sensitive tentacles, these are mainly for foraging and social contact, not for grasping tools. In order to wield instruments, the Liir use telekinesis. A deft Liir can use several tools at once, and can often operate many simple machines simultaneously. With some concentration, they can also hurl objects with astonishing force. The spear was a traditional hunting weapon among the Liir for many centuries.

Although they have large, light-sensitive eyes, the frequency range of Liirian vision is limited. They have a very refined sense of taste and a sophisticated array of sound-producing and sound-receiving equipment to compensate for the lack of optical senses. Liirian echo-location is good enough to allow them to create very sophisticated three-dimensional schematics of any machine or device simply by "singing" to it and reading the sound waves that bounce back.

Old Age Among the Liir

Liir achieve "Elder" status after having lived for more than three hundred years. At this point, they are over 5 meters in length and usually weigh well over 200 kilograms. Liir who have reached this venerable age generally retire from any profession which might put them personally at risk, and adopt a monastic lifestyle. In general, their days are spent contemplating the mysteries of the universe, composing songs and poems, maintaining the oral tradition of the species, and instructing the young in matters of ethics, morality and proper conduct as a sentient being. No Liirian philosopher is taken seriously before the age of 400.

Any given Elder will usually be surrounded by a cloud of younger Liir, who listen to the songs, ask questions, and telepathically explore the complexities and subtleties of the Elder's mind. This period of "swimming alongside" is considered a vitally necessary part of any young person's education. The aged are highly revered in all Liirian subcultures, and younger Liir will gladly sacrifice their own lives or embrace great personal risk to protect an Elder from any possible harm. Their ancestors are living treasures in their eyes. A sizable number of Liir spacers regard their service as a duty to the species, and volunteer to "scout the Black Sea" in order to protect the Elders who must remain behind on Muur.

Decisions regarding government and policy are largely made by Elders. All Liir, from the greatest to the smallest, have a voice in government and society. The word *Liir*, the race's name for itself, translates as "Choir", those who sing together. But because Elders are the strongest, the wisest and the deepest among them, however, their voices are stronger and louder.

Each Liirian world has one Elder who is the largest, the most ancient and most powerful. In general this Liir is given a title of respect by others upon that world, "Eldest". Liir from other worlds often refer to the Eldest upon that world by the name for the whole planet. The Eldest of the planet Muur is simply "Muur", with the implied assumption that the Voice of Muur speaks for all.

The Liir conceive of space as a Black Sea, and members of their space forces are called Black Swimmers. The leader of the Black Swimmers is the Voice of the Void, the largest and loudest voice, known as the Black.

Songs of the Liir

In recent years, a revolution of thought and communication has occurred among the Liir. Up until very recently, the Liir had only limited notions of spoken language. For eons, vocalizations existed only to aid in perception, convey emotion, or for aesthetic appreciation: a traditional Liirian "song" is an artform which has the character of both music and painting. The "words" or "lyrics" of the ancient songs are received telepathically by the audience.

The challenge of commanding and controlling a fleet of starships, however, has forced the Liir to develop new modes of communication. A new class of Liirian "singers" has recently emerged, and they now sing an entirely new type of song. These Liir can now shape sequences of gross physical sounds which are meant to be broadcast by mechanical means... and can be heard at far greater distances than even the strongest telepathic shout can travel.

Once they had developed the concept of "fleet song", and created a code of physical sounds which were analogous to concepts and strings of ideas which would normally be spoken telepathically, the Liir were easily able to grasp the concept of spoken language among other, non-telepathic species. Since most of the species they come in contact with do not possess even the most rudimentary telepathy, they began to assemble a cadre of Liirian specialists who would dedicate their lives to learning the "fleetsongs" of other species. These specially-trained linguists communicate verbally with other species, and develop software to translate any spoken language into Liirian fleetsong.

There was no traditional word for such a profession among the Liir, but they have invented a new title for the job. Members of the diplomatic corps are called "Singers to the Deaf".

Drowning Day: the Liirian Art of War

Culturally speaking, the Liir have a strong pacifistic streak and are inclined to avoid violence whenever possible. Up until recently, the very notion of "war" was unknown to them; they do not war among themselves, historically, and had some difficulty grasping concepts like "conquest", or understanding why such a thing would be desirable.

Because of their empathic and telepathic abilities, the Liir are always keenly aware of the sufferings of others, and they take no joy in causing pain, fear or anger. They revere life and harmony, and abhor needless death or destruction. Nonetheless, they also value their own lives, and over the past two centuries they have come to embrace survival as a necessary virtue. They have formed a military for the first time in their history, with a specific mandate to protect the Liir people from space-faring marauders.

The Liir define space as a Black Sea, and members of their military forces are called Black Swimmers. A military career begins on "Drowning Day", the first day of basic training, when a Liir's lungs are first filled with oxygenated liquid medium and his body is fitted with a battlesuit. The psychological impact of those first few hours, during which a Liir must learn to intake liquid rather than pure air, are extremely powerful and devastating. Often new recruits need to be restrained by other Liir, lest they injure themselves in their struggles. Even those who can retain physical control, however, find the experience very emotionally traumatizing, an overwhelming death experience. Thereafter, it is relatively easy to re-arrange patterns of thought and behaviour in the new recruits, especially given that they are always volunteers.

Black Swimmers quickly learn how to communicate in fleetsong and read steelsong symbols, to operate drive systems and weapons, to engage in personal combat, and various other mental and emotional disciplines, including first aid, and the mental and emotional shielding techniques which allow them to cling to sanity and remain on task under extreme conditions. They also pick up the philosophy and mindset of the Liir warrior through telepathic contact with other Liir warriors.

Black Swimmers have cut themselves off psychologically from the aspects of their character which create and nurture life, for the most part. A Black Swimmer's feminine side, although still present, is not in ascendance; for this reason Black Swimmers are generally regarded as male.

Ishii

Ishii is first and foremost a Black Swimmer, a warrior Liir. His telepathy, his battle suit, his first aid skills and facility with languages, his empathy and his rage are all emblematic of a high-ranking officer in the Liirian military. His name in the Liir language means "primary tentacle", and refers to the appendage that is strongest and most able; it has the same connotation as the phrase "right-hand man" in English. In short, *Ishii* is a title of rank, not a personal name. Cai Rui never knows the personal name of his unlikely ally.

You are not like others-of-the-same-kind. And I thought you might learn.

Ishii here refers to Cai Rui's own latent psionic ability, which is activated over the course of the novel. Every sentient race in the *SotS* universe has some psionic potential; in some species it is simply much more developed.

Suul'ka

Ishii often uses this term in the course of the novel. The literal translation of this term is "Winter Mind". *Ka* is a word with multiple meanings, including "breath", "life", "soul" and "mind"; telepathic communication is called *kanayma*, "souls joining". *Suul* is literally "ice", specifically the pack ice at the poles of Muur, which grows so thick that even an Elder's back cannot break it. *Suul* is killing cold, suffocating cold, cold that shuts out life and breath, that deafens and stills all voices. The two terms knitted together refer to a dreadful, unfeeling enemy, devoid of empathy and motivated by cruelty.

Liir diet

What a Liir eats depends on age. The younger the Liir, the more they rely on hunting and sea vegetables. Optimal hunting age for a Liir is 70–200 years. As they age past this point, they move more and more toward filter feeding, until the most massive Liir are nearly constantly feeding on krill and plankton.

When in space, Liir return to nursing mode, drinking "milk" (a rich high-fat, high-carb, high-protein fluid) from spouts inside the ship. All ships are female to them, for this reason.

The candy game: "Hide the Thought"

Psychic self-defense, especially versus an interrogator, is a subtle art and takes years to learn. This is why the Liir begin the training early, by raising their children to play a little game called "Hide the Thought". It is this game which Ishii is trying to teach Cai Rui to play, using the piece of candy as a metaphor which his sleeping mind is able to understand and manipulate.

The night sea in which your people swim.

Ishii here refers to the subconscious mind. When he says "My people have no such refuge", he means that a Liir mind has no subconscious partition. Liir do not sleep; they are conscious breathers, like our own earthly cetaceans. They can never be fully unconscious, or they would die. They fulfill the need for rest by allowing one lobe of the brain to doze at a time, in three hour cycles, while the other two lobes remain awake and active.

Silence my Song if you can, paingiver.

The Liir spiritual worldview is both simple and profound. They have no separate sense of the divine as we would understand it. They believe that all things are equally sacred; the universe itself is their god, in essence. They make no philosophical or hierarchical separation between themselves and other living things, or even between themselves and non-living bodies like stars and planets.

The Liir conceive the Universe as one great Song—a vast tapestry of harmonious music. To a Liir, every physical object and living thing in the universe is another trembling chord, a pattern of vibrations, a sequence of notes. Everything is part of the Song. Everything that exists, in their eyes, is beautiful and necessary; if one cannot see that beauty, the fault lies within.

When Ishii invites the enemy to silence his Song, he is saying "Kill me if you can."

Heart's Joy

Liir parenting is communal. An infant can nurse from any other "female" Liir in its community. Their language has several variations on the word "mother" which, depending on mental inflection, can mean: "a female Liir", "she who birthed my body", "she who nourishes me physically (or spiritually) ", "she who tears away the blinding caul", etc.

In this case, the memory shared by Ishii with his enemy is a primal moment of Liirian identity, the memory of the telepathic communion between a Liir mother and her lovingly anticipated child. It is a gift, intended to ward off the terror of death: as Ishii puts it, "something to carry with you into the dark."

APPENDIX FIVE: *ZUUL SAPIENS*

*T*he *Deacon's Tale* depicts the emergence of a previously unknown sentient species onto the political scene of the *Sword of the Stars* universe. The Zuul are for the most part a mystery which the protagonist and his allies must solve.

In the months which intervene between chapters 21 and 22 of this novel, however, Sol Force and its allied species have learned a great deal about the Zuul race, thanks to the cooperation of the novel's eponymous villain, the Deacon. SFI eventually released an early briefing on the Zuul, including notes on their biology, culture and technology. The following is excerpted from that briefing.

Basic Overview

The Zuul are a marsupial race, developed in the bio-warfare laboratory of an unknown species. The scientists of White Section are convinced that the Zuul race is not the product of natural evolution; these savage creatures are the result of profound and sophisticated genetic tampering, shaped by bio-science which far surpasses that of any known race. Although it is nearly impossible to say what sort of creatures served as the base stock for the Zuul, or what race created them, a number of their natural attributes have been enormously enhanced.

Rate of reproduction, tendency to aggression, intelligence and psionic abilities have all been artificially increased. The latter two qualities seem to be increasing further with each generation. Other major changes to the Zuul were physiological. Their adult size has been greatly increased, as well as their metabolic rates. Their natural tendencies to disease resistance and environmental adaptability have been enhanced.

The rootstock from which they were bred was a carrion-eating, pack-hunting predator, and they still have the high reproductive and metabolic rates of their ancestors. They live fast, breed fast, and die fast. And along with their many physical abilities, they are also very strongly telepathic, with a talent for coercion and interrogation—dominating the mind of another, crushing the will and forcing the body to obey, and ripping thought, memory and ideas from the cortex of another living thing.

There is a high degree of sexual dimorphism within their species, with enormous physical and psychological differences apparent between males and females. Zuul also undergo an unusual cycle of development from birth to adulthood. Because there are such extreme differences between male and female Zuul as adults, and between all adult Zuul and their offspring in the early phases, a Zuul family seen together might easily be misconstrued as four or five separate species.

Nonetheless, there are some general statements which apply to all Rippers. They are non-placental mammals, warm-blooded and oxygen-breathing. They thrive in a variety of conditions, and adapt with alarming speed to nearly any set of environmental challenges. Zuul of both sexes and all ages are covered with a thick coat of hair; colors vary with the individual. This fur will be considerably less dense on the adult male, and the coat may be greatly reduced in length and thickness on hotter worlds.

Zuul of all ages are omnivores with a taste for carrion. This is especially true in early childhood; a growing Zuul can consume many times its own weight in meat per day. Having been bred from a rootstock of carrion-eating predators, they have an extremely high resistance to infection, especially by bacterial pathogens. Despite their resistance to disease and their native intelligence, however, the maximum lifespan of the average Zuul is not long. If he or she meets with no accidental or violent end, the Ripper metabolism is still so high that most members of the species die of natural causes before the age of 40.

Human spacers dubbed this species "the Rippers" early on for a number of reasons, not least the savagery of their attacks on Sol Force colonies. In only a few decades, however, the Zuul went from a smattering of disorganized raiding parties to a large, organized, and coordinated fighting force. Although the location of their central base was unknown in 2438, Sol Force was able to glean valuable insight into the origins of the Zuul from the ruins of a planet called Irridia-Five.

The Zuul recognize themselves as an artificial species. Their own artificial origin fascinates them, and they have developed an obsessive desire to find the race they call the Creators or the "Great Masters". It is the belief of the Zuul that every aspect of their nature represents a deliberate and purposeful choice on the part of the Creators, who made them strong, rapacious, intelligent, etc. in order to fulfill their role in a greater scheme. They would like to have the details of this scheme revealed to them, and most Zuul appear to believe that their Creators will re-appear and explain a great many things about the universe and the Zuul's place in it when their creations have somehow proven their worth.

Accordingly, all Zuul ventures into space in the year 2438 were essentially part of a crusade, a quest for knowledge and power which would ultimately lead the Rippers to their celestial Fathers, the scientists that created their race.

Zuul Technology

Zuul ships in 2438 were largely assembled from components that were once part of a machine built by another species. Very often their vessels were made up of parts torn from different sources—bits and pieces of several enemy ships, colonial storage crates, even ore carriers or water pods could all be made to serve in a single Zuul cruiser. The disparate parts were welded together into a serviceable whole.

Examination of the vessels destroyed and captured in the Battle of the Jade Mirror revealed that they are made up of bits and pieces stolen from many species. These fragments could often be identified by nose art or serial numbers. It was somewhat disturbing to note that often these random chunks were taken from a vessel lost in battle with a species other than the Zuul. From this evidence it would seem that the Rippers visited the scene of many battles after the main combatants had departed, to comb through the drifting debris looking for anything—or anyone—that they could use.

The only technology unique to the Zuul is their FTL drive, which is based on an unknown branch of gravokinetic theory. The so-called "rip drive" uses a focused energy event to create a miniature black hole. This artificial singularity creates a tiny tear in the fabric of space-time, penetrating to the Node Space layer. What begins as a small puncture immediately opens into a larger "rip", a new gravometric stress fracture which quickly forms a channel between the closest massive stellar body and that of a targeted neighbouring star system. Unlike Node lines, however, a rip-lane is not a stable connection through Node Space. These lanes have a tendency to collapse over time.

Zuul Culture

Zuul of all ages possess a rudimentary telepathic ability, which is strongest in the adult male. This crude telepathic communication is the basis for the basic Zuul social unit, which Sol Force has dubbed the "coterie". Formation of a coterie is an instinctive behavior pattern for the Zuul species. All adult Zuul are members of a coterie, which usually consists of a group of six to twelve females and one male. The male Zuul will take the dominant role and serve as a de facto "brain" for the entire unit. A coterie of Zuul is a single functioning unit, for all intents and purposes, subject to the direction of a single will. In Zuul society, the coterie (specifically, its male) is considered the individual "person".

To say that Zuul society is "male-dominated" would be a grotesque understatement. Among Zuul, females are regarded as beasts at best. In general, a male sees the members of his coterie as expendable tools, and treats them as he might treat a body part that can be easily and painlessly replaced. When Rippers meet in social situations, females are generally concealed from view, draped with cloth or ordered to crouch inconspicuously until they are useful. "Society" as such consists only of male Zuul. In 2438, the race was organized into a loose theocracy. All Zuul males were members of a single religion, focused on the worship of their Creators, and motivated by a single set of ideas and goals which were tenets of this religion.

At the dawning of the Zuul Wars, the Zuul religious worldview recognized two fundamental categories in the universe: the male and the female. The universe and the vast majority of living things in it were generally regarded as female, and categorized as "Mother". All things "mother" were considered worthless and meaningless in and of themselves. Despicable and weak as it may be, however, that which is "mother" is also the wellspring of life—a fecund bed of resources, designed to be ripped apart and devoured in order that the divine masculine spark can come to exist. By contrast, all that was considered pure, admirable, and worthy of respect in some way was categorized as masculine, and given the attributes of "Father".

The only true currency of the Ripper economy is information. The wealth and influence of any given Zuul is measured by the number of ships and slaves he can control. Intelligence and strength of mind is highly valued; higher status is conferred upon those with the strongest psionic abilities. Rank among Zuul tends to be analogous to the organization of a religious faith; more influential Zuul hold their positions by the charismatic power of the will, as well as the ability to educate or enlighten others. "Father", "Lord" or "Master" are the common terms of respect used by those addressing a superior; "brother" is how one addresses an equal, and "son" is the term one uses to politely address an inferior.

The highest ranking members of Zuul society held titles equivalent to that of a bishop or a cardinal, and the nearest human equivalent to the Zuul's "GreatFather" would probably be an ancient pharaoh or pope. The orders given by these high-ranking Zuul are obeyed without question...but there is a good deal of debate as to how long this unity and cooperation among the Zuul can last.

Given the rate at which the Zuul were absorbing information and ideas from alien captives in 2438, some kind of social breakdown or schism was a definite possibility. At the beginning of the Zuul War, the organization of Zuul society was a perverse, distorted reflection of religious and social notions which were somehow "ripped" from other races. Like their ships, Zuul society is a patchwork quilt of stolen parts.

Lifecycle—adult female

The Zuul female is a massive creature, ranging in height from 150-220 centimeters and weighing in at roughly 175 kilograms. Her bones are highly dense and strong, hinting at a species origin on a high-gravity world. Her muscular body is capable of leaping two or three times her own length, or lifting/pressing up to 400 kilos. Although she normally stands and walks upright, her hips and spine are still not fully adapted to running on two legs; she will drop to all fours when she wishes to move at speed.

Her fangs are quite sharp and her jaws are capable of exerting over 200 kilos of crushing force, but the female Zuul's most dangerous physical weapons are undoubtedly the two massive "punchclaws" which protrude from twin sheaths on her forearms. These natural weapons may have evolved from the digging claws of a primitive burrowing ancestor, but at present the claws are more often used to inflict catastrophic damage on enemy soldiers and equipment. With one swipe of her punchclaws, a female Zuul can disembowel a man in heavy armor.

Although her brain is small relative to that of the male, with a maximum mass of roughly 800 grams, the female Zuul is a sensitive and intelligent beast in her own right. Her visual acuity seems to be limited, but her hearing and olfactory senses are quite sharp, and she also possesses a simple empathic ability. With the direction of a male, she is capable of sophisticated tool use, including the operation of heavy machinery; if the male of a Zuul coterie is killed, however, the females will remain highly dangerous. Even without direction, a group of female Zuul is a hunting pack of very large and intelligent predators, and they can always use simple weapons with some skill.

Perhaps the most noteworthy aspect of the female Zuul's physiology is her fertility cycle. An adult female is almost always "pregnant", for want of a better word: she carries a full litter of embryonic Zuul at all times. Although these offspring are conceived within her body, they emerge within 30 days from the aqueous environment of her womb and are placed within a marsupial pouch for safe-keeping. Up to a dozen of these Ripper "proto-worms" will be attached to her nipples at any given time.

Like other marsupials, the Zuul female forcefully ejects her "milk" into the mouths of her offspring while the eyeless, worm-like pups nestle in the safety of her pouch. Unlike ordinary marsupials, however—or ordinary mammals, for that matter—the milk of a Ripper female is not primarily intended to nourish her young. Instead, she secretes a narcotic fluid which is designed to keep her pouchlings dormant. They will remain effectively comatose until the flow of her milk has stopped, and will only awaken and begin to grow and develop when she has died, or removed them from her pouch.

Even though adult female Zuul are considered more as "things" in Zuul society, they are not traded on the open market, as one Zuul's "wife" is useless to another. Zuul females are not especially easy to re-train and control once they have formed coterie bonds. Pre-adolescent females are harvested regularly, however, as Zuul males run through their "wives" every bit as quickly as they do other servants and resources. Young male proteges are also sometimes sought, when a coalition of males is seeking acolytes to perform menial tasks—like, say, herding meat.

Lifecycle—infancy

Once the flow of "milk" to an undeveloped Zuul infant has stopped, it quickly rouses from its dormancy. At this stage of a Ripper's life, the tiny infant has no eyes, no ears, and only vestigial limbs; the full length of its body is not more than 15 centimeters. Shaken from the sleep induced by its mother's milk, however, the infant Ripper will obey its one imperative: to eat. Within minutes it will begin to devour all animal and vegetable matter in its path.

Since they are used almost exclusively for hard and hazardous labor, it is not unusual for a brooding female Zuul to die while carrying a pouch full of young. If she does, the members of her coterie will not be concerned; the mother's own body immediately becomes a host for the proto-worms sleeping in her pouch.

Upon awakening, the larval Rippers will tunnel through flesh and bone until every particle of their mother is devoured. However, it is not necessary for a female Zuul to die in order to provide nourishment for her children: she may also remove proto-worms from her pouch at any time and place them within the corpse of a fallen foe, or into any mound of meat or vegetable matter she may have gathered for the purpose of feeding them.

After an initial burst of growth, the infant Zuul has an average length of 40 centimeters and a mass around two kilograms. Rippers this age greatly resemble the members of the Terran family Mustelidae (weasels, ferrets, etc). Armed with sharp teeth and claws, the young Ripper will also have the keen senses and intelligence of a cat-like predator, combined with a rudimentary telepathic sense. This very primitive instinctive telepathy allows the infant Zuul to detect prey, and to recognize other members of its own species.

Following their instinctive drives, Zuul of this age will usually form a nest with one or two other infants of the same sex and begin a life of hunting and stock-piling kills. Infant rippers have a metabolism so high that they sleep only rarely; they must hunt constantly for the calories to keep their long, slender bodies warm, and support their rapid growth and development.

There is no necessary relationship between infant and adult Zuul at this phase. When living on the surface of a planet, it seems to be common practice for adult Zuul to abandon their offspring during infancy and expose them to the elements, forcing them to adapt to the environment or die. Some xenosociologists claim that this is a cultural practice; the high rate of infant mortality may actually be deemed desirable, because only the fittest Zuul will survive the ordeal.

Lifecycle—children

It can take anywhere from 30-90 days for an infant Zuul to complete the infant phase and enter the pre-adolescent phase of its development. At this stage, the average Zuul has grown considerably, with a mass in the range of 20-50 kilograms.

Males of this age will already be smaller than females, but Zuul of all ages will have gone through significant physiological changes.

The brain of the female Zuul has nearly doubled in size by this point, already approaching the 800 grams of the adult. She has developed significant muscle and bone strength in her limbs and torso, can stand and walk upright when she chooses, and will often launch herself in leaps several times the length of her own body to make a kill. Her two large "punchclaws" are already her primary weapons, used in hunting and in self-defense against other Zuul.

The brain of the male at this age already weighs over a kilogram, and has increased in complexity by an order of magnitude. He will have roughly the intelligence and the curiosity of a very young child from any other sentient species. He can walk upright and climb with great agility, especially if threatened. His under-developed punchclaws are useless as weapons, but do not interfere with his manipulation of objects; he will become increasingly attracted to tool use at this age. His telepathic abilities will begin to flower at a phenomenal rate, allowing him to attract and communicate with females and form a coterie of his own. He will also begin to acquire the language skills to communicate with older males.

It is at this age that the social relationships of Zuul begin to evolve. The members of infant Zuul "nests" will tend to drift apart, if they are male, as the pre-adolescent Zuul male instinctively seeks out a group of females to hunt and care for him. In the case of females, the pre-adolescent children tend to form even stronger bonds with their nest-sisters, and seek out other female Zuul to join into larger groups. Zuul females naturally form the empathic bonds of the coterie at this age, and begin to hunt in coordinated packs. Acting in concert, a group of six to twelve female Zuul can take down a prey animal much larger than themselves.

If left to their own devices, Zuul of this age will eventually form primitive coteries, with a pre-adolescent male providing guidance and direction to a group of females. However, this is also the age at which the adult males of their species will generally begin to take interest in their young. Some will seek new females to fill out gaps left in an adult coterie when one of the "wives" has been killed; other males will take an interest in the fledgling males, taking them on as protégés. Regardless, it is unusual for any Zuul to grow past the age of adolescence in a continued feral state. Most Rippers that survive infancy are adopted as children and raised to adulthood as members of Zuul society.

Lifecycle—adult male

The average Ripper male ranges in height from 85-125 centimeters, with a mass from 45-70 kilograms. Although far smaller than his female cohorts, he is strong and agile, and very adept at climbing. All of his senses are quite acute, but his vision is particularly sophisticated, especially in comparison to the female. Under primitive conditions, he may have been adapted to serve as the "eyes" of his hunting party, helping them to track prey from an elevated position.

Of all Zuul, only the adult male is "sapient" in the fullest sense of the word. His brain is much larger and more complex than that of a female Ripper; he is far more intelligent and has a more sophisticated telepathic ability. This large and complex brain is analogous to that of many other star-faring species, and allows him to understand and communicate complex ideas. Unlike the females of his species, he has both telepathic and verbal language skills, and with his dexterous hands he can build and de-construct various mechanical devices. His forelimbs are equipped with long-fingered, sensitive hands with opposable thumbs; his claws are vestigial and do not interfere with tool use.

The psionic ability of the male Zuul is likely his most dangerous feature. Through a telepathic link he can control his coterie of much larger and stronger females; they obey his telepathic commands instantly and without reflection. The male Zuul can also use telepathic coercion and interrogation on members of enemy species.

Intelligence gathering among the Zuul

Certain peculiarities of the male Zuul's cognitive process must be understood before the behaviour of the species can be fully explained. The male Zuul is an inexhaustibly curious animal, possessed by a hunger for knowledge, information and understanding which might be considered admirable, were it not so inimical to the interests of other sentient beings.

From early childhood onward, male Zuul are driven to seek intellectual stimulation—but the common source of this stimulation is rather horrifying to contemplate. There is a good deal of communication and cooperation among male Zuul, who seem to share information and concepts very readily with one another by verbal and telepathic means. But over and above this cooperative education, male Zuul take great pleasure in invading the minds of other sentient beings, scouring them for information and knowledge by means of psionic interrogation.

The process of harvesting information from an enemy's brain is emotionally painful, psychologically devastating and ultimately destructive for the victim, often leaving large gaps in memory or cognitive function. Most Zuul will try to draw out this process for as long as possible, not only because they find it diverting but because it is more efficient to break down a victim's mind patiently, over a period of months, rather than tear it apart too quickly. The more gifted or educated the victim, the longer a Zuul interrogator will try to extend the unraveling of the mind. A brilliant scientist or engineer is considered a prize among the Zuul, and such a prisoner can expect to spend months or even years in the interrogation room.

When the mind of a captive has been "ripped clean", the process leaves behind an empty shell. The victim's body is catatonic, with no brain activity above the simple autonomic level. Typically such a prisoner will then be turned over to the female Zuul to be eaten, or used as fodder for Zuul offspring.

Not all captives taken prisoner by the Zuul will be subjected to psionic interrogation. The vast majority, in fact, will simply become slaves. Although the mental strength of male Zuul varies, some Zuul specialize in coercion. A Zuul imperator is capable of overpowering his victims very easily. Former slaves of the Zuul often describe themselves as virtual automatons when subjected to the master's will, acting as ordered without being able to physically resist, or consciously form any rational objection or emotional response to their own actions—even when forced to harm friends or loved ones.

Ugly as it is to contemplate, these mental habits of the male Zuul are at the heart of the rapid technological and social advancement of their species. Through psionic coercion, the Zuul have been able to use enemy prisoners to operate their own foreign technology, which has accelerated the back-engineering of that technology to an incredible degree. Through psionic interrogation, the Zuul have increased their fund of scientific and technical information by incalculable leaps and bounds, as well as absorbing numerous abstract notions which have helped to shape their present society.

Irridia V

Assembling notes on the history and culture of the Zuul would have been extremely difficult without the help of the Deacon, a Zuul patriarch who chose to cooperate with his captors. He accompanied Sol Force investigators to the site of Irridia V. Irridia is a hot star surrounded by dense, high–gravity planetary bodies. By the time of their arrival, the ruins on the fifth planet had been abandoned by the Zuul for a number of years, and most of the structures were in a state of weather–beaten disrepair. Nonetheless, with the help and guidance of Deacon, a team of crack xeno–archeologists was able to piece together the tragic history of this world, and find the remains of its former occupants.

Irridia V was the colonial outpost of an initially unknown alien species. Sol Force Intelligence has no name for this unknown race; scientists refer to them as "Species X". Little was known about the physical or social nature of Species X; the remaining bone fragments left on Irridia V are rarely larger than 20 centimeters in length. But we do know that they were a star–faring race with an unknown means of faster–than–light propulsion. They had settled on Irridia V after traveling a significant distance from their own home world; no other remains of their civilization have been found in neighboring star systems, but they were not native to Irridia V. The remains of Species X have been tested extensively for any resemblance to other life forms on the surface; there are only a handful of plants and animals on the planet that share more than 90% of their genome. It can be safely assumed that these organisms were imported as part of a terraforming project, to make Irridia V more livable.

Examining the structures built by Species X suggests that the colony was a scientific research facility. The majority of resources appear to have been devoted to laboratories and machinery designed for high–energy research, possibly in the field of gravity manipulation. It may have been this research which first attracted the attention of "Species Y"—the creators of the Zuul—or there may have been a pre–existing conflict between the two races. It is impossible at present to say. According to the testimony of Deacon, however, the members of Species X did not expect to be attacked in any way, and had made no effort to prepare defenses. They may even have believed they were alone in the universe, prior to first contact with another star–faring race.

Regardless, it is clear that when the first infant Zuul appeared in their area, Species X did not immediately recognize the voracious creatures as a deliberate attack. They may have been mistaken for an infestation of native pests. Species Y, however, had deliberately and maliciously dropped the first Zuul on Irridia V with the intention of destroying Species X. The remains of the drop–pods they used have been found; these were released from low orbit, filled with live female Zuul that were intended to die on impact with the planet's surface.

The mass awakening of Zuul infants following this drop must have created an appalling wave of destruction. Mathematically speaking, most of the agricultural resources of the colony would have been wiped out within a few weeks, and there may also have been deaths among its civilian population. A large number of infant Zuul survived to latter childhood and began to form their first coteries in the undefended perimeter of the colony.

It was here that the original intentions of Species Y may have gone awry. One cannot say precisely what they meant to achieve when they created the Zuul, but it seems unlikely that they realized the full potential of their creation. All that is certain is that they dropped the Zuul on the surface of Irridia V and departed the scene; there is no evidence that they ever returned. It seems probable that they expected the Zuul to survive only long enough to wipe out Species X—they could not have expected this to take long, as the population of Irridia V was small. Thereafter, it would probably have been logical to assume that the Zuul would quickly die out, exhausting the very limited resources of a bleak, half–terraformed world in very short order. The Zuul, by nature a rapacious and highly aggressive species, should have quickly eaten Irridia V down to the bedrock and then suffocated when the last of its oxygen–producing plants were destroyed.

When the scientists of Species Y were tinkering with the intelligence and psionic capabilities of the Zuul, however, they may not have realized the fascination that male Zuul would have for the minds of potential victims. It is horrifyingly obvious, from the evidence found at Irridia V, that the survivors of Species X were not at all quick in dying. The majority were not eaten until years or even decades after the first generation of Zuul reached adulthood. Instead, these colonists were held captive, enslaved, studied, and "ripped" by the primitive forbears of the modern Zuul, who used the alien scientists and their advanced technical knowledge to build the first ships with which fledgling Zuul would reach the stars.

The length of time that some of the Species X captives remained alive is itself astonishing, and seems to indicate that this race may have had some natural, inborn resistance to psionic invasion or attack. Many decades later, all remaining members of Species X are now long gone. It is impossible even to piece together a partial skeleton. Nonetheless, in a very real sense, both Species X and Species Y were the "parents" of the modern Zuul. In their cosmology, the contributions of both species are regarded as sacred, as "Mother" and "Father" of the race.

Psionic Defenses

The Zuul have two forms of psychic attack: the domination of the will, and the interrogation of the mind. Some exceptional individuals, even without training, are able to resist the Zuul to some degree. Cai Rui is such a person, among humans. Hiver Royals are more resistant than Workers and Warriors, as Chezokin demonstrates. It was also Ishii's belief that Tarka males would be exceptionally resistant during the Change, as the Tarka mind becomes a hurricane of tangled thought and emotion during the growth and development phase.

Dominus

Latin, "Master". This is a borrowed term which the Zuul have adopted. It is used as an address only when the Zuul in question has proven superior strength. A Zuul who is in a superior position, but has not been challenged, is called "Lord". A superior who has shared his mind is "Father".

The Vigil

This is the general term for the Zuul search for their Great Masters. It is also called "the Ordeal" and "the Great Silence".

Greatfather

The leader of the Zuul race, their emperor and object of displaced worship.

Communion

The communion of the Zuul is a telepathic broadcast of an event from the distant past. Greatfather is the custodian of the First Memory, a fragmentary vision of light, pain and dawning awareness which Zuul also call the Forging. When Greatfather gathers a rally of thousands or millions of the privileged to his side, he is capable of re-broadcasting the memory of the Forging to all of them simultaneously, and they can all grasp feebly at what it was like for their forebears to be in the presence of the Great Masters, at the moment that they achieved full sapience.

The memory of the Forging is rescinded when Greatfather ceases to broadcast it, and the emotion left behind is a kind of Satanic bereavement and longing. Most Zuul males live in a state of spiritual pain which other races find very difficult to understand. The only Human equivalent is the Islamic conception of Hell: the damned of the Muslim world are deprived of the sight and presence of the Divine for all eternity, and Satan is conceived as the victim of the world's oldest and most painful divorce.

... what no other Zuul had been before: a creature with a name.

The Deacon is an exceptional individual in the history of the Zuul species, the first true apostate and the first to develop an individual sense of identity, and adopt a name which would distinguish him from all other Zuul. As a telepathic race with a very brief span of history, the Zuul did not have names for individual persons prior to this point. It became common for all Zuul to have names by the end of the Zuul War.

Hand

This is what the Zuul call a single male and his coterie of females; the male is the Master, the females are the Claws. The Hand is the smallest social unit of citizenship and personhood, but it is also a unit of military and labor force.

Amnach

In the Zuul language, amnach is the power of authority or lordship, the ability to act without hesitation once granted a position of superiority over others. In this instance, it is the name of the Deacon's command cruiser.

"Please do not make me this mother-thing..."

In his final pleading, the Deacon states his preference: he would rather serve as an inferior for life than have his previous identity destroyed. It is a measure of Ishii's ruthlessness that he does not give his victim this option, and instead chooses to re-define one of the fundamental principles of the Zuul universe.

ABOUT THE AUTHOR

Arinn Dembo has been a professional writer since 1991. Her articles, criticism and reviews of all popular media have appeared in a variety of print and web publications, and her short fiction and poetry have appeared in *The Magazine of Fantasy and Science Fiction, H.P. Lovecraft's Magazine of Horror,* and several anthologies. Since 1996 she has worked as a developer in the computer gaming industry, and her background fiction has enriched a number of popular games for the PC, including *Homeworld, Homeworld: Cataclysm, Ground Control,* and *Arcanum: of Steamworks and Magick Obscura.* Since 2005 she has been the Lead Writer of Kerberos Productions, an independent game development studio in Vancouver, British Columbia. In that capacity she has continued to write fiction and create new worlds for games, including the apocalyptic milieu of the horror role-playing game *Fort Zombie* and the science fiction backdrop of the *Sword of the Stars* franchise.

She holds degrees in both Anthropology and Classical Archaeology, and lives in Vancouver with her family and a menagerie of pets.